With a Twist

Deirdre Martin

D0008919

B

BERKLEY SENSATION, NEW YORK

THE BERKLEY PUBLISHING GROUP
Published by the Penguin Group
Penguin Group (USA) Inc.
375 Hudson Street, New York, New York 10014, USA
Penguin Group (Canada), 90 Eglinton Avenue East, Suite 700, Toronto, Ontario M4P 2Y3, Canada
(a division of Pearson Penguin Canada Inc.)
Penguin Books Ltd., 80 Strand, London WC2R 0RL, England
Penguin Group Ireland, 25 St. Stephen's Green, Dublin 2, Ireland (a division of Penguin Books Ltd.)
Penguin Group (Australia), 250 Camberwell Road, Camberwell, Victoria 3124, Australia
(a division of Pearson Australia Group Pty. Ltd.)
Penguin Books India Pvt. Ltd., 11 Community Centre, Panchsheel Park, New Delhi—110 017, India
Penguin Group (NZ), 67 Apollo Drive, Rosedale, North Shore 0632, New Zealand
(a division of Pearson New Zealand Ltd.)
Penguin Books (South Africa) (Pty.) Ltd., 24 Sturdee Avenue, Rosebank, Johannesburg 2196,
South Africa

Penguin Books Ltd., Registered Offices: 80 Strand, London WC2R 0RL, England

This is a work of fiction. Names, characters, places, and incidents either are the product of the author's imagination or are used fictitiously, and any resemblance to actual persons, living or dead, business establishments, events, or locales is entirely coincidental. The publisher does not have any control over and does not assume any responsibility for author or third-party websites or their content.

Publisher's Note: The recipes contained in this book are to be followed exactly as written. The publisher is not responsible for your specific health or allergy needs that may require medical supervision. The publisher is not responsible for any adverse reactions to the recipes contained in this book.

WITH A TWIST

A Berkley Sensation Book / published by arrangement with the author

PRINTING HISTORY
Berkley Sensation mass-market edition / May 2009

Copyright © 2009 by Deirdre Martin.
Cover art by Andy Lee.
Cover design by George Long.
Interior text design by Tiffany Estreicher.

ISBN: 978-0-425-22803-6

BERKLEY® SENSATION
Berkley Sensation Books are published by The Berkley Publishing Group,
a division of Penguin Group (USA) Inc.,
375 Hudson Street, New York, New York 10014.
BERKLEY® SENSATION and the "B" design are trademarks of Penguin Group (USA) Inc.

PRINTED IN THE UNITED STATES OF AMERICA

10 9 8 7 6 5 4 3 2 1

For my parents, Bill and Barbara Martin,
who always encouraged my dreams.

Acknowledgments

Very special thanks to: Kerry Burke of the *New York Daily News*, who truly is the best damn reporter in all of Manhattan. The staff of the *Ithaca Journal*, especially Dave Hill. Robert Rorke of the *New York Post*. Jennifer Fermini of the *New York Post*.

Thanks to: My husband, Mark; my agent, Miriam Kriss, and my editor, Kate Seaver; Binnie Braunstein, Jeff Schwartzenberg, Eileen Buckholz, and Justin and Amy Knupp; the Actor's Workshop of Ithaca Saturday morning class; the Batshit Crazy Writing Posse; Mom, Dad, Bill, Allison, Frankie, Jane, Dave, and Tom.

1

"*Pardon me, mademoiselle,* could you repeat today's specials? I love listening to that sexy French accent."

Natalie Bocuse smiled sweetly as she honored Quinn O'Brien's request. O'Brien, self-proclaimed "best goddamn reporter in all of New York," ate lunch twice a week at Vivi's, the small bistro owned by Natalie's half sister, Vivi. Quinn loved getting under Natalie's skin, but after nine months of his endless teasing (or flirting, as her sister claimed), she'd learned to hold her sharp tongue.

Quinn took his time contemplating the specials (grilled tuna with herbed tomato, zucchini crepes), tapping his lower lip thoughtfully. "Which would you recommend?"

Natalie suppressed a huff of exasperation. "Both are wonderful. Everything Vivi cooks is wonderful."

"True."

Vivi's cozy little café was a hit in the family-oriented enclave of Bensonhurst, Brooklyn. She served classic French bistro food at affordable prices. There was a neighborhood feeling to the place, enhanced by Vivi's engagement to Anthony Dante, the temperamental chef and owner of the

Italian restaurant across the street, Dante's, a venerable Brooklyn institution. Vivi, born and raised in a small French town, loved the sense of community. Natalie, born and raised in Paris, found Bensonhurst a little too provincial for her taste.

Quinn still hadn't made up his mind. Natalie stared at him, impatiently tapping her pencil on the small pad in her hand. She couldn't hold her tongue anymore. "Well?"

Quinn, knowing he'd pierced her armor, smiled mischieviously. "I think I'll go for the zucchini crepes . . . unless you think the grilled tuna is better, Nat."

Nat. Another of the myriad ways he sought to irk her, by calling her by this stupid nickname, which she couldn't stand.

"Are you saying you're such a simpleton you need me to pick for you?" Natalie asked sweetly.

Quinn, satisfied that he'd gotten her to snap, laughed. "I'll have the crepes."

Natalie scribbled down his order and headed for the kitchen, where she found Vivi standing in front of one of the stoves, joyfully stirring some fish stock. The kitchen was a hive of culinary activity. Vivi's was always packed for lunch and dinner.

Vivi glanced up at Natalie. "Doesn't this smell heavenly?" she rhapsodized.

"Heavenly," Natalie replied flatly. "Mr. Journalist would like the zucchini crepes."

Vivi winked at her. "That isn't all he wants, *cherie.*"

Natalie clucked her tongue. "If he hasn't figured out by now that I'm not going to give him the time of day, then he's not as brilliant as he claims."

"Why can't you just admit you're as attracted to him as he is to you?"

"Because I'm not. How many times do I have to tell you? He's a journalist, which is the lowest of the low. Plus he's an egomaniac."

Lord, when was Vivi going to stop trying to push her into the arms of Quinn O'Brien? Did Vivi really think she would go out with some reporter who looked like he slept in his clothing? Someone whose ego was so huge Natalie was surprised his head didn't tremble under the weight of it? Someone with a horrible New Yawk accent? She'd never go out with a man like that, no matter how striking his sharp blue eyes were or how sexy his salt-and-pepper hair was.

Vivi sighed in resignation as she moved to make Quinn's crepes. "You're stabbing yourself in the toes, you know."

"I believe you mean *shooting myself in the foot.*"

Despite being in America for close to two years, Vivi still had trouble with American colloquialisms. Anthony thought it was adorable, of course. He thought everything Vivi did was adorable. Natalie hated to admit it, but she was envious of their relationship.

"Shooting yourself in the foot," Vivi repeated. "Well, you are. He's not going to keep coming in here forever."

"It doesn't matter, because I'm not going to be around much longer for him to torment."

Vivi looked stricken. "You're not going back to Paris, are you?"

"No, no, nothing like that," Natalie assured her, though the mention of her home city did give her a small pang of melancholy.

"Then what?" Vivi appeared alarmed. "You're not in trouble again, are you?"

"No."

"Trouble" was their euphemism for Natalie's inability to handle money. She was a shopaholic. One of the reasons she was working as a waitress at Vivi's was to help pay off a loan from Bernard Rousseau, a UN diplomat who was an old friend of their late father. They'd needed the loan because Natalie had spent all the money they had to open the restaurant. Bernard had saved them, and Natalie had saved herself, regularly attending Shopaholics Anonymous meetings. She was "in recovery," as they said. And she hadn't slipped up once, which made her proud.

"Then what?" Vivi asked again.

"We'll talk about it tonight, all right? I don't mean to sound ominous. Honestly. It's just something that needs to be discussed in private," she said, nodding toward the two staff cooks working in the kitchen.

"All right," Vivi said, backing off. "I still think you're a stubborn mule not to go out with Quinn," she murmured under her breath.

"Back to him again," Natalie huffed. "Please, just let it go!" She tried to imagine what a date with Quinn O'Brien would be like and stifled a snort. He'd probably take her to a Papaya King and buy her a hot dog and some chemical-tasting phony fruit juice. No doubt that was all he could afford on a reporter's salary.

Vivi handed her the plate of crepes, which looked and smelled lovely. "Here you go."

Natalie took the crepes out to Quinn, putting them down in front of him with an exaggerated flourish. "Bon appétit."

"*Merci, ma petit rougeur.*" Thank you, my little rash. He was always doing this: intentionally making mistakes in her native tongue, trying to get a rise out of her. Natalie ostentatiously covered her mouth, gave a small bored yawn, and walked away. Honestly, the man was so tiresome.

* * *

If home was where the heart was, like the needlepoint hanging in his parents' cramped living room proclaimed, then Quinn's home was the *Sentinel*'s newsroom. The place was alive, pulsing with chaos and tension. Quinn loved the sound of hundreds of frenzied fingers tapping away on keyboards and the curses of frustrated reporters slamming down phones. He loved seeing the messy cubicles piled high with folders and littered with empty coffee cups and the debris of fast-food meals. Home was where the adrenaline rush was. Home was where you triumphed and beat the competition.

The last deadline of the day was 10:30 p.m. He'd hurried in at 10:15 and was frantically writing up his latest story while the city editor, Cindy MacKenzie, hovered over him, looking like she was going to have an embolism any second. "You sure you got all the details?" she asked Quinn repeatedly. "Because if we don't get all the right details—"

"We're fucked," Quinn finished for her with an exasperated sigh. "Have I ever *not* gotten all the details right? Leave me alone so I can finish this up and get the hell out of here."

Cindy backed off. Quinn quickly scanned over what he'd written, knowing it would run on the front page of tomorrow's *Sentinel.* As always, persistence and a willingness to go the extra mile paid off. While finishing up his lunch at Vivi's—a lunch made all the more satisfying, knowing how much he'd irked Natalie, no matter how she'd tried to hide it—he'd gotten a call on his cell from a source in the NYPD that there had been an incident in Queens: some punk had robbed and beat up an old woman on her way home from the grocery store. Thanks to Quinn's connections, he was the first on the scene. He began sniffing around, knocking on doors, and finally found two witnesses willing to talk. Then he went to stake out the punk's parents' house. Unfortunately, by the time they decided to give the media a prepared statement, the competition had shown up. The kid's parents spouted some crap about their son being framed, even though he'd been positively ID'd as the old woman's attacker. Every reporter present knew that by tomorrow, the kid and his attorney would be looking to cop a plea.

Once the parents went back inside, the reporters dispersed, most racing back to file. But not Quinn. He'd found out what hospital the old woman was in and hustled over there as fast as he could to crash her room, something he generally hated doing, but that was necessary if he was going to get that one little nugget of info no one else had. Thankfully, the old woman was awake and lucid. Showing politeness and respect, the two things he'd learned over the years were the magic ingredients in getting people to open up even in the worst circumstances, he'd gotten a few quotes out of granny. He thanked her, jumped in a cab, and raced back to the *Sent*.

"Done," he announced to Cindy, whose eyes were glued to the giant clock mounted high on the wall.

Her tense little body relaxed. "I hate when you cut it this goddamn close, O'Brien."

Quinn grinned. "We've got the story, don't we? You should be kissing my ass, not pawing around in your desk drawer for Xanax."

"Shut up," she replied affectionately. She patted his shoulder as she hustled over to another reporter who was yelling for her. "Good job."

"Always."

Quinn sat back and took a deep breath, scrubbing his hands over his face. The rush would be slow in abating. It always was. He walked over to the cubicle of his longtime buddy, Jeff Rogan. Twenty years older than Quinn, Rogan was a journalist from the old school: tough, hard-drinking, no bullshit. He'd survived six editors in chief getting the axe as well as multiple staff cuts. He was Metro editor now, so most of his time was spent in the newsroom. Quinn knew he wished he were still out on the street, even though the pressure was a killer.

"You comin' to the Wild Hart?" Quinn asked.

The Wild Hart pub, which Quinn's parents owned and ran, was only two blocks from the *Sent*'s offices, making it easy for Quinn and his cronies to pop over after a long day—or night—at work.

Rogan glanced up from his keyboard. "I take it that's a

rhetorical question." He scrutinized Quinn's face. "You look like shit."

"Thank you."

"I'm just saying. You don't have to be in until three tomorrow. So why don't you try not to show up five or six hours early?"

"Can't. You know that."

"Won't, you mean. God forbid you have a fucking life."

Quinn flipped Rogan the bird, knowing that by "life," Rogan meant "a personal life." The idea did cross Quinn's mind—twice a week, in fact, when he strolled into Vivi's and saw Natalie. He adored her, even though she could be a bit of a snob. He liked it that she was so sure of herself. It reminded him . . . of him. But that wasn't all: she was beautiful, she was witty, and whether she'd cop to it or not, he could tell she was as attracted to him as he was to her. He hadn't yet asked her out for one reason: he had no idea where to take someone like Natalie on a date.

Rogan frowned, turning his attention back to his monitor. "Come back for me in twenty minutes, and I'll head over to your folks' place with you."

"Actually, I think I'm going to head over there now. I'm starving."

"Me, too. Make sure your mother saves me some stew."

"Will do."

Quinn grabbed his jacket and backpack, heading outside. The night air was damp, the wide sidewalks still glistening from a downpour ten minutes earlier. Soon his closest buds on the paper would join him at his folks' pub: Rogan; Pete Rodriguez, the *Sent*'s sportswriter who covered the Blades and Jets and drove everyone batshit with his habit of quoting sports statistics; Kenny Durham, the crossword puzzle editor, who was always tossing obscure words around; and Shep Moss, who'd been at the paper forever. No one was quite sure how old Shep really was, what he actually did anymore, or how he managed to hold on to his job. All Quinn knew was that Shep was a newspaper legend and funny as hell.

Quinn couldn't wait to hang out with them, relaxing over a few beers. Spending time at the Wild Hart allowed him to kill two birds with one stone: kick back with his coworkers, and see his parents and his younger brother, Liam. Sometimes one or both of his sisters were there with their husbands, too. Rogan mockingly called Quinn's family "the Waltons," but he loved them as much as anyone else. Hell, everyone loved Quinn's family.

Satisfaction didn't even begin to cover what Quinn was feeling as he strode confidently toward the pub. He let himself indulge in a little self-congratulation on nailing his story and scooping the competition. The city and her stories, always full of surprises, were his life. That was another reason he'd yet to ask Nat out: he wasn't sure he could fit a woman into his life. Besides, she'd probably turn him down anyway.

2

"What is it you want to tell me, *cherie*?"

Natalie slid into the chair opposite Vivi, glass of red wine in hand. As was their tradition after Vivi's closed for the night, they sat down at one of the bistro tables to unwind. Sometimes Vivi's fiancé, Anthony, walked across the street from his restaurant to join them. Despite a cool, standoffish attitude toward each other when they first met, Natalie and Anthony had warmed to each other. Even so, Natalie sometimes wished Anthony wouldn't stop by. She so rarely got Vivi to herself these days, what with Vivi spending large chunks of time with Anthony's family.

Natalie took a small sip of wine. "This is hard to say."

"Since when do you have a hard time saying anything?" Vivi teased.

Natalie cracked a small smile. "Touché."

"Tell me."

"I'm not happy here. In Bensonhurst."

Vivi's face fell. "Oh."

"I understand why you chose this locale for Vivi's, and I understand why you love it here. It has the feel of a small village, like where you grew up in Lyon. But I was raised in Paris, Vivi. I feel more at home in a cosmopolitan atmosphere. I miss living in the city." Natalie took another sip of wine. "Also, I'm single. There's nothing for me to do here on my nights off."

"But you go into Manhattan sometimes," Vivi pointed out.

"During the day. But sometimes I want to go out at night, and there's nowhere to go here. No clubs, no galleries, no theaters . . . You know what a long subway ride it is between here and the city. If I go into Manhattan at night, then I have to worry about what train to take back, so I won't be alone on the subway at some ungodly hour." God, how she missed the days when she was able to take cabs everywhere. The subway . . . she shuddered inwardly. "I'm more social than you. And now that you have Anthony . . ."

Vivi looked upset. "Do you think I'm neglecting you? You know you can always spend time with us."

Natalie reached across the table for her sister's hand. "I know. But I don't like being the third wheel. Especially now that you're engaged."

"You're being ridiculous!" Vivi scoffed. "You're my sister! You could never be a third wheel! And I need you to help me plan my wedding!"

"I will. But you're a homebody, Vivi. You and Anthony are happy to stay in and cook together on your nights off, and that's wonderful. But I need to be out doing things. You know that." She began to tear up. "I miss Manhattan. I miss the energy and all the different things to do there." She took a fortifying sip of wine. "I've decided to move back into the city."

"Natalie." Vivi sounded worried. "You're living here in Bensonhurst because you can't afford to live in the city, remember?"

"Ah, but I can. Our guardian angel Bernard Rousseau has come through again."

Vivi looked distressed. "You didn't ask him for a loan so you could afford an apartment, did you?"

"Of course not," Natalie replied crossly. "Honestly, how could you think that?"

"It's just—your history—"

"I'm well aware of my history, and as you know, I now have control of that area of my life, thank you very much."

"I'm sorry. I didn't mean to insult you."

"It's all right." Natalie brightened. "Bernard is going back to Paris."

"Yes, I know that. His tenure at the UN is done."

"But he wants to hold on to his apartment, and he doesn't want to rent it to strangers. So he's letting me live in it!" Natalie laughed delightedly. "Isn't that fantastic?"

Vivi shook her head, chuckling. "Only you could manage to wind up living rent free in a luxurious apartment on the Upper East Side. That's very, very generous of him."

"Oh, not rent free. I couldn't live with myself if I didn't pay him at least a small amount each month. At first he wouldn't hear of it. But finally I wore him down, and he agreed." Natalie was brimming with happiness. "I still can't quite believe my luck. Papa must be watching out for me from heaven."

"Clearly." Vivi's expression turned cautious. "What do you plan to do for work?"

"Well, after working here with you, I've decided I'd really like to manage a restaurant—one that's slightly more upscale."

The realization had surprised Natalie more than it had Vivi. After being a civil servant in France, she'd assumed it was a field she'd move back into eventually. But working at the bistro, she found she had a real talent for organization and customer service.

"If only you'd open a more upscale French restaurant in the city the way I've been suggesting," Natalie lamented with a heavy sigh. "With you cooking and me running the front of the house? You know it would be a smashing success."

"Natalie, I'm very happy here. You know that. I'm in the right place with the right clientele."

"I know, I know."

Vivi took a sip of wine. "All right, so you've got your living quarters sorted out, and you know what you want to do. Now comes the important question."

"*Oui?*"

"What if you can't find a managing position in a restaurant in the city right away?"

"Oh, I'm sure I will," Natalie replied confidently.

"You don't know that."

Natalie frowned. "Well, I do have a small amount saved, you know. I could live off that for a while."

"A small amount? How much?"

"About a thousand dollars."

Vivi's mouth fell open. "That's nothing! You know that's nothing! It'll run out in no time, and then what?"

Natalie tensed. "Why don't you have any faith in me?"

"It's not a matter of faith, it's a matter of reality! I don't want you to run through your money and get back in a cycle of credit card spending and—"

Natalie scowled at her. "I only have one credit card to be used only in case of emergency, remember? You cut up all the others."

Vivi still looked distressed. "Please, don't move into the city until you have another job lined up to bring in money while you look for your dream job. I won't be able to rest otherwise. Please."

"Vivi." Natalie knew her sister was making a good point, but the thought of spending more time in Bensonhurst when there was a gorgeous apartment just waiting for her on the Upper East Side was torture.

"Please, Natalie."

Natalie hesitated. "I'll think about it."

Vivi sighed. "You're so stubborn. So stubborn."

"Ha! Takes one to know one!"

"We can both thank Papa for that trait." Vivi looked sad. "I'll miss you working here. It won't feel right."

"You're always telling me what a pain in the neck I am."

"Only sometimes." Vivi's gaze turned sly. "Quinn O'Brien is going to be very upset about this."

"I guess he'll just have to find a new waitress to torment," Natalie replied huffily.

"He lives in Manhattan, you know."

Natalie raised an eyebrow. "So—?"

Vivi shrugged. "Nothing. I just thought it was an interesting fact, that's all."

"Millions of people live in the city. My odds of running into him are very small, thank God."

"When you get your dream job, I'm going to tell him where you're working."

"Don't you dare!"

"So you promise you'll keep working here until you find a job to tide you over, at least for now?"

"Yes."

She knew it was the smart thing to do, the sane thing. But that didn't mean she had to like it.

* * *

"Why the long face?"

Quinn had been coming to Vivi's long enough that he could tell when Vivi was upset. Natalie wasn't there today, which disappointed him; he was looking forward to getting her to glare at him before storming off.

Vivi smiled sadly. "It's nothing."

"Gimme a break. What's going on?"

"Natalie gave notice. She's moving back into Manhattan and is going to look for a restaurant job there. She says there's nothing for her here in Bensonhurst."

Quinn said nothing as his heart did a slow free fall

down to his feet. No more Natalie at Vivi's. No more teasing.

"When is she leaving?" he made himself ask, doing his best to hide his disappointment.

"As soon as she finds a job." Vivi sighed. "She wants to manage a restaurant."

"Oh, I can't wait to see that. Have you noticed that her motto seems to be 'The customer is always wrong'? She still thinks she's in Paris, where it's the waitstaff's duty to insult the customer."

Vivi laughed. "Yet no one seems to mind. It makes them feel like they're having an authentic French experience." She paused. "I actually think she'd be a very good manager."

"Yeah, with the masochists."

"She's very organized, and she does treat the other members of the staff here with respect. She's a good waitress. Management is a logical step forward."

"So why are you so worried?"

Vivi tapped the side of her head. "Because sometimes, she just doesn't think! She thinks a job will magically appear for her."

"Does she have any leads?"

"Anthony's given her a few. She's put some calls in."

"Hmm."

"She's already got a place to live."

"Really." Quinn was surprised.

"You know our family friend, Bernard Rousseau?"

Quinn frowned. "Yes."

He couldn't stand the guy. He was one degree too smooth—and whenever he was at Vivi's, Natalie fawned over him like he was the king of France. Still, from what Quinn had heard through Anthony, the guy had saved Vivi from some kind of financial disaster, so he couldn't be all bad.

"Well," Vivi continued, "he's going back to Paris, but he wants to keep his apartment in the city. Guess who's going to live in it?"

"Natalie." Figured. She'd always struck him as one of those people who was saved by the bell at the last minute.

"You should see it!"

"Don't need to," Quinn grumbled. "I can imagine it."

Probably some splendid twelve-roomer on the Upper East Side. Quinn himself still lived in Hell's Kitchen, the neighborhood where he was raised. He saw no point in leaving. He loved it there. It was near his family, and he could walk to work. His apartment was no palace (one bedroom, small bath, kitchen, and living room), but since he was hardly ever home, he didn't need much more. He tried to imagine Natalie at his place and suppressed a snort. She'd probably clean it first. More likely hire someone to clean it. Then she'd refuse to stay.

"When's her last day?" Quinn asked.

"I don't know. I begged her please not to move into the city until she finds a job just to bring in money."

Quinn paused thoughtfully. "You know, I could help her out on the interim job front."

Vivi's eyes lit up. "How?"

"I've told you my folks own an Irish pub in the city, right?"

Vivi nodded.

"Well, my sister Maggie, who's been waitressing there for a while now, is going to massage school. My folks need a new waitress. I'm sure if I recommended Natalie, they'd hire her."

"Yes, I'm sure." Vivi nudged him gently in the ribs. "And that way you'd still get to see her, eh?"

"Hadn't thought of that."

"You're a terrible liar."

Quinn ducked his head sheepishly.

"Quinn, why don't you ask her out? I don't understand."

Vivi asked him this at least once a month. He always replied with the same answer: "I'm too busy. Coming in here to flirt with her is about as much as I can handle." He said it again, except this time, for some inexplicable reason, he found himself adding, "Besides, I'm sure she'd turn me down." Why the hell had he said that? He wasn't someone who liked to cop to insecurity, and for all he knew, Vivi would turn around and tell Natalie, and then she'd really lord it over him.

"No, she wouldn't."

"Don't tell her I said that about my being sure she'd turn me down."

"I would never."

"So, should I float the idea of working in my folks' pub by her? Or do you think she'd snort and walk away?"

"Tell her about it, and if she dismisses it, I'll threaten her. I'm sure she won't. It'll be a way for her to see you all the time, too."

"Yeah, I'm sure that'll really sell her on the idea," he joked. "When's her next shift?"

"Dinner tomorrow."

"I'll be here if nothing comes up at the paper."

Vivi patted his shoulder. "Good. Now, what can I get you?"

* * *

Natalie shot her sister a withering look as Vivi invited Quinn O'Brien to stay and have a drink with them after Vivi's closed. She was up to something. Or Quinn was. Trapped, she sat down at the table opposite Mr. Ego, furious when Vivi immediately excused herself, claiming there was something she forgot to do in the kitchen.

"What can I do for you?" Natalie asked politely, noticing how tired he looked. She almost felt sorry for him. Almost.

"Actually, it's what I can do for you," Quinn replied, throwing back a shot of whiskey. She hadn't figured him for a whiskey drinker. Then again, he was of Irish descent. They were known to be heavy drinkers. Not nice to stereotype, she chided herself, though God knew he threw comments about the French at her all the time.

"I doubt there's anything you can do for me."

"Just hear me out, Princess Nat."

Natalie curled a hand into a fist under the table. He was so—so—smug. Yes, that was the word: *smug*.

"I'm listening."

"Vivi told me you're moving back into the city."

"Yes. Bensonhurst is a little too quiet for me."

"I can understand that. Lots of families. Not too much culture."

"Exactly."

"She said you want to manage a restaurant."

"Yes."

"I'll pay good money to see that."

Natalie scowled. "You're very rude, do you know that?"

"Do you know that phrase about the pot and the kettle?"

Natalie gave him a dirty look, despite the warmth slowly wending its way through her body. Such an egomaniac.

"You were saying?"

"I know you're going to be living in Rousseau's apartment. And I also know you need to bring in some money while you look for a management job."

"And so?" Natalie felt a pinch of annoyance. How much had Vivi told him?

"My parents own a pub in Manhattan called the Wild Hart. They need a waitress. I thought you might want the job."

"What kind of pub?" Natalie asked suspiciously.

Quinn blew out an exasperated breath. "What kind do

you think? An Irish pub. There's a bar, and there's a small dining area that serves Irish food—great Irish food, I might add."

Great Irish food—now there's an oxymoron. She'd been to Dublin once, when she was at university. The food was revolting. Everything was drowned in salt. All meat and potatoes, meat and potatoes, fish and chips. Greasy. Horrible. Still, if she took the job, she wouldn't be eating the food, she'd only be serving it.

An Irish pub. It was probably loud. The Irish were loud. Boisterous. And they drank a lot. Grudge holders, too. Emotional. But admittedly witty sometimes, if Quinn was any indication. Probably good tippers, too.

"What kind of people come in there?"

"What's with the grilling?"

"I'm just curious!"

"Let me think: axe murderers and female impersonators, mostly."

Natalie frowned. "You're not funny."

"What kind of people do you think? It's a working-class neighborhood. We get cops, firefighters . . . old Irish couples that miss 'the ould sod' and want a traditional meal. Locals. Do you want me to describe the decor to you?"

"Don't be an ass."

"Well, don't be so snooty. Beggars can't be choosers, if you ask me."

Natalie drew herself up, offended. "I am not a beggar!"

"No, but you need a job, and this will save you having to look for one."

She narrowed her eyes suspiciously. "Why are you helping me?"

"Could it be because I'm a nice guy?"

Natalie just harrumphed.

"Let's see, what else can I tell you. My younger brother, Liam, is the bartender. He's got that broody, moody Heathcliff thing goin' on; the women love it. Both my folks cook, though Dad sometimes helps out behind the bar, along with a band of merry leprechauns."

"Very funny."

"There's a bunch of regulars who hang at the bar. Real characters."

"What do you mean, 'real characters'?" Natalie asked apprehensively.

"You'll see. Anything else you need to know? My parents' annual income?"

Natalie ignored the barb. "How often will I have to endure seeing you there?"

"Oh, here's the best part," said Quinn with a wicked grin. "I'm there a lot, *ma petite peignoir. A lot.* I tend to come in late at night with my newspaper buddies. It's our established watering hole. You'll like them, too. All nice guys—like *moi.*"

"All asses like you, too, I'll bet."

"Whaddaya say? It'll save you having to job hunt. It'll get you out of Bensonhurst that much faster."

"I can't leave Vivi without any wait help. And by the way, do not ever call me 'your little nightgown' again."

"I'll be fine," Vivi trilled, joining them as if on cue. "You know that lovely teenage girl, Michelle, who sometimes comes in here with her friends?"

Natalie held back a scowl. "Yes." The girls were terrible tippers.

"She has waitressing experience. I told her as soon as you leave, the job is hers."

"Oh." Natalie was hurt, unable to escape the feeling that Vivi couldn't wait to be free of her. But then she took in her sister's face and realized how ridiculous she was being. Vivi just wanted her to be happy as soon as possible.

"My parents could use someone ASAP," Quinn prodded.

"All right," said Natalie with a resigned shrug.

"Great." Quinn handed her a slip of paper. "Meet me at this address tomorrow at noon sharp." He winked at her. "See you tomorrow, Nat."

3

Natalie had never been in this part of Manhattan before: Eleventh Avenue and Forty-third Street. From what she could see, it was primarily a working-class area, though there did seem to be a lot of gentrification going on.

The pub, with its weathered, oval wooden sign hanging over the door featuring a painting of a robust white stag, was unassuming. Standing on the street waiting for Quinn, she was tempted to peek in the pub's front window and then thought better of it. What if his parents or "broody" brother saw her?

Quinn was breathless as he hurried toward her at a quarter past twelve. He looked especially weary today, and there was something angry in his demeanor. "Sorry I'm late."

"No, no, it's all right." Natalie paused. "Are you ill? You don't look very well."

Quinn looked disgusted. "I had to file a story this morning about some kid who was hit on his bike by a drunk driver in a Range Rover. The asshole driver is rich as hell, with a history of DUIs, but every time he's been arrested, he's gotten off because he can afford the best lawyers money can buy."

A lump formed in Natalie's throat. "Is the little boy going to be okay?"

"He's got a pretty bad concussion and most of his bones are broken, but yeah, he's gonna be okay. Eventually," said Quinn, loosening his tie. "The whole thing turns my gut."

That explained the anger.

"I hate doing stories where kids get hurt," Quinn continued vehemently. He pushed the heels of his hands into his eye sockets. "I'll go visit him in the hospital later. See how he's doing."

Natalie gently put her hand on his shoulder. "Maybe you should ask your editor to stop sending you out on stories like that?"

Quinn lowered his hands from his eyes. "Just because I hate it doesn't mean I can't handle it," he snarled. He closed his eyes for a long moment. "I'm sorry. I didn't mean to snap at you."

"No, I understand," Natalie assured him, removing her hand. "Perhaps you're not up to doing this today? If so, I can come back another time."

"No, that's crazy. Besides, I'm not really doing anything, just introducing you to my folks and letting them know they should hire you on the spot."

"This is very nice of you," Natalie admitted, blushing.

"I told you: I'm a nice guy."

Quinn held open the door of the pub for her. *"Entre vous, mademoiselle."*

Natalie smiled nervously as she entered. There was a long black oak bar, behind which hung a mirror that spanned the length of the bar. A large color TV hung high to the left, tuned to a baseball game.

Past the bar was a small dining area with both tables and large, dark maple booths. There were pictures on the walls, though from this distance, she couldn't make out what they were.

"Hey," Quinn said to a well-built man behind the bar. Quinn's brother. Had to be. Quinn was right: he did look the dark, moody type, with his tousled black hair and stormy gray eyes. The type of man that, perhaps, you didn't want to cross.

"Hey."

"This is Natalie," said Quinn, gesturing for her to come closer. "She's gonna take Maggie's place."

The man extended his hand to her. "I'm Liam. Quinn's brother."

Natalie smiled politely. "Nice to meet you."

"C'mon," Quinn urged. "I'll introduce you to my parents first, and then we'll double back here so you can chat with my charming brother and meet the regulars."

Natalie's eyes did a quick scan of the people seated at the bar. It looked like a motley crew, to say the least.

She followed Quinn through to the small dining room. Now she could see what the pictures on the walls were of: pastoral scenes of the Irish countryside, some old tintypes of people she assumed might be Quinn's ancestors in Ireland. It was certainly better than the pictures that hung on the walls of Anthony's restaurant, all those watery paintings of gondolas and autographed photos of priests.

She was nervous as Quinn pushed open the swinging doors of the kitchen. A short, squat woman with a pillowy bosom stood at a large, stainless steel table chopping onions. The familiarity of the sight relaxed Natalie slightly. She couldn't count how many times she'd watched Vivi chop onions.

The woman looked up, smiling at Quinn as she put down her knife and wiped her hands on her apron. Her dark red hair was shot through with gray, and there were lines around her vibrant blue eyes, but they suited her somehow.

"Mom, this is my friend Natalie, the one I told you about."

Natalie held out her hand—"*Bon*—nice to meet you, Mrs. O'Brien."

"You, too, Natalie." The soft, gentle lilt of her Irish brogue relaxed Natalie even more. "Quinn didn't mention you were French."

Quinn shrugged. "I didn't think it mattered."

"True." Mrs. O'Brien turned her attention back to Natalie. "Quinn said you were a very good waitress."

Natalie blushed again, hating it. She knew Quinn: he'd torture her about it later. "I think I'm competent, yes."

"She's more than competent," Quinn boasted. "I've never seen her screw up an order once. And she's personable."

"That's very important in a place like this. We have lots of regulars who come here because it feels like home away from home to them."

"It's the same at my sister's bistro in Bensonhurst," Natalie enthused. "A lot of people from the neighborhood come regularly. It has a very homely atmosphere."

"Homey," Quinn corrected with amusement.

"Oh, yes." Natalie could feel her face get redder. "That's what I meant." *Mon Dieu,* was she that nervous that now she was misusing words? Usually that was Vivi's job.

"I'd need you at least five nights a week, if you're up for it. Maybe fill in for lunch now and then if our other girl, Megan, can't come in for some reason."

Quinn snorted. "I can't believe she's still working here. She's terrible. The only reason you haven't fired her yet is because she's Irish."

Mrs. O'Brien didn't look amused. "We pay a decent salary. Obviously you keep all your tips. I'd need you to come in at around four, if possible."

"That sounds fine."

"Grand." Her whole face lit up: a trait Quinn shared with his mother.

"What else can I tell you?" Quinn's mother continued. "I don't require a uniform, per se. Just look neat."

"That means no chic scarves around your neck," Quinn teased.

His mother looked momentarily worried. "We serve homemade Irish food here: Irish stew, fish and chips, corned beef and cabbage, bangers and mash, champ . . ."

Natalie looked to Quinn for help. "What's bangers and mash? And champ?"

"Bangers and mash is Irish sausages and mashed potatoes, usually served with gravy. Champ is an Irish dish, a type of mashed potatoes with scallions and milk and butter."

"Ah." *Potatoes, potatoes,* Natalie thought. Not that Vivi never used potatoes, but still.

"Mom makes a killer Irish soda bread," Quinn continued proudly. "And her own famous Irish brown bread."

"Brown bread . . . yes . . . I think I had that when I was in Dublin."

"You were in Dublin!" Mrs. O'Brien's face lit up. "When was that?"

Natalie had to think. "Oh, about ten years ago. It was lovely."

"'Tis. Now, did you get out to the countryside at all? Because our people are from Cork, a small town called Ballycraig." Quinn rolled his eyes. "Don't you roll your eyes, you. You've been there. You know how beautiful it is."

"It is," Quinn admitted. He leaned over to whisper in Natalie's ear, "But there's nothing to do there but tip cows. Trust me."

Natalie pressed her lips together, trying not to laugh; she got the distinct sense Mrs. O'Brien would not be amused by what Quinn said or by Natalie's reaction to it.

"I didn't get a chance to see the Irish countryside," Natalie admitted.

Quinn's mother sighed. "It's gorgeous. Gorgeous."

"Here she goes. In two seconds she'll be breaking into 'Danny Boy.'"

His mother scowled at him, but it wasn't without affection. "Rude boy." She winked at him as she turned back to Natalie. "We do traditional Irish desserts as well: bread and butter pudding with custard sauce, mince pie, a lovely lemon sponge—"

"It's killer," said Quinn.

Natalie just nodded, smiling. She didn't know what mince pie was, or lemon sponge. She would have to ask Vivi.

"You and Mr. O'Brien make all this food yourselves?" Natalie asked, amazed at the thought.

Mrs. O'Brien chuckled. "God, no. We've got help. We'd never be able to keep up if we did."

"It's always busy here," Quinn said.

"Can you handle that?" Mrs. O'Brien asked Natalie worriedly. "We don't have too many lulls."

"No prob at all," Quinn answered for Natalie. "This girl is used to busy." He put his arm around her shoulder. "Isn't that right, Nat?"

She wanted to kill him.

"I'm used to busy," she assured Quinn's mother, removing Quinn's arm from her shoulder as delicately as she could.

"Where's Dad?" Quinn asked.

"In the back, going over the books."

"I told him I'd help with that, if he wanted."

"As if you're ever here during the day," Mrs. O'Brien replied dryly. "The man's not an eejit, you know."

"I know that, Mom. I was just trying to be helpful."

"You want to be helpful? Tell your brother out there to lighten up a bit. He's been a dark one lately."

"He's always been a dark one. He came out of the womb a dark one."

"We'll have no talk of wombs here, thank you very much."

Natalie looked down with a small smile. This exchange reminded her a bit of France. At home, people weren't afraid to argue in public. It was considered somewhat of a sport.

"So." Mrs. O'Brien looked at Natalie hopefully. "Do you think you might be interested?"

"Oh yes."

Mrs. O'Brien looked relieved. "Good. Can you start Friday night?"

"Jesus, Ma. Talk about throwing her into the deep end of the pool."

Natalie felt momentarily alarmed.

Mrs. O'Brien put her hands on her hips. "Did you or did you not tell me she could handle busy?"

"I can," Natalie assured her quickly, answering for herself this time.

"Grand. Four o'clock on Friday, then." Mrs. O'Brien extended her hand once again to Natalie. "Welcome to the family."

"Er . . . thanks."

Mrs. O'Brien began shooing Quinn toward the door. "Off with you, now. I've got loads to do."

Quinn kissed his mother's cheek. "Tell Dad I'll stick my head in tonight to say hi."

"Believe it when I see it," his mother grumbled.

Quinn just rolled his eyes.

* * *

"Well?" Quinn asked as soon as they left the kitchen. Every table in the pub was already packed. Natalie assessed the lunchtime crowd; not much different from Vivi's. A bit louder. A few policemen. Some firefighters. There was a group of women in business clothes, probably on their lunch break from a nearby office.

"You didn't need to answer for me, you know. I'm capable of speaking for myself."

"I was trying to help. If I say you know how to handle a busy crowd, she'll believe it."

Natalie softened. "I understand."

"Mom forgot to mention that you're free to eat anything in the kitchen when it's slow."

"Yes, I assumed." She hesitated. "So, there's nothing on the menu like quiche? Or crepes? Coq au vin?"

Quinn stared at her a moment, then burst out laughing. "This isn't Vivi's, honey. This is an Irish pub."

"Don't call me honey," Natalie said crossly.

"Food snob," Quinn accused.

"I most certainly am not."

Quinn looked pained. "Do me a favor, all right? Don't make any suggestions for changes to the menu to my folks. They know what they're doing."

Natalie frowned. "Fine."

"C'mon, I'll introduce you to the bar regulars, and then I have to run."

He started toward the bar.

"Quinn?"

He turned. "Yeah?"

"Thank you," Natalie murmured. She took a step forward, surprising herself when she planted a chaste, measured kiss on Quinn's cheek. Quinn's look of surprise quickly transformed into one of disappointment.

"C'mon, you can do better than that," he teased.

Natalie ignored the quip. "Thank you again," she said.

Quinn bowed, smiling playfully. "Anything for mademoiselle."

It scared her, because she knew he meant it. And she liked it.

4

Natalie felt her nerves return as Quinn led her back to the bar. The group sitting there looked more than motley; they looked somewhat mad. At the far end was a very fat woman with a yellow-and-teal-colored parrot on her shoulder. Natalie was horrified. Wasn't having a bird in a place of dining unsanitary?

Beside the parrot woman sat a thin, scruffy-looking man hunched over his beer. He dressed worse than Quinn, his corduroy jacket bearing the sheen of the threadbare. Two seats down from the scruffy fellow was a rheumy-eyed, middle-aged man with a red nose, engrossed in a battered old paperback. Two policemen sitting side by side had their eyes glued to the baseball game. Last but not least, at the other end of the bar, sat a well-dressed, dignified older man with a wizened face and gleaming silver hair, lost in thought between spoonfuls of what looked like beef stew.

Let me introduce you to the crew," said Quinn with a wicked gleam in his eye. He walked down to the end of the bar where the parrot lady sat. "Natalie, I'd like you to meet Mrs. Colgan and Rudy."

"Grab me a beer out of the fridge, you old hag," Rudy squawked.

Natalie was too stunned to speak.

"Rudy parrots the late Mr. Colgan," Quinn explained helpfully.

God help me, Natalie thought.

"Look what menopause is doing to you!" Rudy cried. "Your beard is heavier than mine!"

"Shut up!" Mrs. Colgan hissed, returning to her drink.

Natalie pulled Quinn aside. "How long has she been coming in with him?" she managed.

"Since her husband died about five years ago. Rudy will probably outlive her. You have any idea how long parrots live?"

Quinn's brother leaned over to them. "Don't pay Rudy too much attention, especially when he screams out about how his balls itch. How'd it go with the folks?"

"I'll be working here."

Liam cocked his head inquisitively. "Did my folks have any problem with you being French?"

Natalie blinked. "No. Why would they?"

Liam shrugged. "Your accent is just kind of high-class for the Hart, is all."

Next Quinn brought her to meet the rumpled man nursing the beer. "This is PJ Leary, our resident novelist." PJ looked up. "PJ, this is Natalie, the new waitress."

"Nice to meet you," Natalie said. "You're working on a book? That's very impressive."

"Yes, my writer's block appears to have lifted. I published a book many years ago—"

"Try forty," said Liam.

"And haven't been able to write a word since—until now."

"What's it about?" Natalie asked politely.

Quinn groaned.

"An army of leprechauns who—"

"Yeah, Peej, Nat here is a little pressed for time," Quinn cut in. "You can tell her all about it on Friday night if she gets a breather."

"Right," said PJ, returning to his gloom.

Natalie couldn't believe Quinn's bluntness. "That was rude."

"We'll see how rude you think it is when he tells you the whole plot one night."

They moved on to the red-nosed man with his face in a book.

"Hey, Joey."

The man shut his book. "Quinn O'Brien. Good to see you."

"We call Joey the Mouth. He never shuts up."

Natalie was once again shocked by Quinn's insult, but Joey didn't seem to mind.

"This is Natalie. She's replacing Maggie."

"Why did you have to say hello to him?" Liam chided his brother, though his expression was affectionate as he regarded the Mouth. "Now he's gonna start up."

"I always say," the Mouth began to pontificate, "that young men who have no respect for their elders will find themselves swallowing a bitter, bitter pill when they themselves grow old."

Liam put his elbows on the bar and leaned over, putting his face right up to the Mouth's. "What about young men who let old men run a tab equal to a month's salary?"

"Ah. Well, it's possible those young men might escape an ignominious fate." The Mouth's eyes shot up to the TV above the bar. Clearly he didn't want to continue the conversation.

Finally, Quinn led her to the older man at the end of the bar. "Major?"

The old man looked up from his stew. "Quinn."

"This is Natalie, the new waitress. Natalie, this is the Major."

The old man held out a shaky hand.

"Pleased to meet you," said Natalie.

The Major just nodded and went back to his meal.

Again Natalie pulled Quinn out of hearing range. "Why is he called the Major?"

"You got me."

"I would think as a reporter, you'd want to know."

"No one will say. Not even my folks. All I know is he's from Dublin. I've learned to let it drop." He looked over his shoulder back at the bar. "Eclectic group, no?"

"You could say that," Natalie replied dryly.

"Feel free to be your usual acerbic self with PJ and Joey. They'll love it."

"I'm not acerbic."

"Yeah, and I don't want to win a Pulitzer. C'mon, let's talk to Heathcliff, and then I have to get out of here. You can stay if you want."

"No, I have a lot to do," Natalie said hastily.

Quinn looked dubious as he gestured for her to follow him behind the bar.

"So, how do you know my brother?" Liam asked Natalie, seeming to make a point of ignoring Quinn.

"He's a regular at my sister's restaurant, Vivi's."

"Wow, you actually take time to sit down to eat now and then?" Liam said to Quinn. He turned to Natalie. "You know about this guy, right?"

Natalie stared at him blankly.

"What, you don't know about Mr. Nominated for the Pulitzer Prize in Journalism Twice? The *Sent* is what he lives for. You know what his motto is? 'I'll sleep when I'm dead.' He spends his life chasing stories."

Natalie was confused. "And you are telling me this because—?"

"Because he's jealous of me," Quinn finished.

"Bite me," said Liam, flipping Quinn off. He moved down the bar to take someone's order.

Natalie swallowed as she looked up at Quinn. "Your brother seems to be a very angry person."

"He is. For some unknown reason, he's got a chip on his shoulder where I'm concerned. Damned if I know why."

"I don't think he likes me."

"He doesn't even know you."

"Yes, but I think since I know you, and he doesn't seem to like you, by extension he will not like me."

"Screw him. Look, just because he's a surly jackass doesn't mean you should be nervous about working here. He can be a great guy. Honestly."

"Why did your mother call him 'dark'?"

"Because he's moody. The girls love it, the whole tormented soul, bad boy persona."

"So it's an act."

"No, he really is that way, poor bastard." Quinn shook his head, his expression playful. "He's not happy-go-lucky like me." Quinn checked his watch. "Fuck—I mean—I gotta run. You gonna be okay?"

Natalie bristled. "Why wouldn't I be?"

"Guess I'll see you Friday night, then. I'll be in with my coworkers, barring unforeseen circumstances."

Natalie frowned. "I'm looking forward to it."

"I know you are," Quinn murmured in her ear.

Natalie wanted to stamp her foot in frustration but refrained. Honestly, he was maddening. Maddening. But he'd done her a big favor, and for that she was grateful. She just hoped she landed the job of her dreams sooner rather than later. She really couldn't picture herself working here for very long.

* * *

"How's it goin', Nat?"

It was Friday night, Natalie's first night of waitressing, and Quinn had determined that come hell or high water, he was going to drop by to see how she fared—that, and he and his cohorts were desperate to unwind after a particularly chaotic week at work. There were a rash of robberies on the Upper West Side. A murder in Brooklyn. A shooting in Queens. Good stuff.

Natalie looked unfazed as she glanced around the small dining room. "I think I'm doing well."

"A little too noisy for you, I bet," Quinn teased.

Natalie said nothing.

"You and Liam getting along okay?"

"Yes. He's very nice. Very personable."

"He damn well better be if he's the bartender." It bugged him that Natalie liked Liam.

"I better get back to work," said Natalie as someone motioned for her to give them their check. "I don't want your mother to think I'm goofing off."

Quinn laughed. It sounded so weird to hear someone say "goofing off" in a French accent.

"Well, I'll be at that booth right over there"—he pointed at the booth farthest in the back—"if you want to come over and flirt with me."

"Arrogant fool."

Eyeing her discreetly as she swung by the table asking for the check, Quinn couldn't help noticing how attractive she was. Lately, he'd been having fantasies about what it might be like to make love to her in every way imaginable. He knew it was just a way to distract himself when he was under so much pressure. He sighed and went to sit in his regular booth.

Within minutes, his cronies appeared. When Rogan, Rodriquez, Durham, and Moss sat down, Natalie was there almost immediately to take their orders. Quinn introduced her to them as a good friend of his; he wanted them to know that he already knew her. Even so, the cavalcade of rude comments started as soon as she was out of hearing range.

"Be still, my horny heart," said Pete Rodriguez. "That is one mighty fine ass."

"Mighty fine ass?" repeated Durham. "That's the best you can come up with? She's ravishing."

"Listen to Mr. Crossword Puzzle," Rodriguez mocked. "Sorry, I happen to think 'mighty fine ass' sounds a helluva lot more manly than 'ravishing.'"

"Hey," said Quinn sharply. "Don't talk about her that way."

"Whoa," said Rodriguez, rearing back. "Sounds to me like someone else at this table wants a piece of that."

"No way," Shep mocked before Quinn could remind them that Natalie was just a friend. "Quinn doesn't have time for beautiful ladies. His only love is New York City. Ain't that right, Quinnie boy?"

"Shut up, Shep," Quinn said with a frown. "At least I do something. What the hell do you do? I've never been quite sure about that."

"He's the Phantom of the *Sent*," Durham cracked. "Prowls the office at night."

Rodriguez was still checking out Natalie, who was chatting amiably with Liam as he filled the drink orders for the table. Quinn watched their easy way with one another, the way they laughed, and found himself percolating with jealousy. Was it possible Natalie and Liam would hook up? He imagined it for a moment and then chided himself for being ridiculous. No way would Natalie ever go out with a bartender. Unless she was falling for his tortured Irishman bullshit.

Rodriguez finally tore his eyes from Natalie, zeroing in on Quinn with a smirk. "Friend, huh?"

"Yeah."

"She have a boyfriend?" Shep asked.

"Why don't you ask her?" Quinn replied snarkily. "Use those interviewing skills you supposedly have, you know? They might come in handy. PS, correct me if I'm wrong, but it seems to me you're old enough to be her father."

Shep scowled at him as Natalie returned to the table

with their drinks. Quinn's friends were more polite to her than he'd ever seen them be to a waitress in their lives.

"You guys are so transparent," he said disgustedly when Natalie walked away.

"Oh, and you aren't," snorted Durham. "*Friend* my derriere. You're smitten with her. Don't repudiate it."

Quinn sipped his Guinness. "You're spending too much time staring at your monitor, trying to think up complicated synonyms for words like *plate* and *oil burner*. It's addling your brain, my friend. You need to get out more."

"Self-denial," Rodriquez murmured to Durham, shaking his head sadly. "One of the more charming Irish traits."

Quinn frowned again. He wanted to get off the topic of Natalie and steer the conversation toward the subject of the *Sent*'s smarmy new editor in chief, Mason Clement, when the bastard himself walked through the door.

"Fuck me with a stick," Durham hissed. "Satan's entered heaven."

"Don't you mean 'Have congress with me with a bough'?" asked Shep.

Rodriguez turned around to look. "I hope he doesn't want to sit here."

"Don't be an idiot," said Quinn. "We're ink-stained wretches. He's management."

"He'd never want to sit here," said Rogan, though he didn't sound entirely sure.

Quinn saw Clement's eyes briefly light on their booth before grabbing a stool at the bar. The guy knew better than to even try approaching them off-hours. Quinn couldn't blame him. From the first day Mason Clement set foot in the *Sent*'s office two weeks earlier after the firing of their previous editor in chief, the hostility toward him had been palpable. Not only was the guy an Aussie, but the paper's new owner—a media mogul from Canada named Darren Hewitt, whose hobby was buying the world's newspapers—wanted to turn the *Sent* into a rag, complete with pages of star gossip and pictures of bikini-clad girls with silicone boobs on page three. Clement was Hewitt's eyes and ears, his henchman. The guy wouldn't know a good story if it bit him in the ass. Quinn disliked him on principle.

Quinn tensed when Natalie breezed by the bar, and Clement actually turned his head to watch her go by, his eyes lingering on her body. He made himself turn back to his friends. "What's the theme of your puzzle for tomorrow?" he asked Durham.

"Aircraft."

"Interesting," Quinn murmured. He turned to Shep with a mischievous twinkle in his eye. "And what are you working on?"

Before Shep could answer, Rodriquez began humming the theme from *The Phantom of the Opera*. They all laughed.

"Anything good come in over the police scanner after I left?" Quinn asked, his eyes magnetically drawn back to Natalie. When he saw Mason Clement call Natalie over and start talking to her, and Natalie smiling, anger surged inside him. The bastard was a charmer, one of those assholes who could fire people and make the person being axed actually feel sorry for him for having to convey such bad news. Must be the accent, Quinn thought.

Unable to help himself, he slid out of the booth. "Be back in a minute."

He strolled over to Natalie and Clement, putting a friendly hand on Natalie's shoulder. "Could you excuse us a minute?"

Natalie looked surprised. "You two know each other?"

"He's the new editor in chief," Quinn said, sounding slightly disdainful.

"Which means I'm his boss." Clement flashed Natalie a charming smile. "I'm looking forward to chatting with you again soon."

Natalie smiled back at him as she walked away.

"What can I do for you?" Clement asked Quinn genially.

Quinn wanted to tell him not to go near Natalie, but he refused to give Clement any ammunition to use against him. He decided to stick to basics.

"Look, I'm gonna say this nicely, and I'm gonna say it once: you're not wanted here."

Clement looked confused as he lifted an eyebrow. "Excuse me?"

"This is the reporters' hangout. Management goes to Barzini's Grill."

"I didn't know that," Clement admitted. Clearly none of the other suits had yet invited him out for an after-work drink with them. Quinn wasn't surprised. It was likely that none of them trusted him, either.

"Well, now that you know, you should hang at Barzini's."

Clement looked bemused. "Why do you care where I go to unwind? As long as I don't sit with you, what does it matter?"

The bastard had a point.

"Look," said Quinn, trying to sound reasonable. "I'm just saying—"

"I promise I'll stay here at the bar if I come in again, okay?"

"Fine," Quinn said begrudgingly.

"Good reporting on the shooting in Queens," said Clement.

"Thanks," said Quinn, not wanting to appear ungracious. God, he wanted this guy to be a total asshole, and he wasn't, at least not right now.

"I'd like to talk to you Monday morning if you can," Clement continued. "We haven't really had a chance to chat on our own. And since you're the paper's star reporter . . ."

"My shift doesn't start until three."

"Yet you're always in the newsroom before noon unless you're out on a story. How does ten sound to you?"

"Great," Quinn said unenthusiastically.

"Talk to you Monday, then."

"Sure thing, lapdog," Quinn muttered under his breath.

Quinn returned to the table, where his cronies were anxiously waiting.

"Well?" Rogan asked. "How'd it go?"

"I told him he belonged at Barzini's."

"And—?" Shep asked.

"He'll probably keep coming here, just to bust our balls. Of course, the fact that this place is ten times homier than Barzini's doesn't help."

"Once he tastes your mother's cooking, we're screwed," said Durham.

"Did you see the way he was looking at your 'friend,' Quinn?" Durham continued, nudging Quinn in the ribs. "I think he wants a piece, too."

Quinn shut him down with a glare.

Rodriguez was still watching Clement at the bar. "God, I hate that prick already."

Quinn drained his Guinness. "Join the club."

5

"It was horrible, Vivi. Just horrible."

It was Saturday morning, the day after Natalie's first night working at the Wild Hart. She was sitting on Vivi's couch, clutching a mug of coffee. She hadn't finished moving all her things from Bensonhurst to Manhattan yet, and Anthony Dante had graciously offered to load the remainder of her possessions in his SUV and drive her into the city, where he and Vivi would help her unpack. So here she was, up bright and early, since both Anthony and Vivi needed to be back at their restaurants at a reasonable hour.

Vivi came and sat beside her, pushing aside a pile of *Bride* magazines on the coffee table so she had room to put her coffee mug down.

"Tell me why it was horrible."

"The regulars are all crazy! There's a woman there with a parrot. A parrot! Who speaks! And a man who never shuts up. Another who never says a word. And some crazy poor writer talking about leprechauns. Oh! There's a TV in the bar, too. And Irish music playing in the background. I can barely hear myself think."

"In other words, the bar is a bar. There have to be some sane people there."

"I suppose," Natalie sniffed begrudgingly. "A lot of police and firemen. But they're loud, too."

"What about the people who come to eat?"

"They seem nice enough, but I have to tell you, every time I look down at those plates heaped high with potatoes of some kind and beef swimming in gravy, I get a little sick. It's not food. Yet people seem to love it."

"It's a different type of food, Natalie. That's all."

"Well, it will never pass my lips."

"I doubt that."

Vivi raised her coffee cup to her lips, smiling impishly at Natalie over the rim. "Was Quinn there?"

Natalie sighed. "Yes. He came in very late with some of his fellow reporters. What a loud, boorish bunch. Like him, they all look like they sleep in their clothes. I could hear them laughing even when I was in the bar." She sipped her coffee, thoughtful. "One very cultured man came in. His name was Mason Clement. He's Quinn's boss. He had a very nice Australian accent."

"Funny, you never think of Quinn having a boss," Vivi mused.

"No." Natalie paused. "Quinn's younger brother, Liam, is the bartender. He seems nice, though a little terse at times. No one seems to mind, though. Not the regulars anyway. They seem to enjoy it when he insults them."

"Ah, so you should fit right in."

"Very funny."

"How did you do in tips?"

"Very well," Natalie grumbled.

"You have nothing to complain about, then."

"But the clientele—"

"For God's sake, Natalie, stop being such a snob! It's an Irish pub. Who do you expect to walk through the door? The rich and famous?"

"No," Natalie replied defensively, "but the people seem a little more déclassé than the customers who come to Vivi's."

Vivi threw up her hands in frustration. "You've worked there for one night! Anthony's been there with Sean—you know, the firefighter who's married to his cousin, Gemma? He says it's a wonderful place. Very warm and welcoming."

"I suppose," Natalie muttered.

"Just give it a chance. Besides, aren't you happy you still get to see Quinn?"

"I couldn't care less," Natalie replied nonchalantly.

Vivi just laughed.

* * *

Quinn loved going to the *Sent*'s newsroom, no matter what time of the day or night. Though things were slower in the morning than late in the afternoon and evening, there was always someone scrambling to finish things up before deadline or trying to get that one extra tidbit of info to add to an article that would squeeze the competition's balls and make them howl.

Today, however, the usual rush he got from entering the fluorescent-lit rat hole was absent, thanks to his having to meet with Mason Clement.

"Whoa, look what the cat dragged in," his editor Cindy said, balancing a phone receiver on her shoulder.

"Not the cat—Clement," Quinn grumbled, the morning edition of the *Sent* tucked under his arm.

"Clement, huh?" Cindy said, rolling her eyes. "You poor bastard. Though I do think his accent is kind of sexy."

"You're pathetic." Quinn gestured at the phone. "Who you on hold for?"

"I'm waiting for some asshole over at Police Plaza to let me know when the kid who whaled on the old lady is doing the shame walk."

Quinn wondered which staff photographer she'd cajoled out this early to stake out the shack to get a photo of the kid being paraded into a vehicle to be transferred to jail.

Cindy looked amused as she regarded Quinn. "I heard there was some serious cock blocking going on between you and Clement at the Hart Friday night."

Quinn thrust his head forward as if he hadn't heard correctly. "What? Who told you that?"

"Rodriguez."

"Excuse me a minute."

Quinn went over to his good buddy's cubicle. Like Quinn, Rodriguez rarely needed to get to the paper early, but he always did, probably because his marriage was on the rocks and he just wanted to get the hell out of the house.

"What's this I hear about you telling Cindy that Clement and I were cock blocking?"

"You were," said Rodriguez, thumbing through the *New York Globe*. Every reporter and every editor read every edition of the competition's papers. It was an unspoken job requirement.

"Bullshit," said Quinn, looking over Rodriquez's shoulders at the hockey standings. The Blades were six and oh, their best start in a few years.

Rodriquez glanced up at him. "Bullshit yourself, man. You went over to him to defend your turf."

"Our turf," Quinn corrected. "You really want him to start hanging out at the Hart?"

"O'Brien, you hustled over there the minute you saw him talking to your 'friend.'"

"Kiss my pale white Irish ass. I would have gone over there anyway." *Bullshit,* whispered a little voice in his head. *Bullshit, bullshit, bullshit.* Natalie *was* the reason he'd gone over to Clement. Defending the Hart as the reporters' lair just provided a convenient excuse. Quinn smothered the taunting voice inside.

"Did you hear what I said?" Quinn asked.

"Yeah, right, whatever; you keep telling yourself you went over for our sake," Rodriquez said wearily. He stood up.

"Where you going?"

"Interview with Ty Gallagher. You know how many goals he scored in his career?"

"No, but I'm sure you're going to tell me right now," Quinn said dryly.

"Three hundred twenty-eight. Do you have any idea how amazing that is?" He blew his nose loudly into a balled-up handkerchief and stuffed it back into his pocket. "You here to talk to our fearless leader?"

"Yeah. Apparently Cindy thinks his accent is sexy."

"Sad. I wonder how sexy she'll find it when he brings the hammer down on her."

"No shit."

Quinn checked his watch. "It's ten now. Think I'll let him cool his heels for a few minutes."

Rodriquez chuckled admiringly. "You were born a ball-buster, and you'll die one."

Quinn put his hand over his heart. "I think that's the nicest thing you've ever said to me, honey."

"Catch you tonight at the Hart." Rodriquez pointed to the closed door of Clement's office. "Have fun."

"Oh yeah," Quinn said sarcastically. "Let the good times roll."

* * *

Quinn didn't bother to knock before entering Clement's office. Clement, studiedly casual, was leaning back in his chair, feet up on the desk, ankles crossed. He was reading the *New York Globe*, the city's trashiest newspaper. Quinn wasn't surprised.

"You wanted to talk to me?"

Quinn was disgusted by how quickly Clement had rid the space of all traces of his predecessor. The office felt sterile now. Corporate. The stale smell of cigarette smoke was gone, the piles of newspapers going back months done away with. You could actually see the desk. The only things that remained were framed blowups on the walls of some of the *Sent*'s best covers.

Clement's feet came back down to earth as he folded up the edition of the *Globe* on his desk. He gestured at one of the chairs before him. "Have a seat."

"I prefer to stand, thanks."

"Suit yourself." He picked up that morning's issue of the *Sent*. "As I said Friday night: good reporting."

"Thanks. Is that why you called me in? To compliment me?"

"No, I called you in because I need to make something clear to you."

Quinn folded his arms, leery. "What's that?"

"I saw how unhappy you looked at the staff meeting the other day when I talked about the Hewitt Corporation wanting to take this paper in another direction."

"You mean into the gutter?"

Clement laughed softly. "Can we try not to make this antagonistic? I think it would make all our jobs easier."

"Fine."

"You've been in this business a long time, O'Brien. I'm sure you've figured out by now that traditional newspapers are dying. The Internet and cable are killing us. For papers to survive today they've either got to be upscale or down-market. For us that's going to mean more sex and more celebrities. That's what sells."

"So do stories about real life. Stories that matter. Two million people read our paper every day. Know why? Because we're a quality tab that lets them know what's going on in their city, in their lives. The city already has the *New*

York Globe for the readers who want nonstop tits and rehab. Newspapers are like a cafeteria, okay? You start serving the same thing, people will stop reading, period."

"The *Sent*'s numbers are already down."

"Oh, and you think boobs on page three and gossip about which actor is banging which actress is going to help?"

"It helped the *Globe*."

"We're not the *Globe*," Quinn reiterated. "We're the *Sentinel*, the workingman's paper."

"Well, right now the workingman isn't buying enough papers. What matters most is selling papers."

"To you and Hewitt."

"Hewitt owns the paper now, Quinn," Clement reminded him. "And if we don't sell papers, we don't get advertisers. And if we don't get advertisers, none of you will have jobs. This is a business." He was beginning to sound irritated.

"What do you want from me, Clement?"

"I'm not looking for you to become a convert. I admire your principles. I don't want you to give them up. But I don't want you flaming the sparks of dissent and leading a revolution out in the newsroom."

"I hate to tell you this, but most of the staff already feel the same way I do."

"That'll only last until they realize their jobs might be on the line," Clement said bluntly. "Look, we'd hate to lose you. You're the best runner in the city, and everyone knows it. You can still keep covering 'real life,' but I need you to get with the program at some point and stay off the soapbox in the newsroom."

"And if I don't?"

Clement's eyes flashed. "I'm your boss. You might want to remember that."

Quinn gave a bored sigh. "That it?"

"For now."

Quinn spun on his heel to go, but a split second later, he turned back to Clement. "About the Wild Hart."

"What about it?"

"The reporters don't want you hanging there. Seriously. You should be at Barzini's."

"Why is it so important to you I keep away from the pub, O'Brien? Your vehemence is a little over-the-top, don't you think? Does it have to do with Natalie?"

He knew her name? Didn't matter, he told himself. Shouldn't matter. Did matter. Shit, Rodriquez was right: he had been cock blocking Clement.

"It has nothing to do with her," Quinn scoffed. "I already told you: the Hart is where staff go to blow off steam after work. We can't do that if you're there, that's all."

"Ah. It's about territory, not competition. You can close the door on the way out. Oh, and O'Brien?"

Quinn frowned. "Yeah?"

"See you later at the Hart."

6

Thank you, Anthony, Natalie thought to herself as she made her way to Mon Plaisir, one of the oldest French restaurants in New York City. Anthony had culinary connections all over the five boroughs, and he'd found out through the grapevine that the restaurant was looking for a manager. Much to Natalie's delight, he'd recommended her to the restaurant's owner. So here she was, hurrying off to a 2 p.m. interview with a chef named Simon Grillet. French, Anthony had told her. Perhaps he'd interview her in their native tongue. That would be delightful.

The restaurant was large: two floors, both with fireplaces and strategically placed antiques to give it a feeling of warmth. She was no sooner through the door than Simon appeared, a short man with an extremely serious demeanor.

"*Bonjour,*" he said politely.

"*Bonjour,*" Natalie replied.

He ushered her to a small table. "Can I get you anything? Some water perhaps?"

All I need is a job, Natalie thought. "No, I'm fine, thank you."

"So, how do you know Anthony Dante?" he asked, slipping easily from English into French. He had a Normandy accent.

Natalie almost slipped and said, "He's engaged to my sister," but caught herself. Nepotism was never helpful. "He owns the restaurant across from my sister's," she explained, also shifting into French.

"Vivi's, yes?"

"Yes."

"I think I may have heard of it. Bistro-style cooking?"

"Yes."

"Hmm. We serve classic Cordon Bleu food here."

Natalie didn't see how that was relevant to managing the restaurant, but she nodded with interest.

"Anthony tells me you're a very good waitress."

"I am."

"What makes you think you'd be a good restaurant manager?"

"I'm good at dealing with the public," said Natalie without hesitation, despite hearing Quinn's guffawing in her head. "I know how important it is to make guests feel special. I know how important it is to treat fellow staff with respect."

"Your sister's restaurant is very small, I believe." He gestured around him. "As you can see, my restaurant is very large." He peered at her closely. "Have you ever waitressed in a restaurant larger than your sister's?"

"No."

"Mmm. You're Parisian, aren't you?"

"Yes," said Natalie proudly.

"It's been my experience that Parisians think they can do anything, even when they can't."

"Perhaps you haven't encountered the right Parisians,"

Natalie replied politely. A provincial who hated Parisians. Forget it. She would never get the job.

"You're from Normandy, *oui*?" she asked him. "I've heard it's beautiful there." She wasn't lying. She had many friends in Paris who regularly went on holiday there. Perhaps, by complimenting where he was from, he'd see she was personable and polite, and not just Parisian.

Simon looked unmoved. "I'll be blunt with you: since you have no real management experience, I think a leap from waitressing at your sister's bistro to a restaurant of this size and reputation is too great. I've known a lot of managers who started out small. But this is a giant step. My recommendation to you would be to try to get a job managing a medium-sized restaurant first. You have to work your way up, you know."

"Of course. I appreciate your advice." She looked at him inquisitively. "May I ask you another question?"

"Certainement."

"Was this even a serious job interview? Or did you speak with me purely as a favor to Anthony Dante?"

Simon was silent.

"I see," Natalie said primly. She rose. "Thank you."

By the time she was out on the sidewalk, she was panicked. What if this interview was a harbinger of those to come? What if every restaurant she managed to get an interview with said the same thing? What if she didn't get another interview for months and was forced to keep working at the Wild Hart?

She'd made enough in tips to take a cab back to her—Bernard's—apartment. As soon as she got home, she'd call and thank Anthony for getting her an interview with Simon. It wasn't Anthony's fault that his acquaintance had no intention of ever taking her seriously.

Disheartened, she hailed a cab and slid into the backseat. She wished she didn't have to work tonight. God help Quinn O'Brien if he went out of his way to make her life difficult, the way he always did. God help him. She was in no mood.

* * *

"Bonjour, mademoiselle."

Natalie turned from helping Liam behind the bar to see Mason Clement sliding onto a stool. He was dressed immaculately in a starched white shirt and navy blue tie, nothing rumpled about him at all. Natalie liked him.

"Bonjour," she replied, approaching him. "What can I get you?"

"A Stella Artois would be great," Clement replied in French.

Stella Artois . . . she wasn't sure what that was. "A Stella Artois?" she said to Liam uncertainly.

Liam nodded, indicating he'd get it.

She turned back to Mason, catching a whiff of his cologne. It was lovely. She liked a man who paid attention to his grooming.

"You speak French?" she asked him.

"Of course," he replied in French. "Having worked for years in Europe, one needs to speak more than just English." Natalie was impressed. A man fluent in French. Sophisticated.

"May I make an observation?" Clement asked, still speaking French as Liam put the beer down in front of him.

Natalie swallowed nervously. "Yes, as long as it's not rude."

Mason laughed. "I don't think it's rude."

"All right, then."

He leaned in close to her. "You seem a bit too classy to be working here."

Natalie flushed with pleasure. This Mason Clement—he saw her. "It's just temporary," she murmured, "until I find a job managing a restaurant. I'm just trying to bring money in."

"I would think a bistro would be more your speed."

"I did work in a bistro," Natalie said, almost feeling as if he might have done research on her. "In Brooklyn. But I missed living in the city, so here I am."

"I can certainly understand that," Mason replied sympathetically. "New York is one of my favorite cities in the world."

"Have you ever been to Paris?"

"Of course," Mason replied, still in French, as if it were self-evident. "Another fantastic city."

"Yes," Natalie replied, feeling almost giddy.

"Tell me: Do you like to go to museums? Concerts?"

"I love to go to museums," Natalie replied. "And I like all different kinds of music."

Mason sipped his beer. "I thought you might. Perhaps sometime . . ."

Natalie felt her face go red. "Yes?"

Out of the corner of her eye, she saw the door swing open. It was Quinn, followed by his friends. Their eyes met, his flashing with displeasure as he and his newspaper buddies made their way to their usual booth. "I should get back to work," said Natalie, even though she wanted to stand there and talk to Mason Clement all night.

"I'll probably be in tomorrow night," he said, momentarily switching to English, raising his beer to her. "*Au revoir.*"

"Yes, *au revoir.*"

She felt slightly disoriented as she approached Quinn's table, especially since the first thing he did was snigger. "Getting to be pals with Crocodile Dundee, are we?"

"What do you care?"

"I don't."

"Then why did you ask?"

"I'm a reporter. My life runs on curiosity, remember?"

She shot a sideways glance at Quinn's colleagues, who were watching this exchange avidly.

"Why doesn't Mason sit with you all?"

All of them laughed, making Natalie feel stupid, which she didn't appreciate.

"It seems rather cruel to me," she continued.

"You want to know why that buttoned-down, pretentious ass doesn't sit with us?" Quinn replied. "Because he's our boss. And if your boss sits with you, you can't bitch about your boss."

"Bitch?"

"Complain."

Natalie glanced back at Mason, who was reading the paper at the bar. Her heart went out to him. Here was a group of men he worked with, and they refused to invite him to join them.

"I think, maybe, if you give him a chance, you will find—"

"What do you care whether he sits here with us or not?" Quinn challenged.

Natalie shrugged. "He seems nice, is all. May I take your orders?"

* * *

As soon as Natalie was out of earshot, the abuse started.

"Pardon moi," said Rodriguez, "but that sure as hell wasn't a discussion between two friends."

"Don't know what you're talking about," Quinn maintained, irked that he had to keep his attention on his friends when really, he wanted to keep an eye on Natalie to see if she and Clement managed any more face time. He couldn't believe she'd come to the table lobbying on the asshole's behalf. He'd charmed her. It was unreal; or maybe not. The guy was suave and rich—just her type, probably. It made him sick.

"How do you know Natalie anyway?" Durham asked.

"She waitressed at this little French place in Brooklyn I go to sometimes named Vivi's."

"And how the hell did you convince her to come work here?"

"I didn't convince her. She needed a job in the city. I helped her out."

"Yeah, I'll bet," Shep said lasciviously.

"I like her," Rodriguez said carefully, "but she's kind of aloof."

"She's French, you idiot," said Rogan. "They're all aloof. Snobby and aloof."

"How the hell do you know?" Quinn asked.

"I attended the International Crossword Puzzle Championships in Paris once," Durham said smugly. "There was this French girl there sitting next to me. Every time I tried to talk to her during breaks, she looked at me like I was a worm."

"You *are* a worm," said Rodriguez.

Natalie's not aloof, Quinn thought. *Not after you get to know her. But snobby?* He managed a quick look at the bar. She was talking to Clement again. Fuck. He knew he shouldn't care; Christ knew the last thing he had time for was a relationship. But he liked Natalie. He didn't want to see her get hurt. He'd hang out until closing time, pop back, and say hi to his folks. And then he was going to do Natalie a great, big favor.

7

Quinn was exhausted by the time the Hart closed for the night. He knew it was insanity to be up this late, but he wouldn't be able to sleep until he spoke with Natalie.

He slipped behind the bar, where Natalie and Liam were stacking clean glasses. Liam glanced up at him. "You're here late," Liam said frostily.

Quinn fought the urge to snap, "What the hell is your problem?" Liam had always had a mountain-sized chip on his shoulder where Quinn was concerned, which baffled him. He'd never done a goddamn thing to him except try to be a big brother. Throughout their childhood, he'd tried to build him up, give him confidence. And what did Liam reward him with? Nonstop resentment. Quinn was surprised to find himself yearning for a confrontation with him. *Let's have it out once and for all. Air your grievances and get it the hell out of your system. Not my fault you chose to punch your way through life. Not my fault you had no ambition when you were a teenager, even though you're smart as hell. Not my fault you took the easy way out. None of it is my fault.*

Quinn ignored his brother's comment. "I need to talk to Natalie a minute."

"Whatever." Liam moved down to the other end of the bar. Maybe he was just in one of his moods.

Natalie's face was blank as she approached Quinn. "Yes?"

"Let's talk over here," Quinn said, motioning to one of the booths in the dining room, Natalie following reluctantly. She looked tired.

"What is it?" she asked, stifling a yawn.

"It's about Mason Clement."

Natalie's expression was guarded. "What about him?"

"You probably think he's nice."

"He is. A good tipper, too."

"I bet you like his accent."

A small, shy smile played across Natalie's lips. "Perhaps."

Jesus, thought Quinn. *What is it with women and foreign accents?*

"He's fluent in French," she added significantly.

"Oooh, he's fluent in French," Quinn mocked. "He's quite fluent in prick, too."

Natalie looked confused. "I beg your pardon?"

"He's a prick," said Quinn, trying to keep his vehemence in check. "He's here to destroy the paper I work at. He's firing people left and right. He may come off as charming, but he's a jerk."

"Why are you telling me this?"

"Because every time I see you talking to him, you look like some kind of enthralled schoolgirl, and it alarms me. You're too smart to fall for a guy like that."

"Perhaps he's only a jerk at work," Natalie murmured. "He's quite personable when talking to me. Very witty and sophisticated."

Oh, and I'm not, Quinn wanted to retort. He quickly scanned her face. She wasn't smirking. She wasn't suppressing a teasing smile. But that didn't mean she wasn't trying to get his goat, the way he was always trying to get hers.

"You can't be a prick at work and a great guy outside the office," Quinn insisted. "The bastard might be attractive and present an oh-so-likable face to the world, but believe me, all he gives a rat's ass about is himself."

"You know him so well?" Natalie challenged.

Quinn sighed wearily. "I've been in the newspaper business a long time, mademoiselle. I know his type."

"Would you like to know what I think?"

Here it comes, Quinn thought. The double-barrel blast Natalie excelled at. The blast that attracted him to her against his better judgment.

"What do you think?" Quinn replied.

"I think you're jealous."

Quinn snorted.

"Don't be embarrassed," Natalie soothed. "I know you've always been attracted to me."

"Takes one to know one."

"Don't flatter yourself," Natalie huffed. "I find you amusing. That's all."

"Yeah, right. You'd be furious if I stopped needling you."

"We were talking about Mason?" Natalie said coolly.

"Yeah, your good buddy, Mason," Quinn jeered. "Just watch out, okay? I'd hate to see you get hurt." Shit, did that sound like a line of bull? No, this was definitely something one friend might say to another. Totally legit reason for bringing the subject up to her.

"I appreciate your concern," Natalie replied wryly, "but I'm quite a good judge of character." She stood up. "Anything else?"

"You seem to be fitting in really well here."

An odd look crossed her face, almost as if she were dismayed by his observation. "Thank you."

Quinn checked his watch. "It's late. How are you getting home?"

"Cab."

He was relieved. He didn't want her on the subway at this hour. "Well, good night, then."

"Good night," said Natalie as she began putting the dining room chairs up on the tables. Quinn headed toward the front door. "Have a good night, Bro," he said to Liam.

"Yeah, you, too," Liam said distractedly.

He was going to have to talk to his kid brother soon and find out what the hell was going on, since he seemed even more sullen than usual. But for now, he was content just to have spoken his piece to Natalie, even though it was clear she was somewhat taken by that Aussie poser. Jealous? Hell yeah. But he'd watch and see what happened. He wasn't about to do anything about it. Not yet.

* * *

The next morning, Quinn headed back to the newsroom after visiting the kid who'd been hit on his bike. He'd slipped into a coma. His parents were there, and Quinn, ever the reporter, knew it was his job to try to get some quotes from them, even though it was clear they were distraught. He always began with an apology when he approached them. "I know this is hard for you. But maybe . . ." Sometimes they wouldn't talk, sometimes they would, especially if he could gently make them understand that the story was bigger than their grief and it was important that they spoke.

The bastard who hit the kid wouldn't talk to him, even though Quinn staked out his house for hours. The lawyer who'd repped the bastard wouldn't speak to him, either. Not surprising. The injustice of it all made Quinn furious. He wanted this bastard to pay. He wanted the justice system to *work*. How naive.

When he got home after leaving the Hart the night before, he tried to read, tried to watch TV, and then finally,

tried to sleep. Years ago, a colleague had advised deep
breathing to help him relax before sleeping. Quinn had
tried it. What a joke. The only thing that ever worked for
him when it came to sleep was pure exhaustion. Plus there
was the little issue of Natalie and Clement keeping him
awake. Just thinking about her being attracted to Clement
made him clench his jaw so tight it gave him a headache.
He didn't want Clement to hurt her. Correction: he didn't
want Clement to have her.

He couldn't afford this kind of distraction, but he
couldn't help himself, and that bugged him. He was a man
who prided himself on control.

Durham walked into the newsroom, pausing behind
Quinn to squeeze his shoulder. "How's it goin', pal? How's
the kid?"

"In a coma."

"Jesus Christ. And the guy who hit him walked again?"

"Yeah."

"You know, when I was growing up and my mother
grounded me for something I thought was unfair and I'd
protest, her standard reply was, 'Whoever said life was fair?'
I hate that she was right."

Durham slurped down some coffee from a huge foam
cup. "Your follow-up gonna be on the cover of the late edition?"

"Depends what they decide at the three o'clock, doesn't
it?"

Every day at three, the editorial staff at the *Sent* met to
discuss what stories had been filed, what stories were still
being worked on, what stories had legs.

"I think it'll be the cover," said Durham.

"Probably."

Durham started to walk to his own cubicle, then turned
back. "Fuck, I forgot to tell you. I've got some info that
could turn out to be something you might want to dig into."

Quinn's ears pricked up. "Yeah?"

"I was talkin' to that guy I know down at City Hall—you know, the one I met at the Metropolitan Crossword Finals?"

"Yeah."

"Remember how we reported the bids for development in your old neighborhood were won by Porco & Sons?"

"Yeah."

"Well, apparently City Hall decided to give the contracts to the Shields Brothers instead."

"No shit." Quinn was surprised. "They didn't award them to the lowest bidder?"

"Yeah. It's very weird."

"What's your friend's name?"

" 'Unnamed Source.' "

"Thanks a lot, you ethical bastard."

"Anytime."

Durham continued on to his own cubicle. Quinn picked up his phone, called information, and got the number for Porco & Sons. Then he dialed.

8

Quinn was delighted when he got through to Carmine Porco right away. He asked if Carmine would be willing to talk to him about the construction bids. Carmine was more than willing; he was dying to. *Yeah, baby,* Quinn thought as Carmine gave him directions to one of their construction sites and told him to meet him there in an hour. *Come to Daddy. Spill it all.*

The last time Quinn had been on a construction site was the previous January, when a construction crane toppled backward into an apartment building on the Upper East Side, killing twelve people including three of the crew. Quinn broke the story that the city's inspector hadn't really inspected the crane as he'd claimed. As a result, the inspector was arrested the next day, and various individuals in the city's building department found themselves under fire. It was one of the stories of which Quinn was most proud.

Entering the site, he headed for the long, white trailer directly to his left. As promised, Carmine was waiting for him, sitting behind a desk almost as messy as Quinn's. He looked up as Quinn slipped inside. Carmine was a hairy-knuckled mountain of a man, the kind whose mere size could intimidate. He slid out from behind the desk to shake Quinn's hand.

"Good to meet you," he said. He motioned for Quinn to sit at a small, square table with two folding chairs. "You want anything to drink? A Coke or something?"

"That would be great." While Porco waddled over to the small fridge, Quinn dug into his backpack, pulling out a pen, a reporter's notebook, and his small digital voice recorder, all of which he laid out on the table.

Porco pointed to the recorder as he handed Quinn a can of Coke. "Do we really need that?"

"I won't identify who you are; don't worry. It's just that sometimes I can't read my own handwriting."

Porco sat down opposite him.

"Before we start," said Quinn, "I need to ask you: Have any other reporters been sniffing around about this?"

"Nope. Just you."

"Great." That's what he wanted to hear.

Quinn picked up his pen. "Okay. So tell me about you guys losing the bid for all that construction that's going on in Hell's Kitchen to Shields Brothers. What happened?"

"Shields donated big money to the mayor's reelection campaign."

"And you guys didn't?"

"Oh, yeah, we made a huge donation. But Shields had a little more muscle and cash behind them."

"Who?"

"You're the reporter. Figure it out."

Quinn knew what that meant. "Why were you so eager to talk to me about this?"

"Because I'm fucking pissed off, that's why."

Carmine looked worriedly at Quinn's notepad. "You're not naming me, right?"

"I already told you that. And there's no article to write yet."

Carmine looked relieved.

"Anything else you want to tell me?"

Carmine scowled. "What, that's not enough for you?"

Quinn extended a hand. "Thanks for talking to me, Carmine."

"No prob. I hear anything else, I swear I'll let you know."

Quinn packed up his things. He had a feeling he knew who was fronting Shields Brothers. Knowing that it was risky, possibly even fruitless, he was going to see if Liam had any info, since Liam tended to know more about what was going on in the neighborhood than he did. It was worth a shot.

*　*　*

Quinn asked Liam to meet him at Longo's coffee shop early the next morning. Though Liam initially hesitated, he eventually agreed.

Longo's was as much a Hell's Kitchen institution as the Wild Hart. Grandpa Longo opened it in the 1950s as a soda shop, and in the past couple of years his grandson Michael had morphed it into a coffee shop.

Quinn was a regular, pretty much popping in every morning for a cup of coffee and a sticky bun, which he wolfed down at the counter before heading over to the *Sent*. He loved that for the most part, the place hadn't changed since his childhood. The tiled floors were still a tiny bit sticky, the red Naughahyde seats of the booths worn and even torn in places. Behind the long lunch counter there were still soda fountains, but the back wall now had espresso machines next to the grill and fryer. The aroma of the place in the morning—eggs cooking and strong coffee—always comforted Quinn.

He pushed through the door, smiling at Grandpa Longo, who still liked to work there.

"There he is. Clark Kent."

Quinn pointed to the nearest booth. "I'm going to sit here today. I'm meeting Liam for breakfast."

Longo looked surprised, then headed off to get Quinn his coffee. Quinn slid into the booth, wondering if Liam would indeed show. He remembered an incident from years ago, when Liam was a kid and he and his juvenile delinquent of a best friend, Tommy Dolan, ran into Longo's, stole some after dinner mints from the bowl beside the cash register, and ran back out. Old Longo thought it was funnier than anything else, though it bothered Quinn. Tommy Dolan had been a punk then, and he was still a punk. Everyone *knew* Tommy was in the mob, because he drove for Whitey Connors, whose crew ran Hell's Kitchen. The fact that Tommy was still Liam's best friend bugged the shit out of Quinn. Yes, they'd known each other since second grade and were still tight, but when Liam and Tommy hit adolescence, they embraced their role of bad boys with abandon, committing petty thievery and mischief all over Manhattan. It still amazed Quinn that Liam and Tommy had managed to avoid doing time.

Liam breezed through the door five minutes past their appointed time. Quinn already had his coffee and paper.

"Hey," said Liam, sliding into the booth opposite him. There were only two other people there: an older man at the counter drinking coffee and spearing a football-sized piece of lemon meringue pie, and an earnest young guy tapping away at a laptop three booths back.

Grandpa Longo waddled over, surprising Quinn by giving Liam an affectionate pat on the shoulder. "Long time, no see. You want some dinner mints?"

Liam laughed, but he looked sheepish. "God, are you ever going to let me forget that?"

"No. Just kidding. I'm just busting your balls. You were

just a little boy. You and that Tommy Dolan." Grandpa's expression darkened. "You still friends with him?"

"Yeah."

"He's trouble, that one," Grandpa groused under his breath. "You need to look at a menu?"

"Nah," said Liam. "Coffee will be fine."

Grandpa nodded and headed back to the counter.

"It's pretty early, Quinn," said Liam with a yawn.

"Yeah, well, I have a lot to do."

"Yeah, well, I was out late last night," Liam returned.

"Date?" Quinn asked mischievously. Quinn was the one in the family always accused of being the inveterate bachelor, but Liam was no better. According to their sister Maggie, he was king of the one-night stands.

Liam shrugged. "Just had some stuff to do."

"Mmm." Quinn wanted to ask but didn't, not wanting to put Liam on the defensive immediately. "How's Natalie working out?"

"Great." Liam took a long gulp of coffee. "Too bad she's not Irish. I think it confuses people to hear her accent in an Irish place." He stared at Quinn sleepily. "So you dragged me out of bed at seven to talk about Natalie?"

"No."

Liam frowned. "What, then?"

"I've been doing some digging."

"Yeah?"

"Yeah. I found out that Shields Brothers Construction is the one *buying* the buildings they're fixing up around the neighborhood, not just fixing them up. I think they might be fronting for Whitey."

Liam looked unfazed. "Yeah?"

"You know anything about that?"

"Why would I?"

"Well, you're still tight with Tommy, right? He's one of Whitey's crew. You involved with Whitey at all, Li?"

Liam just stared at him.

"Because if you are, I've got to warn you: I'm going to pursue this story hard, and I'd hate to think of you being mixed up with these assholes. If you're tied up with Whitey in any way, I suggest you disentangle yourself now."

"I'm not tangled up with Whitey."

"Were you ever?"

"I ran a few errands when I was a teenager, filling in for Tommy. It wasn't a big deal. I needed the money."

"But you're not involved now, right?"

Liam looked annoyed. "I just told you that."

"I'm serious here, Liam."

"Yeah, so am I, Quinn," Liam shot back. "I don't know anything about Whitey and the Shields Brothers."

"Does Tommy?"

"I have no idea, Quinn. Ask him yourself." Liam drained his coffee cup and stood up. "I gotta go."

"Yeah, fine, go," said Quinn. "Just promise me one thing."

Liam looked bored. "What?"

"If you're bullshitting me, and you're still mixed up in any crap that could send you to jail, cut it out now, okay? Because it would kill Mom and Dad if that happened. *Kill* them. Also, if a blue moon should occur and you change your mind about talking to me—"

"Nothing to talk about." Liam slid out of the booth, and walked away.

*   *   *

Later that night, Quinn got to the pub earlier than his friends so he could spend a little time at the bar, trying to ease some of the tension generated between him and Liam earlier that morning. His chance was lost, however, when Liam's friend Tommy strolled through the door, taking the seat right beside him.

"Hey, Quinn," Tommy said affably, patting him on the back as if they were old friends. "Long time, no see."

"Yeah, no kidding," said Quinn dryly. "Guess you've been pretty busy with your limo driving job."

Tommy smirked. "Oh yeah. The money is way too good to pass up."

"I'll bet."

Tommy pulled out a hundred-dollar bill and slapped it down on the bar in front of Liam. "One Newcastle Brown, Bro."

Liam frowned at his friend. "You got anything smaller than that?"

"Sorry, Li. Can't help you out there."

"Asshole," Liam muttered under his breath, but there was affection in his voice. He returned a few seconds later with Tommy's drink as well as a stack of bills. "Thanks for cleaning out the till, pal."

"Anytime."

Tommy turned to look at Quinn. "How's the newspaper biz treating you?"

"Pretty well."

Tommy quickly gulped down some beer. "Still doing investigative shit?"

Quinn threw back a whiskey shot. "Yup."

"You must be making a mint by now," said Tommy, stifling a burp.

Quinn was intrigued. "What's it to you?"

"Just curious." He raised his beer, regarding Liam affectionately. "I keep telling this guy he's never gonna make any serious cash working here with your mom and pop, but he won't listen."

Liam looked disgusted. "It's all money with this guy," he said to Quinn.

Tommy pounded back some more beer. "Makes the world go around, dude," he said to Liam. "Can't believe you haven't figured that out yet."

Jesus, what an asshole, Quinn thought. He tried to

remember if he'd ever liked Tommy. The sad but true answer? No.

"You hook up with that blonde chick with the big tits who was in here the other night?" Tommy asked Liam in a lascivious voice. He nudged Quinn in the ribs as if sharing a confidence. "You should have seen this piece of tail. She was amazing."

"She was also stupid as a bag of hammers," said Liam. "So no, we didn't hook up."

Tommy shook his head in disbelief. "Since when did you give a shit whether any of the babes you give it to can even count to ten?"

Liam looked pissed. "Just drop it now, okay?"

Tommy shrugged. "Sure." He drained his beer, this time wiping his mouth with the back of his hand. "Can you hang when you get off?"

"Yeah."

"Cool." He slid off the barstool, pushing his empty beer toward Liam. "Catch you later, then." He patted Quinn on the back again. "Good to see you, Bro."

"Yeah, you, too," Quinn said dryly, watching him go. He couldn't escape the feeling that Tommy's quick departure might have had something to do with his presence. When he turned back around to talk to his brother, Liam was at the other end of the bar, chatting with PJ Leary. He obviously didn't want to talk to Quinn about Tommy. Quinn let it go. For now.

*   *   *

I don't know how much longer I can work here, Natalie thought desperately, serving a foursome of firefighters their plates of bangers and mash. First, there was the food. One night, she was so ravenous she actually did eat some Irish stew. These Irish knew nothing about spices. Nothing. Everything was salt, salt, salt. When she suggested a few menu changes to Quinn's mother, she was met with a stony stare. Didn't the woman realize she was only trying to help her by suggesting food that actually had some taste? Apparently not.

Then there were the regulars at the bar. Lunatics. Though she could tell they liked her and a few of them enjoyed sparring with her, their oddness often rattled her. No one like this had ever come to Vivi's. What did it say about the Wild Hart that it attracted this sort of clientele, and what was more, let them sit at the bar for hours without really paying anything?

Still, she couldn't afford to alienate them. Diners taken care of, Natalie went to the bar.

"How's the book coming?" she made herself ask PJ, who was shoveling stew into his mouth as if he hadn't eaten for days. *Poor devil,* Natalie thought. *He must not have taste buds.* She'd noticed that whenever she left a bill for PJ, Liam discreetly took it away and put it under the bar.

"Very well," said PJ, looking thrilled to be asked. "The leprechauns have joined with the Galway salmon, and together they've attacked the fairie folk and made them slaves. But I've added a complication: King Seamus has fallen in love with the fairie queen, Lucille."

"Lucille?" asked Liam. "That doesn't sound like a very Irish name. Or a very good name for a queen, either."

These people are crazy, Natalie thought again. Vivi kept talking about visiting the Hart. *Let her come and see the lunacy I have to deal with nightly. Then she'll understand.*

"Names are very, very important," said the Mouth. "For example, my first wife was named Belinda. Same first letter as the word *bitch.* I should have paid attention to that, because she was one."

"Good thing her first name wasn't Catherine," Liam deadpanned. "You have to change the queen's name," he continued. "Something more regal."

"Like—?" PJ asked.

"Natalie."

They all laughed, all sans Natalie, who wasn't sure if Liam was teasing her or trying to make a point.

The door swung open, and in walked Mason Clement. There was an empty stool at the bar, and he slid onto it, saying his hellos to the other regulars. He was always unfailingly polite to them, which impressed Natalie. Quinn's jealousy blinded him; there was no way on earth Mason could be so awful in the office yet be so kind and caring outside of it.

"Bonjour," he said to Natalie as she came to take his order.

"Bonjour," she replied. "What can I get you this evening?"

"Actually, I just stopped by to see you; then I have to go. I'm exhausted."

"Oh." Natalie felt tingly all up and down.

"You told me you liked museums." Mason looked shy. "Well, there's an exhibit opening at MoMA of up-and-coming new artists. Would you like to go with me Saturday afternoon?"

Natalie flushed. "Yes. Very much."

"Terrific. Give me your number, and we'll finalize plans."

Natalie wrote her number down on a page from her notepad and handed it to him. Looking confident, Mason slipped it into his back pocket.

"Au revoir," he said. "See you Saturday."

"Yes. I'm very much looking forward to it."

"Me, too."

She watched him depart. A date with a cultured man; this was what she'd wanted for a long while. Perhaps working at the Wild Hart was going to turn out to be a godsend in disguise.

* * *

"What the hell is this?"

Quinn threw the evening edition of the *Sent* down on Mason Clement's desk. Following his failed conversation with Liam, he'd gone to the paper and busted his ass on a piece about yet another molesting priest. Cindy came out of the morning editorial meeting telling him it wasn't going to be a half page long as originally thought. Instead, it was reduced to two columns. Why? To run a half-page article on Desiree Drake, the nineteen-year-old star of a show on Nickelodeon who'd crashed her Porsche into a utility pole after downing a few Valium and Vicodin cocktails.

Clement slowly lifted his head to look at Quinn. "Calm down."

"Don't tell me to calm down. You cut a major Manhattan story to make room for a piece about a talentless kid too stupid not to know not to drink and drive?"

"People care about this kid, O'Brien, even if you don't."

Quinn snatched the paper back up and, licking the thumb of his right hand, began combing the pages. "You couldn't cut this goddamn half-page picture of the pope in his new hat?" he snapped, showing the picture to Clement. He continued flipping pages furiously. "Or how about this?" He threw the paper back down on Clement's desk, poking a story with his finger. " 'Over Sixty Sex Parlor Raided in Brooklyn.' Gimme a fuckin' break! That could have been covered in one column, and you know it."

"Smut sells."

"Not smut about retirees," Quinn scoffed. "I mean, c'mon. Seriously."

"C'mon what?" Clement looked annoyed. "I told you Hewitt was taking this paper in another direction. Did you think I was kidding?"

"Do you not understand how important my story is?"

"The Drake story is breaking news. We had to bump you."

"You didn't freakin' bump me, Clement—you cut me to shreds."

"We've had this conversation already, remember?" Clement gave a bored sigh. "I don't want you to stop being Mr. Run and Gun, okay? I know it's what you do best. But you need to get it through your thick skull that entertainment is what sells papers."

"Oh, that's right, I forgot: No one bought the *Sent* during the last presidential election. Or in the weeks following 9/11. Thanks for reminding me."

"Different kettle of fish entirely," Clement said dismissively. "Those were stories of international importance. Stories that focus solely on the city? Less important."

"You're wrong."

"No, you're wrong," Clement snapped. "The numbers don't lie."

"Do *not* edit my stories down to minor footnotes in the paper, you got that?"

Clement laughed curtly. "Who the hell do you think you are?"

"The best fuckin' reporter in New York, that's who."

"And I'm your boss, which means I can fire your ass so fast your head will spin," Clement replied angrily.

Quinn shrugged. "So fire me. The *Times* or the *Standard* will snap me up in a heartbeat."

Clement just sighed. "Just do your job, and let me do mine, all right?"

"If you're gonna keep cutting my stories to ribbons, can you at least indulge me where the Wild Hart is concerned?"

"Meaning—?"

"You should be at Barzini's with the rest of editorial. What's the problem?" Quinn sneered. "None of them want to hang with you?"

"You're treading on thin ice here. As a matter of fact, I have gone to Barzini's. The food is terrible, and so is the service. I prefer your mother's cooking and the attentiveness of the Hart's staff."

Prick, Quinn thought. Durham was right: the bastard *was* getting ready to make a move on Natalie. It was none of his business. So why was a slow blaze of anger building in his gut?

"You don't have to worry, O'Brien," Clement continued smoothly. "Let me get this straight, though. You're willing to let me cut your stories if I don't spend time at a certain pub? Something I'm doing there getting under your skin? Somebody you're interested in that might be interested in me? Never mind. Rest assured: I'll never try to sit with you and the reporters."

"Good thing," Quinn muttered, hoping Mason didn't follow up on his shot about Natalie that had obviously been on target.

"We're done," Clement announced. "I have an evening edition of the paper to get out."

"Yeah, we're done," Quinn replied contemptuously. At least where work was concerned.

9

Mason had asked Natalie to meet her at the *Sentinel*, eager to show her where he worked. She agreed, though she was reluctant to admit part of the reason was she wanted to see where Quinn worked.

Natalie had imagined the newsroom would be a frenzy of activity, and she was right. Her first instinct, which she successfully squelched, was to scan the newsroom for Quinn, but she couldn't. First of all, it was far too big. Secondly, the newsroom was broken down into aisle after aisle of individual cubicles. For all she knew, he was hunched over his keyboard somewhere, tucked firmly out of sight. If so, she hoped he stayed there.

Mason was waiting for her by the elevators, ushering her first to his pristine office, where the walls were lined with awards and blowups of some of the newspaper's most famous covers.

"You look beautiful," he murmured appreciatively.

Natalie blushed. Like every self-respecting French-woman, she always dressed well. Today she was wearing pencil-thin black jeans with a wide black patent leather belt, a black-and-white-checked shirt, and a bright pink blazer with black buttons. Perhaps she should have dressed more casually for a day at the museum, but this is what she felt comfortable wearing, and that was the most important thing.

Mason looked handsome, but then, he was a handsome man. Even so, Quinn stole into her thoughts, like a bothersome fly that wouldn't stop buzzing around her head. When it came to personal style, Mason was leagues ahead of Quinn. In fact, Natalie sometimes wondered if Quinn owned a mirror. She knew he worked all hours of the day and night and spent most of them running around the city, but still.

There was pride in Mason's voice as he explained his duties as editor in chief to her. The job sounded pressure-filled, nearly as intense as Quinn's seemed to be, but in a different way. Quinn again. She had to stop this.

"Want a quick tour of the newsroom?"

Natalie smiled nervously. "Sure."

Continuing his narration of what life was like at a daily tabloid, Mason led her up and down the rows of cubicles. Natalie couldn't understand how any of these reporters were able to find anything on their desks: to a person, their small cubbyholes were littered with towers of leaning folders, papers, photos, phone numbers, and old newspapers. She was about to comment on it to Mason when they ran into Quinn's cohort, Kenny Durham.

"Natalie," he drawled, his gaze ping-ponging back and forth between her and Mason. "This is a surprise."

Mason's gaze was cool. "Natalie and I are going to MoMA."

"I see." Kenny raised an eyebrow in surprise, prompting Natalie to glance away somewhat guiltily. This was not the way she should be reacting. Who cared what Quinn's crony thought? She knew Kenny disliked Mason, but she suspected it was on principle more than anything else.

By now, Pete Rodriguez had sauntered over. "Natalie. Good to see you."

She ignored the subtle, sideways glance he shot Kenny Durham. "Nice to see you, too."

"Quinn's out on assignment," said Pete.

Natalie cocked her head, mystified. "So?"

"Just thought you might want to know," he murmured casually. "I'll tell him you popped by."

"I'm on my way out with Mason." Busybodies. She turned to her date. "Shall we?"

"With pleasure." Mason nodded curtly at the two reporters and, putting his hand on the small of Natalie's back, gently guided her out of the office. Out on the street, standing next to Mason while he hailed a cab, Natalie couldn't believe how annoyed she was with Quinn's co-workers. They would tell him she was going out with Mason. She knew they would. She told herself it didn't matter. But it did.

* * *

"Yo, Jimmy Breslin, you're late."

Quinn rolled his eyes at Durham's greeting as he slid into a booth at the Wild Hart.

"Yeah, whatever."

He'd been at the local tailor shop, Franco's, to get a pair of pants taken in. He wasn't surprised he'd lost weight: he'd been running around the city like a madman lately, fueled on nothing but coffee and junk food. He made a mental note to try to eat better.

One of the things that was great about Franco's was that it was open late, even on Saturday nights. Like Longo's and the Wild Hart, it was a longtime fixture of the neighborhood, which was why Quinn was shocked when Franco told him he was closing up shop in two months. When Quinn asked him why he was retiring after thirty-five years, all Franco would offer up was a cryptic "I got an offer for the store that was too good to pass up." Christ, it sounded like something straight out of *The Godfather*, immediately making Quinn sit up and take notice. As subtly as he could, he tried to press Franco for more details, but the man wouldn't budge. By the time Quinn left, he had a pretty good idea of what might be behind Franco's departure, even though he couldn't prove it.

Yet.

Settling in with his cronies, Quinn took a sip of his beer, glancing at the bar. Liam seemed deep in conversation with some petite blonde. The place was hopping, and as a result, Natalie was running her ass off, greeting him and his pals perfunctorily as she took their orders. He hadn't sparred with her for a while and didn't want to get rusty. Maybe he could think of some way to get under her skin after closing time.

"Where's Shep?" Quinn asked. The Hart without Shep was like the city on Saint Patrick's Day without cops and firefighters: incomplete and unimaginable.

"You're never gonna believe this," said Rogan. "Clement actually made him go out on a story." He handed Quinn the evening edition of the paper. "Read it and weep, my friend."

Quinn took the open paper from his friend, scanning the page Rogan tapped with his finger. There, on the lower half of the right-hand page, was a headline reading, "Pied Piper of Lower East Side Lures Rats to River with Flute." And there was Shep's byline.

Quinn skimmed the article, a fluff piece about some lunatic who claimed he'd been able to purge his building of rats by entrancing them with his flute and leading them to jump into the East River.

"Il Duce must have threatened him and told him he was fired unless he filed something," said Durham.

Disgusted, Quinn handed the paper back to his friend. "I hate these kinds of stories."

"We've always had them," Durham pointed out. "Readers love all that 'colorful character' horseshit."

"Yeah, I know. Couple then them with all the celebrity crap, and pretty soon we'll be no better than the *Globe*."

"Welcome to Hewitt World," said Durham dryly. "Guess what story Shep's out on right now?"

"What?" Quinn wasn't sure he wanted to hear the answer.

"Something about a secret army of cats who live in the city's sewers and keep the rat population in check," said Rogan.

Quinn scowled. "I'm not surprised Clement wants a fuckin' story on rats."

"Maybe our fearless leader relates to them because he is one?" Durham offered. "Or maybe he's not," he added, wiggling his eyebrows significantly.

Quinn perked up. "What? You got some dirt?"

"Oh, yeah, we've got dirt, all right," said Rodriguez with a smirk. "Guess who we saw at the *Sent* this afternoon?"

"The ghost of Jimmy Hoffa?" Quinn was starting to get irritated.

"Natalie," Durham murmured mischievously. "With Clement. They were going to MoMA."

Quinn struggled to look unaffected, even though something akin to hatred began clawing at his guts. "Oh, really?"

"Cut the act," said Durham. "We see the way you look at Natalie and the way she looks at you. There's sparks there, buddy. You're an idiot if you don't make a major move now before Mr. Down Under does."

Quinn's eyes tracked Natalie. Oh, he could picture her at MoMA with Clement, all right, Clement spouting shit like, "I prefer Picasso's earlier works, don't you?" in French. And there Natalie would be, thinking the pretentious ass was such an intellectual. The thought made him want to heave.

"You gonna make a move or what?" prodded Durham with a chuckle. "What the hell is wrong with you?"

"What are you talking about?"

"How come you're a ruthless bastard when it comes to getting the story, but when a gorgeous woman you have chemistry with is right under your nose, you're a total pussy?"

"It has nothing to do with being a pussy. I don't have time for a relationship. You guys know that."

"Fine," said Durham with a dubious expression. "Then don't sit here stewing and bitching when she starts going out with your archenemy."

Quinn flashed his friend a dirty look, mostly because he was right. The clawing feeling in his gut was getting worse. "Let's change the subject," he said tersely.

His buddies were right on the money. If he wanted Natalie, he had to make a move. But the thought scared the shit out of him. For one thing, he knew she'd want a relationship, and if his past history was any indication, it wasn't something he was cut out to do. Either he'd wind up ending things because the woman was interfering with his work and making demands on him he couldn't fulfill, or else she'd dump him because she couldn't stand coming in second to his job. Still, the thought of her with Clement rattled him. Mere dating was out of the question; that left open the possibility for her to see him and Clement, which would drive him nuts. No, it was time to try to balance a relationship with work, assuming he could get her to go out on a first date with him.

And he had an idea to help ensure that she said yes.

* * *

"Let me make sure I'm getting this straight." Anthony Dante looked completely mystified as he and Quinn sat at the bar at Dante's after closing time. He pulled out a cigar. "You're asking me for dating advice? You?"

Quinn's idea was to talk to Anthony about Natalie. After all, Anthony had managed to win the heart of Natalie's sister, Vivi, so he had to know something about how to woo classy Frenchwomen, right?

"Why are you surprised?"

"Because you're the man, Quinn. Self-confident, suave . . ."

"True, but I've never gone for anyone like Natalie before."

"You mean a snob?" Anthony said bluntly.

Quinn cringed. "Sounds like you don't like her."

"No, I do, I swear. But I'm not going to lie: I didn't at first. In the beginning she thought I was mean to Vivi. But she's come around." Anthony lit his cigar. "Come on: you know what she's like."

"Yeah. But I kinda like it. Gives me something to tease her about."

"I have noticed you two let it fly sometimes. Vivi says you both have been pussyfooting around this for a long time. So I don't get why you'd need any guidance."

"I've never pursued anyone this high-class."

Anthony took a puff of his cigar. "She's a waitress, Quinn."

"Yeah, but that's just temporary. In France she was some kind of civil servant in the government or something." Quinn realized he barely knew about Natalie's past. She tended to be tight-lipped, and he often got the sense she thought he was rude when he asked about it. But that's how the French were: Ask them questions deemed too personal, and they thought you were rude. Ask them about anything else, and they'd argue with you till death.

"Some guy broke her heart," Anthony told him, filling in a blank. "Upper-level government guy. It was a minor scandal."

"Really?"

"Yeah. She had to resign from her job. The papers raked her over the coals."

Great. She probably thought all journalists were scum.

"Why now?" Anthony asked suddenly. "Why, all of a sudden, do you want to ask her out now?"

"There's some other guy—a real dick—who she's already gone out with once."

He proceeded to tell Anthony all about Mason Clement. Anthony shook his head worriedly.

"Bad news about the accent, my friend. The ladies love accents."

Quinn frowned.

"And you say he took her to a museum? Shit, I don't think I've been to the museum since seventh grade, when we went on a field trip to the Museum of Natural History. You ever been there?"

"Yeah, about two years ago when one of the night watchmen was murdered." Quinn rubbed the back of his neck, frustrated. "Can we get back to Natalie, please?"

"Sure. Just one more question: How do you know she liked going with him to the museum? Maybe she thought it was boring as hell. Maybe you have nothing to worry about with this guy."

"I can't take that risk. Tell me how you won Vivi."

Anthony chuckled. "It wasn't easy. But we started with a common link: we were both chefs. I think it helped sharing that passion."

"The only common link I have with Natalie is a penchant for trying to get each other's goat."

"Reframe that, Bro: You're both quick-witted. And clearly you both have a sense of humor, though hers isn't, uh, apparent right off the bat."

"Yeah, no kidding." Quinn paused. "She is snooty, isn't she? You're right."

"Totally stuck up," Anthony agreed.

"Cultured," Quinn repeated, more to himself than Anthony. That was why she was drawn to Clement, with his goddamn Armani suits and jaunts to the museum.

"She likes expensive restaurants," Anthony said. "She and Vivi are always talking about this or that restaurant in France."

"Mmm." Quinn didn't do expensive restaurants. He couldn't. Reporters didn't make a lot of money. His salary never really mattered to him before; it was the buzz and satisfaction he got from his job that was paramount. Still, if using his AmEx card would get him what he wanted, then he was prepared to use it.

"If I were to take her to an expensive restaurant in the city, which one would you recommend?"

Anthony took another puff of his cigar. "How expensive?"

"The most expensive. One that you have to make reservations for weeks in advance. One she would have heard of."

"You talking French?"

Quinn snorted. "Of course."

Anthony puffed on his cigar thoughtfully. "L'Orangerie. It's one of the most expensive restaurants in Manhattan. I'd be shocked if she hadn't heard of it. I took Vivi there once, and she nearly fainted with ecstasy. The food is really amazing."

"I bet the prices are, too."

Anthony turned up his palms apologetically. "Hey, you're talking to the wrong guy here. I think it was worth every penny, but then again, I'm a chef."

"You think that's the way to go? Take her there?"

"Natalie? Oh yeah. You'll need a tie, though."

Quinn was mildly offended. "I own a few ties."

"Just checking." Anthony snuffed out his cigar. "I can pull some strings and get you in. When do you want to take her?"

"You mean if she accepts?"

"She'll accept. Because if she doesn't, Vivi will kick her ass from here to gay Paree."

Quinn chuckled. "Sunday night would be good. She works Friday and Saturday."

"Time?"

"Eight?"

"Don't think it'll be a prob. Call me and let me know if she accepts, and I'll set it all up."

Quinn clamped a hand on Anthony's shoulder. "I owe you for this, Anthony. Seriously."

"Don't be an *idiota*. Vivi is going to be thrilled about this."

"How're the wedding plans going?"

Anthony groaned. "It's giving me constant *agita*. You want the definition of hell? Two chefs trying to select a caterer."

"Yeah, but it'll all be worth it in the end, right?"

Anthony's face lit up. "Totally."

Quinn slid off his stool. "All right, I'm off. Give my love to Vivi, Mikey, and Theresa, too." Michael was Anthony's brother, assistant head coach of the New York Blades. Theresa was his wife. Quinn knew them fairly well because they, too, often dined at Vivi's. "Tell Vivi I'll stop in soon."

"Can I tell her you're finally gonna to ask her sister out?"

"Yeah, just don't say anything until I give you the green light. She could say no."

"Ain't gonna happen, my friend. Mark my words."

10

"Forgive me, Mrs. O'Brien. I was only trying to help."

Quinn's mother nodded tersely as Natalie brought the last few empty beer glasses from the bar into the kitchen while Liam locked up. Quinn had warned her not to suggest any menu changes to his mother, but Natalie couldn't help herself. She didn't see how adding a wine list, as well as a few classic dishes like quiche and coq au vin, could do any harm. Apparently, Mrs. O'Brien didn't agree. "We're an Irish pub, and we serve Irish food, period. We've been open close to forty years, and to the best of my knowledge, no one has ever complained about the menu," she'd told Natalie frostily. Natalie apologized, but deep down she believed the O'Briens were making a mistake. Expanding the menu might bring in even more customers.

Humbly ducking her head, she left the kitchen, knowing Quinn was waiting for her. He'd made a point of pulling her aside during her shift, saying he wanted to talk to her. She saw no reason not to, even though she could guess what it was about: he was going to give her a hard time about Mason Clement. She knew his friends had told him about their date. If there was one thing she'd learned about Quinn and his fellow reporters, it was that they were a pack of gossiping biddies.

Her date with Mason had gone well. He was knowledgeable about art, which impressed her. They'd gone for coffee afterward, and he'd talked about all the different, exciting places where he'd worked: Tokyo, London . . . he was so erudite and sophisticated. So well traveled.

"I had a really nice time today," he'd said to her when they finished their coffee.

"Me, too."

"I'd like to see you again."

"That would be nice," she'd said, ignoring the lack of excitement she felt. Mason was nice. He was good-looking. He was funny. But she didn't feel the kind of spark that shot through her whenever she tangled with Quinn. Still, she wasn't going to turn down another date with such a charming man.

Mason looked delighted. "That's great. I'll ring you." He kissed her lightly on the cheek. No pressure, no big passion play. He was ever the gentleman. Natalie was glad; she wasn't sure she was a good enough actress to fake pleasure if he'd kissed her and it left her cold. Still, perhaps over time a spark might ignite?

Quinn was waiting for her at his regular booth. He'd had two whiskey shots over the course of the night, in addition to his usual pint of Guinness. Natalie truly wished there was a wine list. It was so much more refined than beer and whiskey.

Quinn motioned for her to sit down opposite him.

"I can't for very long," said Natalie. "I'm supposed to be helping your brother clean up."

"You're with me. He hassles you, he can answer to me."

"Oh yes, I'm sure he'd enjoy that," Natalie said sarcastically.

Natalie checked over her shoulder to make sure. Liam was talking on his cell phone, frowning. She turned back to Quinn.

"So, I hear the drongo gave you a tour of the newsroom," Quinn said sardonically.

I knew it, thought Natalie. *I knew his friends told him.* She lowered her head for a split second so he couldn't see the quick smile that passed over her face. He was jealous. What's more, she was pleased.

"I have no idea what a drongo is," she replied coolly as she lifted her eyes to his, "but if you're talking about Mason showing me around the newsroom, then yes, I had a very nice tour on Saturday."

"Ask him to tell you what a drongo is. I assure you, it isn't a compliment." Quinn looked amused. "How was the museum?"

Natalie put an elbow on the table, cupping her chin in the palm of her hand. "My, you newspapermen are gossips."

"Let me guess: He paints in his spare time. And fences. Yeah, he definitely looks like a guy who fences."

"Perhaps he does. At the very least, he knows about art."

"So do I. Ever see that painting of dogs playing poker? I've got the original oil hanging in my living room."

Sarcastic ass. "You're jealous Mason asked me out."

"Not jealous; disappointed. In you."

"In me?" Natalie's ire began to rise, but she tamped it down. That was what he wanted, and there was no way she was going to give him that satisfaction.

"Yeah, in you. You could do so much better than Clement."

"Oh, yes, here it comes, Mr. Know-It-All holds forth." She folded her arms across her chest. "Go on."

"How would you like to go to dinner with me next Sunday night at L'Orangerie?"

Natalie stared at him. She knew all about L'Orangerie; Vivi had raved about it, and it was supposedly one of the most expensive restaurants in the city.

"Something wrong?" Quinn drawled. "Cat got your tongue? That's an American expression, you know."

"Yes, I *know*." She paused, *"Connard,"* she added under her breath.

"Congratulations! You've just called me a drongo in your native tongue."

So, he'd called Mason an idiot. Arrogant swine. At least the man pressed his clothing, which was more than one could say for Quinn.

Natalie narrowed her eyes suspiciously. "I don't understand how this could be possible."

"How what could be possible?"

"Getting into L'Orangerie. People wait months to get into that restaurant."

"I'm not *people*," Quinn said smugly. "I've got connections all over this city. You say yes, and there'll be a table waiting for us at eight."

Natalie was impressed, but again, she was not going to give Mr. Arrogant the satisfaction of showing it. "Why do you want to take me out to dinner?"

Quinn grinned. "Because I like you, Nat. You know that."

Natalie gritted her teeth. "You know I hate being called that."

"And you know that's why I do it." He shook his head, clucking his tongue. "God, I've missed annoying you."

"Your mere presence annoys me."

"So we're still in love, then. I'm glad."

Natalie just huffed.

"You want to have dinner with me or not?"

"Certainly," Natalie said, trying to sound nonchalant. "I just need to check my schedule first and make sure I have no other commitments."

Ha! Who's annoyed now, she thought, as irritation flashed across Quinn's face.

"Yeah, well, let me know as soon as you can." He stood. "You and Liam want help cleaning up?"

"No, we'll be fine."

Quinn slung his sports jacket over his shoulder. "Talk to you soon, *ma petite olivier.*"

My little olive tree. God, what an ass! Yet there was no denying it; she enjoyed the way he teased her. L'Orangerie indeed. She couldn't wait to see what happened.

11

"I hope the appetizer was to mademoiselle's liking?"

Natalie was on the verge of an ecstatic swoon as the waiter at L'Orangerie took the empty plates of the appetizer she and Quinn had just completed: duck liver served with fresh fig chutney. She'd been dubious about Quinn's boast that he could get them reservations at the drop of a hat. But apparently he wasn't lying, and now here they were, being served in New York's finest French restaurant by a waiter who was French. She was in heaven.

She felt slightly guilty about doubting him, as well as the fact she was worried about how he might dress. But he looked wonderful, his pants pressed, his white shirt starched, a lovely tie, a blue blazer. She'd never seen him look this smooth and put-together before. Even his thick salt-and-pepper hair, which he often unconsciously mussed himself raking his hands through in frustration, was neat and tidy. She was proud to walk into such a fine establishment on his arm.

"Impressed so far?" Quinn asked. He sounded just the tiniest bit smug, but she didn't mind.

"Very much so," Natalie admitted. "You must have lots of connections, as you boasted." She paused. "You're very well-known in the city, aren't you?"

"Yup," said Quinn.

His blatant egotism made her laugh. In fact, he often made her laugh. He was funny, and she prized wit.

"You look—very handsome."

Quinn laughed. "How hard was that for you to say, Nat—I mean Natalie."

"Not hard," Natalie insisted. "It's just that—"

"You're used to seeing me after I've been running my ass off all day."

She studied his face. "Your job is very hard, isn't it?"

He took a sip of the wine the sommelier had recommended, a semisweet white wine produced along the Layon River, an area Natalie knew well. "You're just figuring that out, huh?"

"It's difficult, but you love it."

"Passionately."

Natalie felt a small tingle inside her as she wondered what else he might be passionate about.

Quinn's gaze was penetrating. "What are you passionate about?"

Natalie stared back at him. Americans—so blunt! So rude! But she enjoyed the subtext of his question.

"I'm passionate about culture, I guess. I like the theater, museums . . . I love going to the symphony."

"Me, too!"

"Really?" Natalie's insides began jangling with excitement. They did have more in common than teasing each other. She never would have figured him for someone who enjoyed going to the symphony. Such an interesting man . . .

Meanwhile, Quinn was pouring on the charm. "You know, there's a lot about you I don't know." He was right, of course. He knew very little about her life before she came to the States, unless Vivi had told him some things. Alarm pierced her, and she wondered if Vivi had told him she'd been a shopaholic. But then she realized Vivi would never do that to her. He reached across the table to take her hand in his.

Natalie tried to look nonplussed. "What do you wish to know?"

"Tell me about your family. Your job in Paris. Your romantic past."

Bold, Natalie thought. *Pushy.*

"If I tell you some things about me, then you must tell me some things about you."

"Of course."

"Well, I'm not going to just start babbling about my life," Natalie scoffed, trying to ignore how much she was enjoying the physical contact between them. "You need to ask me specific questions."

As they spoke over their entrée—a mouthwatering fillet of salmon simmered in dill and braised with vanilla essence—Natalie found herself wishing she hadn't left the questioning to a reporter. He had a very subtle way of making her trust him, a gentle way of drawing facts out of her. By the time dessert came around, he knew all about her sour mother, the relationship that had ruined her career, all of it—even her problem with money, which she'd decided to tell him of her own volition. She waited for him to look disgusted, even shocked. But no, he understood addiction: one of his best friends at the *Sent,* long fired, had a gambling addiction that had cost him everything. Quinn told her she should be proud of taking hold of herself. His admiration for her made her like him even more.

"Your turn now," she insisted over dessert, a delicious citron sorbet. She couldn't wait to discuss this meal with Vivi! She was touched by how deeply he loved his family and how close-knit they were. She'd seen it at the Hart, but hearing him verbalize it so fiercely and tenderly was different. She was envious. The only relative in her family she could stand was Vivi.

Quinn skimmed the surface of his romantic past, just as she had. But it was talking about his job where he came most alive. Natalie could not shake the feeling that he was one of those people who thrived on adrenaline. "Anything to get the story," he told her. There wasn't an ounce of humility in his voice when he told her he'd been nominated for two Pulitzer Prizes in journalism, which further impressed her. She loved the way he couldn't talk without using his hands and the way passion flashed in his blue eyes, eyes she could drown in if she lost control of herself. Quinn O'Brien was an impressive man, one with drive, soul, and passion. Charming and handsome. Vivi was right; they'd been doing this dance around each other for too long, and much as she hated to admit it, she was intensely attracted to him. Worried that he could tell, she excused herself to go to the ladies' room.

*   *   *

Quinn's first thought when Natalie excused herself was, *Moron! Why did you lie to impress her? Telling her you loved the symphony? What a load of horseshit!* Classical music bored the hell out of him.

Their waiter hustled over to the table. "How'd I do?" he asked Quinn, dropping the French accent to speak to Quinn in his normal New Yawkese.

"Great. Thanks for doing this for me."

"Hey, anything for Anthony Dante."

"Where'd you learn such a good French accent?"

"I do a little theater on the side," the waiter said modestly.

"Well, you're terrific. I really appreciate it. And I think she's impressed."

"She seems like a classy broad."

"Probably too classy for me, but we'll see." Quinn held

out his hand. "All right, I've steeled myself. Hand over the check."

Quinn suppressed a choke when he saw the damage; the meal cost $350. He looked up at the waiter. "Holy shit."

"Yeah, no kidding."

Quinn pulled his AmEx card out of his pocket.

"Thanks again, man. You saved my ass in a major way."

* * *

Standing outside her apartment building, Natalie debated whether she should ask Quinn upstairs. She knew that in many instances, it was a euphemism for something else, and she certainly didn't want him to think she was cheap or fast, because she wasn't. Still, she could stand here and flirt with him a little, couldn't she?

"So, now that you know everything about me—"

"Not everything."

"What's left?" she murmured.

"This."

Quinn took her in his arms, crushing his mouth to hers. The rush of it made her feel so exhilaratingly alive it almost hurt. When he slipped his tongue into her mouth, deepening their connection, she felt weak-kneed, almost giddy. God help her, she'd let him make love to her right here in the doorway of this building if he wanted. She was dissolving in his arms, drowning in a whirlpool of need and desire and lust. He was, too. She could feel it in the urgency with which he pressed his body against hers, heat matching heat. Which was why it was such a jolt when he abruptly tore himself away.

"I think we should call it a night," he said gruffly. He appeared to be trying to regain his breath. Natalie nodded dumbly, trying not to stare at his mouth. She'd never noticed before now how sensual his lips were. And now that she knew the pleasure they could give, it was even harder not to want more.

"I suppose you'll go home now and roll around in your clothing to rumple it a bit," Natalie ribbed. "Actually, I feel honored that you made an effort to dress up for me."

"It wasn't for you. Didn't you see the No Wrinkled Clothing sign posted in the window?"

"Ah. I seem to have missed that."

"Distracted by my handsomeness."

"*Oui.*"

"So, how would you like to go see the New York Philharmonic next week?" Quinn asked.

Natalie's breath caught. "Really? Rachmaninoff's Second Piano Concerto?"

Quinn rocked on his heels. "Yup."

Natalie clasped her hands together excitedly. "Oh, I would love to see that. He's one of my favorite composers."

"Mine, too."

"What's your favorite piece?"

"The Second Piano Concerto, of course."

"I love Prelude opus twenty-three, number three."

"Another favorite of mine."

Natalie was intrigued. "You're really full of surprises, aren't you?"

"I'm going to try not to take that as an insult." He smoothed a stray lock of hair off her face. "We can talk about the concert at the Hart the next time I see you."

Natalie nodded. She felt somewhat cheated; the night had passed by so quickly. "I had a wonderful evening."

"See? I'm not such a crude jackass once you get to know me."

"At least not all the time."

He put his lips softly to hers. "See you in a few days, Nat."

She smiled shyly. God help her, she was starting to like him calling her that. It was like his own private nickname for her. She watched as he ducked into a cab, and then she went upstairs to her—Bernard's—apartment, the memory of their kiss a small torture. Vivi had been right all along.

* * *

Quinn directed the cabdriver to the Hart. If he went home, he'd be forced to admit just how much Natalie got under his skin: enough to make him lie about liking classical music and ask her out on a date to see a concert that might be sold out, for all he knew. When had he become so pathetic? Answer: the second he saw how easily Natalie was entranced by Mason Clement. He'd never gone out on a limb like this for any woman, and it scared the shit out of him.

Entering the pub, he was shocked to see Mason Clement perched on his usual seat at the bar, talking to PJ Leary. Clement? On a Sunday? Maybe the drongo thought he might catch Natalie filling in for Megan. Quinn hated that Mason was now a regular, well-known enough to be on cozy chatting terms with the old-timers. Catching sight of Quinn, Mason raised his pint glass to him. Quinn ignored it.

"Unusual to see you here on a Sunday night," Quinn observed dryly after asking his eternally glaring brother to get him some Jameson. He didn't have the energy to deal with two assholes tonight, so he just let it go.

"Came over after work."

"Since when do you work seven days a week?"

"Much like you, O'Brien, I'm always working. You should know that by now."

Yeah, working on turning the Sent *into a rag.* "So, what's on tomorrow's front page? A story about a secret army of dogs that keeps the secret army of cats in check?"

Clement ignored the barb. "The actress Geraldine Carr has cancer. Rumor has it she only has weeks to live."

"That's the fucking front page? Jesus Christ. Liam, make that a double, will ya?" he called to his brother. He turned his attention back to Clement, not bothering to hide his contempt. "Let's see if I can guess the headline. 'Carr's Last Drive'? 'Carr Crash Looming'?"

"Read the paper tomorrow and find out." Clement took a sip of beer. "Oh, and to save us both the displeasure of another debate on the proper focus of big-city tabloids, let me just cut to the chase and remind you that celebrity sells, and selling papers is my job."

Quinn picked up the glass his brother handed him and threw his first whiskey down his throat, relishing the burning sensation blazing a trail all the way down to his stomach.

"Celebrity does sell, Quinn," PJ chimed in.

"How the hell do you know?" Quinn snapped. "You sit in a crappy room with peeling paint writing about leprechauns."

The minute the words were out, Quinn regretted them. "Shit," he said, putting a conciliatory arm around PJ's shoulders. "I'm sorry I said that, man. I didn't mean it."

"No offense taken," PJ insisted, quickly covering his pained expression. "Were you out on a story tonight?" He sounded so interested that Quinn felt even worse. Sometimes he got the feeling PJ lived vicariously through him.

"No story. I had a date." There was no mistaking the flicker of interest that passed across Clement's face.

"A date," PJ repeated, impressed. "You haven't had a real date in years."

"Haven't had time. But this was one woman I'm more than willing to make time for."

"Don't hold out on your old friend!" PJ continued with a wicked gleam in his eye. "Details, my man, I want details."

"She's an incredible woman," said Quinn, knowing that Clement was listening to every word. "Sexy, intelligent, witty, cultured, feisty . . ."

"I take it you're going to see her again?"

"Oh yeah," Quinn boasted. "We're going out again next week."

"Best of luck. I hope if it ends up becoming serious, you'll bring her in here to meet everyone."

"That goes without saying." He patted PJ's shoulder. "I'm gonna go in the back and say hi to my folks."

"Well, good luck on your next date."

"Thanks," said Quinn in a voice brimming with confidence, "but I don't think I'll need it." He nodded curtly at his boss. "See you, Clement."

"O'Brien."

God, that felt good, sticking it to that pretentious Aussie number cruncher. Cock blocking indeed.

12

Two hundred bucks each. That's what it cost Quinn for two tickets to the New York Philharmonic. He'd almost stroked out from sheer shock.

Despite a crazy schedule, he'd managed to find time to hit Best Buys to pick up a CD of Rachmaninoff's Second Piano Concerto so he at least knew what he'd be hearing. Jesus Christ, it was boring. Long, torturous, and boring. He didn't know how the hell he was going to stay awake for the whole thing, unless he guzzled at least a few cups of joe before meeting Natalie at Avery Fisher Hall. He also Googled Rachmaninoff, just in case Natalie brought him up. Russian, influenced by Tchaikovsky, blah blah blah. Two dates with Natalie, and he was already down $750. If they continued seeing each other, he was going to have to introduce her to some of the less expensive things in life, or he'd be broke within two months. Then again, both the ritzy restaurant and the Philharmonic had been his idea, not hers.

No doubt $750 was a drop in the bucket for Mason Clement. Clearly he'd gotten to the bastard. Clement had been a prick to Quinn and his cronies all week. Nothing anyone did was up to snuff—as if the asshole knew or even cared about news, sports, or crossword puzzles. It was pure ballbusting. It bugged Quinn that Clement wasn't just riding him but his friends as well, part of some kind of twisted spite by association thing. If it didn't stop soon, Quinn was going to call him on it.

He was cooling his heels outside Lincoln Center while he waited for Nat, watching all the well-dressed people make their way inside. Quinn loved people watching, maybe because reading faces was a big part of his job. He wondered if people knew how much their expressions, even if they were only fleeting, revealed about them. An older couple who looked to be in their seventies walked toward him. The frail, slightly hunched guy was decked out in a tux, while the woman, wizened yet bosomy, waddled beside him in some kind of gauzy, floor-length peach dress. The man was talking a mile minute in that croaky old-guy voice, and for a split second, the woman looked like she wanted to plunge a dagger into his heart. The old man didn't catch it at all. Quinn loved noticing stuff like this.

"Bonjour."

Hearing Natalie's voice behind him, Quinn turned. There she was, his four-hundred-dollar date, looking so happy and relaxed that he had no choice but to ignore the feeling he was about to descend into musical hell.

Quinn gave a small bow. *"Bonjour, Mademoiselle Bocuse.* You look rather beautiful tonight."

Natalie ducked her head shyly. "Thank you."

She did indeed look beautiful, dressed in a sleek black dress and pearls, her long, wavy brown hair pulled back.

"Frenchwomen really do know how to get decked out."

Natalie jokingly tilted her nose up in the air. "We pride ourselves on it."

"You've got a booger in your left nostril."

Natalie's hand flew to her nose, horrified. "What?"

"Just kidding."

"You're an immature ass," Natalie hissed.

"Yeah, I know. But you love me anyway."

Quinn quickly glanced down at his own outfit, wondering if Natalie noticed he was wearing the same thing he'd worn to L'Orangerie. He owned two sports jackets, and the other one was at the cleaners because he'd dripped mustard on the sleeve eating a hot dog on the run.

He offered her his arm. "Shall we?"

"Oui."

Natalie threaded his arm through hers, and together they walked to Avery Fisher Hall. When he led Natalie to their third-row seats, there was no mistaking the shock on her face.

"How did you—?" she asked breathlessly.

Quinn almost lied and said he was a season ticket holder and then caught himself, fearing it would be a recipe for poverty. Instead, he just winked and said, "I have my ways."

They settled into their seats. Quinn was struck by the volume of the murmuring crowd: so low and respectful it reminded him of being at a wake. Meanwhile, Natalie was gazing around in elation.

She finally turned to him. "This was a wonderful idea. Thank you for inviting me."

"Thank you for accepting."

He took her hand in his. Her fingers were long and delicate, her hand tiny and soft. *Christ, listen to yourself. You're rhapsodizing over her hands.* The effect she was having on him was downright unnerving. He couldn't help himself: without warning, he gently put his mouth to hers, enthralled by the myriad sensations tumbling through him. Though it seemed a sweet kiss on the surface, he could feel need rising up in him, spurred on in part by her lack of resistance. He longed to deepen contact, but this wasn't the time or place. He slowly lifted his mouth from hers. Natalie looked slightly dazed. He waited for some sort of teasing rebuke, but none came. Still holding her hand, he tightened his grip. No resistance.

Eventually the orchestra filed onstage and began tuning up. The audience fell silent. The house lights went down. The conductor came to stand behind the podium, the orchestra poised for direction, and the music began.

For the first half hour or so, Natalie's happiness was enough to keep Quinn's boredom at bay. But then he began losing the battle, stifling yawns, trying to sit up straight in his seat, feigning concentration. Ultimately, the only thing that kept his head from slumping down onto his chest was thinking about the next piece of research he might need to delve into about the possible connection between Shields Construction and Whitey Connors. That's when his cell phone vibrated.

Quinn quickly pulled the phone out of his pocket and checked to see who was calling. It was Liam. Panic seized him: Liam never called him. Something bad had happened.

"I have to go," he whispered to Natalie.

"What?" she whispered back, looking stunned.

"I have to go. I'm really sorry. I'll call you."

He kissed her quickly on the cheek, turned his phone off, and began his litany of "excuse me's" as he made his way to the aisle. He could feel Natalie's eyes burning into his back. He couldn't worry about that. Something bad had happened. One thing was certain: he sure as hell was awake now.

* * *

"Jesus Christ, PJ."

Quinn tried not to wince as he pulled up a chair beside the writer's hospital bed. He'd hated leaving Natalie in the middle of the concert, but he didn't have a choice. Liam had called to tell him that the Mouth had rushed into the Hart after seeing PJ being loaded, bloodied and unconscious, onto a stretcher and taken away in an ambulance. The "family" at the Hart was close-knit; what happened to any one of them affected them all. Someone beating up mild-mannered PJ certainly fit the bill.

Quinn prayed in the cab that he wouldn't have to go hospital hopping to find PJ, and his prayers were answered: PJ was in the first hospital he hit, Roosevelt. Unsurprisingly, Quinn found him in a small cubicle awaiting triage, his cuts and bruises pretty low on the emergency room's totem pole. Even so, it was a shock to see him: there was blood caked to his head, his left eye was a bloodied slit, and he was missing a front tooth. His face was virtually swollen beyond recognition.

"Quinn." PJ looked pleased to see him and began to smile, then stopped. "Shit, that hurts."

"Any idea when they'll fix you up?"

"Nurse said they've got two heart attacks and a gunshot wound. I'll probably be here all night." He touched his left cheek, grimacing. "I must look a sight."

"That's putting it mildly."

"Who called you?"

"Liam. The Mouth saw you being loaded into an ambulance—where? Outside your apartment building?"

"No, the building where I rent my writing room."

"Wanna tell me what happened?" Quinn murmured.

PJ's eyes turned toward the wall. "I got mugged. It's nothing."

"It's nothing? PJ, your face has been rearranged. That's not nothing."

PJ didn't say anything.

"Did some guys rob you and then decide to kick the shit out of you just for fun?"

"Just let it go, Quinn, okay? It's not important."

Quinn drew his chair closer. "You know what, PJ? For an Irishman, you're a terrible liar. Don't hold out on me here, pal."

"I can't go into it, Quinn," PJ replied evasively.

"Why not?"

PJ hesitated. "Because it could make things worse for me."

"Worse for you? Did the guys who beat you up threaten you?"

PJ looked exasperated. "Quinn, just—"

"No. I'm not moving from this chair until you give me at least the bare bones of what happened. I'm serious." Quinn sat there, knowing that if push came to shove, he could wait PJ out. Hell, he could wait anyone out if he had to; he was the master of the journalistic stakeout. He just never thought he'd be staking out a friend lying in a hospital bed.

As Quinn predicted, PJ eventually caved. "I was in my writing room," he began woodenly, "working on my book— you know the one based on Celtic myth with a touch of—"

"Yeah, yeah, I know the book." Quinn hated sounding impatient, but he knew PJ: once he got started rhapsodizing about his magnum opus, it could be hours before he got round to the meat of the story—and Quinn wanted the meat badly.

PJ glared at him with his one good eye. "Anyway, I was working on my book, when three young thugs burst into the room. All of them were wearing balaclavas. I thought, 'Shit, they're here to rob me, and all I have to give them is my precious Underwood and a bottle of Johnnie Walker Blue.' But they weren't there to rob me," he said quietly.

"What happened?"

"They asked if I knew that the building had a new owner. I said no. Then they said they were putting me on notice that I had a week to get out of there. I told them I had a lease, and I didn't see why I couldn't just keep paying rent to the new owner. Their charming, erudite response? 'There's no way you're going to be able to afford this room anymore, fuck face.'"

PJ took a long breath, gritting his teeth. Obviously his ribs were hurting. "I said, well, could I just talk to the owner and see? That's when they beat me up, reiterating I had a week to get out or else."

"They didn't say who the new owner of the building was?"

"No."

"So then what happened?"

"What do you think happened?" PJ retorted. "They left, I pissed my pants from pure fear, and I called an ambulance."

"You're gonna file a police report, right?"

PJ's swollen lips fell open in disbelief. "What are you, out of your mind? Those guys almost killed me. They want me out, I'm out."

"Peej—"

"Don't push me on this, Quinn. I wish Liam had never called you. I knew you'd come running down here sniffing blood."

"That's what I do for a living, PJ. I sniff blood. Besides, you're my friend."

"I guess," PJ mumbled.

Quinn shook his head, distressed. "I can't believe this shit is going on in our own neighborhood."

"Well," said PJ, groaning in pain as he shifted position, "I got the message loud and clear, and I'm getting the hell out of there." He sighed. "At least they didn't break my typewriter."

Fuck your typewriter, Quinn thought. "I'm gonna write this up for the *Sent.*"

"Don't," PJ hissed vehemently. "You wanna get me killed?"

"It won't get you killed."

"Look at my face, you bullheaded idiot. If even one of them sees the article, I'm dead. I'm begging you as a friend:

forget I ever told you about this, okay?" He looked desperate.

Quinn gently patted his shoulder. "Okay, don't worry about it. I won't write up the story. I'll just wait here until they fix you up."

"Actually, I'd be much happier if you went and got my typewriter and manuscript."

"I can do that. You sure you gonna be okay here? Let me at least go get you some magazines or something. Even better." He dug into his backpack, pulling out his iPod and earbuds and handing them to PJ. "Close your eyes and just relax. I'll go get your typewriter and keep it safe."

"You're a gentleman and a scholar, Quinn O'Brien."

Quinn walked out of the emergency room, his mind racing. PJ had had his ass beaten and was told to vacate his room within the week. Franco the tailor was mysteriously retiring after being made "an offer" he couldn't turn down. Porco & Sons' higher bid was rejected by the mayor's office. It didn't take a scholar to connect the dots.

*   *   *

"Let's hear you sing the praises of that oaf Quinn O'Brien now."

Natalie was standing in the kitchen at Vivi's, watching her sister and her two cooks prepare for the inevitable lunch rush. Natalie had barely slept, her anger over Quinn's abrupt departure from the concert keeping her awake.

For a few brief seconds after he left, the surrounding concertgoers glared at her as if she were somehow responsible for his behavior. Natalie glared back, then spent the rest of the concert seething.

His flimsy exit line "I have to go," was downright insulting in its vagueness. They were on a date, for God's sake. Didn't she deserve a real explanation? Something along the lines of "There's a family emergency," if indeed that's what it was? "I have to go" told her nothing. Go where? To the newspaper office? Out on a story? To see another woman, who just found out she's pregnant? By the time she got home, her imagination was out of control, and she was dangerously close to irrationality, intending to quit waitressing at the Wild Hart so she'd never have to see him again. But then she realized she *wanted* to see him again; she wanted to berate him for the way he'd treated her. It was the least he deserved.

Vivi pressed the crust of a quiche into a pie plate. "I'm sure he had a very good reason for running out on you, Natalie."

"Well, if he did, he could have told me."

"I'm sure he will, as soon as he can." She motioned for Natalie to pass her the plate of crisped bacon in front of her, which Vivi began crumbling. "How's the job hunt going?"

Natalie groaned. "Only one interview so far. A waste of time. The owner was a buffoon from Normandy who hates Parisians. He as much as told me he was only talking to me as a favor to Anthony. He also told me I wasn't ready to manage a restaurant of medium size. That I should start small and work my way up."

"That sounds like good advice."

"What does he know? He's from Normandy." Vivi caught her eye, and they both laughed.

"I miss you," Natalie blurted. "I miss working here."

"I thought you said there's nothing to do here for someone single."

"There isn't," Natalie said glumly.

"Don't be so impatient, Natalie. Things will work out."

"That's easy for you to say. You have your own business, a good man who loves you . . ." Natalie looked down, trailing her index finger back and forth across the stainless steel table. "I'm envious of you," she admitted quietly.

Vivi stopped crumbling bacon and came to Natalie's side, forcing her to look up at her. "You're being ridiculous. Where's that imperious Parisian I know and love?"

Natalie cracked a small smile.

"If I may put my four dollars in—"

"The expression is 'two cents,' Vivi."

"If I may put my two cents in, I think he's a good man who's been fond of you for a very long time, and if you give him a chance, you'll find love, too."

Natalie hesitated. "I'm not sure he's as refined as I'd like."

"He took you to the symphony!"

"Yes, but I could tell he didn't like it, even though he claims it's one of his favorite things to do! He was fidgety and distracted."

"You're just looking to find things that are wrong with him because you're scared. Didn't you tell me on the phone the other day that he took you to L'Orangerie and the two of you had a lovely time? That he made you laugh and was very interesting? That he impressed you?"

Natalie cast down her eyes. "Yes." She paused. "But there's another man who impresses me, too. One who presents a more sophisticated face to the world."

"Who, that Mason Clement you told me about?" Vivi sounded dubious.

Natalie looked back up at her. "Yes."

"You said there was no spark between you."

Natalie squirmed. "Yes, but maybe a spark could ignite. He wants to see me again."

"Do you want to see him?"

"Maybe. I don't know. It's not like Quinn and I are a couple." Natalie paused thoughtfully. "Yes, I think I will see Mason again. Why not?"

Vivi scowled. "Are you just trying to get back at Quinn for leaving you at the symphony?"

"No!" *Well, maybe,* Natalie thought. Maybe it would teach him that she was not the type of woman you could just dash out on without explaining why.

"I think you're overreacting. I'm sure Quinn has a perfectly good explanation for leaving in the middle of the concert."

"He better have. In the meantime, I see no harm in seeing Mason again."

13

This was a mistake, Natalie thought to herself, sitting with Mason in a cozy little candlelit bistro in the Village. As charming and witty as Mason was, all she could think about was that baboon, Quinn O'Brien. It wasn't fair to Mason. Natalie had to tell him that as much as she enjoyed his company, she just wanted to be friends.

Mason must have been reading her mind, because he unexpectedly introduced the topic of Quinn into the conversation.

"I was at the Hart last week, and Quinn O'Brien came in raving about what a wonderful date he'd been on. I kept thinking there was only one person he could be talking about: you."

Natalie grew guarded. "We had dinner, yes."

"Are you seeing him?"

"I'm not sure what you mean by that."

Mason looked irritated. "Are you going to go out with him again?"

"I don't think that's any of your business."

"Well, I want it to be."

Natalie blinked. "Pardon?"

Mason's hand came across the table to rest firmly atop hers. "I really enjoy your company, Natalie. I would like— I would love—if we started dating each other exclusively."

"Exclusively," Natalie repeated dumbly. As delicately as she could without being hurtful, she slid her hand from beneath his and took a deep breath. "Mason, I think you are a wonderful, very interesting man. But—"

He cut her off, frowning. "Is this about O'Brien?"

"No," she lied.

"Then why not go out with me?"

His arrogance reminded her of Quinn, but with one difference: had Quinn said that, her heart would secretly beat a little faster. Irksome and egotistical as Quinn was, at least she felt alive in his presence—not that she still wasn't angry with him. With Mason, there was nothing beyond casual fondness.

"I enjoy talking to you, Mason. But I can't see us being anything more than friends. I'm sorry."

Mason's eyes fixed on a spot over her shoulder. "I see," he said coldly.

This is horrible. Totally horrible and painful, to hurt a nice person this way. Not wanting to prolong the agony for either of them, she rose. "What do I owe for my half of dinner?"

"Don't be silly," Mason scoffed.

"I just feel—"

"Like you owe me something for letting me down? That's silly, Natalie. Sit down and finish your coffee." He motioned for the check. "I'm glad we'll still be friends."

"Me, too."

"I'll see you home when we're done."

"I'll be fine."

Mason looked deflated. "Then I guess I'll see you at the Wild Hart."

* * *

"Gimme five minutes."

Quinn could *feel* Kenny Durham's eyes burning a hole in his back as he frantically hammered out some notes from a recent conversation on his computer.

"Five minutes," Quinn repeated when Durham didn't move. He had to get all the info down while it was still fresh in his head, especially since he couldn't read half the shit he'd jotted down on his notepad. It didn't help that he typed using only two fingers, his brain racing faster than his fingers could keep pace with.

Durham sighed, walking away, but Quinn couldn't worry about him right now. The notes he was typing—he was pretty sure he had a possible lead on something pretty big going down right in his own neighborhood. God bless connections, discontent, and unnamed sources.

He finished his typing with a final flourish and went to find Durham. His friend was sitting with his feet up on his desk, his fingers laced behind his head, deep in thought.

"What's up?" Quinn asked.

Durham turned to look at him. "What's up with *you*?"

Quinn tapped the side of his head. "Had to get down what's in here. You know I can't read my own handwriting half the time."

"Use your damn digital voice recorder."

"I do. But in general I hate that thing. Looking at notes is easier for me."

"God, you're such a Luddite." Durham rubbed his eyes wearily. "I have no goddamn idea what the theme for Thursday's crossword puzzle should be, and it's due in half an hour."

"Monkeys? Nuns? Lindsay Lohan?"

"I'm being serious here," Durham whined. "Help me out, you pain in the ass."

Quinn thought. "Mayors of New York."

"Good one." He jerked his head in the direction of Quinn's desk. "You ever follow up on the stuff about the Porcos losing the bid?"

Quinn grinned. "Oh yeah."

Durham's eyebrows lifted. "Care to elaborate?"

"Not yet."

"Quinn O'Brien, International Man of Mystery."

"You know it."

"There *are* some things you *should* tell your friends, though."

"Like—?"

"I heard through the grapevine that you were out on a date the other night."

"So?"

"Was it with *Natalie*?" Durham prodded.

Quinn readjusted his watch. "Maybe."

Christ, he'd been so busy he hadn't been to the Hart in a few days. Crime tended to come in waves. Things would be relatively quiet for a while, and then bam! He'd be running his ass off all over the five boroughs. Of course, Mademoiselle Natalie probably assumed he was just avoiding her. She had been royally pissed at him when he called to apologize. She understood the emergency but reamed him out for not explaining what was going on before bolting from the concert. He knew she was right.

"You've got some serious competition, you know."

Quinn yawned with boredom. "You already told me she went out with Clement. Old news."

"No, *new* news: she went out with him again. Met him here last night, and they left together."

What the hell? After he'd shelled out four hundred smackers to take her to the symphony? Yeah, she had a right to be upset with him, but this was spite. And it pissed him off.

"You look kinda pale, Quinnie boy."

"I just need coffee," Quinn growled.

She wasn't the only one who deserved an explanation.

* * *

Natalie hated cleaning. She knew it was the result of growing up with a maid, but all that dusting and vacuuming and sink scrubbing and whatnot—it all seemed so futile, especially since things just got dirty again so quickly. Vivi, of course, loved to clean, claiming it gave her a sense of accomplishment. All it gave Natalie was a feeling of having wasted a morning of her life. Still, she didn't like dirt, and since the apartment was Bernard Rousseau's, she felt an obligation to maintain it.

She was in the middle of dusting the giant telescope in the living room when the intercom buzzed, startling her so much she nearly shot to the cathedral ceiling. She glanced at her watch: 11 a.m. on a Friday morning. Maybe it was another package from her mother in Paris, who claimed to miss her, while in the same breath saying she was a "selfish and atrocious daughter" for choosing to live in America.

Natalie pressed the intercom button. "*Oui*—uh yes, Mikel?"

"There's someone here to see you named Quinn. Should I let him up?"

She told Mikel to send him up, regretting it immediately. She was barefoot, in jeans and a plain blue T-shirt, sans makeup—completely unpresentable. Panicked, she ran into the bathroom to put some lipstick on and at least run a comb through her hair. There was no time to change into something a bit more stylish. *Merde.*

Her doorbell rang, and she squared her shoulders, opening the door. There he was, the man who had dashed out on her in the middle of one of the most glorious piano concertos of all time, one he claimed to love. She found herself wishing that he wasn't quite so good-looking. Even with what looked like a small spaghetti sauce stain on his tie, he still emitted charisma. It was maddening.

"Come in."

Quinn entered the apartment, whistling through his teeth. "Wow. Impressive. I figured Bernard had to have a nice place, but I didn't think it would be this nice."

"He's a diplomat, remember?"

"Maybe I should switch careers."

"I believe diplomats need to be diplomatic. I don't think it would be the right job for you."

Quinn chuckled, still glancing around. He pointed to the dust rag Natalie had carelessly thrown on the coffee table in her haste to answer the intercom.

"Did I interrupt your cleaning, Cinderella?"

Natalie just stared at him.

Quinn leaned toward her. "Can I ask you a question?"

"Even if I say no, you'll ask anyway, so go right ahead."

"Who the hell cleans house with lipstick on?"

"Who shows up unannounced at someone's door?" Natalie snapped.

"You put it on for me, didn't you?" Quinn continued in a teasing voice.

"Don't flatter yourself."

He studied her face. "You really don't need makeup, you know. You look fine without it." He looked down at her feet. "Nice toes. Very well-groomed."

I hate you! Natalie thought.

"Enough with your sarcastic compliments. Why are you here?"

"Because I owe you another apology. Can I sit down on Bernie's couch? Or do you want to have this entire conversation standing by the door?"

"Sit," Natalie muttered begrudgingly.

"Are you going to join me?"

"Of course, you oaf."

She saw Quinn suppress a smile, which irritated her no end. He thought this was a joke, did he? Well, he'd soon find out it wasn't.

She sat down on the opposite end of the couch, hoping to send a clear message. Now Quinn looked amused.

"Aren't you even going to offer me a cup of coffee?"

"You're not going to be here long enough to drink it."

"God, you're feisty."

"And you're maddening." She crossed her arms. "Well? I'm waiting."

"You're absolutely right. I should have told you there was an emergency. I was wrong to just run out of there without an explanation. I'm terribly sorry."

"Apology accepted under one condition."

"I don't do it again."

"That's not the condition. I want you to give me an honest answer to one question."

"Of course, ask away."

"You were bored at that concert, weren't you? Bored to tears."

Quinn scratched his chin absently. "Yeah, I was. I'm pretty sure that if I go to hell when I die, part of my eternal punishment will be an endless loop of that concerto."

Natalie shook her head, her exasperation beginning to fade, even though she wished she could hold on to it longer. "Why did you lie to me, then? Why did you say you loved classical music and that concerto?"

"Because I wanted to impress you. Jesus Christ, what was I supposed to do? Take you to the movies and buy you a tub of popcorn after Mr. Down Under took you to the museum, and you acted like you'd spent the afternoon with the art critic for the *New York Times*?"

"So this is really all about you and Mason, then. Trying to outdo each other."

"No, you mule-headed woman," Quinn spat out in frustration. "It's all about wanting to make sure you had a good time."

Natalie narrowed her eyes. "But Mason did figure into it, too, didn't he?"

Quinn threw his hands up in the air. "Fine! Yes! Crocodile Dundee figured into it! It drives me crazy that you like that putz!" Quinn was scowling. "Durham told me you went out with him again."

"I saw no reason not to," Natalie replied, sounding blasé.

"You going to see him again?"

Natalie shrugged, a frisson of excitement going through her as she waited to see what he would do.

"Need a reason not to?" Quinn growled. He looked dangerous, thrilling Natalie even more. "Here, I'll give you one."

One minute Quinn was practically snarling at her from the other end of the couch; the next he had snatched her up into his arms, pressing his lips against hers so hard that an uncontrolled current of electricity shot through her, making her gasp. Quinn pulled back to look at her, an evil little smile on his face.

"Liked that, huh, Miss Bocuse?"

Natalie's head was swimming.

"Here's a little more."

He crushed his mouth to hers again, the force of the kiss one of unmistakable dominance. His mouth was claiming hers so fiercely, so roughly, that she began to quiver. She liked a man who took control, and clearly Quinn O'Brien was one of those men. When he pulled back a little to nip at her lower lip, a small groan escaped Natalie's lips.

"Clement kiss you like that? Huh?"

"He—he never kissed me," Natalie managed.

His expression was triumphant. "Good."

Had any other man acted as if she were a prize he'd won, she would have pushed him off her and given him a piece of her mind. But that wasn't what she wanted. What she wanted was to pull his face down to hers, taste his mouth, run her hands through that thick tangle of his hair.

She reached for him, confused when he pulled away. "Quinn—?"

His expression was all innocence. "Yes?"

Natalie swallowed, trying to hide how vulnerable she suddenly felt. "If you want to, you can keep kissing me."

"You still haven't said you've forgiven me."

"Obviously I've forgiven you, you fool! I'm kissing you, aren't I?"

"And Clement—?"

"Dear God, have you suddenly turned into an idiot who needs everything spelled out for you? I told him we would only ever just be friends."

"Oh, he must have loved that."

"Can we stop speaking about him?"

"Sure." Quinn stood up.

"What are you doing?!" Natalie's heart was still thumping away in her chest for want of him.

"I think it's good to keep your lady eager for more, you know?"

Natalie's mouth fell open. "You bastard!"

"That's me," Quinn grinned mischievously. "Should I give you a call and we'll figure out our next rendezvous, mademoiselle?"

"Oh, you're maddening! *Maddening!*"

"I'll take that as a yes." He leaned over and planted a chaste, gentle kiss on her cheek. "Talk to you soon."

14

"Well, if it isn't himself."

Quinn ignored his mother's affectionate barb and bent down to kiss her cheek. She was at the breakfast table with his father and Liam. This was the way the three of them started most every day: Liam would come over to talk inventory and the previous night's take, etc., with his folks, and then his parents would go downstairs into the kitchen at the Hart and start preparing for lunch while Liam dealt with deliveries and the bills. It was Liam with whom Quinn wanted to speak, but he thought that by stopping by he'd kill two birds with one stone.

"And just where have you been keeping yourself, boyo?" his father asked while Quinn grabbed a mug from the cabinet and poured himself a cup of coffee.

"Working."

"You're going to drive yourself into the ground with that job," his father chided.

"I could say the same to you," Quinn replied, sliding into the empty seat next to his brother.

"No doubt you've heard about what happened to PJ Leary," said his father, shaking his head sadly.

Quinn's eyes flicked to Liam's. "Yeah, Liam told me."

"I don't like what's going on in this neighborhood," his father continued. "All those perfectly good buildings being torn down or renovated by the Shields Brothers."

"You know them at all?" Quinn asked suddenly. Jesus, why hadn't he thought of asking this earlier? Well, at least he had the presence of mind to ask now.

"Not really. They've come in a few times over the years but never really became regulars."

"The wife of the younger one—what's his name, Larry?—she's nice," said his mother. "I see her at Mass every Sunday with their two little ones."

His mother was the only family member who still attended Mass regularly. His once-devout father had stopped going, disgusted by the priest sex scandals. But his mother's faith ran deep. Sunday remained a ritual for the family in another way, however; it was when they all gathered for a big afternoon dinner.

"Why are you asking about the Shields Brothers?" asked his mother.

"The boy's a reporter," his father answered with pride in his voice. "He asks about everything."

Quinn sipped his coffee. "How's Natalie working out?"

His mother's expression darkened. "God knows she's a good waitress, but Jesus, Mary, and Saint Joseph, the gall of her to suggest we change the menu . . ."

"She's just trying to help, Mom."

"Yes, well, I do find it a wee bit insulting."

"Call her on it," Quinn suggested, knowing Natalie would kill him if she knew what he was about to suggest. "Next time she suggests a menu change, say, 'Fine, but you cook it.' I bet that'll shut her up fast."

His mother laughed. "Perhaps I will."

"I hear you two are sweet on each other," said his father.

Quinn's gaze shot to Liam.

"Don't look at me!" Liam protested.

"It was your crossword puzzle friend who told us," his mother confessed. "Is it true?"

"We're dating," Quinn replied evasively.

Quinn's father coughed nervously. "You sure she's the type of girl for you, Quinn? She seems a bit—"

"Posh," his mother finished.

"Because of her accent?"

His mother sighed. "Because of all of it, I guess. Her accent, the way she carries herself . . . I noticed her nails are always manicured and painted."

This was just the sort of thing his no-nonsense mother would notice. As far as Quinn knew, his mother had never had her nails done, claiming it didn't make sense, since she cooked so much. Still, there were times he'd caught his mother looking enviously at the well-dressed women who came into the pub.

"You should have your nails done sometime," Quinn suggested.

His mother snorted as if that was the most ridiculous suggestion she'd ever heard. "I'm not that type of woman."

"No, it's that you don't think you deserve it," said Liam. "You've got that Irish denial thing going on."

Quinn's mother turned to his father. "You hearing this? My own sons ganging up on me?"

Quinn's dad just chuckled, eyeing Quinn. "We were on the subject of your sweetheart before all this talk of nails sidetracked them."

"Yeah, you were characterizing her as posh." Quinn chose his words carefully. "Natalie was raised wealthy, but that doesn't mean she's had it easy." He filled his parents and Liam in on what he knew: her diplomat father's love-less marriage to her mother, being a lonely, only child until she found out about Vivi. He omitted the part about a romantic relationship driving her to make a new life for herself here in the States. He also saw no point in telling them she was a recovering shopaholic. That wouldn't go down well with his frugal mother.

"Does she plan to stay here in America?" his mother asked. Quinn knew what she was angling at: always protective, she wanted to make sure her eldest son wasn't left high and dry with a broken heart. As if he'd ever had his heart broken; usually it was the other way around.

"She loves it here."

"And what, exactly, is it you like about her?" his father asked.

Quinn would never admit it, but the question pleased him; he loved the fact that his family was interested in her. "She's funny, smart—"

"Beautiful," Liam interjected, pissing Quinn off.

"She gives as good as she gets with me," Quinn continued. "She's very sharp. Feisty."

"Well, she'd have to be to hold her own with you," said his father.

"She's not the warmest soul on earth," his mother observed coolly.

"She's reserved, Ma. There's a difference. French people don't let down their guard right away and tell their life story within five minutes of meeting someone the way the Irish do. She's warm once you get to know her."

"She is," Liam agreed. "The regulars love her."

Quinn glanced at Liam, surprised. He had no idea.

"Let us get to know her, then," said his father. "Bring her for Sunday dinner sometime."

Quinn wasn't sure how to react. His parents usually held off asking one of their kids' significant others to their sacred family dinner unless they assumed the relationship was serious. Was it serious?

"Let me think about it."

"Quinn O'Brien, the man who couldn't commit," said Liam.

Quinn shot Liam a quick sideways glance. He could see from his expression that Liam was razzing him, not zinging him, which was unusual.

"Look who's talking," Quinn shot back.

"I brought a girl here once: Terry O'Neill. Remember?"

"Yeah, then you dumped her two days later."

"Better than your track record. You've never brought anyone to Sunday dinner that I can recall."

Quinn flashed Liam a dirty look. It was true. He'd never felt strongly enough about any of his former girlfriends to bring them to Sunday dinner. He tried to picture Natalie with his loud, boisterous family. Would she be overwhelmed? Or reserved? Clearly his mother mistook shyness for snobbishness. Not that Nat wasn't a snob sometimes. But she was getting better, and he knew part of that came from working at the Hart. Plus, it wasn't like she'd be meeting them for the first time. He really had to think about this.

His parents rose from the table, rinsing their coffee cups in the sink. "You got a minute after they go downstairs?" Quinn murmured to Liam.

Liam looked wary. "Sure."

"You coming down?" their father asked Liam.

"In a minute. Quinn's going to impart the meaning of life to me." No razzing this time; sarcastic Liam was back.

Quinn waited for his parents to go downstairs, and then started talking.

"Thanks for defending Natalie to Mom and Dad," he said.

Liam shrugged. "No problem."

"I was surprised to hear the regulars like her."

"Oh yeah. She horns in on their conversations and puts her two cents in, especially if it's politics."

Quinn grinned. "Sounds like Natalie. The French are like that. They love a good argument."

"You two really serious?"

Quinn raked his hand through his hair. "I'm not sure what that word means."

"Exclusive?"

"Why?" Quinn asked tersely. "You interested?"

"If I was interested, I would have made a move by now. Besides, it was obvious from the minute you introduced her that you were crazy about her."

"Bullshit."

"Not bullshit."

Quinn frowned. The thought that he might have been so transparent bugged the hell out of him. "Anyway, as far as exclusivity goes, then yeah, I guess we are. I sure as hell shoved Mason Clement out of the picture."

"No offense, but he seems like a nice guy."

"He's a prick, Liam. Take it from me."

"If you say so." Liam looked antsy. "Is Natalie what you wanted to talk to me about?"

"No. I wanted to thank you for calling me about PJ."

"No prob. How come you didn't write it up for the paper?"

"PJ asked me not to. He was afraid he'd get his ass beaten again, or get killed."

Liam seemed to ponder this.

"Li, if you know anything else about this, you gotta tell me, okay?"

"I heard some shit from Tommy," Liam said guardedly.

"I knew it. What did that piece of shit have to say?"

"Hey!" Liam looked pissed. "He's my best friend."

"Christ knows why, but anyway."

"He kinda boasted that something was gonna go down with PJ."

"Before it happened?"

"Yeah."

Quinn was incredulous. "Why the fuck didn't you tell me this as soon as you found out?!"

"Because sometimes Tommy is an asshole. He makes shit up when he's drunk. I usually take what he says with a grain of salt."

"Yeah, well, he didn't make this up, did he?" Quinn sighed. "Okay, here's what I want to know."

Liam frowned. "What?"

"You say Tommy is your best friend. Then you turn around and tell your reporter brother that he was talking about how something was going to go down. Why? Why tell me something that could wind up with Tommy's ass rotting in jail when he's your best friend?"

"It's complicated," Liam said evasively.

"So help me, God, Liam, if you're mixed up in this in any way—"

"I'm not! Jesus Christ, how many times do I have to tell you?"

"Then why tell me?"

"Because I'm trying to do the right thing, okay?" Liam's voice was fierce. "PJ's an eejit, but he's our eejit. He's family."

Quinn nodded. He understood what Liam felt. People always accused the Irish of being tribal. Well, tribal was just another word for loyal.

"If Tommy tells you anything else, you'll tell me, right?"

"Yeah, yeah, yeah," Liam said distractedly. He drained his coffee cup and stood. "That it?"

Conversation closed. When Mr. Moody didn't want to talk anymore, that was it; you were done.

Quinn rose, too. "Yeah, that's it. Thanks again for the call, Heathcliff."

"Up yours, Jimmy Olson."

Liam headed downstairs to the pub, leaving Quinn staring after him. Liam was always a tight-lipped, broody bastard. But something else was up with him, which worried Quinn. Liam would come to him in his own good time. All Quinn had to do was wait.

15

After speaking with Liam and his folks, Quinn headed directly to the *Sent.* As always, his cubicle was a mess, despite his weekly vow to tidy it up. There were no messages for him and no e-mails, either, but his editor, Cindy, was there. As usual, she looked like she was on the verge of a complete nervous breakdown.

"What's up?" he asked.

"It's Shep."

"What about him?"

"Yesterday he went out on a piece about the new clown college that opened in the Bronx. He's gone MIA."

"Maybe he's run away with the circus." Quinn couldn't hide his disgust. "Please tell me this idea was generated by Clement himself. Please tell me it's not something *you* or any of the other esteemed editors came up with."

"Mal Evans at the Metro desk came up with it."

Before Quinn even had a chance to move in the direction of Mal's desk, Cindy grabbed Quinn's forearm in a death grip. "Don't. All you'd be doing is stirring up trouble, and that's the last thing we need right now, okay?"

Quinn frowned disdainfully. "Drank the Kool-Aid, did we?"

"Just let it go for now, please?"

"Fine."

She looked relieved, but only for a split second. "Clement wants to see you."

"Me? What the hell for?"

"If I knew, I'd tell you, wouldn't I?" Quinn contemplated lobbing an equally snarky comment back but changed his mind since Cindy was so stressed she was having a hard time checking her cell phone for messages.

"I don't understand why Clement can't just call me on my cell like the rest of the world," he muttered. "When does he want to see me?"

"As soon as you came in, he said."

"And what if I hadn't come in until late tonight? What if I'd gotten a tip and was out on a story?"

"Then I would have told him that, because you would have called in to *let me know* that's what you were up to. *Right*?"

Quinn just grumbled. He'd given Cindy a rough idea of what he was working on with the proviso she didn't say anything to Clement about it yet. He wanted to wait until the story was so airtight the bastard couldn't give him any reason not to run it.

Cindy snapped her cell phone shut with unusual vehemence. "Shit. No word from Shep." She began shooing Quinn away from her. "Go talk to Clement. Just get it over with."

"You know, Darby over in photo has a big stash of Valium. You should—"

"*Get out of here.*"

Quinn squeezed her shoulder. "I'm officially out of your hair, Cin. We'll talk later."

* * *

Clement's office door was open, which was unusual. Perhaps he'd figured out by now that everyone hated him, and he was trying to reach out to the staff and prove he was an approachable guy. *Good luck with that.*

Quinn thrust his head through the open doorway. "You wanted to see me?" he asked tersely.

Clement barely looked up from his desk as he waved his hand vaguely in the air, motioning for Quinn to step inside. "I have an assignment for you."

"It doesn't have to do with clowns, does it? 'Cause I don't do clowns."

Clement looked up but ignored the shot. "I want you to cover a movie premiere."

"What?"

"The new Spielberg movie is premiering Friday, and as I'm sure you know, it's got that rising young star Susan Gambor in it."

"Never heard of her."

Clement's expression was dubious, but he continued. "I want you talking to fans waiting outside the theater to get in. I want you on the red carpet talking to Spielberg, Gambor, getting as many quotes from as many celebs as you can. Then I want you to go to the after party."

"Excuse me, but don't we have an entertainment reporter—*two* entertainment reporters, if I remember correctly—to cover this kind of fluff?"

"Yes, but I want you to get used to writing other types of stories."

"I have written other types of stories," said Quinn, trying to keep a lid on his fury. "I've even done some of these bullshit celebrity stories, okay? I hate them. I loathe those people. What the hell do they do all day? What do they contribute to society? Nothing."

"You need to stretch your wings."

Quinn snorted. "You are so full of shit."

Clement raised an eyebrow. "Pardon me?"

"This is about Natalie. You're pissed she chose me over you. You're trying to belittle me. You're totally deluded if you seriously believe I'm going to do this story."

Clement's gaze was steely. "You don't have a choice."

"There's always a choice." Quinn stared at him. "God, you're one petty bastard."

"And you're a hypocrite," Clement sneered.

"Oh, I can't wait to hear this."

"You paint yourself as a man of the people, the reporter chronicling the stories of the city, so virtuous and principled, only caring about the average Joe. I've done a little checking up on you, O'Brien: seems to me you've attended lots of A-list, celebrity parties in your day."

Quinn was unfazed. "Yeah, so what? Usually it's as a guest of someone from the mayor's office or someone from the Blades. Big deal."

"Well, whether you like it or not, you're what passes for a celebrity journalist in this town. Since you're a regular at these types of bashes, you should have no problem covering one for the paper."

"I'm not a regular."

"Fine, but you know how they work. Besides, your being there raises the *Sent*'s profile among people who we want in our corner."

"Why not give this piece to Shep? You seem to be sending him out on every other idiotic story in the city."

"He's working on something else."

"Yeah, well, so am I, in addition to being the main runner around here."

"I heard you've been poking around the mayor's office."

Quinn was momentarily thrown, but hid it. "That's what reporters do, Clement. They sniff. They poke. They dig. Sounds like you're doing quite a bit of poking around yourself—about me, for some inexplicable reason. Oh, wait, it's not inexplicable: you want to know about the man Natalie chose over you."

Loathing flickered in Clement's eyes. "What are you working on that concerns the mayor's office?"

"I really don't like to talk about investigative pieces until I'm sure I've really got something there," Quinn told him, enjoying busting Clement's balls, especially now that he sensed Clement was displeased with the fact that he was sniffing out *news* behind his back. "What do you care what I'm working on?" Quinn continued. "I thought all you gave a shit about was putting actresses who are dying of cancer on the front page."

"You keep forgetting that all I have to do is snap my fingers, and you'll be collecting unemployment."

Quinn held his tongue. They'd already had this discussion, and he'd already told Clement that if he wanted to fire him, he should just go ahead. But he knew Clement wasn't that stupid, and to be honest, Quinn didn't want to go. It was the *Sent* in which he wanted his exposé to appear, because the *Sent* was where his heart was, the place where he'd honed his skills and learned to be the best. He wasn't about to let Clement drive him out.

Quinn frowned. "What time is this stupid thing? And where?"

"Friday night at the Loew's on Forty-second Street." Clement handed him the invitation lying on his desk.

Fuck, thought Quinn. *The middle of the theater district on Friday night. Wall-to-wall people.*

"Who you sending down to take pictures?"

"Randi Schimmelman."

Quinn nodded his approval. Randi was as tenacious as a bulldog. Shooting celebs would be a piece of cake for her.

"No point filing Friday," Quinn pointed out. "The paper will be in bed by the time the party's over. You'll have it for the Sunday edition."

"Good man," said Clement, like they were old buddies. Jesus, he hated this guy more and more.

"That it?" Quinn concluded curtly.

"That's it," said Clement. "Have fun Friday night."

Quinn could have sworn there was a faint undertone of contempt in Clement's voice, but he couldn't be sure.

* * *

Natalie never thought of herself as starstruck, but the sight of so many celebrities gathered in one place was very exciting. When Quinn had invited her to accompany him to the new Steven Spielberg film, as well as the after party, she'd initially been hesitant, especially when he told her he'd be working part of the time, "courtesy of your spiteful, brokenhearted ex-paramour, Clement." But then she thought, when would she ever again have a chance to experience something like this? So she accepted. Besides, it would be interesting to see Quinn working, even if he had been given an assignment he loathed.

She met Quinn at the theater, the throng both outside and inside the lobby overwhelming. He was wound so tightly she feared he might give himself a stroke as he fumed about having to talk to "idiot actors." She hung back, watching him interview famed director Steven Spielberg, whom he said was witty and sharp. Natalie could see he also enjoyed talking to the fans waiting on line, some of whom had camped out for days. But the stars of the film? "Vapid, shallow, self-absorbed"—his laundry list of criticisms was endless. Thankfully, the film was wonderful, which seemed to appease him somewhat.

The after party was held at Cipriani's. She and Vivi had Googled it, marveling at its majestic interior and the clientele it catered to. "Maybe that's where you should have your reception," Natalie teased Anthony, who'd just laughed his head off and walked away. He and Vivi were still locking horns over caterers, as well as where to hold their reception.

The only thing they agreed upon was where they would actually marry: Saint Finbar's in Bensonhurst, the Catholic church Anthony's family had been attending for as long as he could remember. Vivi wasn't thrilled about being married in church, but it was important to Anthony, so she acquiesced. Natalie, whose only experiences with church were accompanying visitors to Notre Dame, was curious to see what it would be like.

"What do you think?" Quinn asked as he put his hand in Natalie's as they entered Cipriani's. "They got any restaurants this ornate in gay Paree? I bet not."

"You bet wrong."

Quinn gripped her hand a little tighter as he nabbed a glass of champagne from the tray of a passing waiter, handing it to her. "People are turning to look at you," he whispered, nuzzling her ear. Heat warmed her body, but she wondered . . .

"Aren't you working? Isn't it unprofessional for me to be here with you?"

"I don't think anyone gives a rat's ass."

"Charming expression."

"Oh, has the crude New Yawker offended mademoiselle's delicate sensibilities? I really don't believe anyone will be perturbed. Is that better?"

"Much."

They found a place to stand and chat. It astounded Natalie how many people sought out Quinn rather than the other way around. She hadn't realized how well-known he was. There was just one embarrassing problem. Every time he introduced her to someone, they inevitably asked her, "What do you do?" She had no choice but to answer honestly, then watch their expression deflate as they uttered a polite "Oh" and redirected their attention to Quinn, who always, always, made the point to tell them that she had been in the French government, and her working as a waitress was part of a career change toward restaurant management. She was grateful for his explanation, yet part of her wondered: Was he embarrassed that she was a waitress?

She studied him in action. Instead of being crude, he was being witty and charming and never at a loss for words. He had to drop her hand to take notes when he talked to celebs attending the party, but that was all right. When he was mingling with other reporters, she was surprised how collegial they all were. Quinn explained that it wasn't unusual for reporters to hop from paper to paper in the course of their career. Half of them used to work at the *Sent*.

Quinn turned, pointing out a tall man to Natalie looking at them from across the room.

"You see that thin guy in the expensive suit?"

Natalie nodded.

"Well, he's one of the mayor's top aides." He paused. "I really need to go over there and talk to him. Will you be okay if I leave you alone for just a few minutes?"

"Certainly." Obviously, Quinn wanted to talk to the man privately, and she wasn't going to press him for the reason. If he wanted her to know, he would have told her. Besides, she'd spotted someone she wanted to talk to: British chef Sebastian Thompson, owner of highly regarded restaurants in London and New York who was about to open a new place in Manhattan.

"You sure you'll be okay?" Quinn asked.

"Yes, perfectly fine." She tipped her head in the direction of Thompson. "I'm going to go talk to Sebastian Thompson."

Quinn glanced Thompson's way. "Isn't he supposed to be totally nuts?"

"He's brilliant. He's opening a new restaurant very soon. He might be in need of a manager."

"He well might be." Quinn discreetly pinched her butt. "Go for it, Nat. What have you got to lose?"

His confidence in her buoyed her. "Exactly."

"We'll meet up when I'm done with the mayor's aide. Good luck."

"You, too," Natalie said.

Then Natalie took a deep breath, squared her shoulders, and began moving in the direction of Sebastian Thompson.

16

Natalie had never been shy, and the thought of approaching Sebastian Thompson in no way intimidated her. She knew she was good-looking. In addition, most English and American men were enchanted when they heard her accent.

Thompson was holding court at a small, round table beneath one of the soaring stone archways. Natalie strode confidently to the table and tapped his shoulder. Thompson looked up at her, his eyes immediately sweeping her body. She smiled.

"*Bonjour.* My name is Natalie Bocuse. I wanted to let you know that I've eaten at Shepherd's Pie in London, and it was wonderful. You are an amazing, amazing chef."

"Well, thank you," said Thompson, looking immensely pleased. "You're not from around here, aye, love?" Despite the pedigree of his restaurants, his accent was pure cockney. Natalie was surprised to find it charming.

"*Oui.*"

"On holiday in New York?"

"Actually, I live here."

"Interesting." Thompson rose and dragged over an empty chair from the next table, placing it next to his own. "Have a seat, love. Join the party," he urged as he poured her a glass of champagne.

Natalie sat down beside him and took a demure sip of champagne. The constellation of people surrounding Thompson didn't seem to resent her presence, for which she was grateful. Most of them were what the Americans referred to as "foodies." Because Vivi was a chef, Natalie knew a bit about food and how restaurants worked, so she was able to hold her own in conversation. In fact, Thompson said he'd heard about Vivi's, claiming he wanted to check it out. Natalie couldn't wait to tell her sister. She'd be beside herself.

Her chance for an in with him came when he asked what she did. "I'm a restaurant manager."

Thompson's eyes lit up. "Yeah? Where?"

"Well, I'm unemployed right now. But I'm actively looking for a job."

"What kind of experience you got?"

"Well, I was a manager at my sister's bistro." A lie. "And I was also a manager at a medium-sized brasserie in Paris after I left the civil service." Oh, God, another lie. But she had a feeling if she admitted she had no experience at all, he'd dismiss her outright. Right now, he was looking very interested.

"Wot you doing right now?"

"Helping out some friends who have an Irish pub."

"The Irish are mad as hatters," he declared. "Good with salmon, though. You do know I'm opening a new restaurant called Seb's in about a month or so?" Thompson asked casually.

"Yes, of course."

His eyes bored into hers. "Haven't picked a manager yet. You think you might want to come in for an interview?"

"That would be wonderful." Calm on the outside, she was giddy with excitement inside.

"How 'bout you give me your number, and I give you a ring in the next couple of days?"

"Again, that would be wonderful. Thank you so much."

"My pleasure, darlin'. More champers?"

* * *

Quinn took his time making his way to Larry Mullen, pausing to chat a moment with Kirsty Perry, a bubbly former *Sent* reporter now covering entertainment for the *New York Globe*. She was surprised to see him there. "I'm surprised to be here," Quinn replied dryly. He promised to give her a call soon, then continued on his way.

"Larry Mullen." Quinn extended his hand and Mullen shook it.

"Quinn O'Brien. Long time, no see."

"Been busy," Quinn replied enigmatically.

"You always are." Mullen's smile was as broad and fake as Pamela Anderson's tits.

"I've been digging into the gentrification that's going on in Hell's Kitchen. I've been struck by how many of the buildings being renovated by the Shields Brothers were also purchased by them. I mean, that's kind of rare, isn't it?" Quinn cocked his head inquisitively. "Shields Brothers were major contributors to Mayor Dunphy's reelection campaign, weren't they?"

Mullen smiled tersely. "I don't see your point."

Quinn shrugged. "Just making conversation, Lar."

"You know, the mayor really likes you, Quinn."

"Does he? I didn't think City Hall was very pleased with the piece I did after the crane accident."

"No, not at all. You revealed an oversight that needed to be corrected. But as for the Shields Brothers, well, I don't think you'll find what you're looking for down at Gracie Mansion. That would be a waste of time. And I know how busy you are. I think you'd be better off looking a little closer to home."

"Larry, how considerate of you. I'm touched that you care."

"Oh, I care. And so does the mayor. We care that you find what you're looking for, rather than getting diverted by, let's say, side issues that really aren't pertinent."

"Larry, please tell the mayor that I appreciate his concern, and that I don't intend to be diverted."

Mullen smiled broadly. "That's great news, Quinn. I'll be sure to tell the mayor that you're focused on what really matters. Enjoy the rest of your night."

"You, too, Larry."

Quinn spun on his heels quickly so Mullen couldn't see the glee overtaking his face. He couldn't wait to file this insipid movie premiere story, then get back to the work that really mattered.

Quinn caught Natalie's eye as soon as he was done talking to Mullen. She seemed to be having the time of her life at the crazy chef's table. A few minutes later, Natalie was by his side.

"How'd it go?" he asked.

"He's going to call me in a few days to interview me about a managing position when he opens Seb's!" Natalie said excitedly. She bit her lower lip. "I lied, though."

"What do you mean, you lied?"

"I told him I had more experience than I did."

Quinn laughed. "Well, if he doesn't hire you, it won't matter. If he does hire you and you do a good job, he won't give a shit. And if he hires you and you don't do a good job, you'll get fired anyway."

They were on the sidewalk now. Quinn raised an arm to hail a cab.

"Where are we going?" Quinn asked as one pulled over.

"Your place?" Natalie was pleased their evening wasn't coming to an end quite yet.

"Oh, no, no, no, no, no," Quinn chuckled. "That's simply not happening. How about your place?"

"Fine."

They slid into the back of the cab.

"Why not your place?" she wanted to know.

"It's a sty," Quinn said simply. He reached into his coat pocket and pulled out his reporter's pad, thumbing quickly through the pages. "More than enough crap to give Clement what he wants," he muttered, shoving it back into his coat.

Natalie smiled at him. "Thank you for inviting me. You seemed to find it much less excruciating than the symphony."

"A little bit, but not much." He put his arm around her shoulders. "I'm glad you had a good time."

"I did."

"Thompson was staring at your chest."

"Everyone stares at my chest."

"God, your lack of humility turns me on." He leaned over, lightly brushing his lips over hers. Natalie felt an excited flutter low in her belly as Quinn sat back, smiling seductively. Would he tease her again tonight? Would she let him?

It was then she realized: she'd let him do anything.

17

Should I offer him a drink? Natalie wondered as she led Quinn into her—Bernard's—apartment. She'd been vigilant about not letting herself think of the apartment as hers, no matter how much she wished otherwise.

The minute Quinn stepped over the threshold, he loosened his tie, carelessly tossing his sports jacket over the back of the couch. He was one of those men who, by the end of the evening, had developed a five o'clock shadow. On any other man, Natalie might have thought it scruffy. But on Quinn it seemed attractive. She remembered the roughness against the skin of her face and swallowed nervously.

"I hate ties," Quinn announced as he sank down onto the couch. "I bet you like them. I bet you think they're classy."

"They give men a polished look."

"They're uncomfortable as hell. If you had to wear them all the time for work, you'd know."

"Moan moan moan."

Quinn laughed. Natalie loved that sound, and that she could make such an intelligent man with such a wonderful sense of humor laugh. So many people thought her humorless. They didn't understand that she had a hard time letting down her hair. She'd been raised to be ladylike and polite, a true politician's daughter. She envied her sister's free spirit. Still, she was learning. You couldn't work at the Wild Hart and be reserved; almost everyone there was a talker, friendly as can be. It was as if everyone was gathered in one big living room chattering away.

She paused, hand on the back of the couch. "Can I get you something to drink?"

Quinn craned his neck to look at her. "Do you have any whiskey?"

"Well, I don't. But Bernard might have some somewhere."

She headed toward the kitchen, halting when Quinn called out to her.

"Know what? Forget it. If I have a shot of whiskey now, I'll fall asleep."

Natalie nodded, joining him on the couch. He certainly didn't look tired to her. In fact, his blue eyes seemed as awake and intense as ever, sending a bolt of lust through her body. She wondered if he felt the same way. Well, there was only one way to find out.

Slowly, seductively, she brushed an index finger back and forth over his lower lip. "You like that, yes?" she murmured.

Quinn's eyes hooded. "Who wouldn't?" He removed her index finger from his lip and slowly, with eyes burrowing into hers, took it into his mouth, sucking on it. Natalie's breath hitched. How embarrassing that such a simple action could arouse her so quickly.

Quinn took her finger out of his mouth, kissing the tip before returning it to her lap. "Close your eyes," he commanded quietly.

Natalie complied, butterflies in her stomach. She held her breath for what felt like an eternity. Finally, she could feel Quinn's face close to hers, his breath on her face, his scent filling her senses. When he finally pressed his lips to her cheek, it was so exciting she felt weak.

"Tell me how that feels," said Quinn.

Natalie swallowed. "Nice," she managed, her heartbeat beginning to gallop. With her eyes closed, Quinn could do anything he wanted to her; he could make any move he wanted, and she wouldn't see it coming. A delicious feeling of vertigo overcame her.

"How about this?" Quinn's lips moved to within a fraction of an inch of hers, lingering, not moving. Again Natalie held her breath, the warmth wending through her almost unbearable. Finally Quinn attacked, kissing her roughly as he spoke in between bouts of ravishing her mouth.

"I'm a journalist," he said in a low, seductive voice. "I like words. Tell me what I'm doing to you."

"Kissing me," she whispered with a moan.

"And how . . . is it making you . . . feel?"

"Wonderful." Oh, Jesus God, her body was on fire.

"Just what I wanted to hear," said Quinn, teasing her lower lip with his teeth. "Except I want you to be a little bit more descriptive."

"I—I—oh, it feels so good." Her blood was sizzling.

"Correct answer." Quinn gently pulled Natalie's head back as he began running his lips over her neck. "Describe what I'm doing now." Natalie let out a small gasp at the feel of his mouth running over her flesh. The fever beginning to build in her body couldn't be ignored. She opened her eyes.

"Close them," Quinn growled roughly.

"Oh, God." Natalie took a shaky breath, doing as he commanded, unable to suppress a moan as his mouth returned to feast on her neck. His mouth pressed to her skin, her own galloping heartbeat in her ears—it was a wonderful kind of madness. She almost jumped out of her skin when Quinn began slowly unzipping the back of her dress, fingers grazing the sensitive skin of her back.

"What am I doing now?" he whispered.

"Driving me insane!" Natalie cried out in frustration.

Quinn laughed wickedly. "Tell me what you want me to do, Natalie."

She was trembling uncontrollably now, drunk on the feel of him, wondering if it were even possible to form the words she longed to say.

"Tell me," he commanded again.

"I—I want you to undress me and put your mouth on my breasts and—and—"

She didn't have to finish. Quinn pushed up her bra and dipped his head to her breasts, his tongue circling and flicking as she fisted her hands in his hair. It had been so long . . . If he kept it up, she was going to explode. The rough stubble of his chin against her skin as he suckled . . . unbearable. And then he took one hand to reach under her dress and cup her between her legs with his palm, rubbing it against her. Natalie couldn't hold back anymore. She bucked with pleasure as lightning crashed through her body.

Slowly, dazedly, Natalie returned to herself. What she saw when she was finally able to focus was Quinn with a somewhat devilish yet amused smile on his face.

Natalie raised an eyebrow. "Pleased with yourself, are you?"

"Very pleased." He kissed the tip of her nose. "Did you like that?"

"You know the answer. You're just fishing for compliments." She stroked his hair. "Now you."

Quinn kissed her hand. "Let's save that for next time."

Natalie stared at him. "You don't want me to pleasure you?" She felt a quick jab of rejection. Did he think she might not be good at it? The French were known as lovers. Had he forgotten that?

Quinn kissed her palm. "Of course I want it. But not tonight. Not when I'm so tired I can't fully enjoy it."

"All right," Natalie acquiesced, still surprised. She nestled into his arms. "I had a wonderful time tonight."

"Me, too—when I was with you."

"I've been thinking, though. You've taken me on three very fancy dates—all, I think, to impress me, no?"

"I already told you that. Yes."

"You don't need to impress me. I am impressed, even though you are the most trying man on earth. Why don't we do something you would like to do?"

Quinn smoothed her hair. "Funny you should say that. Would you like to come to dinner with me at my parents' on Sunday afternoon?"

"Your parents?"

"Yeah, you know, that plump white-haired couple with brogues who sign your paycheck?"

Natalie scowled at him. "No need to be sarcastic." She took a deep breath. "The thought is very scary to me."

"Why's that?"

"Because your mother doesn't like me."

"My mother doesn't know you. That's one of the reasons I want you to come." Quinn paused. "I've never taken anyone home for Sunday dinner before," he said quietly.

"Really?"

"Really."

So you love me? Natalie longed to say.

"Look, it's not a fancy affair. You don't need to get dressed up or anything. If everyone shows, there will be nine of us."

Nine. That was nothing compared to the Sunday dinners the Dantes had, where it wasn't uncommon for fifteen or more people to be gathered around the table, the decibel level deafening. Natalie realized that maybe she no longer needed to envy Vivi's being welcomed as a member into a large, loving family. Maybe it was her turn now, even though she didn't want to think about what the food would be like.

"All right, then. I'll come. Shall I bring a bottle of wine?"

Quinn hesitated. "You could, but my family really doesn't drink it. Why don't you bring some flowers? And an appetite."

Natalie smiled. "All right." She ran an index finger up and down Quinn's arm languidly. "Are you sure you don't want to stay?" she murmured. If she could be forward with Sebastian Thompson, who meant nothing to her, why couldn't she be bold with the man she was falling in love with?

Quinn cupped Natalie's cheek. "Tempting as that offer is, I think I better take off." He kissed her fully on the mouth. "I'll call you tomorrow about Sunday, all right?"

"I'll be working tomorrow night if you want to stop in."

"I definitely will, depending on what's going on work-wise."

"Of course," Natalie said, trying not to sound disappointed. Work, work, always work.

Quinn picked up his jacket, Natalie following him to the door. He kissed her again—slowly, torturously—then pulled back with yet another of those roguish grins he excelled at.

"Talk to you tomorrow, Nat."

She shook her head affectionately. "Go home now, Quinn O'Brien. Before I stop you."

And with that, he was gone.

18

"Come in, darlin', come in."

Quinn's father was gracious as he welcomed Natalie into the apartment where Quinn and his siblings had grown up. Despite already knowing the O'Briens, Natalie was anxious. She hoped it didn't show on her face.

She handed the bouquet of flowers she'd bought to Quinn's father. "For you and Mrs. O'Brien. Thank you for inviting me."

"It's our pleasure."

Mr. O'Brien reached out, clamping down on Quinn's shoulder affectionately. "You'd best have that damn cell phone off unless you want your arse kicked from here to Canarsie."

"It's off, Da, okay?"

They were standing in the kitchen. Natalie had to admit, whatever it was Quinn's mother was cooking smelled delicious. She clasped her hands in front of her nervously, waiting for Quinn's mother to appear. In the meantime, Quinn's father had taken the flowers from her and was on his hands and knees in front of a cabinet under one of the kitchen counters, searching for a vase. "There. Found one."

She looked up at Quinn, who winked at her. She wished his laid-back style allayed her nerves, but no such luck. Natalie forced a smile, her attention now focusing on the sound of talking interspersed with laughter coming from beyond the kitchen.

"Sounds like everyone is here," said Quinn.

Natalie's stomach did a flip-flop. Nine people who'd be sizing her up. She discreetly glanced down at what she was wearing, hoping it qualified as casual: a simple pair of black jeans paired with a royal blue turtleneck. Vivi told her the color of the turtleneck brought out her eyes. Natalie had contemplated accessorizing the turtleneck with a deep magenta scarf, but Vivi told her not to. Too French, she said. Too chic. Keep it simple. Natalie, who adored scarves, couldn't believe how naked she felt; it was almost as if she'd lost her security blanket. She'd worn her hair up, soft tendrils falling around her face. Small, simple gold hoops in her ears. No perfume (which she adored), in case anyone was allergic. She was relieved when Quinn showed up at her—Bernard's—apartment in jeans himself, though his, of course, hadn't been ironed, nor had his blue oxford shirt. Natalie couldn't help herself: she asked him if he wanted her to quickly press his clothes before they left for his parents'. Quinn just laughed at her. "Take me as I am, baby, or don't take me at all," he jested. Natalie just sighed.

Just as Quinn's father exited the kitchen with the flowers, Quinn's mother appeared, her ubiquitous white apron wrapped around her stout form. She smiled at Quinn and Natalie.

"Welcome," she said to Natalie. "We're so pleased you could come."

"Thank you for inviting me," Natalie replied, momentarily seized by awkwardness. Should she kiss her once on each cheek, as was the French custom? Was that too forward? Too foreign? Too odd? God knows, at Dante family dinners, everyone was always kissing everyone else when they walked through the door. The first time she'd gone with Anthony and Vivi to Michael and Theresa's, and Michael had greeted her with a big kiss, she'd been taken aback, almost shocked at the invasion of her personal space. She decided she'd take her cue from Quinn's mother. No kiss, but a soft press of the arm.

"Why don't you and Quinn go into the living room so you can meet the rest of the clan? Dinner will be done in a moment."

"It smells wonderful. What is it—if you don't mind me asking?" Natalie added hastily. She didn't want Mrs. O'Brien to think she was about to offer up any culinary advice.

"Roast pork with gingersnap gravy, scalloped potatoes, and glazed carrots."

"Oooh, glazed carrots," Quinn teased. "Trying to impress your guest, huh?"

"As a matter of fact," Quinn's mother replied, "it was your sister. Sinead requested it."

"God forbid Sinead has regular steamed carrots with butter." Quinn looked at Natalie. "My sister Sinead's an attorney at a very prestigious law firm," he explained. "She makes a lot of money. With each pay raise, her culinary tastes have gone up."

"Don't be so hard on your sister," Mrs. O'Brien chided. "She works like a dog. Like someone else I know." She leaned in close to Quinn. "Brian's not with her," she said in a low voice. "Don't say anything. I think they're still rowing over the baby issue."

"Fine. I won't even ask where he is. How's that? He can be the pink elephant in the room."

"I'll give you pink elephant. Get on with you, now. Get out of my kitchen."

Quinn took Natalie's hand, which she wished he hadn't

done. Her nerves had made her palms somewhat sweaty. "Hurdle number one complete," he whispered. "Now you just have three hundred more to go."

Conversation died down as she and Quinn entered the living room. Her anxiety surged, until she noticed that the four faces there were all smiling at her.

"Everyone," said Quinn, "I want you to meet Natalie, my—friend."

"Friend?" Liam snorted. "That's lame, Bro."

Thank you, thought Natalie.

"Girlfriend," Quinn corrected. "That better?"

"Why don't you ask Natalie?"

"I'm sorry," Quinn murmured to Natalie. "I'm just not used—"

"No, no, I understand," Natalie assured him quietly, even though she didn't understand at all. Oh, they would be speaking about this after dinner. His friend?

Quinn led her over to a gorgeous woman with red hair, sitting on the couch with a man with dark, tousled hair and eyes nearly as gorgeous as Quinn's. "Nat, this is my sister Maggie, and her husband, Brendan."

Maggie got up and gave Natalie a quick peck on the cheek. "Nice to meet you."

"You, too." Natalie could see a strong family resemblance between her and Quinn around the nose and mouth.

Brendan didn't stand, but he leaned forward, proffering a firm handshake. "Nice to meet you." His Irish accent was as thick of that of Quinn's parents.

"You, too."

"Nice accent," said Brendan.

"You, too."

Everyone laughed.

Natalie discreetly wiped her palm on the side of her pants in anticipation of Quinn taking her hand again and leading her toward his other sister, who looked more tired than Quinn often did, if that were possible.

"This is my sister Sinead. She works too hard, which is probably why she gets three migraines a week."

Sinead sighed. "Once an ass, always an ass." She, too, stood but didn't give Natalie a kiss like Maggie did. "It's nice to meet you. We've heard a lot about you."

Quinn blinked, looking confused.

Before he could even ask, Sinead pointed to Liam.

Quinn shook his head incredulously as he looked at his brother. "You know, we should call you the Mouth, not Joey."

"I make time to see my sisters," said Liam smugly, "unlike someone else in this room. And I'm not the only source of info. Mom and Dad—"

"How 'bout we stop talking about Natalie like she's not here?" Quinn cut in.

Natalie blushed.

"Good point," said Sinead.

"Dinner," Quinn's mother called, saving Natalie from being the subject of any further sibling exchanges. Grateful, she followed Quinn to the table.

Natalie was pleased one of her fears about dinner was misplaced: everything was delicious.

And everyone was solicitous. Natalie worked hard at being as personable as she could be without overdoing it. She let her humor shine through whenever she could as she and Quinn teased each other, which fit right in with the family, since they all seemed to thrive on it. She could have sworn a look of approval passed between Quinn's parents, but she wasn't sure.

Eventually they got around to the subject of Vivi's wedding.

"Where is your sister getting married?" Quinn's mother asked.

"In Bensonhurst. The ceremony will be in the church my future brother-in-law has attended since childhood. They have to start meeting with the priest once a week, where he talks to them about marriage. Imagine! A man who has never been married and is celibate talking to an engaged couple about marriage! It's ridiculous!"

"Does your sister agree it's ridiculous?" Quinn's mother asked coolly.

"Yes, she does."

Quinn shot Natalie a quick warning glance, which she ignored. She was entitled to an opinion, was she not? They were well past the niceties of "Tell us about growing up in France." Why not finally have a lively, interesting conversation, the kind Quinn and she had all the time?

"Are you and your sister both Catholic?"

"Yes, but we're French."

Quinn's mother furrowed her brows on confusion. "I'm not understanding what you mean."

"The French aren't very religious. We tend to be a bit more rational."

"Oh, so religious people are irrational, are they?" Quinn's mother asked curtly.

"That's not what she meant, Ma," said Quinn, squeezing Natalie's thigh hard under the table.

"Oh?" Quinn's mother looked very upset.

"I didn't mean to offend you, Mrs. O'Brien, truly," said Natalie contritely, feeling all Quinn's mother's goodwill caving in on her. "It's just that my sister doesn't wish to be a hypocrite. She's not religious at all, and it feels very false to her to see this priest before her marriage, especially since she and her fiancé already live together."

Quinn let out a small groan under his breath.

"I don't really approve of that," Quinn's mother sniffed, helping herself to more carrots. "As for your sister not wanting to be a hypocrite, perhaps Pre-Cana might give her a bit more insight into the Church and the sacred bond of matrimony she's about to enter into."

Natalie didn't know what to say, and obviously no one else did, either. There were a few seconds of silence and

one nervous cough from Quinn's father before Liam asked
Natalie to pass him the potatoes, and the topic was changed
to one less rife with the potential for misunderstanding.
Natalie knew she'd made a mistake. She just didn't understand what it was.

* * *

"Well, at least it wasn't a total disaster."

Quinn sounded grim as he and Natalie left the Wild
Hart. There was still a slight chill in the air when she and
Quinn said good-bye to his parents, though both his parents had kissed her on the cheek. She wondered if anything
would be different when she came to work on Tuesday. She
hoped not.

"I don't understand."

"We have a saying here in America," said Quinn, taking
her hand. "Never discuss politics or religion—especially
the first time you're meeting someone."

"That's silly," Natalie scoffed. "Those are two of our
favorite things to discuss and debate at home."

"You're not at home," Quinn reminded her gently.

"If I offended your mother, I'm truly sorry. But I had no
idea she was a devout Catholic. You could have told me."

"I didn't think I had to, because I assumed you knew
not to talk about politics and religion."

"Well, obviously I didn't," Natalie said defensively. "She
must hate me more than ever now."

"She doesn't hate you. She just doesn't get you. You
were doing great until then."

Natalie wasn't listening. "I should have asked if I could
bring Vivi with me. I'm relaxed around Vivi."

"I'm not going out with Vivi. I'm going out with you."

Natalie halted in the middle of the sidewalk. "Oh, we're
going out? I wasn't sure, since I'm just your 'friend.'"

"Yeah, about that." Quinn looked apologetic. "I was just
trying to avoid my siblings ragging on me, okay?"

"Ragging on you?"

"Teasing me."

"But you teased each other all through dinner! And they teased me, with that 'What are you doing with this loser?' stuff. I was very hurt when you introduced me as your friend. Hurt and confused. What are we? I need to know. I deserve to know."

Quinn winked. "You're my gal."

Natalie stamped her foot in frustration. "Just for once, could you not obfuscate?"

"Obfuscate? Have you been doing Durham's crossword puzzles?"

Natalie was about to tear her hair out in frustration. "Stop deflecting! Tell me in plain language what I am to you!"

Quinn took her in his arms. "You're my girlfriend," he said after a small pause, brushing the back of his hand across her cheek.

"Do you have any idea how uneasy you sound saying that?"

"I am uneasy." He broke their embrace. "I'm not good at relationships, Natalie, okay?"

"What does that mean?"

"What I said. The women I've been with—they either don't understand how important my work is to me, or they demand so much I bolt because I can't stand being roped and tied."

"What do they dare to demand? A commitment?"

"*The* commitment. The big one."

"So marriage scares you."

"Right now it does!"

"This might surprise you, Quinn, but I have no desire to marry you."

Which was true, at least for now. She needed to be settled in her life. And seeing the madness surrounding Vivi and Anthony as they tried to plan their wedding certainly didn't make it look very appealing.

Her jaw fell in shock when she saw that Quinn looked mildly insulted. "You say marriage scares you, but you have the nerve to look upset when I say I don't want to marry you?! You can't have it both ways, you know!"

Quinn held up his hands in surrender. "You're right, you're right. Guilty as charged."

"I'll apologize to your mother as soon as I get in to work tomorrow."

"Just let it go for now. I'm sure that by tomorrow, she'll have forgotten all about it." He paused, looking at her uncertainly. "Are you sure you can deal with how unpredictable my job is?"

"Yes."

"Good. Because my phone is on, and it's vibrating in my pocket."

"Take it," Natalie said resignedly, waving a hand in the air. "I know it will drive you mad if you don't."

"See, that's the kind of woman I've been looking for. One who gets it." He pulled the phone from his pocket, flipping it open. "O'Brien."

Natalie watched his face closely as he listened to the caller on the other end and pulled his reporter's pad out, scribbling. He was concentrating intently, yet there was an animation in his eyes she wasn't sure she'd ever seen before.

"Yup . . . on it. Bye." He flipped the phone closed. "Nat, I'm sorry, but I have to go. There was a body found in an elevator shaft in the East Village." He dug in his pocket, handing her some crumpled bills. "Let me at least pay your cab fare, since I have to run out this way."

You don't have to run out this way, Natalie thought, *you choose to. There must be other reporters at the paper who could cover this.* She pushed the thought away. Someone had chosen to call Quinn specifically; obviously they wanted him on the story. She was determined to prove she was the only one who "got it."

"No need to worry. I can pay my own cab fare."

"You sure?"

"Just go." Natalie kissed him on the cheek.

"I'll call you later, okay? And don't fret about my mother. Everything will be fine."

* * *

Later that night, after filing a story about the body in the elevator shaft and another on the movie premiere, Quinn headed back to the Wild Hart. His mother was on him the minute he walked through the door.

"Let me guess," Quinn said wearily. "You want to talk about Natalie."

"I'm not sure about her, Quinn. I'm not sure she's the right one for you."

Quinn moved behind the bar, pulling himself a pint of Guinness. "And why's that? Because she's not religious?"

"She mocked our religion!"

"Mom, she did not."

"She said meeting with a priest before marriage was ridiculous!"

Quinn took a sip of his beer. "It is." He turned to Liam. "What do you think, Liam?"

"I'm keeping out of this one."

"Coward." Quinn turned back to his mother. "Why don't you just admit it: you're just looking for excuses not to like her."

"She doesn't fit in with us, son. With our family."

"Funny, you seemed to act otherwise until the religious issue came up."

"Well, I'm not sure she's the right girl for you."

"Oh, here it comes," Quinn scoffed. "I need to find myself a nice Irish girl."

"Is that so bad?"

Quinn scrubbed his hands over his face in frustration. "Mom, it's Natalie I care about, all right?"

"I'm still not sure she's right for you," his mother repeated obstinately.

"No offense, but you have no idea who's right for me, okay?"

"A mother knows."

"Are you listening to this?" Quinn asked his brother.

Quinn's mother snorted. "Don't look to him for backup! He's just as bad as you!"

"What the hell does that mean?" Liam asked.

"You should have a nice girl by your side by now. But do you? No. Mr. Moody Bachelor. Any number of nice girls come in here. I see the way they look at you."

"Yeah, and I've dated a number of them."

"You need a steady."

Liam shook his head disbelief. "I don't want a steady."

"Mary Clooney's daughter just broke up with her boyfriend," their mother murmured nonchalantly.

"Brenda?" Quinn snorted. "One-Brow Clooney?"

"Ma, she's got a face like a horse!" said Liam. The two brothers looked at each other and broke up laughing.

"She's a nice girl," their mother huffed.

"She's not a *girl*, Mom, just like Quinn and I aren't boys," said Liam. "We're grown men who know what they want when it comes to dating, okay? So just leave it out."

Their mother clucked her tongue in wonder. "You two are so alike sometimes it astounds me."

This was the last thing Quinn expected to hear, and obviously Liam felt the same way, despite the laugh they'd just shared together. There was a split second of uncomfortable silence, and then Liam went to tend to a customer at the opposite end of the bar.

Quinn was about to add his two cents to what Liam had just said when there came the sound of an explosion and shattering glass out on the street. For a split second, no one moved. But then, as if on cue, everyone in the pub rushed outside.

Sweeney's Hardware Store, another longtime fixture of the neighborhood, was engulfed in flames.

Quinn pulled out his notebook and began running up the street.

19

Everyone was gathered watching Sweeney's burn, the crackle and hiss of the fire as it licked its way through the store one of the worst sounds in the world. Smoke billowed out onto the street. By now, it wasn't only the pub goers who crowded the sidewalks; tenants from surrounding buildings had also heard the explosion and were gathered outside.

"Someone better call Sweeney," Quinn said. Adrenaline was pounding through him, one of his favorite feelings in the world. PJ, Franco's . . . the story was getting juicier and juicier. His story.

His eyes cut to his parents; his mother was crying. Quinn walked over, putting an arm around her soft shoulders. "You okay?"

"God, what are Declan and Marianne going to do? What are they going to do?"

Quinn's father squeezed his wife's hand. "I'm sure they've got insurance, darlin'. They'll open a new store."

Everyone turned simultaneously to look down the street as the wail of the fire trucks grew closer and closer. As soon as the trucks arrived, the fire chief was flying out of his Bronco, barking at the bystanders to get the hell back. Quinn, who knew the chief well, ignored the edict, watching while the firefighters prepared to drag hose into the store.

"Jesus, O'Brien, you got here fast," Chief Greenberg said when he finally spotted Quinn.

"I was four doors down at my folks' pub." He paused a moment. "Once the fire's out, you think you'll be able to tell what happened right away? Whether someone chucked a Molotov cocktail through the front window or something like that?"

"Probably." The chief kept looking back and forth between his men and Quinn. "You know who owns the store?"

"A guy named Declan Sweeney. He's lived here forever."

"Right, right. The name is familiar. I think he donates to the FDNY Widows and Orphans Fund. Poor bastard."

"No shit." Quinn looked around. He noticed that whenever there was a fire, bystanders were unable to tear themselves away. It was a drama, and like all dramas, they wanted to see how it played out. It was too late at night for the store to be open, thank God. He doubted anyone had been inside.

The sound of a woman wailing made everyone turn around. The Sweeneys had arrived. Marianne Sweeney was running toward the store, but Chief Greenberg grabbed her and pulled her back. "I need you to step back, ma'am."

"That's our store," she sobbed.

"I know that. But you need to step back for now."

Greenberg gently handed Marianne Sweeney over to Quinn, who steered her back toward her husband. "C'mon. Let's do as Chief Greenberg says, okay?" The devastation and shock on Declan Sweeney's face was painful to see. He was looking through Quinn as if he wasn't even there.

"I've been here for twenty-five years," he said dazedly to no one in particular.

"I know," said Quinn quietly. It was the only hardware store in the area. If something went wrong in the pub that needed fixing, Sweeney's was where his parents went. He remembered the Sweeneys giving free nails to Liam and Tommy when they got the crazy idea to build a go-cart when they were ten. They were good people, part of the tight-knit community that was the neighborhood.

Quinn stood with the devastated couple, watching as the firemen doused the flames. Because the store was fairly small, they were able to put out the fire in a matter of minutes.

Quinn continued to hang back a moment, watching as the firefighters emerged and went over to talk to Greenberg. He was nodding and then glanced over at the Sweeneys. Quinn felt his pulse pick up as the chief walked over to the distraught couple who'd poured their guts into making their business a success. All ashes now. All gone.

The chief doffed his helmet. "I'm very sorry about your store."

The Sweeneys nodded numbly.

"Look, I'm not supposed to say anything, but it looks like someone torched the place."

Quinn felt that pinch inside that he always got when one of his hunches turned out to be right. The minute he'd seen the fire, he had a good idea of who might have set it.

"You got any idea who might do something like this?" Quinn asked.

Declan Sweeney glanced away. "None," he said in a dead voice.

He's lying, Quinn thought. He'd been a reporter for too many years not to be able to read people's faces. Chief Greenberg explained to the Sweeneys that his comments were totally unofficial. There would be a formal arson investigation conducted by the department, but he'd do his best to keep them unofficially informed of what was going on. The Sweeneys looked like zombies as the crowd slowly dispersed. Quinn pulled the chief aside as he made his way back to his Bronco.

"You willing to go on record about it being suspicious?"

"You know I can't do that, Quinn," he said with an air of exasperation. "On background I can tell you it was definitely arson, done by someone who's a pro at this kind of work. It was a firebomb, just big enough to get the job done but not so big that it would damage neighboring buildings."

Quinn nodded.

* * *

Part of Quinn's job was trying to pry info from people on what was possibly the worst day of their lives, and the Sweeneys were no exception. As soon as the fire trucks left and the crowd slowly dispersed, Quinn approached the defeated couple, who seemed unable to tear their eyes from the burned-out shell of their store. He was hopeful that because they knew him, they might be more willing to talk.

"Mr. and Mrs. Sweeney?"

They turned, and Quinn experienced a brief moment of awkwardness. They'd known him since he was a child, but once he reached adulthood, they'd insisted he call them Declan and Marianne. But he never did; in his mind, they were forever Mrs. and Mrs. Sweeney. They always looked amused when he still addressed them that way. But not tonight. Nothing could amuse them tonight.

"Hello, Quinn."

Quinn squeezed Mr. Sweeney's shoulder. "Jesus, I'm really sorry about the store."

"Thank you," said Mr. Sweeney.

"Look," Quinn said carefully, "would you mind if I asked you a few questions? It won't take long."

Mr. Sweeney looked wary. "What kind of questions?"

"About the fire."

"I'm tired," said Mrs. Sweeney. "I'm just going to wait in the car."

Quinn watched her go, her shoulders sunken in defeat, and then turned back to Mr. Sweeney. "Mr. Sweeney—"

"Declan—"

"Declan. You know what I do for a living. I've been doing some digging into the gentrification that's going on here, and I've got a feeling what happened tonight is somehow connected to what happened to PJ Leary and Franco's."

"Mmm."

"Is it?"

Mr. Sweeney said nothing.

"It would be very helpful to me if you could tell me anything—*anything*—about who you think might have torched your store."

Mr. Sweeney retained his silence.

"Anything," Quinn repeated. "Totally off the record. Nothing that would put you in danger."

Mr. Sweeney looked away.

"Please," said Quinn. "Did someone threaten you?"

Mr. Sweeney sighed heavily. "Quinn, look, Marianne and I are very tired. We've been through a terrible shock. Our livelihood has been destroyed. Can't you see that?"

"Of course I do," said Quinn. "But the more information you give me, the greater the odds that whoever did this can be brought to justice." He paused. "Please."

Declan Sweeney looked at his burned-out store and then back to Quinn. He turned away for a moment and then looked back. "Quinn, I want to tell you something about your brother Liam."

Quinn felt sick to his stomach.

"I know Liam's a good man," Declan continued.

Quinn's nausea started to pass.

"Tell Liam there's an old saying that while a man can't choose his family, he can choose his friends. I'll be going to look after the missus now. Good night."

* * *

Quinn couldn't help but notice the feeling of shock continuing to linger in the air as he went back to the Wild Hart following the Sweeneys' departure. There was no music on in the bar or in the back dining area. It was almost as if his parents thought it would be disrespectful to play light, happy tunes after what had just occurred. Voices were muted and solemn. It seemed like no one wanted to go home yet, like everyone wanted to try to process what had happened all together.

He didn't even have to ask his brother for his usual shot. Their eyes met and held for a brief moment before Liam poured Quinn's Jameson and handed it to him. The door opened, and in strolled Tommy and Whitey Connors. The pub instantly fell silent.

Quinn watched as his father, who'd been talking quietly to Liam behind the bar, came around to greet the two men.

"Tommy," he said with a curt nod. "Whitey."

"Charlie," said Whitey. As always, he was impeccably dressed in a dapper black suit and tie, his gleaming white hair concealed for the most part under his Donegal tweed cap.

"Haven't seen you in a while," said Quinn's father politely.

"I've been busy. But tonight I was overcome by an urge for your lovely Kathleen's beef and Guinness stew."

Quinn's father shook his head mournfully. "I assume you two heard about Sweeney's?"

"Yes," said Whitey. "Terrible. Just terrible."

Quinn quickly scanned the bar. No one was looking at Whitey and Tommy except for Liam. Silence crashed around

the room except for the polite exchange taking place between his father and Whitey.

"Might it be possible for us to eat at a table in the back?"
asked Whitey. "I'm not much for dining in the bar."

"Yes, of course," said Quinn's father. He began walking
toward the back of the pub. The only patron who looked up
as they walked through the bar was the Major. Whitey
lifted his Donegal tweed cap to him as he passed. The Major just turned back to his paper. Tommy and Whitey seated,
the low murmur of conversation resumed at the bar, shot
through now with palpable anxiety. Quinn filed it all away
in the back of his mind. He felt awful for the Sweeneys, but
from his perspective as a reporter, things just kept getting
more and more interesting, and he loved it.

*   *   *

"His parents hate me," Natalie lamented as she followed
Vivi around Kleinfeld, a bridal shop. This was their second time shopping here, and so far, Vivi hadn't seen one
wedding gown she liked, at least not at a price she thought
reasonable.

"I give up," Vivi said with a sigh of resignation. "I can't
afford anything here."

Put it on a credit card, Natalie thought reflexively and
then caught herself. That was the old shopaholic Natalie's
solution to everything: put it on your credit card.

"There has to be somewhere else we can go that's
cheaper," said Natalie.

"I doubt it." Vivi held open the door for her as the two
walked out onto the sidewalk. Vivi's expression was glum.
But suddenly, her face lit up. "I know what I'm going to do."

"What?"

"I'll wear my *grand-mère*'s wedding dress. She still has
it. It's very beautiful and simple."

"Do that."

"Hmm." Vivi seemed lost in thought for a moment, and then shook her head as if clearing out cobwebs. "I'm sorry, you said something before, and I wasn't paying attention."

"I said, Quinn's parents hate me."

"Don't be ridiculous."

"I stumbled badly at dinner."

She told Vivi about the comments she made about her and Anthony having to see the priest at Anthony's church before they were wed, and how upset Quinn's mother became by the fact both she and Vivi thought it crazy.

Vivi looked sympathetic. "Americans are much more sensitive about religion than we are. They're much more— well, religious."

"Well, I didn't know that, and now they hate me—at least his mother does."

Vivi linked her arm through Natalie's. "I doubt that."

"No, it's true. She'll probably fire me," Natalie said miserably.

"Don't you have an interview in a few days with Sebastian Thompson?"

Natalie brightened a bit. "Yes."

"Well, perhaps you'll get the job, and it won't matter if you're fired."

"Maybe."

Vivi looked concerned. "Do you really think they'll fire you?"

"I don't know. Probably not. They'll probably just give me the cold shoulder." Natalie was surprised to find herself getting tearful. "I want them to like me so badly. I want what you have with Anthony: to be welcomed and embraced into a big, loving family."

"You will, *cherie*. You just need to be patient. You told me Quinn's brother likes you, *oui*?" Natalie nodded. Thankfully, she and Liam got on well.

"And his father?"

"Yes, he seems to like me. His sisters seemed to like me, too. Only his mother was offended."

"She'll get over it," Vivi reassured her breezily.

"But what if she doesn't?"

Vivi shrugged. "Well, then, she doesn't. You can't control it, so you may as well not fret over it." She paused. "Didn't Quinn come to your defense when you stumbled?"

"He tried to. But his mother was having none of it."

"How's it going with you two?" Vivi asked.

"I think things are going well," Natalie replied thoughtfully.

"You *think*? You're not sure?"

"It's hard to tell," Natalie said, frustrated. "He's always dashing off here and there. Work, work, work. He seems to have no set hours. He asked me if I could cope with how unpredictable his job was, and I said yes."

"Is that true?"

"I can make it true, if that's what I need to do to be with him."

"Ah. So you love him."

"Yes," Natalie said softly. It was the first time she'd admitted it out loud.

"Does he love you?"

Did he? Much to her distress, Natalie was unsure. "I think so. He hasn't said it yet, and neither have I. But apparently, his bringing me to Sunday dinner with his family was significant."

"Cherie." Vivi's eyes glistened with happy tears. "It's so wonderful the two of you are finally together! You're so perfect for each other!" She sighed sadly. "It's too bad Papa isn't alive. I think they would have liked each other."

"I think so, too." Talk of their father inevitably brought to mind Natalie's mother, and what she would think of Quinn. She would disapprove, thinking him too rough around the edges, which of course was Natalie's first impression, too. Her mother would disapprove of his family as well. Too boisterous, she would say. Too coarse. Natalie knew she should give her a call, but the thought of being hung up on again was unbearable.

"Do you want to go to lunch?" Natalie asked.

"Yes! Why don't you take me to the Wild Hart? Show me where you work."

"It's my day off, Vivi. The last thing I want to do is go in there. Why don't you and Anthony just come down one night while I'm working? At least then you can see what I'm talking about with the food."

"I'm sure it's not as bad as you say. But yes, we'll come down one night. Let's just walk along and see if we find a bistro that strikes our fancy."

"All right."

"I'm sure she doesn't hate you, Natalie. Just relax and keep being yourself. Once they get to know you and see how much you love their son, all will be well."

"Vivi, the eternal optimist," Natalie said dryly. "I'll try."

20

Rather than approach Liam at the Hart about Mr. Sweeney's cryptic comment, Quinn decided he'd visit him at home. He'd never been to his younger brother's apartment, which struck him as kind of sad. Come to think of it, Liam had never been to his place, either.

Quinn pushed the buzzer once, waited, and then pushed again. Liam's voice over the intercom was groggy.

"Yeah?"

"Li? It's Quinn."

There was a long pause. "Come on up."

After being buzzed in, Quinn looked around the lobby. No elevator. By the time he got up to Liam's apartment on the third floor, he was slightly winded. Jesus Christ, he was out of shape. Time to cut out the office donuts.

The apartment door was open. Quinn was surprised by what he found inside. The small, sparse apartment was tidy, despite Liam's being a slob all through adolescence. Quinn's eyes were immediately drawn to a picture of the family that hung in a prominent place above an old gas fireplace.

Does his best to hide it, but he's as sentimental as the rest of us, Quinn thought.

"What's up?" Liam asked, wandering out of the kitchen in sweatpants, bleary-eyed and sporting one of the worst cases of bed head Quinn had ever seen.

"I need to talk to you about Sweeney's."

"Christ, you're relentless. I'm not even awake yet. But I'll tell you what I know: nothing."

"Fine. Then I need to talk to you about Tommy."

Liam groaned, motioning for Quinn to follow him into the kitchen. "I need to get some coffee in my system. You want some?"

"Sure."

Liam's kitchen was one of the tiniest Quinn had ever seen. Instead of a stove there was a hot plate with two burners. He did have a microwave, but his refrigerator was one of those small cubes college kids keep in their dorm rooms. The only open wall space sported an Ireland 2009 calendar.

Liam began pouring coffee from a French press. "Sorry, I don't have anything here to go with this," he said with a yawn. "I usually steal a hunk of soda bread when I get to Mom and Dad's."

"Nothing better."

Liam cracked a small, sleepy smile. "You can say that again."

Quinn looked around the kitchen again. "Nice place."

"It's okay." Liam put a cup of coffee down in front of his brother.

"Thanks." Quinn took a sip and gagged. "Think you made this strong enough?"

Liam shrugged unapologetically. "That's the way I like it."

Quinn forced down another sip, reasoning that no matter how awful it might taste, a man could never have enough coffee. "When's the last time you saw Tommy?"

"A few days ago. Why?"

"He say anything interesting? Boast about anything stupid?"

"Apart from the fact he's been banging some rich widow on the Upper East Side? No. Why? What's up?"

"I'm gonna tell you something that you can't tell anyone."

Liam looked wary. "Yeah?"

"I talked to Declan Sweeney last night and, while he was afraid to come right out and say it, he hinted Tommy was involved. Has Tommy said anything to you about what's been going on in the neighborhood?"

"All he's talked about lately is this MILF he's been screwing."

"He ever say anything further about PJ's getting beat up?"

"Don't you think I would have told you if he did?"

Quinn rubbed his temples in frustration. "Li, I really need your help here. Seriously. Your best friend is one of Whitey's guys. The more info you can get for me, the bigger my chances that my article could take Whitey down."

"Yeah, you told me that already, Quinn. But for such a brilliant reporter, I would have thought you'd realize that if I all of a sudden show interest in what Tommy's up to, it's going to look really suspicious. Whitey might think I want in."

"He never pressured you to come in when you ran errands for him as a kid?"

Annoyance crossed Liam's face. "Believe it or not, no. He knew I was just doing it as a favor to Tommy."

"And Tommy's never tried to persuade you to come in over the years?" Quinn prodded.

Liam rose and went to the fridge, his back to Quinn. "Sometimes," he said tersely. "But he drops it when I make it clear that I don't have any interest."

"Have you ever wondered why he's never tried to extort

protection money from Mom and Dad, since the Hart is on his turf?"

"Yeah, I've thought about that, too. I've never had the balls to ask them about it, though. I just figured Whitey must be scared of Mom."

"They must hate Tommy coming in."

Liam looked irked. "Quinn, he's my oldest friend, and they've known him since he was little. I'm sorry that he's not perfect like you," Liam sneered. "It must be a real burden."

"I never claimed to be perfect."

"You didn't have to; Mom and Dad do it for you. They've always thought the sun shines out your ass."

"They think the sun shines out your ass, too," Quinn retorted, "but you've spent so much time being angry at me for God knows what, you couldn't see it." Quinn leaned forward across the table. "I've spent my whole goddamn life trying to be a good big brother to you, and all I've ever gotten is resentment. What the hell gives?"

Liam's jaw clenched. "Nothing gives."

"Oh, *bullshit*. Let's just get it out once and for all, all right, so we can move past it. What's the deal? Was it jealousy?"

"Maybe," Liam muttered reluctantly. "Maybe I figured out pretty young that I couldn't compete with you in any way, shape, or form. Quinn, the star athlete. Quinn, the valedictorian. You walk in a room, and everyone is drawn to you. You have any idea what it's like to be in your shadow?"

"So you decided to become a bad boy underachiever?"

"Fuck you, Quinn."

"No, fuck you, Liam!" Quinn was surprised to find himself losing it. "Don't pin your lack of ambition on me! You're the one who chose to hang out with Tommy and goof off in school! At any point along the way, you could have made a different decision, but you didn't."

Liam pushed back from the table and stood, rigid with anger. "So you think I'm a failure." He jerked his chin up defiantly. "Go ahead. Say what you've always wanted to say to me: that you think I'm a fuckin' failure."

Quinn could tell Liam was itching to punch him, and part of Quinn wanted to tell him to, to take a swing so he could get it out of his system and they could clear the air once and for all. But he knew it would turn into an out-and-out brawl, and considering he got winded walking up three flights of stairs, he was pretty sure he'd lose, so he kept his mouth shut, sighing wearily. "I don't think you're a fuckin' failure, Liam, okay? I know that, unlike Tommy, you work your ass off at a legitimate job. I just think you sell yourself short, and that pains me, because you could be anything you want to be. You could have gone to college like Sinead and me. You've got the brains."

"How is being a bartender selling myself short?" Liam challenged. "I know this might be incomprehensible to you, but I actually enjoy it. I like meeting different kinds of people. I like the tradition of keeping it in the family. You're a goddamn snob, Quinn, you know that, implying that working at a bar is somehow *beneath* me."

Liam's observation hit like a soft blow to the gut. He was right. What he'd just said to his brother indeed implied he thought what Liam did was somehow lesser than what he did.

"You're right," Quinn admitted quietly. "You're totally right."

Liam looked surprised. "Thanks for admitting it," he mumbled.

"Look, Liam. It bugs me that you've spent most of your life resenting me, that you can't see what a great guy you are, too. You gotta let it go. Grudges eat people alive. Don't you know that?"

"We're Irish, Quinn," Liam said wryly. "We love a good grudge."

Quinn chuckled. "Sad but true." He stood up and approached his brother. "Can we at least agree to cut each other a little slack?"

Quinn held out a hand for his brother to shake.

"What's this handshake bullshit?" Liam enveloped him in a tentative hug.

Sensing they were both clearly uncomfortable with the display of affection, Quinn broke contact and changed the subject. "What's on your agenda for today?"

"Hitting the gym, then helping Dad with the books. You?"

"Not sure. I might head over to the *Sent*, then call Natalie."

"Shouldn't it be the other way around?"

Quinn tried not to get defensive. "That's not the way I roll," he said as he walked to the door.

"I guess as long as she's fine with that," Liam said as he watched Quinn head down the hallway to the steps.

Quinn turned to look back. "She is . . . so far."

* * *

Natalie took a deep, fortifying breath as she walked through the door of Sebastian Thompson's restaurant for her interview. In just a few weeks, his new restaurant, Seb's, would open. She was both surprised and flattered by how soon he'd called her after their meeting at the premiere party. While Quinn's parents hadn't fired her, his mother had been rather cool toward her, which hurt. But it also struck her as somewhat hypocritical. Weren't Christians supposed to forgive? Why hadn't his mother forgiven her, then?

The restaurant was empty when she entered, but it was not silent. In the kitchen, she could hear Thompson screaming at the staff. Thanks to having dealt with Anthony Dante, she knew chefs could be emotional, but from the sound of it, Sebastian made Anthony seem like a saint.

Every other word was either "fuck" or "cunt." Unsure

of what to do with herself, she sat down at a small table for two in the middle of the restaurant, waiting for Thompson to finish his tirade. She hoped he hadn't forgotten their interview.

Five minutes later, Thompson stormed through the swinging doors of the kitchen, his face still contorted with rage. *Great. Another waste of my time. Oh, well, it was good practice.*

"Sorry I'm late, love."

Natalie rose to shake his hand. "Only a few minutes."

"Yeah, well, still. I expect punctuality from my staff. Not fuckin' right for me to be a hypocrite, innit?"

Natalie smiled tightly, unsure of how to respond.

"You thirsty? Want anything from the bar?"

"No, I'm fine, thank you."

"Lucky you. I'm just going to grab a double scotch for myself, won't be a mo. I deserve it after dealing with those stupid cunts."

Natalie suppressed a wince as Thompson headed off to fix himself a drink. Her heart was pounding wildly. She was afraid of him.

Thompson swaggered back to the table, sliding into the seat opposite her, the ice in his glass tinkling. "That's better." Natalie felt distinctly uncomfortable as he eyed her up and down. "How's life treatin' you, doll? Still at the Paddy pub?"

"Yes."

"Bit beneath you, innit? Sophisticated French lady like you."

"As I told you, I'm helping out some friends. I'll be fine until I find the perfect managing job."

Thompson winked at her. "Well, perhaps you have." He glanced around his restaurant proudly. "You said you ate at Shepherd's Pie when you were in London?"

"Yes." *When I was thousands of dollars in debt and just*

charged the meal on my credit card, she thought to herself.

"Wotcha think?"

"I told you: it was amazing."

Thompson slumped down in his chair, eyeing her suspiciously. "You just blowin' smoke up my ass because you want a job?"

Natalie colored. *Smoke? Ass?* "I don't understand. Do you mean to ask if I'm giving you a false compliment?"

"Yeah, yeah, exactly." He belted down some scotch. "I love your accent. So posh. Sexy."

Natalie's face turned even redder. "So, about the job?" she asked, trying to steer the conversation away from herself.

"Yeah, yeah, we'll get to that." He threw more scotch down his throat. Natalie was still intimidated by him, but at least he was calming down a bit with each gulp of scotch. "I was thinking of changing the name of the new restaurant."

"To what?"

"Flaming Bitch. That way it would still be dedicated to my ex. Would you eat in a restaurant called Flaming Bitch?"

"I think it would depend more on the food than the name."

"Good answer, angel," Thompson replied. "You know my restaurants in England and Scotland have, collectively, earned over ten Michelin stars? You're French. You know about Michelin stars. Highest fuckin' honor there is."

Natalie was admittedly impressed. "I had no idea you'd garnered that many."

"Yeah, well, the reason is, I'm creative, and I know what the fuck I'm doing. I only hire the best, even if they *are* a pack of stupid cunts sometimes. I demand perfection, both in the kitchen and in the front of the house."

"Of course."

"It's gonna be the same philosophy at Seb's." He drained his scotch. "Tell me about managing the brasserie in Paris."

Natalie swallowed, relieved that she had Googled "Skills needed to be a restaurant manager" on the Internet and had basically memorized what she found. She felt guilty lying about the experience, but she wanted this job so badly, she was willing to do anything.

Or so she thought.

"Sounds like you know your stuff, Miss Bocuse. Would you like to manage Seb's?"

"I would love it." She was so excited, it was hard to restrain herself from jumping up and down in her chair.

"Well, I'm gonna need to know if we're on the same wavelength. If we can connect, not just intellectually but emotionally . . . and physically. Know wot I mean, love? How about you come to my place tonight to close the deal?"

Natalie froze, her elation quickly turning to anger. He had no interest in hiring her for herself. He just wanted to sleep with her.

"I don't think that's a very good idea," Natalie said coolly. "In fact, on second thought, I don't think Seb's would be the right fit for me. But thank you for considering me."

"Suit yourself, angel. I've got three more birds coming in this afternoon."

Irate, Natalie walked out of the restaurant. By the time she managed to quell her anger, despondency had taken its place. She tried to bolster herself up. She'd only been on two interviews so far. Perhaps she was being punished for lying. Her imagination began spinning out of control. She would never find a job. Never. She'd be stuck working at the pub until Quinn's mother's fired her after having some religious vision. Quinn would find her so pathetic he would dump her and take up with a beautiful young reporter whom he could mentor. Humiliated, she would crawl back to Brooklyn, where she'd live out her days as the spinster aunt to Anthony and Vivi's children.

She knew she was being ridiculous, but she couldn't help it. It was easier to spin these fantasies than admit she'd been overconfident and naive about how soon she'd find a job in Manhattan.

She slowed her pace, stopping to peer into the window of a very chichi boutique called Rula's. She fished out the sole credit card she possessed that was to be used for emergencies only, staring at it hard. *Do it, do it, do it. Don't do it, don't do it, don't do it.* She closed her eyes, picturing how Quinn and Vivi would react if she "fell off the wagon," as they said here. She imagined the disappointment on their faces. Worry, too, maybe even anger. She snapped open her eyes and put the card away, hurrying up the street. She would get a job eventually. She would. She just had to have faith.

21

"I should go over there and beat his limey ass."

Natalie was sitting beside Quinn on a bench in Central Park, eating lunch. Her temptation to pull out her credit card and go wild had scared her. When she couldn't get hold of her Shopaholics Anonymous sponsor, she called Quinn. He had wanted to hear from her anyway following her interview with Thompson. Luckily, she caught him as he was on his way to grab some food. Quinn told her he'd pick up sandwiches for both of them and meet her at the entrance to the park, right across from the Plaza Hotel, in half an hour or so. Natalie took the subway, which she still despised. So dirty compared to the Metro in Paris.

Because she didn't want to appear snobby or ungrateful, she forced herself to eat the somewhat revolting tuna sandwich Quinn had purchased for her. The tuna was drowning in mayonnaise, the lettuce limp. She knew why he'd picked tuna for her: she'd once told him she loved fish. He'd bought himself a ham and Swiss cheese sandwich, which Natalie found herself coveting. How sad, she thought, coveting a soggy, prepackaged sandwich. She really needed to get herself out to Vivi's for a real meal.

When she'd told Quinn about her interview with Thompson, his expression had quickly changed from annoyance to sheer swagger. Natalie found his show of machismo sexy.

"I don't need you to beat his ass. I handled it myself."

Natalie took another bite of her sandwich, washing it down with a healthy dose of bottled water. Quinn, of course, was drinking coffee from some deli. He'd always said he'd rather shoot himself than ever set foot in a Starbuck's. She might be a food snob, but *he* was a coffee snob.

Quinn grunted in agreement. "I hate guys who talk to women that way. They're scum."

Natalie wiped her mouth. She wasn't going to tell him this, but she decided that she wanted no secrets between them. "I was so upset afterward, I almost went on a spending spree. But I didn't."

"That's great, honey," Quinn said, admiration in his voice. "I'm really proud of you."

"It's so hard sometimes," Natalie admitted. Had she not resisted, she would probably be in her third boutique by now, charging away, ruining her life.

"Of course it is. It's a legitimate addiction, just like anything else. You have to go day by day, right?"

"Right."

"Well, like I said, I'm really proud of you."

"Thank you." It was just what she needed to hear.

Quinn gazed out at the bank of trees before them, branches swaying back and forth in the breeze. Natalie gazed at his profile. She loved the way the wind tousled his hair.

She rested her head on his shoulder. "You're looking very handsome today."

"Despite the mysterious hole that's managed to appear in the right elbow of my jacket?" He held it up for her to see.

"Please tell me you're going to have it mended. I can't bear the thought of you walking around looking like some kind of tramp."

"A *tramp*?" Quinn looked amused. "Oh yeah, I forgot, you're French. Anything less than perfection when it comes to clothing, and you're one step away from the gutter."

Natalie slapped his shoulder playfully. "Not true."

"Is true." Quinn looked at her with concern. "You cold? You're shivering a little. You can wear my tramp jacket if you want."

Natalie gave him a warning look but then broke into a smile. "Yes, please."

Quinn wrapped the jacket around her shoulders, putting his arm around her for good measure. "You hate that sandwich, don't you? Go on. You can admit it."

"It's horrible."

Quinn laughed. "You once told me you liked fish. Tuna is a fish."

"I like fish when it's not drowning in mayonnaise."

"Jesus, you're a pill." He held up the remainder of his own sandwich with his free hand. "Wanna switch?"

"Oh, God, yes."

"As mademoiselle wishes."

He lifted a strand of her hair, kissed it. "I'm really sorry I haven't been around the past few days. I've been running my ass off on this story I'm working on."

"Oh, the one you haven't told me about?"

"If I tell you, do you promise you won't breathe a word about it to anyone?"

"Who would I tell?"

"Vivi?"

"I promise you, I won't tell a soul."

He proceeded to tell her about his investigations into Shields Brothers Construction and their ties to the Irish mob. He was more animated than she'd ever heard him before. But by the time he was done, she was deeply uneasy.

She lifted her head from his shoulder to look at him. "Aren't you in danger, pursuing this story?"

Quinn looked mystified. "Danger?"

"Can't they hurt you? Come after you if they learn you're poking around?"

"I suppose. But I can't think about that."

"Well, I can." She stroked his cheek. "Please be careful."

Quinn rolled his eyes.

"Don't dismiss me!"

"Fine, I'll be careful." He kissed her mouth softly. "I've missed you."

"Me, too." She hesitated a moment, then took his face in her hands and began kissing him. Quinn responded instantly, wrapping his arms around her in a crushing embrace. Natalie was thrilled that he wasn't shy about expressing affection in public. In France, that was one way couples displayed to the world the strength of the relationship. Another was arguing.

She wondered if he could sense her giddiness, the sheer pleasure shooting through her as he took the lead, his mouth conquering hers roughly. It was intoxicating. Magical.

And then his phone rang.

Natalie broke their embrace with a glare. "You don't have to answer it. You're eating lunch and relaxing. Whoever is on the other end can leave a message, *non*?"

"It'll only take a second," Quinn promised. Natalie pushed back against the bench, folding her arms across her chest crossly like a petulant child. *You chose this,* she reminded herself.

"It's not work, it's Liam," Quinn whispered, looking worried.

Merde, had something happened to someone in the family? Worried now herself, Natalie put a comforting hand on his leg, avidly watching his face as she listened to his side of the conversation.

"What's up? . . . He's dead?! . . . When?! . . . She must be out of her mind with grief . . . When's the service? . . . Yeah, I can make it, no problem . . . Natalie and I will both be there. You, too."

"What's happened?" Natalie asked nervously as soon as Quinn shoved his cell back in his pocket.

Quinn looked sad. "Rudy the parrot is dead. Mrs. Colgan found him at the bottom of his cage this morning, stiff as a board. There's going to be a memorial service at the Wild Hart tomorrow morning."

Natalie stared at him in disbelief. "A memorial service. For a parrot."

"Yeah," said Quinn, looking mildly offended. "Mrs. Colgan is a regular, Natalie. And so is Rudy. It's only right people pay their respects."

Natalie pinched the bridge of her nose. "You're joking, yes? You're making this up."

"I am not making it up," said Quinn, his voice tinged with annoyance. "Look, if you don't want to go, I can represent the both of us."

He was crazy. They were all crazy. She should have stayed in Bensonhurst. So what if there was nothing to do? The people there might have an obsession with putting religious statues on their front lawns, but at least they didn't hold memorial services in pubs for dead parrots.

"Stop looking so shocked. I guarantee you that when you go to work tomorrow night and Rudy isn't there, you're going to be really sad. Haven't you grown just a tiny bit fond of him?"

"No!"

"My parents are going," Quinn continued slyly. "It'd definitely earn you brownie points with my mother if you were there."

"You're all mad," Natalie muttered.

"Hell yeah. We're Irish." He put his arm around her again. "C'mon. Say you'll go."

"Yes, yes, I'll go. Should I wear black?" she asked dryly.

"I'm going to wear my best black suit."

"You are not!" It couldn't be so. The man couldn't even dress decently for work yet he'd don a black suit for a deceased parrot?

"No, I'm not," Quinn admitted. "I was just teasing you. Wear whatever you want." He pointed to the tuna sandwich on the bench on the other side of her. "If you don't want that, I'll eat it."

"By all means."

"A memorial for a parrot," Natalie murmured incredulously. "And I'm going. God help me."

* * *

The minute she and Quinn parted after lunch, Natalie phoned Vivi, who insisted that before anything else, Natalie tell her how her interview went with Sebastian Thompson. Vivi didn't sound surprised.

"I was worried that might happen," Vivi admitted. "He has a reputation, and the kitchen is one of the only places left in the civilized world where men feel free to be pigs."

Natalie then told Vivi about the memorial service for the parrot she was attending tomorrow.

Vivi laughed with delight. "How wonderful!"

"You are such a hypocrite, Vivi!" Natalie snorted. "You would never allow a parrot to be at Vivi's night after night! You'd be too afraid the board of health would shut you down, and rightfully so."

"Perhaps. But it's such a lovely gesture."

"I'm only going because Quinn's parents are going to be there. Quinn says it might help with his mother."

"I want a full report, *cherie*," said Vivi.

"Oh, you'll get one, believe me."

* * *

Quinn was the last to arrive for the service. It was all Natalie could do to keep from gasping aloud when he strolled through the door in a black suit and tie. "So what do you think?" he whispered, coming to stand beside her. "Not bad for a rental."

"You're unbelievable."

She'd already—insanely—paid her condolences to Mrs. Colgan, who was sobbing so loudly she was barely coherent. Most of the regulars were there—The Mouth, PJ, Quinn's parents—all of them looking a little teary save for Liam, who was glad the bird was gone. The Major, unable to attend, had sent a giant floral arrangement, as had Quinn's two sisters. *These people are all crazy,* thought Natalie. *Insane.*

"Flowers for a parrot," Liam muttered under his breath as he came to stand on the other side of Natalie. "Jesus Christ."

She'd noticed when she'd entered that Quinn's mother initially looked shocked to see her. But soon after, she seemed to be looking at Natalie with begrudging respect. Quinn had been right: coming to the memorial was softening his mother's attitude toward her a bit. Now, if she could only find a time machine and undo what she'd said at Sunday dinner, everything would be perfect.

PJ cleared his throat. "I think it would be appropriate if everyone here said a word or two about Rudy."

Liam shot a glance at the Mouth. "Note PJ said *a word or two.*"

"Who wants to start?" PJ asked. His face had healed nicely, but it still made Natalie uneasy when she looked at it, especially after what Quinn had told her yesterday.

There was a second of uncomfortable silence before Mr. O'Brien stepped forward. "Rudy was a lovely bird, a lovely bird. We'll miss him very much."

"I won't," Liam muttered. Natalie gave him a discreet jab in the ribs with her elbow.

"I agree with my husband," said Mrs. O'Brien, squeezing Mrs. Colgan's hand. "He was lovely. I'm going to write out a Mass card for him as soon as I'm done here."

"Thank you," Mrs. Colgan choked out.

Mrs. O'Brien disappeared into the kitchen to start preparing for lunch, while Mr. O'Brien stayed. PJ glanced around at the small band still gathered. "Natalie? Perhaps you'd like to say something?"

"Yeah, go ahead, Natalie," Quinn said with a smirk.

She shot him a dirty look. "All I can say is, *au revoir,* Rudy. The Wild Hart just won't be the same without you."

"Natalie's right," PJ added. "Who else is going to shout out, 'You fat whore'? Who else is going to squawk, 'There's nothing but crap on TV'?"

The Mouth shook his head sadly. "Too true. Too true." He took a step forward. "I'd like to say a few words."

"A *few* words," Liam reminded him.

"'Twill never be another bird like Rudy. Proud, with an enviable plumage, he was friendly to all who came here."

"Oh my effin' God," Liam murmured in disbelief to Natalie. "He's lost his mind."

"Did he ever have one?" Natalie whispered, genuinely curious.

"Many is the time I was feeling low, and the mere sight of our Rudy perched on Mary Colgan's shoulder perked me right up."

"He never nipped you," Mrs. Colgan agreed, sniffling. "You two loved each other."

"That's right."

The Mouth opened his arms wide. "Fly, fly, proud fellow! Fly home to your maker!"

"Do you know that if I had a cyanide pill in my pocket, I'd bite down on it right now?" Liam whispered to Natalie. He leaned over to Quinn. "You *are* writing this up for the *Sent,* aren't you?"

"That asshole Clement would probably love it," Quinn grumbled.

"Boys!" Mr. O'Brien hissed indignantly. "Some respect!" Quinn and Liam both looked down, shamefaced. They were like two little boys stifling laughs in school after being reprimanded by their teacher.

"Liam?" asked PJ.

Liam lifted his head, biting his lower lip to suppress laughter. "Yeah?"

"I think you should say a few words about our fine feathered friend, and then I'll finish up after Quinn has said his piece as well."

"Shit," Quinn whispered.

"It's your own fault," said Natalie.

Liam dug his hands deep into the back pockets of his jeans. "Um . . . I remember when Mrs. C and Rudy started coming here, right after Mr. C died." Everyone nodded solemnly. "My family knew right off the bat that Rudy was special. So we'll miss him. I, especially, will miss giving him the occasional sip of Cuervo."

"He loved that," Mrs. Colgan said, her bottom lip quivering.

"Over to Quinn," said Liam. Natalie noticed they refused to look at one another, probably for fear of bursting into laughter.

"I'm better when it comes to writing words than speaking them," Quinn said, "but I believe in keeping things simple on both scores. So I'll just say: Rudy was a great bird. Irreplaceable. He will truly be missed."

"That's all you could come up with?" Liam whispered. "Wimp."

"Lovely sentiments, lovely sentiments," said PJ. "And now, if I may, I have a few words of my own to add.

"There's an old Irish blessing, 'May the light of heaven shine on your grave.' Each of us here knows how appropriate a blessing that is, for Rudy himself was a giver of light.

He might not have been one of our species, true, and there were a few times he bit me hard and made my finger bleed and ate all the peanuts down at our end of the bar, but he was family. I know that we will keep him in our hearts, and as a way to ensure we do, I've created a memorial to him."

"If this goes on much longer I'm going to lose it," Liam told Natalie under his breath. She looked at Quinn. He was back to staring at the floor, his shoulders shaking with silent laughter.

PJ walked over to his battered shoulder bag and pulled out an eight-by-ten color photo of Rudy perched on Mrs. Colgan's shoulder at the bar. Across the bottom of the picture he'd written, "Rudy, We Hardly Knew Ye." With a solemn face, he passed the picture to Mr. O'Brien. "Please, put this up behind the bar in honor of our good friend who has passed, so we can gaze upon his countenance each time we're here."

"Of course, of course," Mr. O'Brien assured him.

"Anyone else want to say anything?" PJ asked. "Mary?"

"I have a request, too," Mrs. Colgan said quietly.

"Okay," Mr. O'Brien said uncertainly.

The widow Colgan reached down into the shopping bag at her feet and took out a small wooden urn, which she placed on the bar. "Can we put Rudy behind the bar? It would mean so much to me and to him, too. He loved it here."

"Just let me check with the missus," said Mr. O'Brien.

"Thank you." She tucked her crumpled hankie into the sleeve of her blouse. "Well, I guess I'll go home now. See you all later at six."

PJ offered her his arm. "I'll see you home."

"Me as well," said the Mouth.

As soon as the three of them departed, Liam turned to his father. "You're not really gonna put that stuff behind the bar, are you?"

"Ah, why not? It'll do no harm." He glanced toward the

back of the pub. "I best be gettin' in the kitchen." He squeezed Natalie's arm. "See you tonight."

Natalie was warmed by his affection. "Of course."

Mr. O'Brien disappeared.

"Good omen that he squeezed your arm," Quinn said to Natalie. He loosened his tie. "Thank Christ that's over."

"No shit," said Liam. "What's with the suit?"

"A little joke between me and Natalie."

"Feel free to keep it to yourselves. I have to hit the basement and check out inventory. Catch you both later."

Alone, Natalie smoothed Quinn's tie. "You should wear suits more often," she murmured. "You look very handsome."

"I'll wear one when the Mouth's gerbil dies. How about that?"

"Always the sarcasm with you. Let me guess: you don't have time to have breakfast with me."

"Nope. Meeting at the newspaper. I doubt we lowly reporters will be included, but Clement wants everyone there anyway."

Natalie hid her frustration. "So when will I see you again?"

"I'll probably come in tonight with the guys." He kissed her. "Walk with me?"

"Actually," Natalie said as an idea slowly began forming in her head, "I want to talk to your mother about something."

"Good luck," said Quinn.

But Natalie wasn't so sure she'd need it.

22

"Mrs. O'Brien?"

At the sound of Natalie's voice, Quinn's mother looked up in surprise from where she stood making the dough for her famous Irish soda bread. She'd been chatting away animatedly with Megan, the daytime waitress, but as soon as she heard Natalie, she adopted a more professional demeanor than usual.

"Excuse me," she said to Megan. She approached Natalie, where she stood right by the swinging doors of the kitchen. "Yes? How can I help you, Natalie?"

"I'm so sorry about what I said the other day at dinner. I didn't mean to offend you. Honestly. Quinn never told me you adhered to your faith so strongly. Had I known, I never would have said anything that would be an affront to you."

She wished she hadn't listened to Quinn, with his "Just let it go for now" advice. He'd been wrong, and her faux pas had been haunting Natalie all week. She didn't want Quinn's mother thinking she didn't care about offending her, because she did. Deeply.

Quinn's mother looked appreciative. "Apology accepted," she said quietly, reaching out to squeeze Natalie's hand.

Natalie heaved a sigh of relief. "Oh, I'm so glad. I've hated the tension between us since it happened. I've come to feel so close to your family, and it pained me very much to feel estranged from you." She blinked tears away.

"Now, now, don't cry. Water under the bridge, as they say."

"I was wondering: you were so gracious, inviting me for a meal at your home. May I invite you for a meal at mine? I would love for you to meet my family—well, it's only my sister and future brother-in-law really, but still, they are the only family I have here."

Mrs. O'Brien's face lit up. "Now that would be lovely, having a meal and meeting your family. And you know what? You could make that coq au vin you're always going on about. I've never had it."

Natalie forced a smile. "That's a wonderful idea."

Merde, merde, merde. She had no idea how to make coq au vin. She had no idea how to make anything, for that matter. The idea to invite the O'Briens over to her— Bernard's—apartment was impulsive, but she was desperate to smooth things over, and fast. She figured that she'd just have Vivi make dinner.

"Shall we make it Sunday afternoon?" Natalie asked. "That seemed to work very well for everyone in your family."

"Only if it works for you," Mrs. O'Brien replied, suddenly solicitous.

"Oh yes, it works very well, and I believe it works for my sister and her fiancé as well." For a split second, it occurred to Natalie that perhaps having Vivi and Anthony there was a stupid idea. They were the ones, after all, who were the main offenders in the meeting with the priest before marriage debate.

"It'll be lovely to meet them. Now what shall I bring?"

"Please, you needn't bring anything."

"No, I'd like to. What if I bring dessert?"

"That would be wonderful."

Mrs. O'Brien looked excited. "We'll chat a wee bit more about it as the week wears on, shall we?"

"Yes. Finalize plans."

"Lovely." Natalie was stunned when Quinn's mother gave her a tiny peck on the cheek. "Run along with you, now, and enjoy your day. We'll be seeing you later tonight."

Spirits lifted, Natalie left the pub and hopped on the subway out to Bensonhurst.

*   *   *

Quinn wished to hell he'd changed out of his suit before heading over to the *Sent*; he hated the thought that Clement might think he was starting to dress better.

Bizarre though the event was, he was glad Natalie had turned up for Rudy's funeral. He knew his mother: seeing Natalie there had softened her a bit; he could see it on her face. To say he was relieved was an understatement. He didn't think he could handle a cold war between the two most headstrong women he'd ever met in his life. The mere thought gave him the willies.

He strolled into the newspaper office. As usual, it was buzzing, but there was an underlying tension. Everyone knew what might be coming. Everyone was afraid it would be him or her.

"Nice suit," Durham cracked the minute he set eyes on Quinn. "What'd that set you back? Ten bucks at the Salvation Army?"

"Hey, show some respect—or, as you crossword geeks might say, some reverence. I just came from a memorial service."

Durham's demeanor turned serious. "Shit, I'm sorry. Who died?"

"Rudy."

Durham thrust his head forward. "Rudy the fuckin' parrot at the pub?"

"Yeah."

"And you didn't invite me? Or any of the other guys?" Durham was indignant. "We've been going there for years, too, man."

"Liam was in charge of the invites. Bitch to him."

"Hey!" Durham called out. "Rodriguez! Shep!"

"Shep's back?" Quinn asked. As far as he knew, his friend was still MIA.

"Yeah. Where the hell have you been? Came back after he finished that article about that killer sheep in Jersey." He cupped hands on either side of his mouth and called out "Guys! Major news here! Rudy bit it!"

"Whaattt?" Shep hurried over, looking distraught. "You're kidding."

"Nope." Durham jerked a thumb at Quinn. "That's why this putz is all purtied up: he just came from his memorial."

Rodriguez looked hurt. "Hey, thanks for not inviting us, dude. I mean really."

"You can pay your respects if we head down there tonight, okay?" Quinn replied with mild exasperation. "His urn is behind the bar."

"Fitting," said Durham, nodding approvingly. "Good thing Clement doesn't know. He would have sent Shep to cover it."

"Where's Rogan?" Quinn asked.

"Rogan's in the meeting."

Quinn pulled his tie off completely and tossed it on his desk. "I'm gonna burn all my ties when I retire; I swear to God."

"Who the hell are you kidding?" Durham jeered. "You're never gonna retire. You're gonna be eighty, sneaking into buildings and hospitals trying to get that one, final juicy quote."

"Probably right—if I don't die first from lack of exercise and donut consumption."

"Hey, you've an image to uphold: Mr. Reporter on the Go."

Quinn glanced toward the conference room. He had a pretty good idea what was going on in there—and when his editor Cindy emerged, her skin as pale as chalk, he knew his hunch was right.

"So," said Quinn, "how many of us is he canning?"

Cindy pressed a thumb and forefinger to the bridge of her nose. "Quinn."

"Has he even got the balls to do it himself? Or is he gonna make his editors do it?" Quinn leaned back against the lip of his desk, his feet crossed at the ankles. "Let me guess. They've got to trim the budget. Never mind the fact that the Hewitt Corporation is a multinational, multimillion-dollar publishing juggernaut."

"Quinn."

"Come on, Cin; admit it."

She ignored him and turned to Shep. "Clement wants to see you. He wants to see you, too, Durham. And you, Quinn. Rodriquez, you need to talk to your own editor."

"Rogan still in there with Clement?"

Cindy nodded.

"Asshole," Quinn said. "Clement, I mean, not Rogan. They better be giving the old-timers a decent retirement incentive package is all I can say." He pushed off his desk. "Well, time to start boxing up my crap," he said with a heavy sigh. "That way, I'll be ready to roll right after my head does."

* * *

Shep was fired. Rogan was fired. Durham could stay if he made the crossword puzzle a "little less esoteric" and was willing to take a pay cut. He was. Rodriquez was spared the axe.

Watching his friends and other coworkers box up their things, Quinn couldn't help but wonder who'd replace them. It wasn't uncommon for newspapers to fire existing staff when there was a regime change and bring in their own people. By the time he was called in to Clement's office, he was already calculating in his head which of his contacts to call at the *Times* and the *Standard*.

Clement nodded curtly.

"Quinn."

"Mason."

"Have a seat."

"No, thanks." He yawned and stretched. "So, what's the deal? Two weeks' severance pay?"

"We're not letting you go. In fact, we'd like you to replace Jeff Rogan as Metro editor."

"You have got to be kidding me."

Clement frowned. "Do I look like I'm kidding?"

"Thanks, but no thanks. I have no interest in being stuck behind a desk all day. Besides, do you really think I'd take a position that you just fired one of my best friends from? Get real."

"It would mean a significant pay increase."

"I thought you were trimming the budget."

"Getting rid of excess fat. You're not fat."

"Well, that's good to know," Quinn replied scornfully.

Clement told him how much more he'd be earning if he took the editorial job. It was a significant amount. Fuck. He made crap money. Then again, it had never been about the money. Hell, a hefty pay raise would be nice, but stuck in the newsroom most of the time? The thought nearly made him bust out in hives.

"You'd still get to write," Clement continued.

"Hard news?"

"We'd see."

Quinn chuckled softly. "No offense, but how much of a

moron do you think I am? You just want me off the street so you can keep an eye on me. I'm too much of a cowboy for you."

"Your ego astounds me. You really think Hewitt Corporation spends that much time worrying about what you're up to? The simple fact is that we'd thought you'd make an excellent editor."

"Based on?"

"Your years of experience as a writer." Clement's gaze was coolly appraising as he took a sip of tea, which Quinn didn't appreciate. He didn't like feeling like he was being sized up, especially by some corporate drone from Down Under.

"Wasn't Jeff Rogan a reporter for years before he became an editor?"

"Yeah, but he wanted off his beat. He was burned out."

Quinn paused. "Interesting you know that bit of *Sent* history. You check out all our backgrounds?"

Clement just smiled.

"I know the *Sent* is where you cut your teeth, O'Brien. I know it's the only paper you've ever worked at, and I know how much you'd like to stay. So here's our offer: either you take the Metro editor position, or you're fired."

"How's about we make a deal?"

"A deal." Clement's voice was so condescending it set Quinn's teeth on edge. "What kind of deal?"

"I finish up the big article I'm working on, and then I take over the Metro desk."

"Interesting. When will you be done with the article?"

"When I'm done."

"Don't be coy. I need a timetable, O'Brien."

"I'm not being coy. Does your boss want to own a paper that gets nominated for a Pulitzer in journalism or not? Might give him some legitimacy and respect, which Christ knows he doesn't have in the news world. If he does, then let me finish my article."

"Let me float the idea, and I'll get back to you as soon as possible."

"Fine. In the meantime, this conversation is between you and me, got it? It leaks, and I'm outta here."

"Certainly," Clement murmured. His gaze was reptilian. "I'm sure I'll see you at the Hart tonight."

"You know, it might help prove you're not a totally sadistic bastard if you don't stop by the Hart tonight, considering the fact that some of the people you fired will be there, and you're probably the last person on earth they want to see."

"I'll think about it."

"Anything else?"

"Not for now."

"Always a pleasure."

Quinn turned and left the office, suppressing a smile. *What an idiot.*

* * *

"This is a nice surprise."

Vivi's face lit up as Natalie pushed through the swinging doors of the kitchen at Vivi's. It felt like an eternity since she'd been there. Wiping her hands on her apron, Vivi came and embraced her but quickly pulled away as if suddenly remembering something. "I'm sorry. I reek of fish. Tonight's special is going to be my grilled tuna with herbs, garlic, oil, and lemon sauce. You know I like to debone all the fish myself."

"Funny you should mention tuna." Natalie told her about Quinn buying her the soggy, prepackaged sandwich. "I tried to gag down as much as I could, Vivi. Truly."

"Well, it's the thought that counts." Vivi returned to the long steel table to continue working on the fish. "How was the memorial service for the *perroquet*?"

"It was like being in a Roddy Doyle novel. Honestly, I wish you and Anthony had come to the pub before the bird died so you could have seen what a bizarre creature it was."

"Yes, well, we haven't had time to do much of anything, have we?" Vivi said tartly.

"*Cherie?* What's wrong?"

Vivi threw down the knife. "I'm thinking of calling off the wedding! I don't think I can spend eternity with that obstinate, opinionated, bullheaded man!"

Natalie hid her amusement. "What happened?"

"First I agree to marry in his church! Then he tells me he wants to have the reception at Dante's. Reasonable enough. It's convenient, and the banquet room is enormous. But then—oh, oh, here is the pièce de résistance—he tells me he thinks we should serve Italian food at the wedding.

"Well, I put my foot down." Vivi was so angry her nostrils were flaring like an adorable little bull, not that Natalie would ever tell her sister that. "I want the food to be classy, I tell him. Of course he gets all cold under the sleeve—"

"Hot under the collar, Vivi—"

"He gets all hot and cold under the collar and says, 'Oh, so you think the food of my people isn't classy, eh? I suppose you want French food.' And I said, 'Yes, I do.' Natalie, I agreed to getting married in a church! I agreed to have the reception at his restaurant! I think I have the right to pick the menu, don't you?"

Natalie heartily agreed.

"We've been at each other's throats like two crazy dogs. I hate it!" Vivi pushed her slipping bandanna farther back on her head. "Oh, I'm not done. I wanted to keep the wedding small. Intimate. Of course, he wants to invite half of Bensonhurst! He has more relatives than the population of my hometown, I swear to you! And every third cousin twice removed has to be invited, or else it's an insult to the entire clan."

Natalie put a consoling arm around her sister's shoulder. "He's proud to be marrying you, Vivi. Is that so bad?"

"But so many people?"

"He's lived here his whole life. There are people here who've known him since he was a little boy. His family is beloved."

Vivi pressed her lips into a thin, angry line. "So you think I should capitulate."

"Compromise," Natalie urged. "Tell him you'll agree to having a large wedding if he'll agree to letting you choose the menu and the band."

Vivi stamped her foot. "Oh! How could I have forgotten to tell you about the music! An ex-teammate of his brother has a band called the Tarantulas. Anthony and Michael say they're great. I am not having a band called the Tarantulas play at my wedding reception! I am not!"

"You know, I'm sure Quinn and his brother know some good bands in the city you can hire for weddings. Shall I ask them?"

"Yes. I'm open to anything, as long as they're not named after poisonous spiders." Vivi picked up her knife, pointing it at Natalie. "Take my advice: don't get married. It's not worth the stress of planning the wedding. If we can get through this without killing each other—and God knows we each possess the utensils to do it—it will be a major miracle."

"It'll all work out. You'll see."

"I say that all the time to you, don't I? No wonder you always look so annoyed," Vivi grumbled. She was in such a bad mood that Natalie wondered if this might be the wrong time to ask for a favor. Then again, focusing on something other than planning the wedding might be a welcome relief for Vivi, and this was something Natalie really couldn't afford to leave too late. She had to risk it.

"Vivi, I need your help."

"Yes?" Vivi replied, not looking up from her fish.

"I made peace with Quinn's mother."

Vivi smiled. "See? I told you she didn't hate you."

Natalie's reply poured out in a torrent. "And I invited the family over to dinner next Sunday and she accepted but she wants me to make the coq au vin I've been trying to convince them to put on the menu and I had no choice but to say yes so I need you to help me with it or I'm doomed."

Vivi shrugged. "Of course," she said simply.

"Oh, God, thank you. She's looking forward to meeting you. And Anthony."

Vivi scowled at her. "Anthony won't be there. I'll have murdered him by then."

"Vivi."

"Fine, all right, I'll bring the hot-tempered prima donna with me. Just don't be surprised if he tries to take over the kitchen."

"That's all right with me," Natalie assured her, perhaps a bit too hastily. Vivi narrowed her eyes at her a moment, then went back to deboning.

"Can you stay for lunch?"

"Yes, I would love to. Can you spare a piece of that tuna now?"

"*Oui.* How would you like it?"

"Broiled with a little lemon, *merci.*"

"Go sit, then, and I'll bring it out to you. And don't fret about having Quinn's family over. It will be fine. Trust me."

23

"This was a mistake. A *très, très* large mistake."

Natalie looked to Quinn for confirmation as the two of them set the huge table for twelve in Bernard's dining room. In the background, Vivi and Anthony were arguing loudly in the kitchen. Something about mashing up garlic.

"I'm sure that once my family arrives, they'll be on their best behavior."

"If they don't murder each other in the next ten minutes."

"Well, it would certainly make for an extra exciting meal, that's for sure."

Natalie wished she could appreciate Quinn's wit, but she was too nervous. She'd been up since early morning, fretting. What if she put a foot wrong again? What if Anthony did? He was as opinionated as Quinn. What if, when his family saw where she lived, they thought she was a rich girl slumming it by working at their pub? She had to remember to tell then this was not really her apartment, that she was subletting it from a friend—very cheaply—while its owner was out of town.

She and Vivi had arranged things so that by the time Quinn's family arrived, the meal would be virtually ready to go. All she'd have to do was check it once or twice during the conversation as if she'd made it, and then serve it.

The whole family would be there save Liam, who'd made previous plans with a friend of his named Tommy, whom Natalie had never met. An odd look—half interest, half concern—flashed across Quinn's face when Natalie told him the reason for Liam's absence. When she asked him about it, he said it was nothing.

Quinn came up behind her as she set the final place, rubbing her shoulders. "You've got to relax."

Natalie leaned her head back against his chest. "I know. But I want everything to go perfectly."

"As long as you steer clear of the subject of religion, you should be okay."

The doorbell rang, and Natalie immediately tensed. *Please let this go well,* she prayed to whomever might rule people's fates. *Please.*

"Out of the kitchen, out of the kitchen," she urged Anthony and Vivi as she hurried to the front door.

Vivi shot her an annoyed look, but within seconds, she and Anthony were casually arranged on Bernard's sumptuous leather couch, looking like they'd been chatting away just waiting for the other guests to arrive.

Natalie opened the front door, greeting Quinn's family with a warm smile. *"Bonjour."*

"Bonjour," Quinn's father replied, giving her a quick peck on the cheek as he came in. He gazed around, whistling through his teeth. "This is quite a place you've got here."

"It's not mine," Natalie said quickly. "I'm just subletting it from a friend."

"A very rich friend," noted Quinn's mother, handing Natalie two foil-wrapped plates.

"Can't have too many rich friends," Quinn's dad quipped.

"It would be nice if we had just one," his mother quipped back. Quinn's sister Maggie and her husband, Brendan, followed behind Quinn's parents. More kisses on the cheek. Last in was Sinead.

"I'll probably have to leave before dessert," she apologized. "I'm a little behind on my work."

Natalie nodded. "I understand." She looked at Quinn affectionately. "You're just like your brother, *non*? Always working."

"Except her brother doesn't get three headaches a week, and she does," said Mrs. O'Brien.

"Just drop it, Mom, okay?" Sinead pleaded wearily.

The plates in Natalie's hands were still warm. She lifted them to her nostrils, inhaling deeply. "Something with apples, yes?"

"Your basic apple pie."

"She's trying to prove she's absorbed *some* American traditions after all these years living here, eh, *macushla*?" said Quinn's father, squeezing his wife's shoulder.

"*Macushla* is Gaelic for 'my darling,' " Quinn explained before Natalie could even ask.

Everyone inside now, Quinn closed the door, relieving Natalie of one of the pies. She was glad; she was so anxious she was trembling and afraid she was going to drop them.

"Come, I want you to meet my family." Natalie led the O'Briens over to the couch, where Vivi and Anthony now stood waiting to greet Quinn's family. "This is my sister, Vivi," Natalie said proudly, "and this is my future brother-in-law, Anthony. They're both chefs. Right across the street from each other, as a matter of fact. In Brooklyn."

"I hear congratulations are in order," said Quinn's mother. Natalie tensed. "You're getting married soon, isn't that right?"

"Yes," said Vivi.

Natalie prayed that Mrs. O'Brien's pious side didn't emerge, even if it was only for a moment. Luckily, it didn't. She was all smiles, asking Vivi all about her dress. Natalie wondered if Quinn had asked her not to say anything. She'd have to remember to ask him later.

"I'm just going to put these in the kitchen and check on dinner." Natalie turned with a smile, heading for the kitchen. A few minutes later, Vivi appeared.

"Quinn's family seems very nice," she observed.

Natalie put the pies down on the counter. "They are. I just wish Liam were here. He's the one I know best. We get along very well."

"Who's the serious one?"

"Sinead. I think she's a very high-strung person."

"You should introduce her to Anthony. She'd probably be better suited to him than I."

"There's no one better suited to you than Anthony, so just hush."

Vivi checked the coq au vin. "This will be ready soon. All you need to do is baste it two more times in the next twenty minutes. We'll set the oven timer. When it's done, have Quinn arrange it on that big platter. He can then slice the baguettes and toss a nice salad while you prepare the creamed green beans."

"Honestly, it would be so much easier if we just microwave—"

"Do not even finish that sentence," Vivi interrupted with mock seriousness. "Not in the presence of a chef." She sighed wistfully. "It's very nice to see Quinn again. He never comes in anymore—proof that he was only coming in so he could see you."

Natalie blushed a moment, then grabbed her sister up into a spontaneous hug. "I can't thank you enough for today," she whispered. "I'd be doomed were it not for you. Come on, we'd best go back out there."

* * *

Natalie knew it made her look anxious, but she couldn't stop glancing in the direction of the kitchen every couple of minutes, despite Vivi's having set the timer. As she'd told Quinn, she wanted everything to go perfectly.

Inevitably, talk turned to Anthony and Vivi's wedding. Anthony was unable to resist asking Quinn's family's opinion about whether he was right in wanting the reception to be large, or whether Vivi was right, wanting it to be, in his words, "a sad little affair."

"Oh, you gotta go big, darlin', big," Quinn's father said without hesitating. "The more the merrier."

"I told you," Anthony said to Vivi smugly as she shot him daggers.

"Wouldn't you agree, darlin'?" Quinn's dad asked his mother.

"Now, I do think it's a matter of personal taste," Quinn's mother said cautiously. "However, we Irish do like to have big weddings." She gave Quinn and Natalie a none-too-subtle glance before continuing. "And if the music is good, well, that guarantees everyone will have a good time. They'll be dancing into the wee hours."

Anthony looked triumphant.

"I'll think about it," Vivi murmured noncommittally.

The timer went off in the kitchen, and Natalie and Quinn rose simultaneously.

"Why don't you all head into the dining room, and mademoiselle and I will bring out her culinary delights just as soon as we can?" said Quinn. Natalie was the only one who caught the brief flash of mischief in his eyes. He thought it hilarious that she was pretending to make dinner. *Connard.*

"Need any help, darlin?" Quinn's mother asked Natalie.

"Oh, no, no, I'm fine," Natalie assured her quickly. "Please, go make yourself comfortable at the table."

She hustled into the kitchen, turned the timer off, and put the coq au vin on the counter. "Vivi says you're to arrange this on the platter, toss the salad, which I have already cut up, and slice the baguettes while I try to cook these infernal green beans in cream sauce, which I'm sure we could have microwaved."

"I can't decide who's bossier: you or your sister."

"When it comes to food, Vivi." She turned to Quinn anxiously. "They'll like this, right? It's not too fancy? It doesn't look like I'm showing off?"

"They'll like it," Quinn assured her. "Please relax, Nat. *Please*. Although it is kind of cute to see Miss Calm, Cool, and Collected a little flustered. It makes you deliciously vulnerable."

"I'm going to give you a deliciously vulnerable kick in your derriere if you don't get started on the chicken."

"Ah, there's the feisty girl I—adore."

The air around them charged. Quinn turned quickly to the task before him, while Natalie, heartbeat banging, went to the stove to start on the string beans, which Vivi claimed would only take a few minutes. She tucked away in her heart what Quinn had nearly said and got to work.

* * *

"This is delicious, darlin', truly delicious," Quinn's father raved enthusiastically. "Though at this giant table for twelve, I feel like I'm at the Last Supper."

"It might be, depending on how well Natalie followed the recipe," said Quinn.

Everyone laughed, Natalie included. The meal was going very, very well. She was glad Vivi was there, helping to bolster her at every turn, telling stories that couldn't help but make Natalie look good in the O'Briens' eyes. Most important of all, she was beginning to feel as though she was really getting to know Quinn's family. Sinead was still somewhat quiet, but she liked Maggie very much. She was free-spirited and open, reminding her of Vivi. Her husband, Brendan, was nice, too, with a charming sense of humor. In fact, all the men round this table had a pretty good sense of humor. So far, it had been a wonderful, relaxed meal.

"Now, this coq au vin," said Quinn's mother. "What all is in it exactly?"

Merde. Why hadn't she realized that Quinn's mother would ask that, being a cook herself?

Vivi jumped in. "This is *grand-mère*'s recipe, isn't it? The one you make with the mashed-up garlic and the bacon and the Beaujolais?"

"I knew you'd recognize it!" Natalie replied, wishing she could duck beneath the table right now to kiss her sister's feet.

"If I remember correctly, it has just a soupçon of cognac in it as well, right?"

"You don't make it at your bistro?" Quinn's mother asked Vivi skeptically.

Double *merde*.

Vivi covered beautifully. "I use a different recipe. One that's a little easier to prepare."

Quinn's mother nodded, seeming satisfied.

"Vivi made it," Natalie suddenly blurted out, cheeks flaming. "I can't cook. I wanted to impress you."

Quinn's mother looked touched. "There was no need to impress us, love. The invite alone was a lovely gesture. Anything you served would have been fine."

"But you suggested the coq au vin."

"That's kind of my fault," Quinn interjected ruefully.

Natalie turned to him. "How?"

"Uh, Mom and I were talking once, and she mentioned that you kept pressing her to add coq au vin to the menu. So I suggested that the next time you brought it up, she call you on it and say, 'Fine, but *you* have to make it.'" He winced. "Sorry?"

"That's not why I asked you to make it, though," Quinn's mother hastily assured her. "I wasn't trying to trick you into putting your money where your mouth is. I genuinely wanted to try it, because I've never had it. So don't be blaming Quinn here."

"Yeah, don't be blaming me," Quinn chimed in with an Irish brogue.

Natalie wanted to kick him hard under the table.

"I hope you can forgive me," Natalie said humbly.

"There's nothing to forgive," said Quinn's mother. She turned to Vivi. "Delicious," she said.

"Natalie did do the green beans," Vivi pointed out.

Quinn's mother winked at Natalie. "Delicious."

Brendan put an arm around Maggie's shoulders. "Don't feel bad, Natalie. This one here can't cook worth a tinker's damn, either."

Maggie's mouth fell open. "That's not true!"

"Doesn't matter." Brendan kissed the side of her cheek. "You give a bloody good massage."

"And it doesn't matter to me if you can't cook, either," Quinn told Natalie, kissing her cheek. She felt radiant. This was the first time he'd kissed her in front of his family. His parents were practically beaming. *They do like me,* she thought ecstatically. What a wonderful day it had turned out to be.

* * *

"I thought that went really well, don't you?" Natalie asked Quinn after his family, Anthony, and Vivi had departed. By the time the meal was over, Natalie's anxiety had evaporated. Telling them the truth about Vivi preparing the coq au vin had been the right thing to do. Had she not, her deception would have gnawed at her.

"I thought it went great."

Quinn and she had cleaned up the kitchen and dining room, loaded the dishwasher, and were now relaxing in the living room. Quinn's feet were stretched out on the coffee table, his arm around Natalie, who had her feet curled up beneath her, her head resting on Quinn's shoulder.

"I told you my mother didn't hate you," Quinn continued.

He swung his feet off the coffee table, taking his arm from her shoulder. "I'm going to go check out Bernie's CDs."

"All right." Music would be nice, though Natalie didn't mind it being just the sound of their two voices.

Quinn's head was tilted sideways as he walked up and down the shelves of CDs, his eyes scouring Bernard's massive collection. Natalie thought there had to be at least four hundred CDs, maybe more. Odd that she'd never thought once to listen to any of them. He'd told her to make herself at home, but clearly, she hadn't yet, not really. Bernard also had an incredible collection of DVDs she hadn't investigated, either.

"See if he has Rachmaninoff's Second Piano Concerto," Natalie called to Quinn. "You know, your favorite Rachmaninoff piece?"

Quinn raised an eyebrow. "Do I detect a note of sarcasm in mademoiselle's voice?"

Natalie put her hand over her heart. "*Moi?* Never."

Quinn reached up and plucked a CD out from a high shelf, examining it.

"Do you like Kenny G?"

"He plays that mellow saxophone music, yes?"

"I think so."

"Let's try it, then."

Quinn nodded, loading the CD in Bernard's sound system. The smooth, mellifluous sound of a saxophone filled the large, airy space, light and relaxing.

"What's the name of the CD?" Natalie asked.

"Oh. Didn't even bother to check." He picked up the CD

cover. "Uh . . . *I'm in the Mood for Love: The Most Romantic Melodies of All Time*," he murmured uncomfortably.

"Oh." Natalie felt a surge of heat crackle through her as Quinn sat back down beside her, his hand reaching up to caress her cheek.

"I think it's an appropriate title," Quinn murmured seductively.

"Oui." Natalie took a deep breath, then began running her fingers through the thick, beautiful tangle of his hair. She didn't want to be teased tonight. She wanted to be loved fully and love fully in return. "I want you," she whispered.

"Really." Quinn drew her into his arms, his lips just barely touching hers. "Tell me more."

"It's not just what I want," Natalie managed with a jagged breath. "It's what *you* want."

Quinn's gaze, already intense with desire, sharpened. "And what would that be?"

"Me."

She began running her palms up and down his broad, muscular shoulders, the simple act exciting her beyond belief. Despite her bold declaration, she was feeling a little tentative. Still, she would not stop. She moved to nuzzle his neck, gratified when a small groan escaped his mouth.

"You like that?" she whispered as she began planting hot, tiny kisses along his jawline.

"What do you think?"

"I think yes."

"You think right."

With torturous, almost infinitesimal slowness, Quinn lowered his mouth to hers, their tongues beginning their delicate dance, which soon turned frenzied. Natalie knew if she tried to explain it to anyone, they'd think she was crazy, but he tasted unmistakably of Quinn, just as he

smelled unmistakably of Quinn. All her senses knew him
intimately.

Quinn's hand moved to her breasts, his fingers circling
her nipples through the material of her shirt, producing
such an agony of lust she almost couldn't take it. "Take me
to bed," she whimpered. "Please, God, take me to bed."

Quinn chuckled. "You're a very demanding lady."

"Yes, but you like it. Don't deny it."

"Believe me, I'm not."

He stood, extending a hand to her. Trembling, Natalie
took it, leading him down the hallway to the master bedroom, trying hard not to betray the eagerness threatening
to overtake her as she led him into the room toward the
king-sized bed. She untwined her fingers from his to switch
on the bedside lamp, its muted light perfect for just this
occasion. Head swimming, she pulled back the bedspread
to reveal the crisp white sheets she had just laundered that
morning, their fresh scent wafting up to tickle her nose.

Eyes pinned to hers, Quinn kicked off his shoes, and
Natalie did the same. She could still hear the slow, smoky
jazz playing in the living room, distant now but no less
seductive.

"C'mere," Quinn said as he stretched himself out on the
bed, pulling her down beside him so they faced one another. He cradled her face in his hands, his gaze quietly
intense as he once again put his mouth to hers, the taste of
him familiar yet so intoxicating at the same time.

"Quinn," she whispered.

"Mmm?" he murmured, wrapping his arms around her
as his mouth moved to nip at her earlobe. Natalie closed
her eyes a moment, luxuriating in the feel of their being
stretched out together like this, the fit of her body against
his still perfect.

"I want you to use the word you were originally going
to say in the kitchen—you know, when you said I was the
feisty girl you adore."

Quinn pulled back slightly to look at her, his eyes dark with desire. "I was going to say you were the feisty girl I love." His voice turned hoarse with emotion. "God help me, but I do love you, Natalie."

"I love you, too," she said, tears filling her eyes. She'd dreamed of him saying this for so long. He was the only man she'd ever truly loved; no other had ever inspired such passion in her. His touch made her feel obscenely alive.

Desire crossed over the line to lust as she crushed her mouth against his, a small groan escaping her lips. Quinn drew her tighter to him, feeding her want. Wanting to touch, wanting to memorize the body that had always inflamed her, though she was loathe to admit it for so long, she moved her hands beneath the back of his shirt, caressing him with her curious fingers. Quinn inhaled sharply as her exploration took her lower down his body. She touched his hips tentatively and then grew bolder in her touch. His entire body tensed; she could tell he was fighting the desire within him to take her right now. But he held back, exciting her even more. He wanted it to be as good as she did. Crazed with need, she pulled her hands up to again drag his mouth to hers, her hands fisting in his hair.

It was too much for him. Groaning, Quinn rolled on top of her, his hardness against her nearly driving her to the brink. He looked down at her, the naked desire in his eyes so heart-stopping that she could not prevent herself from rubbing against him gently. Breathing hard, Quinn pressed his forehead to hers.

"I want this to be good. I want it to be worth the wait."

Joy shot through Natalie. "Me, too."

Quinn lowered his mouth to her throat, his kisses seductive and undeniably authoritative. She let her head drop back, reveling in the sensation. When he raised himself up to begin undoing the buttons of her blouse, her mind fogged. He was undoing the buttons very slowly, very deliberately. She could see it in his eyes, the way he was watching her, gauging her reaction. She decided to forgo words and show him with her body what he was doing to her as she rubbed herself against him more insistently.

His breath ragged, Quinn hastily pushed up her bra, his greedy mouth latching onto her left breast as one hand teased and circled the nipple of the right. Natalie gasped, pleasure possessing her as his teeth nipped, grazed, bit lightly. Each masterful lick of his tongue intensified the frenzy creeping up on her. She wanted this never to end, yet at the same time, she craved him desperately.

When he pressed into her with his whole body, Natalie thought she would explode. Panting wildly, she tugged on the hem of his shirt. Quinn reluctantly tore his mouth from her breast and, sitting up, quickly shucked his shirt, throwing it onto the floor. His bare chest was breathtaking: muscled, hard, with a line of dark hair trailing down the middle of his abdomen before disappearing beneath the waistband of his briefs. He carefully lowered himself back down, burying his face in her neck before whispering things in her ear no man had ever said to her before: tender words mingled with dirty ones that left her gasping with wild desire.

Quinn began a slow descent down her body, his hot mouth pressed against her skin as he kissed her hips, her belly, all the flesh she had that was revealed to him. And then he paused. And then she begged.

"Please . . ."

Possession in his wild eyes, he undid the zip of her jeans and tugged them off, followed by her panties. His hands began blazing a slow, heated path up and down the insides of her thighs. Unable to control herself, she began rocking her hips as wave after wave of pure, unabashed pleasure assaulted her. The longing to have him moving inside her was overtaking everything. She could think of nothing else.

"Now," she urged, hearing the desperation in her own voice.

Quinn's groan was pure animal as he tore off the remainder of her clothing before stripping off his own. She thought he would take her now, as she'd pleaded, but he didn't. Instead, his fingers began exploring her again, stroking the terrain of her hips before trailing ever lower. He paused, panting, then cupped her between the legs. Natalie could not control her quivering now.

"Please," she rasped.

Quinn chuckled wickedly, then began to use his fingers to slowly circle her, the pressure unbearably light at first, then gradually becoming harder and faster in rhythm with Natalie's body. Desperate for release, she let herself go, convulsing beneath his touch as her screams of pleasure filled the room. It seemed to go on and on, glorious in its perfection.

She was just beginning to return to herself when Quinn sat up a moment, grabbing his pants from the floor to pull out protection with which he sheathed himself. He slid back up her body and, carefully parting her legs, plunged into her. Barely able to hold on to consciousness, she wrapped herself around him, reveling in the sensation of him moving inside her, the white-hot pressure within her body beginning to build again, sharp and steep, until once more she was lost, crying out a second time, driving Quinn to madness.

Natalie clutched hard as his body shuddered with its own release. Finally, he was fully and completely hers.

24

"Nat. Natalie."

Natalie was one of those people who awakened instantly. Hearing Quinn's voice in the dark bedroom, she bolted upright, blinking as he gently shook her shoulder.

"What is it?"

The light shining in from the hallway showed he was perched on her side of the bed, holding a large, steaming mug in his hand.

"I have to go," he whispered. "I made you some coffee."

"Go?"

He kissed her forehead. "I'm sorry about this, but I got a call from one of my NYPD contacts that some business owner was found beaten to a pulp in a warehouse he owns on Twelfth Avenue and Fifty-sixth."

"I didn't hear your phone."

Quinn brushed her hair off her forehead affectionately. "You were out like a light."

Natalie accepted the mug of coffee woodenly, doing her best to hide her disappointment. This was not the way she pictured their first morning together. She'd imagined cuddling, spooning, and more sex as the day got away from them until finally, she had to rush into the shower to make her shift at the Hart on time. Once there, there would be a new level of ease and affection between herself and Quinn's parents.

Instead, he was leaving her alone with a steaming cup of coffee and an empty bed.

Natalie squinted at the digital clock atop the night table. "*Chere*, it's only seven o'clock."

Quinn looked perplexed. "So—?"

"Well, can't you tell your police friend to call another reporter at your newspaper?" Natalie asked, trying to stifle her frustration. "There must be others."

"No." Quinn sounded irritated. "Nat, I told you—"

"Yes, yes, I know. It just would have been nice . . ."

"I know." He picked up a strand of her hair and kissed it. "Look, honey, I have to run." Her disappointment retreated for a moment when he treated her to a long, slow kiss. "I'll try to shoot you a call at some point. Otherwise, I'll probably see you at the Hart tonight."

Natalie sighed resignedly. "Okay." She reached up, wrapping her arms around his neck. "Last night was beautiful."

Quinn grinned. *"Très magnifique."*

Natalie kissed him. "I love you."

"Love you, too. Later," he said, walking back into the hall. Seconds later, she heard the front door close.

Natalie took a sip of the coffee, then put the mug down on the nightstand and stood, rubbing her arms to ward off the room's chill. Her gaze played over the tangle of bedsheets, a reminder of last night's passion. The sight should have made her bloom with happiness; instead, she felt hollowed out and lonely.

She sat back down on the edge of the bed, taking a sip of coffee. How many women before her had sat just as she was sitting now, alone in the early morning as he'd flown out the door on his way to what might or might not be a major story? She cast it from her mind. She was the one who was different from them. She was the one who would let him be who he was. Right?

She threw on her robe and, mug in hand, walked out into the living room to sit on the couch, her feet curled up beneath her. She knew Quinn loved her, yet his not being here now was bittersweet. It had never been a word that she'd particularly liked.

* * *

Quinn sat at his desk at the *Sent*, digging the heels of his palms into his eye sockets in sheer frustration. He'd arrived at the warehouse only a few minutes after the cops, where they all gathered the same information: the owner was a guy named Dominick Tallia, and he'd been found, bloodied and semi-incoherent, by one of his workers on the early morning shift. Both the cops and Quinn talked to the worker, who claimed not to know anything. The poor bastard looked so rattled Quinn knew he was telling the truth. Either that or he deserved an Academy Award.

Leaving the warehouse after they'd gleaned all they could, both he and the cops headed over to Roosevelt Hospital, where Tallia had been taken by ambulance. Beating wise, Tallia was far worse off than PJ, but like PJ, three hooded thugs had attacked him. The cops asked if someone had been extorting him. Turned out he hadn't even been offered that option; he was told by one of the masked thugs that someone wanted the warehouse and his business, and if didn't like it, he'd find himself chopped up in a Dumpster in Red Hook. To bring the point home, they beat him up.

A few more questions, and he passed out. Quinn and the cops left Tallia to languish in peace, and then Quinn headed over to the *Sent*. He hated it when he didn't have enough info for a story beyond "Business Owner Threatened, Found Beaten in Hell's Kitchen Warehouse," though he did mention the mysterious torching of Sweeney's Hardware Store. And at least Tallia was willing to talk about it, which was more than he could say for PJ. He wrote it up, which took all of five minutes, and then he called his brother.

"We have to stop meeting this way," Liam groused, sliding into the booth at Longo's, where Quinn sat waiting for him. Technically, Quinn could have waited until later in the day to talk to Liam. Hell, he could have waited until later that night, when he and his pals descended on the Hart. But Dominick Tallia's beating was eating at him. Natalie said Liam couldn't come to dinner at her place yesterday because he was doing something with Tommy. While Quinn was fairly certain that "something" wasn't beating up a middle-aged Italian warehouse owner, Quinn's craving for any possible tidbit of Whitey-related information, be it large or small, was overwhelming. And so he'd called Liam and lured him to Longo's with the promise of lunch.

The senior Longo waddled over to the table as soon as Liam sat.

"Afternoon." He playfully pushed Liam's shoulder. "What, you only come here when you're with your brother?"

"I usually eat with my folks, Rocco."

"So bring them, too, sometime. I won't tell them you stole those mints from me when you were a kid."

Liam chuckled.

Quinn pointed at him. "One of your famous omelettes for this man here."

Liam held up a hand and put the other to his stomach. "Actually, I'm fine. I already had some soda bread at Mom and Dad's," he explained to Quinn.

"Coffee?" the old man asked.

"Hell yeah," said Liam. He turned his gaze to Quinn.

"You don't have to buy me off with food, you know. I told you I'd tell you if I found out anything."

"I'm not buying you off," Quinn replied, offended. "I was just trying to be nice. Christ."

"Yeah, well, whatever," Liam muttered. Clearly he was in one of his moods. Maybe he was still wary of Quinn and their newfound relationship.

Perhaps sensing he was being a prick, Liam switched to a more amicable tone.

"I hear it went great at Natalie's yesterday. Mom and Dad really like her. And Mom even liked her sister, despite the whole church flap."

"Yeah, it went great."

"So, this is the one, huh?" Liam asked as he gratefully accepted his cup of coffee from the old man.

"I guess," Quinn mumbled.

"What?"

"It's early days yet, you know? We're taking it slow." Quinn felt pensive as he took a gulp of coffee.

"She know that?"

"Of course. It's not like we're planning a wedding or anything," Quinn scoffed. He tried to imagine being married and couldn't, at least not right now. And Natalie had made a point a few weeks earlier of saying she had no interest in marrying him. Which irked him. *Which is it, Quinnie boy,* he asked himself. *Can't have it both ways.* See? He was already starting to worry about losing his edge. Not good. Not good at all.

"Mom say anything else?" Quinn pressed.

"She busted my balls a bit about not being there, but I'd already explained to her I'd committed to this thing with Tommy."

"That's what I wanted to talk to you about."

"I figured."

"Tell me what you got."

"He asked me if I wanted to come hang at a party a

friend of his was having, some guy named Gerald who I've met a few times."

"One of Whitey's guys?"

"Oh yeah. Works for Shields Brothers. Big surprise, huh? You should have seen this guy's apartment.

"Anyway, some of the other guys there were suspicious when I came in, because they have no idea who the hell I am, despite my walking in with Tommy. Morons. But once Tommy explained that I was his best friend and Gerald said I was cool, it was okay. Everyone was talking about mundane stuff at first, the Mets, the Blades, blah blah blah. But once Tommy had a snootful, I was able to get some info—kind of."

Quinn took a deep breath. "Like—?"

"Well, he asked me if I was sick of living in my crappy little apartment—which I don't think is crappy, by the way. When I asked him why, he said one of the warehouses in the neighborhood was being turned into luxury apartments, and if I wanted, he'd see if he could have one set aside for me, since he knows the owner. Like it's hard to figure out who that is, right? I asked him how the hell he thought I could afford a luxury apartment, and he just smiled at me and walked away. He's such a feckin' idiot when he's drunk."

"No, he's a useful idiot, at least to me." Quinn gulped down more coffee. "Some warehouse owner had the shit beaten out of him last night. Same situation as PJ—three masked assholes."

Liam frowned. "Not surprised."

"You get anything else?"

"Hell yeah. Whitey Connors was there. He asked about you."

"I can't wait to hear this."

"I'm standing on the terrace talking to Tommy and some other goon, and Whitey comes out. Asks how tending the bar is going. Asks about Mom and Dad. Then asks about you. 'Still working hard as a reporter? Still got his ear to the street?' " Liam sucked down some coffee. "He knows, Quinn."

"Of course he fuckin' knows." Quinn shrugged dismissively. "It's not a big deal. Stupid as he is, he'd never kill a journalist. Threaten? Sure. Beat up? Maybe. But kill? No. I don't need to worry."

"Well, maybe you don't, but I'm sure Natalie will. She know what you're working on?"

Quinn frowned. "A little. And before you even ask, yeah, she's worried. But it's not like I'm going to stop."

"Mom and Dad know?" Liam asked.

"What are you, crazy? They'd drive me up the friggin' wall with worry and tell half of Manhattan."

Quinn leaned forward. "Look, Li, I really appreciate you keeping your ear to the ground on all this stuff."

Liam looked uncomfortable. "No problem." He drained his coffee cup. "You comin' in tonight?"

"Probably. Depends. Gotta help keep up Rogan and Shep's spirits, you know?"

"You surprised you weren't axed?"

"A little. But like it or not, they still need some hard news runners around."

"Clement likes Natalie."

Quinn scowled. "No shit. But he had his shot. I really wish he'd find somewhere else to hang out. He does it on purpose just to irk me and the guys."

"I think he does it to see Natalie."

"Are you deliberately trying to piss me off? Because you're doing a good job."

"Jesus, relax. It was just a bartender's observation." Liam shook his head. "And they claim I'm the moody one," he said under his breath.

Quinn changed the subject. "You headin' back to the Hart?"

"Yeah, of course. You know there's always a ton of shit to do. You coming with? Say hi to Mom and Dad?"

"Not today. I have some poking around I need to do. But like I said, I'll probably be in tonight."

"Okay." Liam stood. "Well, thanks for the coffee."

"Thanks for the info," Quinn said gratefully.

"No problem. I just hope it doesn't result in you getting beaten up."

"Quit being such an old lady. I told you: there's nothing to worry about. Trust me."

25

TWO MONTHS LATER

"You're still up?"

Quinn glanced up from his laptop to see Natalie in the doorway of her dining room, rubbing sleep from her eyes. It was 3 a.m. He'd been plagued with insomnia for three weeks running. Just as he'd feared, trying to balance his job and a relationship had caused him to lose his edge as a reporter. Sometimes he found himself distracted, daydreaming about making love to her when he should have been focused. Sometimes he found himself watching her when he should have been listening to what his friends were saying. They'd kid him about it, but it made him feel bad. To top it all off, his parents were dropping hints about marriage.

Quinn had come back to Natalie's place every night since they'd first slept together. He hated that it felt obligatory. Not that he didn't love her, but it was making him feel roped and tied.

He had to tell her the truth, even though it risked wounding her. If he didn't come clean, his unease would turn into resentment, which was the last thing he wanted.

Natalie came and stood behind him, tenderly rubbing his shoulders. "Work. Always work."

"Yeah, well, that's me." Quinn turned around to look at her. "We need to talk."

Trepidation rippled through the room as Natalie slowly dropped her hands. "Can we go where it's more comfortable?" she asked quietly.

"Of course." Quinn playfully tugged a strand of her hair, trying to lighten the mood. "Don't sound so afraid. It's not bad."

Natalie was silent, leading the way to the living room. Quinn made sure to sit right beside her as she curled up on the couch. Even with her face a little puffy from sleep and her long brown hair somewhat of a tangled mess, she looked beautiful. In fact, this was one of the ways he liked her best: no makeup, unguarded, just pure, unvarnished Natalie.

Despite his telling her not to be fearful, there was no mistaking the anxiety in her eyes. "What is it?"

Quinn took a deep breath and blew it out. "I need a little more space for myself. I'm feeling a little—pressured."

Natalie drew her knees up to her chest, wrapping her arms around her shins. She looked like a vulnerable little girl. "Pressured?"

"Nat, I told you when we got together that my work is extremely important to me. And sometimes, to do it well, I need to be alone. To think. I don't feel like I can do that when we go home together every night. You think I don't see you bristle every time my phone rings?"

"Because you work too hard. Because you never stop working."

"It's who I am."

She was quick to disagree. "*Non. Non.* It's who you choose to be."

"All right, it's who I choose to be. Especially now, working on this story."

"Yes, the story that will get you killed."

Quinn suppressed his exasperation. "How many times do I have to tell you? It won't get me killed."

"When will you be done with it?"

"Soon."

She looked hopeful. "And maybe then—?"

"Maybe then what?"

"You'll cut back a little?"

Frustrated, Quinn ran his hand through his hair. "You're not understanding me. I can't cut back."

"Not even a little bit? Why can't you compromise?" she asked plaintively as she feathered her fingertips across his cheek. "I love you, and I'm proud of what you do. But it's difficult sometimes, knowing that in the back of your mind, even when we are out to dinner or just relaxing here, you are always thinking about work. You're obsessed with it." She looked sad. "I wish you were obsessed with me, even if it was just a little bit."

"I am obsessed with you," Quinn said, trying to express his misery and confusion. "That's part of the problem. I find myself thinking of you when I should be focusing on my work. I'm not paying attention to my friends when we're hanging out at the Hart."

She looked wounded. "Because of me."

"Because of us," Quinn said softly. For someone who worked with words, he was having a hard time coming up with the right ones. "I don't want to lose you. I just need a few nights a week to myself so I can concentrate on my work."

"Let's say we do that," said Natalie, sounding reasonable. "Does that mean the nights we are together you'll turn off your cell phone? Mmm?"

"I can't right now," Quinn said bluntly. "Not until I'm done with this story."

"Is this what's been keeping you awake? This story? Or not having time to yourself?"

"Both. Plus, I've always gone through spells of insomnia. I try to use it, though. Do research on the Web. And sometimes the pieces of a puzzle come together in the middle of the night when I least expect it. I do crash eventually."

"Precisely what I'm afraid of: the word *crash*."

Quinn wrapped his arms around her. "I need you to try to understand this."

"I'm trying to understand, truly I am. It's just hard when I feel envious of your job."

"Envious or neglected?"

Natalie looked thoughtful. "Not neglected exactly. More like"—she fluttered her long, pale fingers in the air, searching for the right word—"second best. I can't compare to the excitement I see in your eyes when you run out to cover a story."

Quinn felt terrible. That's not how he wanted her to feel, but he knew she was right. She had every right to ask him why he couldn't compromise a little bit. He knew the answer: he was an uncompromising bastard, which was why he was such a success at work and so crappy when it came to relationships. But maybe it was time to bend. Just a little.

"Look," said Quinn, brushing a silky tangle of hair away from her face. "All I need is a few nights a week on my own, and things will balance themselves out. I swear."

Natalie looked skeptical.

"What, you don't believe me?"

"*Chere*, don't be offended when I say this, but I'll believe it when I see it. In the meantime, how do we work this? Do we come up with a schedule for when you're here and when you're not? Or do I wait for you to walk into the pub or call me late at night to tell me whether you'll be coming home with me or not?"

She sounded angry. *Bend, you selfish bastard. Bend.*

"I would never leave you hanging. You decide on a schedule, if that's what works best for you."

"I get you on my two nights off, Monday and Wednesday, and Saturday and Sunday during the day as well."

"Agreed."

She looked satisfied and rubbed her nose against his. "Are you coming to bed?"

"In a little bit. I promise."

Natalie clucked her tongue. "You are so exasperating."

Quinn grinned. "I do my best."

"You succeed admirably."

They rose, Quinn taking her hand, pausing when they came to the bedroom door. "Sleep tight," he murmured, kissing her gently. He wished he wasn't so wide-awake so he could lie down next to her, spooning as they both drifted off together.

"Please try to get some sleep," she begged. "Even if it's just a little."

"I will. I promise."

He kissed her again, continuing on to the dining room, where his laptop sat waiting for him. He sat down, reflexively taking his cell out of his pocket. He stared at it a moment, then turned it off, even though it killed him to do so. With that, he got down to work.

* * *

The next day, Natalie took the subway out to Bensonhurst to see Vivi. It was early morning, the only time to catch her at home. Natalie entered the house to find Vivi in the living room, dramatically sealing up a large cardboard box sitting on the coffee table.

"Bonjour," said Natalie, kissing her sister on both cheeks. "What's that?"

"My *grand-mère*'s wedding dress. I'm sending it back to Lyon. The wedding is off."

Natalie sighed heavily. "Again?" At least once a week, Vivi or Anthony broke their engagement. It was becoming tiresome.

"For real this time," Vivi insisted with a scowl. "I can't marry him. Truly I can't. Isn't the wedding day really supposed to be the bride's day? Eh?"

"Yes, I believe so," said Natalie, sitting down on the couch.

"Ha! I knew it! Yet he's trying to control everything. Everything."

"I thought you two had agreed on the church. And where to hold the reception. And didn't you two just hire a band you both liked?"

"Yes," Vivi said impatiently, "but he was still pushing for that *stupide* Tarantulas band right up until the last moment!"

"What does it matter? In the end, they're not playing."

"He still wants to invite three hundred people! It's absurd! And he wants a wedding party! The only person I want standing up for me is you. But he wants Michael as his best man, and Aldo as a groomsman as well as his cousin Gemma's husband. I love all of them, but I don't want a wedding party!"

"Vivi—"

Vivi plopped down on the couch, close to tears. "Him, him, him. All about him."

"I understand that," Natalie commiserated under her breath. "Where is he?"

"At his brother's, I imagine. I threw him out last night. He better not walk across the street to Vivi's later to try to make up. I'll chase him with that damn cleaver he bought me last year."

"I've never met two more stubborn, temperamental people in my life."

"*Oui*, and that's why it's a match made in hell."

"Maybe you shouldn't get married," Natalie suggested. "You've been living together for a year, and it's been fine. If the planning is going to drive you apart, is it worth it?"

Vivi's eyes began watering. "I've always wanted to get

married," she sniffled. "Ever since I was a little girl. And I want to have children."

"Your mother had you, and she wasn't married."

"My mother couldn't marry my father, remember?" Vivi snapped. "He was married to your mother." She clamped her eyes shut for a moment, looking like she was trying to regain control. "I'm sorry. I didn't mean to sound nasty."

"No, it's true."

"But not accurate. Even if our father was free, I don't think my *maman* would have married him. She was always *très* bohemian."

"Yes, I know. I'm looking forward to meeting your *grand-mère*. Wait until she sees you in her dress. You're going to look so beautiful. I know I'm going to cry the minute you walk down the aisle."

Vivi was silent.

"All this stress will be over soon, you'll see. And you'll live happily ever after and have a passel of strong-willed, temperamental children."

Vivi laughed, cheering up. "We still need to shop for your dress. Something chic and lovely, not one of those *atroce* wedding party dresses that you'll never wear again in your life."

"Chic and lovely and reasonably priced."

"Oh, no, no, I'm buying it for you," Vivi insisted. "It's my present to you for being such a good sister, and helping to keep me sane."

Now it was Natalie's turn to tear up. "You don't have to do that, but I know you: you'll dig your heels in. So thank you."

"Enough of me," Vivi declared, slapping the top of her thighs as she stood and began untaping the box containing her wedding dress. "Time to hear about you."

"I'm with a selfish man as well." Natalie rubbed the back of her neck, suddenly aware of the knot of tension forming there. "Do you remember me telling you that he asked me early on if I could deal with the unpredictable nature of his work, and I told him yes, and then told you I would make it work if that's what it took to be with him?"

"Yeeesss."

"Well, it goes beyond unpredictable," Natalie lamented. "He's addicted to it. I'm not exaggerating, Vivi. It's all he lives for. He tries to put me first when we're together, but I can tell that his mind is often elsewhere. He rarely has his phone off, but when he does, he turns it on all the time to check for messages! I feel like work is his mistress. No, that's wrong; I feel as if I were the mistress, and his job is his wife. I love him, but it's harder to be with him than I thought."

Vivi looked concerned. "Have you told him this?"

"Yes. We talked about it last night—after he told me he didn't want to stay with me every night. He said he needs a few evenings a week alone to concentrate on his job. He's working on a particularly difficult article right now. But he swears that once it's done, we'll have more time together."

"Maybe that's so. Maybe you just need to be patient."

"Or maybe it's crazy for me to think he'll change." She paused. "It hurts me that he doesn't want to spend every night with me. Of course I understand it intellectually. But emotionally, it feels like he's distancing himself."

Vivi looked apprehensive. "Are you thinking of breaking up with him?"

"I don't want to," Natalie said miserably. "I love him so. But it's very hard to play second fiddle to his work."

"Yes, that would be painful."

"All his relationships before me ended because of his work or his feeling that too many demands were being put on him. He told me that himself. I've been trying so hard to prove I'm different from all the others, that I accept him as he is. But maybe I'm the same as them. Maybe I need and deserve more than he can give, the same as all the others did."

"I think you should give him a chance to prove himself. He obviously loves you and doesn't want to lose you. You've always been very impatient, Natalie, don't deny it. Wait and see what happens."

"And if nothing changes?"

"You can make a decision then. But for now, I'd just sit cheap."

"*Sit tight*, Vivi," Natalie corrected with a chuckle. "The expression is *sit tight*." She stopped massaging her neck. "That's what I'll do then, right after I have a chat with your pigheaded fiancé."

26

Natalie followed Vivi to her bistro. There was no mistaking the look in Vivi's eyes—part relief, part sourness—when she glanced across the street at Dante's and saw Anthony's SUV parked there. "Well, at least he's still alive," she muttered, opening the door of her restaurant. She kissed Natalie on each cheek. "Don't fret about Quinn."

"Don't fret about Anthony," Natalie returned.

"I'll call you, and we'll figure out when we can go shopping for your dress."

"Yes."

Natalie waited until Vivi was inside her restaurant, then headed across the street. It was ironic, really, how when she and Vivi had first moved to Brooklyn, she'd thought both Anthony and Quinn somewhat déclassé. She still wished Quinn dressed better, but there were worse things in life than loving a man who didn't know a Bastian from a Boateng. Perhaps she'd go to Bloomingdale's and buy him a shirt. It wouldn't cost too much.

She decided she'd go round back and knock on the

kitchen door, since the kitchen was probably where Anthony was.

She opened the screen door of the kitchen and popped her head in. None of the kitchen staff knew who she was, so when numerous pairs of eyes lit on her questioningly, she told them she was Vivi's sister. They nodded pleasantly, gesturing for her to come in as they returned to their work.

The heat, the noise . . . the kitchen at Dante's was so much larger than Vivi's. Natalie found it somewhat overwhelming.

Much to her surprise, Anthony's brother Michael was there. His face lit up when he saw her. "Natalie! Long time, no see."

"I know."

Michael enveloped her in a big bear hug.

"What are you doing here?" Natalie asked.

"Day off. Thought I'd stop in and bust the big guy's balls."

"Mmm."

"I hear they broke up again," Michael continued, looking amused as he shook his head. "They're more melodramatic than a freakin' Italian opera."

"I agree completely. Is he here?"

"He's in the dining room mulling over some new recipes."

"And his mood?"

"What do you think? He's a crab's ass as always." Michael's expression was curious. "You here to blast him on Vivi's behalf?"

"Lobby would be more accurate. I hope I don't have to resort to blasting."

"Yeah, from what I've heard from Vivi, he has been somewhat of a stubborn bastard. But he's always been a stubborn bastard."

"Vivi's always been stubborn, too, which doesn't help." They shared a laugh.

Natalie cocked her head quizzically. "Was he this obstinate when planning his first wedding?" Anthony's first wife, a policewoman, had been killed in the line of duty. Vivi had been reluctant to get involved with a widower, but ultimately decided to take the chance. Clearly she'd made the right decision.

"Don't remember. Probably." Michael patted her shoulder. "Well, good luck. If I hear him yelling, I'll come out and rescue you."

"Thank you," Natalie said appreciatively. The thought of Anthony yelling was very unpleasant. She certainly wouldn't yell back; that wasn't her style at all.

Michael began walking away, then turned back. "Oh, wait—how's Quinn? Vivi said he hasn't come in to eat in quite a while."

"He's doing very well. I'll tell him you asked."

"Tell him if he ever wants tickets to a Blades game for him and his cronies, just let me know."

"I will."

Natalie gently pushed through the swinging doors of the kitchen and went out into the dining room. Anthony was sitting at a table for four, poring over three large, spiral-bound notebooks, jotting notes on a legal pad. He turned when he heard the doors open, unmistakable surprise on his face.

"Let me guess," he said sardonically as Natalie approached the table. "Vivi sent you here to give the engagement ring back to me."

"Wrong." Natalie gestured at the seat opposite Anthony. "May I?"

"By all means. Can I get you anything?"

"*Non*, I'm fine. Thank you for asking."

Natalie slid into the seat opposite her future brother-in-law, feeling awkward. She and Anthony had never had a serious talk before. She wondered if he would accuse her of overstepping her bounds, or if he'd lose that famous temper of his. Maybe both. Well, Quinn always said she could give as good as she got, even if she could be some-what tart. She hoped it wouldn't come to that, but if that's what it took to make Vivi's dream wedding come true, then she'd do it.

Anthony closed up his notebooks. "What can I do for you?"

"It isn't what you can do for me," said Natalie, seeing no reason to beat around the bush. "It's what you can do for Vivi. Anthony, she's been very accommodating regarding your wedding. A religious ceremony. Italian food. Having the reception at Dante's. Now she tells me you want her to have a wedding party."

"I don't think it's asking a lot."

"There's no reason why you can't just have your brother and me be your witnesses. It's a small thing."

"But it will be, I dunno, weird."

Natalie blinked. "It won't be weird. Do you really think anyone cares? Do you think your loved ones will be sitting in church thinking about that?"

"No," Anthony admitted sheepishly.

"So we've taken care of that."

"No offense, Natalie, but—"

"Vivi's entitled to get some of the things she wants," Natalie interrupted fiercely. "This is her first wedding and, she hopes, her only wedding. You've been married before. Yes, it's a day for both of you, but the wedding day should be all about the bride. Your bride loves you so much that she acquiesced on things that were important to her. The least you can do is give her what she wants on what's left to decide—which is not a lot!"

Anthony leaned back in his chair, sizing her up. "Did Vivi send you here to talk to me?"

"No. I'm here because I want her to be happy on the most important day of her life."

Anthony's expression softened. "Believe it or not, I do, too."

"I know that," Natalie said, heartfelt. "I used to think you weren't good enough for Vivi."

"And I thought you were a snob."

Natalie leaned forward. "I still am—a bit," she confessed in a stage whisper.

"That's okay. I'm probably *not* good enough for Vivi."

They both laughed.

"You and Quinn doing good?"

"Very well," Natalie said politely.

"Maybe you'll be next at the altar, huh?"

Natalie cleared her throat uncomfortably. "Maybe." She felt ill at ease discussing this issue, even though she could see it was just his way of being friendly.

Anthony scrubbed his hands over his tired face. "Okay. Whatever Vivi wants from now on, she gets. You're right: she's the bride. Obviously I've been walking around with my head up my ass."

Natalie chuckled. "Another charming American expression."

"Any thoughts about her bridal shower?" Anthony asked.

"I was just thinking about that. Maybe we should have it at my—Bernard Rousseau's—apartment." Natalie saw the small flash of displeasure in Anthony's eyes at the mention of Bernard's name and held back a bemused smile. Anthony had once thought Bernard was his competition for Vivi and was very jealous.

"That sounds good." Anthony rubbed his chin. "Want me to make the food? It would save money."

"That would be lovely," Natalie said with relief. She needed to save as much money as she could. "I'll need you to tell me what I should buy her for a present," she continued.

"Some tranquilizers might be good."

"I'm being serious."

"I'll let you know."

"Thank you, Anthony. For everything." Natalie stood. "I'll let you get back to work."

"You want some olive oil cake to take back to the city with you? Fresh made this morning."

Did all chefs want to fill everyone up with food all the time? Natalie wondered. Vivi did the same thing.

"No thank you."

"Ah, well, your loss," Anthony teased. He rose.

She came around the table and kissed him on both cheeks. "Tell Michael it was wonderful to see him." She wagged a finger at him as she departed. "And no more breaking up!"

* * *

Quinn was sitting at Longo's having his coffee and a cinnamon roll, reading that morning's edition of the *Sent*. He nearly choked on his pastry when he saw a cover story about a three-alarm fire in Chelsea that killed four and looked to be the work of an arsonist. These were his stories. Yet the byline read Chris Truelsen—a goddamn new hire, a kid straight out of J school. Pissed, he finished his breakfast, making a beeline for Cindy the minute he hit the newsroom.

He tossed the newspaper down on her desk. "Care to tell me why I wasn't sent out to cover this?"

Cindy looked up at him wearily. "Your cell was off. Truelsen's was on."

Shit. He knew he shouldn't have turned his phone off. He knew it.

Quinn glanced back down at the story. "Has it got legs?"

"Don't know yet," said Cindy, looking like death warmed over.

"Give me the follow-up," he demanded.

Cindy looked incredulous. "Quinn, it's Truelson's story. He does the follow-up."

"You're not looking too hot," he noted with concern.

"Thanks a lot. In case you haven't noticed, since the cuts I've been doing the work of three damn editors. I still can't believe they let Rogan go and that they're not refilling that position. I don't care what kind of rag Hewitt wants to turn us into; we *need* a Metro editor."

"Mmm."

Cindy looked troubled as she put her computer to sleep. "Look, there's a couple of things I need to talk to you about."

"What's that?"

"Lewis from the *Times* beat you out on two stories in the past month. Neither were earth-shattering, but that's not a good trend. Is something going on?"

Yeah, Natalie. Distraction. Being stupid enough to turn his cell off. Shit.

"It's just this article I'm working on," Quinn lied. "I've been really absorbed in it." That much was true.

Cindy rubbed her eyes. "Please tell me your magnum opus is almost done."

"Oh yeah." Another lie.

"Because Clement's been on my ass about it. Which is weird."

"Let me handle Clement," said Quinn.

Cindy glanced away uncomfortably. "The other thing is . . ."

Quinn tensed. "What?"

"Clement's pushing me to use Truelsen more. He told me to start giving him more of the hard news assignments, even if you're available."

Quinn didn't bother saying anything to Cindy. He just barreled down the hall and, without knocking or even popping his head in the door, barged right into Clement's office. Clement was on the phone, his feet up on the desk, the very image of a casual commander in chief, which annoyed Quinn no end. He waved Quinn in, pointing at the chair in front of his desk, but as usual, Quinn rejected the offer to sit. Clement wound up the conversation quickly. *He doesn't want me to figure out who he's talking to,* thought Quinn.

Clement smiled pleasantly as he hung up the phone. "What can I do for you?"

"What's this I hear about you pushing for more assignments for Truelsen?"

"You're going to be an editor soon, Quinn." His mildly condescending tone prickled. "I'm going to need someone to replace you, and I think Truelsen has potential."

"Give me a break. You and I both know this is about you breaking my balls, pure and simple."

"Actually, I'm trying to help you. I figure the less you have on your plate, the sooner you'll hand in that master-piece you're working on, and the sooner you'll assume your duties here in the office. Believe it or not, this paper doesn't revolve around you. Cindy is swamped. The sooner you join her in editorial, the less the odds the poor woman is going to have a nervous breakdown."

That he was in part responsible for Cindy's currently insane workload filled Quinn with guilt.

"When's the big exposé going to be done?" Clement pressed.

"When it's done," Quinn maintained obstinately.

"You can keep working on your story, but you've got to assume some light editorial duties here in the office right now. You can leave if you get some tip or info that relates to your story so you can wrap it up as soon as possible. But otherwise? I want you here—say, Monday, Wednesday, and Friday mornings."

"I'll do two mornings a week: Monday and Wednesday. Any more than that, and I walk."

"You'd best stop threatening that, because one of these days, I might take you up on it."

"Go ahead. It would be your loss, and we both know it."

"I'll see you here bright and early Wednesday morning, O'Brien. Enjoy the rest of your day."

"You, too."

Quinn walked out of the office. Bastard thought he'd won. But he didn't know Quinn O'Brien.

27

"Go on. Open it."

Sitting together on the couch at her place, Natalie excitedly thrust a Bloomingdale's box at Quinn. She'd been waiting all day to be able to give him the present she'd bought him, her first ever.

Quinn picked up the box, shaking it. "Well, it's not a computer. Or a pet parrot."

"I can't believe all the grieving that's still going on over that ridiculous parrot. It's madness."

"Haven't you ever loved and lost a pet?"

"No. My mother thought pets were disgusting, and when I was on my own, I didn't have enough time to care for a pet properly." She tapped the box. "Stop torturing me! Open it!"

Quinn smiled wearily and opened the box, pulling out the beautiful Marc Jacobs shirt she'd bought him. It was a long-sleeve, blue-and-white-striped button-down with a chest pocket, and it would go beautifully under that blue blazer he raced around in. Quinn held it up for inspection.

"Wow. Nice."

"It's a Marc Jacobs," Natalie said excitedly. Quinn's face was a blank. "He's a very popular designer."

"Oh." Quinn carefully folded it back into the box.

"That's it? Just 'Oh'?"

"It's nice, Nat. But I don't get the point of designer stuff. I mean, who's going to know, unless I walk around telling people, 'Hey, I'm wearing a Marc Jacobs shirt.' "

Natalie felt stupid. "I can take it back."

"No, no, I like it. I just hate the thought of you spending a lot of money on something you probably could have gotten at half the price at L.L. Bean."

"Who is L.L. Bean? Is he American?"

"It's a what, not a who. It's a catalog company that puts out all sorts of clothes at an affordable price."

"This was affordable."

"Really?" Quinn's gaze was uneasy. "How much did this set you back?"

"Not a lot. Besides, it's a present. I'm not going to tell you what it cost."

"You didn't put it on your credit card, did you?"

"No," she lied. She had put it on her card, but it was such a small amount—$79—that it would be no problem paying it off. She was insulted that he still assumed she couldn't handle money. She could.

Quinn looked relieved. He leaned over and kissed her. "Thanks for the present, Nat."

"I can't wait to see you in it! You'll look so handsome. The sleeves of your other shirts were beginning to fray."

Quinn grinned that teasing smile of his that always made her heart skip. "Still tryin' to make me look presentable, huh?"

"As much as I can. Especially now that you're going to be an editor."

It was the wrong thing to say. Quinn's gaze hardened. "Clement tell you that?"

"Yes. Was he not supposed to?"

"Hell yeah, he wasn't supposed to! He's got no right telling you things I haven't had a chance to discuss with you yet."

"But it sounded like it was a very big deal, you becoming an editor. He said it was a step up."

Quinn's voice was vehement. "It's not a big deal. I'm only editing part-time. And contrary to what your boyfriend thinks, I've been using the time in the office to work on my own stuff, not direct editorial traffic."

"Why do you still insist on calling Mason my boyfriend? He never was."

"Yeah, well, sometimes . . ." he muttered.

"Sometimes what?"

"Sometimes I think he's better suited to you than I am."

Natalie stared at him, speechless. "What are you saying? Do you want to end things? I must say, you seem very miserable lately."

Which was painful but true. She was giving him space, vigilantly holding to the schedule they'd worked out, even though she wished they could be together every night. But instead of him being happy with this new arrangement, he seemed more preoccupied than ever. It was beginning to make her nervous.

"The misery has nothing to do with you," Quinn assured her, looking apologetic. "It's being stuck behind a fucking desk at the *Sent* two mornings a week. The prick is doing it on purpose, the same way he continues to come to the Hart every night to chat with you. He'll do anything to piss me off."

"May I point something out to you?"

Quinn looked guarded. "Sure."

"You are, without a doubt, the most egotistical man I've ever met."

Quinn laughed loudly. "You're just figuring that out?"

"I'm not just talking about your feud or whatever you

want to call it with Mason. I'm talking about you and me."

"Explain."

"You, you, you. It's always about you," Natalie said quietly, surprised to find herself blinking back tears. "You say you love me, but do you ever ask what is going on in my life? *Non.*"

"I know what's going on in your life," Quinn protested. "We talk about it every night at the bar."

"No, we don't. You come in with your friends, and you ask what's new at the bar, or what's new with your family since I see them more than you do. We come back here and you complain about Mason or brood over your article. The only time I have your full attention is when we're in bed. But never do you ask me how my job hunt is going, or how the planning for Vivi's wedding is going."

"Why don't you tell me about it, then?" Quinn offered softly.

"I shouldn't have to tell you," Natalie replied tearfully. "You should be asking me! You should be as interested in my life as I am in yours."

"I am interested. I'm just a little preoccupied right now." Quinn wrapped his arms around her. "I'm sorry, honey. I'll try to be more attentive, I swear. Just be patient."

Natalie swallowed. Be patient—the same thing Vivi was always telling her. But when did patience cross over the line to becoming a doormat? She had rights, too, but she felt so shrewish bringing them up to him. She did not want him to think she was a demanding prima donna who needed his attention all the time. All she wanted was a few small glimmers of hope that when this damn story was done, she might figure more prominently in his life.

A friend of hers in Paris had once told her that all women wind up with men like their fathers. Like her father, Quinn was addicted to his job. Her father loved what he did, but work was also a way to spend time away from her mother. Natalie had always been desperate for her father's attention, and now she was desperate for Quinn's. The parallel unnerved her.

"Please be patient, Natalie," Quinn repeated. He sounded vulnerable, which shocked her.

"I'm trying. I'm trying so, so hard, *chere*."

"I know you are. And I'm going to try harder, too. I promise."

*   *   *

"Might I have a word with my eldest son?"

Quinn had been sitting at the bar politely listening to PJ Leary talk about his tedious leprechaun chronicle when his mother snuck up behind him.

"Hey, Ma." He kissed her cheek. "What's up?"

"I need a word with you. In private."

Quinn slid off the stool, trying to ignore Mason Clement at his usual seat at the end of the bar where he appeared to have gotten somewhat chummy with the Mouth. Of course, the bastard still spent half his time watching Natalie. The fact that he'd told her about his supposed editing gig—info that wasn't his to tell—made Quinn despise him all the more.

He followed his mother into the kitchen, lightly brushing Natalie's arm as he walked by where she stood tallying up a bill. He was trying to be less self-absorbed, more tuned in to small, simple gestures like this that seemed to let her know he cared.

He had a feeling that his mother was going to give him her "All work and no play will leave Quinn a lonely man" speech, and girded himself. Instead, she looked excited.

"I'm planning a surprise party for Natalie."

Quinn was confused. "What?"

"I overheard her on the phone with her sister the other night during a break. Her birthday is in three weeks. I want to have a wee party for her here that Sunday after-noon. Nothing huge, mind."

Quinn nodded cautiously. "Sounds good."

His mother pressed her lips into a thin, disapproving line. "You had no idea it was her birthday, did you?"

"How would I?" Quinn retorted. "She hasn't said a word to me!"

"Maybe she did, and someone wasn't paying attention."

"You don't think I'd remember if my own girlfriend told me her birthday?"

"No, I do not."

She folded her arms across her chest. That's when Quinn noticed her frosty pink fingernails. He tapped a shimmery index finger. "Well, well, what have we here?"

Quinn's mother flushed, looking defensive. "Natalie took me for a manicure."

"I see." Quinn couldn't resist a good tease. "I seem to remember you telling me that you thought manicures were frivolous. A waste. Especially in your line of work."

"Well, maybe I've changed my mind." She held out her hands in front of her admiringly. "Looks nice, no?"

"Very nice."

She lowered her arms. "It'll chip off in no time, but no matter."

So, Natalie had bought him a shirt, and she'd taken his mother for a manicure. She seemed to be getting very gen-erous.

He glanced around the kitchen. "Where's Dad?"

"Upstairs watching the Mets game, lying on the couch like a lummox," his mother said affectionately. "He hurt his back."

Quinn sighed heavily. His father's back had been both-ering him more and more, and it concerned him. His par-ents were getting on in years, yet they showed no signs of cutting back on the time they spent at work. Even when they were exhausted or under the weather, they soldiered on, spouting that "the devil makes work for idle hands." Well, apparently the devil could also throw your back out.

"He should see a doctor."

"Who'll do what? Tell him to rest it the way he is right now."

"You don't know that."

"I do, and so does your father. Waste of money."

Quinn gave up. This was an argument he couldn't win.

He squeezed his mother's arm affectionately. "I'm really touched you want to throw Natalie a party, Ma. That's very sweet."

"Well, I like her." She held up a hand to stay him. "I know I didn't at first; you needn't remind me. But all in all, she's a lovely girl, and she genuinely seems to love your sorry arse, which is all a mother could hope for. That and grandchildren."

Quinn groaned. "Talk to Maggie and Brendan about that, okay?"

"You're not getting any younger," his mother reminded him.

"Neither are they. Let's get back to the party. If there's anything you need me to do, let me know."

"As if I wouldn't." She paused. "You know what would make a lovely gift?" she said brightly. "An engagement ring."

"Ma." Now he was getting annoyed. "Stop pushing."

Getting engaged—as if they were even remotely ready for that. As if he could afford a ring, or even want to take on that whole premarital headache. In his efforts to pay more attention to what was going on with Natalie, he'd been hearing all about the high drama of Vivi and Anthony's wedding plans. The amount of time being eaten up, the money being laid out on everything from flowers to catering was mind-boggling as well as scary. Half the reporters he knew were divorced as a direct result of their jobs. He was in no rush to say, "I do." Thankfully, Natalie wasn't, either.

He was beginning to get restless. "Anything else?"

His mother looked amused as she raised an eyebrow. "Being dismissed, am I?"

Quinn put his hand over his heart. "My sainted mother? Never."

She rose up on tiptoes to kiss his cheek. "Go up and see your father."

"I was planning to." He loved the way she still tried to boss him around.

She patted his cheek and then moved off to deliver an extrathick slice of brown bread to the Major, as she did nearly every evening. "You're a good boy, Quinn. I raised good boys. Now, if you'd just get your priorities—"

He put his index finger to her lips, shushing her. "Night, Mom. See you soon."

28

"Tommy fucked me over. I'm screwed. You're screwed."

Quinn watched in alarm as Liam paced the length of Quinn's tiny living room like a caged animal, his voice sawing back and forth between anger and incredulity. It was one of Quinn's "work nights," and when his cell rang at 2 a.m., he was wide-awake, hours into doing research on the 'net. He assumed something had come in over the police or fire scanner at the *Sent*, and one of the overnight editors was sending him to check it out.

He was wrong.

It was Liam, distraught, asking if he could come over and talk to him *now*. And here he was, emanating dark, dangerous anger as only Liam could.

"Calm down," Quinn urged.

Liam halted, laughing with disbelief. "When I tell you what went down, you'll see why calm is the last thing I can muster up right now."

"Well, at least sit." Quinn gestured toward his crappy old couch, its cushions covered in old files and newspapers that he promptly transferred to the floor.

"You sure I won't catch some kind of disease from this thing?" Liam joked before sitting down. Quinn thought it was a good sign that Liam still had his sense of humor.

"You want a shot of whiskey? Calm your nerves?"

"You sound like Dad."

"We do share some of the same genetic material."

"True. Yeah, whiskey would be great. Thanks."

Quinn nodded and went into the kitchen and pulled a half-empty bottle of Jameson from one of the cabinets. He poured a shot for each of them and returned to the living room.

"*Sláinte.*" Liam threw the shot down his throat.

"*Sláinte,*" said Quinn in return, doing the same. He sat down beside his brother. "What the hell is going on?"

"Two days ago, Tommy came to me and asked me if I could drive a moving truck out to Long Island tonight so he could help one of his longtime clients move. He can't drive a stick, and I can. Said he'd pay me. So I said yes. I mean, what the hell, right?"

"Okay. So you moved the guy's stuff and—?"

Liam looked pained as he ran a hand through the tangle of his dark, curly hair. "We drove back into the city. Tommy said he needed to drop some DVDs off at the video store or else they'd be late. He was just going to throw them in the drop box, you know? Again, no big deal. So we pulled up in front of the store, and thinking he'd only be a minute, I kept the engine running while he jumped out."

"What time was this?"

"I don't know. Midnight, maybe."

"Whoa, back up. You moved the Long Island guy's stuff at night?"

"Yeah."

"That didn't strike you as weird?"

"No."

Quinn shook his head. "So what happened next?"

Liam's eyes flashed with anger. "Tommy hops out of the

truck, grabs something from under his seat, smashes the door of the store, and runs inside. He loads up a couple of duffel bags full of shit, and then *sets the fucking place on fire*. Then he hops in the front seat and tells me to get the hell out of there as fast as I can."

Quinn pressed his palm to his forehead as he tried to take this all in. "Li. You saw him break into this store and you just sat there? It never crossed your mind to just drive away?"

"What the hell was I supposed to do, Quinn?" Liam snarled. "Leave him there? Besides I was too shocked to even move!"

"Do you have any idea if anyone saw you were driving the truck?"

Liam frowned. "I'm pretty sure no one did."

"But you're not hundred percent certain. Jesus Christ." He went back into the kitchen, grabbed the bottle of whiskey, came back to the couch, and poured them both another shot. Without a word the brothers both tossed the second shot down. "Then what?" Quinn asked, wiping his mouth with his sleeve.

"Tommy directs me to a warehouse on Twelfth Avenue. I'm screaming at him the whole way about how he used me. And you know what he says? He says he had no choice, that Whitey told him to. That now that I was involved, you'd stop nosing around." Liam put his head in his heads. "Can you believe this? My oldest friend in the world, Quinn."

"Shit." Quinn felt waves of guilt break inside him. "This is all my fault."

"No, it's my fault, because I was stupid enough to trust that asshole. I never thought he'd screw me this way. I'm going to fucking kill him."

"Maybe he wasn't bullshitting you when he said he had no choice."

"Screw that. You've always got a choice," Liam said bitterly. "Oh, and by the way, this warehouse? Two down from the one that was torched."

"Anyone at the warehouse?"

"I don't know. As soon as we pulled up, I jumped out of the truck and told Tommy to go fuck himself. He tried to throw some money at me, but I started jogging away, trying to wrap my head around all this. That's when I decided to call you and walk over here."

Quinn put a consoling arm around his brother's shoulder. Liam hung his head. When he lifted it, his expression was pure despair. "What the hell am I gonna do if Tommy comes strolling through the door of the Hart with some 'job' Whitey wants me to do? If I say no, they'll nail the video store robbery on me or threaten the pub or Mom and Dad."

"Don't worry about Mom and Dad. Whitey's never offered them weekly protection, as far as I know. Don't know why, but he hasn't. There's always been something about the Hart that's kept Whitey from throwing his weight around. I don't think he'd threaten them."

"But he can drop a dime on me."

Quinn grimaced. "Yeah, he can." His guilt was all-enveloping now as he realized his story might well have screwed up his brother's life for good. "I'm gonna quit working on this story," he declared. "It's not worth it."

"Yes, it is," Liam insisted. "They beat the shit out of PJ, threatened Franco, and torched the Sweeneys' store. You gotta nail their asses."

"I don't cave, and you're screwed."

"We'll figure something out." Liam stood. "I'm wired. Wanna go to that all-night diner, get some food?"

Quinn gave a small wince. "No. I'm gonna call my contacts at NYPD and see what they know about the video store."

"Okay." Liam dug his hands into the front pockets of his jeans. "I guess I'll be going, then," he mumbled.

"Yeah."

Quinn hated how it was still two steps forward, one back with him and Liam, moments of closeness alternating with moments of awkwardness. At least he got the sense that Liam's long-held resentment was fading. That was something.

He walked Liam to the door. "Hang in there."

"I'll try." Liam glanced back over his shoulder at Quinn's living room. "Word of advice: don't ever have Mom here. She'd have a heart attack if she saw how filthy it is."

"Yeah, I know," Quinn said, mildly mortified.

Quinn patted his brother on the back. "Talk to you tomorrow. Probably see you at the pub after work."

"I'll be there," Liam said dryly, "unless I'm off torching a store for Whitey."

* * *

"I'm sure he's on his way, *cherie.* You've said he tends to be late."

Natalie put her best smile on as she tried to believe Vivi's assurance. All around her, people were having a great time at her surprise party. All the regulars were there: Mrs. Colgan, PJ, and Joey. Quinn's sister, Maggie, was there, too, with her husband Brendan. Quinn's sister Sinead was tied up at her office, but she'd sent her apologies with Maggie. Even Anthony and his sister-in-law Theresa were there. Michael Dante had a hockey game but said he'd try to stop by afterward.

It seemed like everyone was there but Quinn.

She never suspected a surprise party. She and Vivi were going shopping for her bridesmaid's dress in the city. When Vivi expressed curiosity about visiting the Wild Hart since she'd never been there, Natalie decided there would be no harm in bringing her over.

She'd nearly leapt out of her skin with shock when she walked through the door of the Hart and heard the loud, enthusiastic shouts of "Surprise!" Above the bar hung a hand-painted banner that said, "Happy Birthday, Natalie!" She quickly scanned the cluster of faces gathered in front of her. No Quinn. Maybe Vivi was right. Maybe he was just running late. But Natalie couldn't help but notice Quinn's mother glancing at her watch every ten minutes.

Her first thought when she'd walked through the door was that the party was Quinn's idea, but it wasn't. She soon realized it was all Quinn's mother's doing. At first Natalie was incredulous. Then she understood it was Quinn's mother's way of showing her that she was now part of the family. That meant more to her than any gift. When she went to thank Quinn's mother, she found herself crying tears of happiness.

Natalie chatted with her sister for a bit before Vivi moved off to talk to Quinn's mother (about cooking, no doubt), and Anthony took her place, nodding approvingly as he looked around the pub. "Nice place. Not as small as it looks from the outside. The dining room goes far back."

"Yes."

"They play Irish music here?"

"All the time."

Anthony screwed up his face. "Too maudlin for me. All those songs about ghosts and the pipes calling and lovers away over the sea leaving the other one behind to dig potatoes and all that crap. I can't stand it."

"Oh, and songs about the moon hitting your eye like a big pizza pie are better?" Natalie challenged.

"Hey, watch it," Anthony warned, playfully wagging his index finger at her. "That's my heritage you're talking about there."

"Yes, well, Irish music is their heritage. I don't mind the harp music. Up front in the bar, they play more rock music. U2 and things like that."

"I bet. They don't want everyone crying into their beers." He leaned in to her confidentially. "Just so you know," he murmured, "I told Vivi she didn't need anyone to stand up for her but you. *And* she picked out the flowers. *And* the invitations. And where we're going on our honeymoon."

"Yes, she told me when we were shopping. She's very happy. She's especially thrilled about going to Hawaii."

"Yeah, me, too. I've never been. That's where Mikey went on his honeymoon. He said it's fantastic."

Anthony moved off to talk to Quinn's father, giving PJ the opening to come up over to Natalie to give her a big, sloppy kiss on the cheek. They were only an hour into the celebrations, and he was already drunk. "Marry me," he slurred.

"Can't. I've already got a boyfriend."

PJ looked around. "Don't see him here."

"He's running a little late," Natalie said with a weak smile.

She was relieved when PJ staggered away, but the relief evaporated when Joey Evans immediately came to take his place. She was beginning to feel like a queen receiving visitors at court. "Birthdays are milestones," he began solemnly. "They are a way for us to measure the progress of our lives. A means for every man and woman to—"

"Can you please not run your mouth for one day? Just one?"

Natalie peered past Joey's shoulder, relieved, as Liam approached. Joey looked offended. "I was merely trying to offer young Natalie here some important advice."

"She doesn't need advice, Joey," said Liam. "She needs to have a good time. Why don't you go join Mrs. Colgan at the bar? She's crying over Rudy again."

Natalie glanced with trepidation in the direction of the bar. Mrs. Colgan was cradling the urn holding the dead parrot's ashes.

Flashing Liam a dirty look, Joey went to the bar to console his friend.

Liam leaned over and kissed her cheek, touching Natalie immensely. "He'll be here."

Natalie felt a lump form in her throat.

"He'll be here," Liam repeated. "I talked to him yesterday. He'll be here."

"Yes, I know. It's just hard sometimes." She scoured Liam's face with concern. "Are you feeling better? Your mother said you were sick last night, and that's why you missed work."

"I'm fine," Liam replied somewhat gruffly. "Just a little twenty-four-hour bug." He changed the subject. "You got some nice presents."

"Very nice," Natalie agreed.

It was odd: she'd found it hard being the center of attention as she opened them, feeling like she didn't deserve them somehow. Vivi had given her a beautiful brocade blazer, while Mr. and Mrs. O'Brien had given her a gorgeous midnight blue shawl from Ireland. Maggie gave her a gift certificate for a massage, while Liam gave her a pair of dangly silver earrings she was certain Maggie had picked out. The regulars had pooled their resources and given her a hideous fluorescent pink scarf.

She mingled and chatted, all the while feigning happiness while trying not to watch the door.

It never opened, because Quinn never showed up.

29

Quinn knew he was cutting it close, but he had thought he'd make Nat's surprise party in the nick of time. He'd been at the *Sent* a bit longer than he'd planned, finishing up a piece on a shooting spree that had taken place in Harlem in the early morning hours. Six people had been killed, three wounded. It was believed the shooter was a twenty-three-year-old man taking revenge for being beaten up the day before. After visiting the crime scene, Quinn had spoken to the three survivors in the hospital before heading down to Police Plaza to see if there were any final details. He hated stories that involved people winding up dead. Still, something like this was better than a story involving a child being tortured or beaten.

He was hustling down Forty-third Street when a black limo pulled up beside him. The black-tinted back window rolled down, and a man with a giant head and ruddy face poked his head out. "Get in."

Quinn just laughed. "Kiss my Irish ass," he said as he continued walking. Seconds later, he heard the car door open, and a big, beefy hand gripped his shoulder. "Whitey

Connors wants to talk to you," said Ruddy Face. "Get in the fucking car."

Quinn halted, glancing down at his watch. Shit . . . the party . . . but Whitey wanting to talk to him . . . this was a reporter's dream. Maybe he wouldn't be there long. He might be *late* to the party, but at least he'd get there. Natalie knew how important this article was to him; she'd understand. The limo sat there idling, Ruddy Face glaring down at him in what Quinn assumed was supposed to be an expression of intimidation. Too bad it had no effect on him.

He followed Ruddy Face back to the limo, sliding into the plush leather backseat. Natalie would understand, he told himself again. Ruddy Face blindfolded him as the limo slowly pulled away from the curb.

The ride took about half an hour, with Quinn the only one talking. "How you guys doin'?" he cheerily asked Ruddy Face and the driver. "Enjoying this beautiful Sunday?" He couldn't help himself. The whole situation seemed absurd, as though he were guest starring in an episode of *The Sopranos*. Neither man responded.

When they finally guided him out of the car and took off his blindfold, Quinn found himself inside a dark, shabby bar, almost a seedy version of the Hart. There were tattered posters of Ireland scattered on the walls, and a huge Irish flag hung behind the bar. Quinn could have done without the shamrock and leprechaun lights strung from the ceiling, but to each his tacky own.

Ruddy Face locked the door behind them, his expression deadly serious. Quinn stifled a laugh, wondering if he was supposed to be scared. He wasn't. He was excited. A one-on-one chat with Whitey Connors.

Predictably, Whitey sat waiting for him at a back table, the farthest from the door. Were Whitey Italian, Quinn was certain he would be sipping from a tiny cup of espresso. Instead, he had what looked to be a regular cup of coffee in front of him.

As always, Whitey was impeccably dressed in a dapper suit and tie, his gleaming white hair brushed back off his pale, craggy face. Quinn started toward him but was stopped by Ruddy Face and another man who had quickly slipped out from behind the bar. Quinn recognized him from around the neighborhood: Mickey "Shoes" McCourt, so nicknamed because of his passion for expensive, hand-made Italian shoes. Quinn glanced down at Mickey's feet: they were shod in alligator loafers polished to a high sheen. They had to cost a mint.

"Hold up your arms," Mickey commanded.

"What?" Quinn was momentarily confused. But when Mickey began patting him down, Quinn couldn't hold back a laugh. "You think I walk around with a gun? I'm a re-porter, for chrissakes."

"We still have to check."

When Mickey was through, he told Quinn to hand over his backpack. He rifled through it, pulling out his digital voice recorder. Fuck. Hopefully the idiot wouldn't think to listen to it. As far as Quinn knew, his chat with Carmine Porco was still on it.

Mickey pocketed the voice recorder and demanded that Quinn hand over his cell phone as well, which he turned off. "Go on." He jerked his head in Whitey's direction. "And don't worry; you can have your toys back when you're done."

Quinn surreptitiously checked his watch. Natalie's party must have started by now. He tried to imagine what her ex-pression was when she walked in and everyone shouted, "Surprise!" He wished he were there to see it. He wondered what she made of his not being there. She was probably hurt. Or furious. Or both. He didn't even want to think about how his mother had to be reacting to his absence.

"Quinn O'Brien. Good to see you again." Whitey, as polite as ever, rose to shake Quinn's hand. Quinn noticed he was wearing a gold Claddagh ring with a ruby heart in the middle in addition to a simple gold wedding band. Quinn knew nothing about his missus—nothing at all, really, about Whitey's personal life, apart from the fact that he supposedly lived in a pretty plush mansion on Long Island's North Shore. Obviously the "customer" whose stuff Liam and Tommy moved was part of Whitey's circle. It pained Quinn to think that right up until Tommy screwed him, Liam still trusted his friend, holding on to the belief that somewhere deep within Tommy there existed a shred of decency. Stupid Irish loyalty, Quinn thought. He really felt for his brother.

Whitey gestured at the chair across from him. "Sit. Please."

Quinn sat.

"You're looking well," Whitey observed.

"I'm feeling well. You?"

"Fit as a fiddle. Can I get you anything? Coffee?"

"I was hoping I wouldn't be here long enough to drink a cup of coffee."

"You might, you might not. Why don't you let Mickey make you an Irish coffee?"

"Fine."

Whitey barked out his order, Mickey delivered the coffee, and then Whitey began to make small talk—lots of it. Quinn soon realized that Whitey was dragging things out on purpose, showing him he was the one controlling things after Quinn's comment about not wanting to be here long. Quinn had no choice but to go along with it. It wasn't as if he could say, "Could you cut to the chase?" though he was tempted. Tempted but not stupid. A memory flashed through his mind of his mother once warning him, "That mouth of yours will get you in trouble one day." It already had on numerous occasions, but this wasn't going to be one of them.

"So." Whitey splayed his veiny hands on the nicked wooden table in front of him. "I hear you've been asking a lot of questions around the neighborhood." His tone was amused, almost nonchalant.

"That's right."

"Just out of curiosity, what are you hoping to find?"

Quinn smiled enigmatically. "The one big story behind the little stories."

"And what stories would those be?"

"You know: the beatings, the torchings, the building renovations by the Shields Brothers . . ."

Whitey chuckled derisively as he withdrew his hands, his expression thoughtful as he raised his coffee cup to his lips. "And you think they're all connected somehow, do you?"

Quinn's gaze pinned his. "I know they are."

"Hmm." Whitey's thoughtful expression turned unsmiling. "Son, take a word of advice from me: this will lead to no good."

"What do you mean?"

"Sometimes people, good people, get caught up in webs they don't understand and can't control. It's always been that way. It'll always be that way. Sometimes other people, who think they're doing their jobs, overreact, trying to impress. Often, it's best to let those who understand what's going on handle things."

"Can you be a bit more specific?" Quinn pressed.

"If things progress the way they should, those who've been harmed by excessive zeal will find recompense."

Christ, Quinn thought, he talks like a cross between Yoda and a leprechaun.

Whitey cocked his head inquisitively, his smile reptilian. "Tell your brother that I'm grateful he hasn't kicked Tommy Dolan's ass. They're both good boys, and no one wants to see them have any troubles."

Whitey was staring at him, waiting for a reaction to his comment about Liam, but there was no way in hell Quinn was going to give him one. It took every ounce of self-control Quinn possessed not to lean across the table, grab the old bastard by his turkey-wattled throat, and throttle him. *You hurt my brother and you die,* he wanted to growl. Instead, he just stared Whitey down.

Whitey's smile broadened, and he stood. "I know you said you were under some time pressure, but please, feel free to stay until you've finished your coffee. Give my best to your ma and da." He squeezed Quinn's shoulder on his way out the door.

Quinn tilted his head back, finished his coffee, and then went over to Mickey, who was watching him like a hawk from behind the bar.

"Give me my fuckin' voice recorder. And my phone."

"Of course." Mickey was a study in politeness as he handed both over to Quinn. Then he pulled out the silk scarf that had been used to blindfold Quinn. "Time to go home now."

Quinn rolled his eyes and allowed himself to be blindfolded and led back to the limo by Ruddy Face, whose name, apparently was Dennis.

"Where we taking you?" Dennis grunted.

"The Wild Hart. I need to get there fast."

The driver sniggered. "You get there when you get there. Right, Dennis?"

"Oh yeah. In fact, I feel like driving around a bit."

"Me, too. Nice day for a drive."

Shit, thought Quinn. What kind of a moron tells mob guys what to do? He knew now that by the time they delivered him to the Hart, Natalie's party would be over. Maybe she'd still be there, upstairs with his parents. He just hoped she'd forgive him. Again.

* * *

"Jesus, Mary, and Saint Joseph, who the hell do you think you are?"

Were his mother a dragon, Quinn had no doubt flames

would be shooting from her needle-sharp tongue, enveloping him in enough fire to incinerate him. The moment he set foot in the family kitchen, a nimbus of rage began shimmering around her, rage he knew he deserved. He wished he could tell her where he'd been, though in her current state, it might not have made any difference.

"Ma—"

"Shut your gob. I don't want to hear any of your shite. You didn't show up for your girlfriend's birthday party, and we all know why: because you're a selfish bastard. Work always comes first—before people's feelings, even the feelings of those you supposedly love. Natalie was heartbroken. *Heartbroken.* She tried to cover it, but you could see it in her eyes. The hurt. The disappointment. As for your father and me, you know what we were? Plain bloody ashamed of you. I never in my life thought I could be so ashamed of my firstborn son."

Quinn's eyes cut to his father, standing in the doorway leading to the living room, watching this unfold from a safe distance. He shook his head sadly and walked away.

Quinn wheeled back to face his mother. "Trust me when I tell you I had a good reason for not being there."

"There can be no good reason for you not being there, not if it has to do with your bloody work! Natalie didn't say it, but I could tell she was thinking you don't love her. And you know what? I don't believe you do. I don't believe you love anyone but yourself.

"I hope she tells you to stick it where the sun doesn't shine, boy. Because she deserves better than you, a selfish eejit who doesn't appreciate her and who's too stupid to grasp what's really important in life. I hope that Pulitzer you're always chasing after keeps you warm on winter nights. I truly do."

Quinn swallowed and looked away. Never in his life had his mother upbraided him like that, and it was worse for it was happening now, when he was an adult. Thoroughly ashamed, he moved past her into the living room, feeling her eyes like darts on his back. Maggie and Brendan were there. Maggie glared at him, a disgusted expression on her face. Brendan kept his nose buried in the newspaper, clearly determined to avoid being drawn into the conversation. Liam wasn't there. Shit. As soon as he left, he had to call him.

Not knowing what else to do, Quinn returned to the kitchen. "I guess I'll go," he said sheepishly.

"You do that," said his mother, refusing to look at him as she cracked eggs into a bowl. "Because right now, I can't stand the very sight of you. Truly. And I wouldn't be surprised if she can't, either."

* * *

"She doesn't want to see you."

It was Vivi's voice, not Natalie's, that came through the intercom loud and clear at the front desk in the lobby of Natalie's building. Quinn had come directly from his parents' place, his mother's blistering speech still ringing in his ears. He had a feeling that Vivi's being there wasn't a good sign.

"Tell her she's got to hear me out. Tell her I'm going to sit down here and wait as long as it takes for her to see me. I'm a reporter; I'm used to stakeouts. I can wait for hours."

The intercom went dead for at least thirty seconds. Then Vivi's voice came back on. "You can come up, but not for long," she said crisply.

"Thank you."

Be prepared for Natalie to yell at you, because you deserve it. Be prepared for her telling you to go to hell, because you deserve that, too. Be prepared to beg if you want to keep her.

Vivi was waiting for him at the apartment door, a formidable gatekeeper. "I don't like you much right now," she said coldly. "None of us do."

"Yeah, I can see that. Can I come in?"

"I guess," she sniffed.

Quinn took off his jacket, tossing it over the back of the couch. Thinking he'd be at the party, he'd worn the shirt Natalie bought him, knowing it would make her happy.

"Where is she?" he asked Vivi quietly.

"In the bathroom, putting on makeup. She doesn't want you to see how terrible she looks from crying." Vivi looked him up and down contemptuously. "You know, I've been telling her to be patient with you. I know all about this big article you're working on and how you've been promising her that once it's done, you'll have more time for her. But if you were my man, well, I'd slice your neck."

"You mean slit my throat. Vivi, I swear to you, I had a very good reason for not being there," said Quinn, heart-felt.

Vivi didn't say a word and flashed him one final glare before she disappeared down the hallway. He heard the bathroom door quietly open, then close. Quinn sat down on the couch and waited for Natalie.

30

"I can explain."

Natalie suppressed a bitter laugh. Somehow, she knew those would be the first words out of his mouth. "I can explain." She'd heard it before.

Quinn watched her anxiously as she sat on the opposite end of the couch, away from him. Childish? Maybe. But it sent a message. Her makeup was applied expertly enough that he wouldn't be able to tell she'd been crying, though maybe that had been a mistake. Maybe she should have agreed to see him with her red nose and puffy eyes so he felt guilty.

She was silent. She would give him nothing, even though, for the first time in her life, she had the urge to rail at him. But Natalie Bocuse didn't rail. Instead, she drew herself up, dignified, the way she'd been taught as a child. She would always be the consummate French politician's daughter.

Quinn looked nervous. "Can I explain?"

Natalie nodded curtly.

"First, let me apologize for missing the party." He edged toward her, but her glare stopped him dead. "Honey, I really wanted to be there," he said remorsefully. "It killed me to miss it." He pulled forward the material of his shirt. "See, I even wore the shirt you bought me."

He paused, waiting for her to react to his showing her he was wearing the shirt, which, admittedly, looked fabulous on him. But she wouldn't soften. It would take more than a shirt for him to redeem himself.

"Here's what happened: I was on my way to the party, when a limo pulled up beside me, and this beefy guy told me to get in."

"Was it an alien come to abduct you?" Natalie asked, unable to resist using his mother's line.

"No. It was one of Whitey Connors's henchmen."

Natalie looked at him blankly.

"The head of the Irish mob," Quinn prompted.

"Ah. I see. Go on."

"I told them to go to hell, but the guy got out of the car and grabbed me and told me Whitey wanted to see me. I couldn't turn them down."

"You mean, you couldn't turn down the opportunity."

"You're right: I couldn't turn down the opportunity," Quinn admitted honestly. "You know how hard I've been working on this article, and I knew that when I told you what happened, you'd understand, especially when I explained that this kind of one-on-one with a mob boss is something every reporter dreams of."

He slid a little bit closer to her, and though she was regarding him warily, she let him. "Baby, we didn't talk long, and I really thought his thugs would get me back to the Hart so I could at least attend some of your party. Instead, they drove me around for hours after I finished talking to Whitey just to bust my balls. By the time they dropped me off at the pub, the party was done."

"People pitied me," she found herself telling him. "Poor Natalie, whose boyfriend couldn't even make a brief appearance at her birthday party. You could see it in their eyes and in the way they kept trying to make me jolly. Vivi especially."

"Well, obviously if they knew why I wasn't there, they wouldn't have thought that," Quinn countered.

"You could have called me."

"They took my phone."

What could she say to that?

"Baby, I am so, so sorry," Quinn repeated. "Look, if it's any comfort, I went upstairs to see my folks, and my mother really lit into me. She told me I didn't deserve you. And I don't." His voice turned plaintive, yanking hard at her heartstrings. "She said she wouldn't be surprised if you dump me."

Natalie clenched her jaw, holding back the sudden rush of tears that threatened. "I'm thinking of it."

"Nat, please. One more chance," Quinn begged. "Just let me get this article done, and I swear to God, I'll figure out a way to make this all work. I'll give you all you deserve."

Natalie looked at him sadly. "You're deluding yourself. When this story is done, there will be another, and another. Our relationship will always come second."

"It won't. You've got to believe me. I love you."

God, please, help me believe. Natalie's mind was fogging with confusion. What if she gave him one more chance, and he let her down again? The pain would be unendurable. Once again, everyone would pity her. Stupid, blind Natalie, the doormat. But what if the opposite happened?

"I'm afraid you're going to hurt me," she confessed in a tiny voice.

Quinn grabbed her hands and kissed them fiercely. "Never. Never again. I swear."

Natalie sighed. "What am I going to do with you, Quinn O'Brien?" she asked softly.

"You're going to give me another chance. Right?"

Natalie caved. She didn't say anything. She just nodded.

Quinn whooped with relief. "Thank you, *cherie*. Thank you." His hands still held hers. He lifted them to his mouth, brushing his lips seductively across her knuckles. "Wait until you see the fantastic birthday present I have for you."

"Oh yes? Where is it?"

"I'll give it to you tomorrow. It's all planned, and I have the day off."

"Are you staying here tonight?" she asked tentatively.

Quinn rubbed his thumb back and forth across her lower lip. "If you'll let me."

"Yes."

"I'll stay here. And not just for tonight. For forever."

Natalie closed her eyes. She loved this man. She had no choice but to believe him.

* * *

"This is wonderful. I never thought about doing this."

Natalie snuggled against Quinn as a bright blue horse-drawn carriage drove them through Central Park at twilight. She knew it was an experience usually limited to tourists, but right now, it struck her as romantic—which it was.

She'd been so absorbed in work and Vivi's wedding planning that she'd failed to notice that spring had arrived, and the natural world was bursting back to life. Even though they were in the heart of the city, Natalie felt as though they were riding through an oasis of tranquillity. She turned to look at him, loving the feeling of his arm tight around her shoulder. He looked somewhat contented and relaxed, a rare look for him. It made her happy.

Quinn smiled at her. "I'm glad you're enjoying this. I had a feeling you would."

"I feel kind of silly," Natalie confessed.

"Why?"

"This is such a touristy thing to do."

"Maybe. But who cares? Believe it or not, it's something *I've* always wanted to do."

That he'd never done this with any woman before her delighted her.

He squeezed her tight. "This is only the first part of your present, you know."

"What?" Natalie drew back in surprise. "This is more than enough."

Quinn kissed her forehead softly. "I can never do enough for you."

Natalie rested her head on his shoulder. This was perfection. If only she could always have him to herself just like this. She closed her eyes. She could imagine a future with Quinn. A bumpy one, maybe, but a future nonetheless.

As the horses clip-clopped along, Quinn pointed out various landmarks to her, telling her a little bit about each: the Bandshell, the Boathouse, Tavern on the Green, Cherry Hill . . . he knew them all.

"How do you know all this?"

"I'm a lifelong New Yawker." He looked thoughtful. "I come here a lot just to think."

"About what?"

"Ah, everything."

She put her head back down on his shoulder.

"I'm so sorry about missing the party, Nat."

He'd been apologizing nonstop—at the pub, at her flat, on the phone. What had Vivi called it? Ah, yes: "Bowing and scraping." Part of her wanted to tell him he didn't have to keep apologizing . . . but she was still enjoying it.

The carriage ride lasted for a full magical hour. Natalie was feeling closer to him than ever before, loving how easy it was to talk to him, the way they teased each other. It felt so easy and uncomplicated.

She fought a small twinge of disappointment as the ride came to a stop just where they started at, Fifth Avenue and Central Park South. Quinn hopped down first, extending a hand to help her down from the carriage. She took one last, wistful look at the carriage and then slipped her hand into his.

"Now what?" she asked, excited yet nervous at the same time.

Quinn pointed across the street as he drew her close, nuzzling her as his voice dropped seductively low. "Now we spend a night at the Plaza."

Natalie impulsively threw her arms around his neck. "Oh, Quinn! I love you so much!"

He put an arm around her waist and squeezed tight. "Ready, *ma petit pamplemousse*?" *My little grapefruit.* She hit his arm playfully, and together they walked across the street.

* * *

Natalie resisted the urge to bounce up and down on the enormous king-sized bed like an excited little girl. He'd booked them into a beautiful suite overlooking the park.

Her overnight bag was already there. Quinn had packed it when she was away at work, filling it with a few items from her bra and panty drawer, all those lacy push-up bras and thongs he loved. Quinn was inspecting the champagne bucket. Sometimes, just the sight of him took her breath away. It wasn't just that he was handsome, or that his shoulders were broad, or that his voice was deep and sexy. It was his love for his family, his sense of humor, his passion for what he did—his passion, period. It still amazed her that of all the women in the world he could have had, he'd picked her.

He held up two champagne flutes. "Champagne?"

"Oh, yes, please."

Quinn poured out the champagne and handed her a glass, coming to sit beside her on the bed.

"To love," he said softly, kissing her.

Tears sprang to Natalie eyes. "To love," she whispered

back. They clinked glasses and sipped their champagne. The bubbly went down Natalie's throat smooth and easy.

Quinn went to sit with his back against the headboard, his feet stretched out in front of him. He patted the space beside him, and Natalie joined him.

Quinn sighed contentedly. This is the life, aye, Nat?"

"Oh, please. You must have done this before."

"Done what? Take a carriage ride and stay at a fancy hotel, sipping champagne with a gorgeous woman? Nope, I've never done it."

"I don't believe you."

"I swear on Rudy's ashes."

Natalie almost passed champagne through her nose. "Has the Wild Hart always attracted such unique characters?"

"Oh yeah. There was one woman who came in for about ten years we called Sasquatch Judy because she claimed she'd seen Sasquatch on line at the Thirty-fourth Street post office. Then there were these identical twin firefighters, Patrick and Daniel Brady, who no one could tell apart, not even their wives. They'd sit together at the bar and flip a coin to decide who'd go home to which family."

"Whatever happened to them?"

"They both died on 9/11," Quinn said quietly.

"Oh."

"The big joke at the wake was that their families probably flipped a coin to decide who'd be buried in which grave."

Quinn took a drink of champagne and changed the subject. "You glad you emigrated? Ever have any regrets?"

"Never."

He kissed her cheek. "Glad to hear it."

Happiness was expanding inside her like a balloon. She felt she would burst.

He brushed her hair away from her face. "I wish I could do more. Give you more."

Natalie slowly lifted her head. "All I want is more of your time, Quinn. You know that."

The words slid out so effortlessly it was a second or two before she realized what she'd said. She glanced up at him, expecting to see a defensive expression on his face. Instead, he looked guilty.

"Soon. I swear. You know that." His palm gently cupped the back of her neck. "Because there's nothing in the world I want more than you."

His mouth on hers was so tender that Natalie felt her entire body go weak. She was trembling, experiencing a split second of hesitation before she grabbed Quinn tightly to her, showing him she desperately longed for more than tenderness right now; she wanted passion, the straight road to blissful oblivion. Quinn delivered, his hungry mouth bruising hers, his fingers pressing so hard into her skin that she gasped. She pulled him down on the bed atop her, impatient, her hips instinctively pushing against his. Quinn responded with a growl as he tore his lips from hers and locked eyes with her, his own eyes dark with lust. It was too much; frustrated by the clothing between them interfering with pure touch, she yanked Quinn's shirt out of his jeans and slipped her hands beneath it, splaying her fingers on his chest, slowly pressing and caressing the muscled skin beneath her touch.

Quinn's reaction sent a thrill through her. He was breathing hard, his pupils enlarged as he continued staring down at her eyes, his expression daring her to do more. And so she did. With an uncharacteristically wanton smile, she let her hands roam lower and lower until her fingertips gently slipped beneath the waist of his jeans. Quinn groaned, spurring her on to more boldness. She unzipped his fly, moving her fingers beneath his briefs to take him in her hand, her touch featherlight as she moved her hand up and down.

Quinn's eyes flashed. The slow seduction was over. His

gaze was now smoldering with pent-up desire so fierce it almost scared her. He sat up and hurriedly took off her shirt, then with impatient hands he pushed up her bra and began suckling her with an intensity that made her cry out. She arched against him, raising her arms high above her head, pushing more of herself into his mouth. Quinn laughed wickedly, Natalie teetering on the edge as his teeth began nipping a sharp trail down her body, the bites punctuated with hot licks of his tongue and lingering kisses. She was becoming a quivering wreck. Throwing her head back, she gasped and brought her legs up, wrapping them tightly around his hips. Quinn, breath ragged, gently pushed her legs down and apart. With a husky, seductive laugh, he hurriedly undid her jeans, tugged them down, and then, with a gaze now bordering on feral, plunged his fingers deep inside her.

It was too much. She cried out as she thrust against him, climaxing. Quinn was still watching her, his expression thrilled, his breath coming harder than she'd ever heard it. Moaning with lingering need, Natalie pulled him down to her. Quinn growled once, bit her neck, and then freed himself from the confines of his own clothing. Natalie held her breath, eager, waiting. He sheathed himself. And then he plunged into her.

"Oh, God!" Natalie cried out and squeezed herself tightly around him. The burning blue of his eyes told her he was greedy for her, greedy for speed and force and total possession. "Yes, God, please. Do it," she whispered hoarsely. She watched his eyes darken again, thrilled by his instant transformation from man to beast.

"Beg me again," he commanded.

"Please . . . do it."

It was what he wanted to hear. Again and again he drove into her. Deeper. Harder. Sensation after sensation soared through Natalie, leaving her raw, quivering, completely at his mercy. She climaxed again, the feeling one of being lifted up by a tornado and slammed back down to earth, rendering her insensible. When lucidity returned, she caught the dark thrill of pleasure in Quinn's eyes at having pleased her, which she gladly returned.

"Your turn," she panted. Natalie watched as his eyes went blind, and he gave himself over to raw need, his hips pumping, the mild sheen of sweat coating his muscular body one of the sexiest things she'd ever seen. Her eyes never left his face as she matched her frenzied rhythm to his own, until finally he gave one final thrust and with a strangulated cry of relief, emptied himself inside her. Spent, he collapsed on her, but not before he flashed her a devilish grin. "Happy, happy birthday, Nat."

"My best ever."

And it was.

31

It was wrong, and Quinn knew it. The minute Natalie went to run a bubble bath for them, he hopped out of bed and grabbed his cell from his backpack to check his messages. There was one from Liam.

"Quinn . . . hey. I really need you to call me back as soon as you can. Please."

He sounded stressed. Quinn stared at the time of the message. Liam had called a few hours before his carriage ride with Natalie. Quinn had turned off his phone hours before, determined that nothing spoil his birthday surprise for her, especially after missing the party.

He listened to the message again. Fuck a duck. He'd called Liam yesterday as soon as he'd left his folks, and Liam had never called him back.

Quinn deleted the message and sank down on the bed. He glanced quickly at the bathroom door. Natalie was sweetly singing to herself in French over the cascade of water filling the luxurious marble tub; he could probably shoot a quick call to Liam if he wanted. He hit his speed dial, and then thought better of it. He felt furtive, like a married man sneaking a call to his mistress. He closed his eyes and took a deep breath as he let his head fall back. Years ago, Durham had once asked him, "If you had a choice between winning a Pulitzer or settling down with a good woman who'd love your sorry ass for the rest of your life, which would you take?" Quinn didn't miss a beat: "A Pulitzer." If Durham asked the same question now, how would he answer? *It's just this one story,* he told himself. *And besides, she's inside running a bath.* It wasn't as though returning his brother's call was cutting into their time together. He picked up the phone and dialed. Liam picked up on the first ring.

"Quinn." He sounded relieved.

"Li, what's up?"

"Uh, I'm fucked, okay? Totally and completely fucked. Quinn?"

Quinn squeezed his eyes shut. He knew he was tempting the Fates by calling his brother back. Knew it. He turned. Natalie was poised in the bathroom doorway, staring at the phone in his hand. She stood there a second, then retreated back into the bathroom, closing the door. Fuck.

"I gotta call you back, okay?"

"Quinn—"

"I'll call as soon as I can."

He hung up the phone, bounding to the bathroom door. It was locked. The water had stopped running. He knocked gently. "Nat?"

"Allez en enfer!"

"Nat—"

"I'm telling you to go to hell! Go! To! Hell!"

"Natalie—"

" 'I can explain'—that's what you're going to say!"

Quinn closed his eyes, leaning his forehead against the door. "Nat. Please hear me out."

"You told me your phone was off!"

"I don't see what the big deal is checking my messages when you're running a bath!"

"God forbid you don't check them. Tell me all about it, then, your big important messages."

"Message."

"Go on." He knew she had her arms crossed expectantly on the other side of the door. He knew it.

"It was Liam. I don't know what he was calling about since I hung up as soon as you came out of the bathroom."

"Of course you did. Because you felt guilty. Because you promised you wouldn't be checking that damn phone the second you got the chance. Tell me, Quinn: What if the call had to do with your big story, eh? Would you have ignored it until tomorrow after we parted? Or would you have left me here, high and dry, with the promise of returning as soon as you can?"

His silence was damning. Liam's call did have to do with his story; he felt it in his bones. Not that he could tell her that.

"No answer. I thought so." The bathroom door swung open, and Natalie pushed past him. "I'm going." She went directly to the closet to pull out her overnight bag. How vulnerable she looked in the plush, terry cloth robe the hotel had provided. It was swimming on her, making her look so tiny.

Quinn followed her. "Don't. Please."

Her shoulders drooped with exhaustion. "I can't do this anymore. I was deluding myself yesterday. You'll never change. Your work will always come first." She shook her head, chuckling bitterly. "I was so confident that it wouldn't matter to me. That I'd be the one who'd let you be who you are. But I was wrong. I'm just like all the others. I want to come first."

Quinn grasped her arm. "You're not like the others. I didn't love the others."

Natalie shook him off. "So what? That's doesn't matter, does it? I'm tired of being patient. I'm tired of waiting, feeling like I should be grateful for any little crumbs of time you can give me. I don't want a lifetime of 'I'm sorry, Natalie,' or a lifetime of 'I can explain, Natalie.' Your job is the love of your life. Not me. I saw what not coming first did to my mother. It turned her into an angry, bitter woman. I will not let you do to me what my father did to my mother."

She marched to the bed and put the bag down, hurriedly pulling out clean clothing. Halting abruptly, she turned to him. "You know what? Why am I going? It's *my* birthday. You should be the one to go. Leave! I'm going to take that bath, and then I'm going to call room service and order anything I damn well please and think about how sad you are, Quinn O'Brien. Sad, selfish, and stupid. And when I'm done, I'm going to sleep in this big bed and love it."

She walked back into the bathroom, closing the door and locking it behind her. Quinn didn't want to think about how she was right; his mother, too. He'd gotten what he deserved. He swallowed, trying not to heave his guts up.

He collected his things and walked to the bathroom door, rapping gently. No reply. He left the suite, closing the door quietly behind him.

* * *

The minute Quinn exited the Plaza, he called Liam. The two agreed to meet at the Hart.

He walked all the way from the Plaza to the pub, trying to silence the disgusted voice in his head berating him for losing Natalie. He should have told her what was going on with Liam. Who the hell would she have told? But that wasn't the point. The point was that no matter how hard he tried, the siren call of work was always there. She wasn't the only one who'd thought this time would be different; he was certain that because he loved her, he'd find a way to balance a personal life with his job—after this article was done. But Natalie was right: he was kidding himself if he thought he could change his stripes. This was how he rolled. This was how he always had rolled and probably always would: solo, just like so many other obsessed reporters he knew.

He just hated how much he'd hurt her. It killed him, as did the thought she probably hated him. The thought streaked through his mind that she'd wind up with Clement. Talk about something that would drive him insane.

He walked into the pub, surprised to find the Major sitting at the bar, reading the *Irish Independent*. Quinn felt sorry for the guy. He'd never married, and he had to be pretty damn lonely to spend so much time here, probably to avoid being home alone. *Look who's talking.*

"Hello, Major," Quinn said as he slipped behind the bar. The Major nodded politely. "Evening, Quinn."

"You doing well?"

"Very well. Thank you for asking. Yourself?"

"I've been a little better," Quinn admitted ruefully.

"Sorry to hear that," the Major sympathized and went back to his paper.

Liam was stacking glasses, listening in on the exchange. "What do you mean, you've been a little better? Natalie tore you a new one for missing the birthday party, didn't she?"

"She went one better: she dumped me."

"Well, I can't say I blame her."

"Yeah, well, whatever," Quinn said impatiently, not wanting to get into it. "I had a pretty goddamn good reason for missing the party."

Liam tossed him a bar towel. "Tell me while you make yourself useful."

"I missed the party because your pal Tommy's boss wanted to see me." He was trying to be as oblique as possible in front of the Major. "What was I supposed to do? Say no?"

Liam's face fell. "Shit. What happened?"

"In a nutshell, he told me that if I dropped the article, he'd help out those who'd been hurt, but if I didn't, he'd drop a dime on you."

"They sent me the same message tonight—that's why I called."

"What happened?"

"Shoes strolls in like he owns the place and walks behind the bar. Tells me Tommy's going to ask me for help again and that I shouldn't let friends down. Says my family will be heartbroken if I forget how important that kind of loyalty is. And then he leaves. I have to tell you, I was shaking so bad I had to down to two shots of Wild Turkey. I don't know whether it was because I was so scared or because I wanted to kill him. Thank God he was in and out so quick I couldn't make up my mind. What the hell are we going to do?"

Quinn glanced quickly at the Major sitting at the other end of the bar. "Li, keep it down."

"No need," murmured the Major casually. Stunned, Quinn and Liam turned to him simultaneously.

The Major closed his paper. "I think maybe you boys should tell me what's going on. What did Shoes have to say to you, Liam?"

Liam and Quinn looked at each other in amazement. The Major had never said more than a few words to them before. And now he was asking them to open up to him? The Major obviously knew what they were thinking.

"Come over here," he said in a voice that commanded obedience. They did what they were told.

"Quinn, look at me. Look into my eyes."

As if under a spell, Quinn did just that. He'd never noticed it before, but the Major had dark blue eyes, almost black in their intensity. And as Quinn looked into them, he saw something he'd seen only a couple of times before in the eyes of cops he knew. Rogan called it "the shark." It was a blackness, Rogan said, that came when a man had killed so often that he'd lost the part of his soul that hesitated to take a life.

Still looking into that frightening emptiness, Quinn started telling the whole story to the Major. Liam followed suit, describing everything that had happened. The Major listened closely and, Quinn later swore, didn't blink the whole time. When they were done, the Major looked them both in the eye before slowly closing his own eyes and folding his newspaper. When he opened them again, the blackness seemed to have passed. He was back to being the quiet, distinguished gentleman they'd always known. He got up slowly from his stool.

"You boys go home and get a good night's sleep. Don't worry about anything. It will be taken care of. We'll talk tomorrow."

With that, the Major slowly walked out the door of the Wild Hart.

"What the fuck just happened?" Liam asked.

"I have no idea."

* * *

Merde, what have I done? Natalie sat on her couch, cradling her head in her hands, staring down at the small mountain of bags and boxes at her feet. After checking out of the Plaza the next morning, she'd headed down Fifth Avenue and hurried from store to store, buying whatever struck her fancy. Shoes at Ferragamo. Earrings at Tiffany's. Two blouses at Bergdorf's. A handbag from Gucci. Price didn't matter; she charged it all, telling herself she deserved a consolation prize after what she'd put up with from Quinn all these months. Why shouldn't she pamper herself? So what if she was the one who ended things? It still hurt.

As soon as she sank down deep in the tub at the Plaza, she realized *she* should have been the one to leave. It was torture being there alone in the plush suite they should have been enjoying together. His gift to her, and still he couldn't keep away from the phone. That was when she'd known he'd never change.

After her bath, she'd gotten tipsy on champagne and was tempted several times to call Vivi to let her know what had happened. But she was afraid that in her distraught state, she'd let slip the envy she felt toward her half sister, who seemed so effortlessly to have it all: a successful business and a man who loved her more than life itself and who wanted to spend the rest of his life with her. Why couldn't she get it right? Why did she always pick jerks? First that career-wrecking, lying bastard Thierry when she was still back in Paris, telling her he was separated from his wife when he wasn't, and now Quinn.

She'd cried herself to sleep in the big bed, sleeping fitfully, waking up with a skull-shattering headache. Thankfully, it was gone by the time she'd finished the sumptuous breakfast she'd ordered, courtesy of Quinn O'Brien.

She rose from the couch, surprised to find her hand trembling when she poured herself a glass of water in the kitchen. She wished she could hide there. Her headache was returning. When she forced herself back to the living room, a fresh wave of despair assaulted her. *Stupid girl,* as her mother used to say. *Stupid, stupid girl.*

Knowing she had to take responsibility for what she'd done, she forced herself to go to her purse and fish out all the credit card receipts, tallying up the damage. A small cry of horror escaped her lips when she came to the grand total: six thousand dollars. She'd spent six thousand dollars in three dazed hours. There was no way she could afford this. And yet, the addict inside her wanted to keep it all. All the old familiar lies and justifications came rushing back to the fore. *You'll figure out a way to pay it off; just get a second job. It's not really that much. Besides, you deserve it.*

She closed her eyes tight, clenching her hands into fists,

knowing that if she allowed herself to keep it, she'd start buying more and more and would be unable to stop. She had to take it all back, or disaster would ensue. She would lose Vivi. She would lose her job. Worst of all, she would lose self-respect. She resolved to return it all tomorrow. But right now, she was going to find out when the soonest SA meeting was, and she was going to go—and keep going for as long as she needed to. At least there would be one thing in her life she could control.

*   *   *

The next night at work, Natalie decided she had best tell Quinn's parents that she and Quinn had split, and that she'd leave just as soon as she could find another job, since it was probably best for everyone. The truth was, she'd gotten somewhat complacent in her job search, since she liked working at the Hart, especially now that she was considered part of the family.

"You're not going anywhere," Quinn's mother declared. "I'd rather that eejit son of mine and his friends find somewhere else to wet their whistles than lose you. You're a good waitress. And you're family. You stay."

Natalie teared up. "That means so much to me." She didn't have the heart to add that a part of her wanted to leave, since she didn't know if she could stand seeing Quinn night after night. It would be too painful. Not that she'd ever let that show.

Quinn's mother embraced her. Natalie had come to love the way she smelled: like fresh-baked bread and fried onions and love all mixed together. It occurred to her that she had no idea of her own mother's scent, so rarely had her mother hugged her.

Quinn's mother pulled back, running a tender finger down Natalie's cheek. "I'm sorry he hurt you, love. And it pains me to say this about my own flesh and blood, but you deserve better."

"He's a good man; he just—"

"Has his head up his arse," Quinn's mother finished tartly. "Mark my words: one day the chickens will come home to roost, and he'll rue the day he let you go."

Not likely, Natalie thought sadly, but she appreciated the sentiment.

She gave Quinn's mother a quick peck on the cheek. "I'd better get to work."

* * *

Natalie desperately hoped tonight would be one of the rare nights Quinn didn't make an appearance, but of course he did, coming in late with his coworkers. For a split second she refused to look at him. Then she gathered her pride and used it to build a wall around her heart. Quinn came over to speak with her while she was waiting at the bar for a drink order from Liam.

"Did you enjoy the rest of your evening?" he asked quietly.

"Oh, yes. It's always been my dream to spend a night at a fancy hotel all alone."

"I'm sorry." He looked miserable. "I'll say it as many times as it takes for you to believe me."

"I believe you," she said as coldly as she could.

Quinn grimaced as he glanced past her shoulder in the direction of the kitchen. "Did you tell—?"

"Yes."

Looking uncomfortable, he'd shoved his hands deep into the front pockets of his pants. "I guess I'll go sit with my friends."

"I take it you'll all want your usual?" Natalie asked, all business.

"Yeah."

"Very good."

He turned to go, then spun back around. "Nat."

"What?" She was becoming desperate to get away from

him, tortured by those dancing blue eyes of his that she loved and by the weary handsomeness of his face. *Stupid girl. Harden your heart.*

He looked sheepish. "Again . . . sorry."

"Go to your friends, Quinn," she said wearily, "and let me do my job."

* * *

"You okay?"

Liam's question surprised Natalie as he began filling the drink order for Quinn's table. Liam hadn't spoken with his folks since she'd arrived at work, so she assumed it was Quinn who had told him they'd split.

"I'm fine."

Liam put Quinn's traditional whiskey shot down on the tray. "I wasn't shocked when he told me, but I was kind of bummed. You and Quinn were a great couple."

No, Natalie thought, *Quinn and Manhattan are a great couple.*

"Were?" The Mouth's eyes widened with shock. "You and Quinn have parted ways?"

"Yes." Natalie wished Liam hadn't brought it up in front of the bar regulars. Now the news would spread like wildfire. Maybe it really didn't matter. Everyone would have eventually found out anyway.

PJ Leary held a declamatory index finger in the air. "'The course of true love never did run smooth.'" He lowered his finger. "Shakespeare."

"I thought it was Elizabeth Taylor," said Liam. He looked hopeful as he regarded Natalie. "Who knows? Maybe you guys will get back together."

"I don't think so," she replied coolly. Eager to keep busy, she scoured the bar for empty glasses or to check if anyone needed a refill. She found herself looking right into the face of Mason Clement, who, with his usual kind smile, was holding his glass aloft.

"Hello, Mason." She took his glass. "The usual?"

"Yes, thank you." There was a small, awkward pause. "I'm sorry to hear you're no longer seeing Quinn."

"Yes, well, these things happen," she said briskly. "I'll just be a minute."

She went to get his Stella Artois, knowing he wasn't sorry at all. She served him and then carried the usual array of cocktails and beers over to the booth where Quinn and his cronies sat. The mood was somber. Natalie didn't know if it was work related or whether Quinn had told them of their breakup. It didn't really matter.

32

The next night, Quinn lingered at the bar after closing time. He'd been called a "pitiful specimen" by his mother, a "loser" by his friends, and he'd had to endure the ultimate insult of Mason Clement smirking at him.

It shocked him how painful it was to see Natalie. She was brisk and businesslike with him, even as she joked and chatted with his coworkers. And each time Mason Clement flagged her down for a refill and she lingered to talk to him, it was like a hammer blow to his solar plexus. Smarmy bastard.

Door locked, parents safely tucked upstairs after chatting a bit with the Major about the recent flooding in Ireland due to endless rain, the Major motioned for Quinn and Liam to come closer to his usual perch. He pushed an envelope toward Liam. Puzzled, Liam opened it, rendered speechless. Then he passed it to Quinn. It was a voucher for a one-way ticket to Ireland.

"I—I don't—" Liam stuttered.

"You're to leave the country as soon as possible. I can't protect you here, but you can go wherever you'd like in

Ireland. I'd suggest Ballycraig, where your people are from. You have my word that you'll be perfectly safe. Whitey won't dare trouble you when he hears I'm the one who sent you away."

Liam looked stunned. "Am I ever going to be able to come home?"

"I expect so. But don't worry about that yet. Just get yourself to safety."

"What do I tell my parents?" Liam asked.

"Quinn will help you tell them the story, and if they resist the idea of your going, just tell them I'm the one who's sending you. They'll be heartbroken, but they'll know it's the right thing to do. Right, then; I'm off home."

Quinn finally overcame his stunned silence. "Major, no disrespect intended, but who the hell are you?"

The Major smiled. It was the first time either of the brothers had ever seen him smile, and it was in some ways just as terrifying as the dark look they'd seen the night before. "Let's just say that Whitey Connors knows there are forces far more powerful and frightening than his little band of thugs."

"Why are you doing this for me?" Liam sputtered.

"You're a good boy, Liam. And so are you, Quinn. But I'm not doing it for you. I'm doing it for your ma and da. They helped me find a peace I sorely needed, and so I'm forever in their debt. Good night then."

With that, the Major left the Wild Hart.

* * *

Liam turned to Quinn. "Holy shit."

"I know." Quinn hated to bring up the obvious, but he was worried that Liam might be so overwhelmed he wasn't thinking clearly. Not that he was himself. "We should tell Mom and Dad as soon as possible."

"Yeah, like now." Liam suddenly scrubbed his hands

over his face. "Jesus Christ, Quinn. What the hell am I going to do in Ballycraig? There's nothing there but the pub, the church, the gas station, and that crappy supermarket!"

"Aunt Bridget and Uncle Paul are there. Cousin Erin. Cousin Brian. And the countryside is beautiful." Liam scowled at him. "Let's not think about this right now, okay? Let's go upstairs."

"You're right. It is what it is," Liam said with a weary sigh. "Let's just get this over with."

* * *

Shock and despair didn't even begin to cover Quinn's parents' reaction to the news about Liam.

Quinn spoke first, as the Major had suggested. By the time Liam finished telling them his part of the story, their mother's face was as white as chalk, their father's breathing labored. Quinn was afraid he was going to have a heart attack. As far as he knew, the old man had never exercised in his life, unless you counted jackassing boxes of booze and restaurant supplies up and down the basement steps for forty years.

Quinn's mother began to cry, her face contorted with grief. "You can't go," she said to Liam. "You can't."

The look on their father's face changed. "If the Major says he has to go, he has to go," he snapped.

"Yes, but . . ."

"No buts. That feckin' Tommy Dolan," Quinn's father growled. "He's never been anything but trouble. Did I or did I not tell you years ago to get the hell away from him?" he yelled at Liam.

"Dad, calm down." Liam came to sit beside the old man. "Take a few breaths. C'mon."

"Your father's right," their mother murmured. "That Tommy—"

"It's a moot point, all right?" Liam snapped.

"Look," Quinn intervened cautiously, "I know we're all really upset here, but I think we should all try to calm down a bit."

His mother snorted derisively. "Will you listen to this one, telling us to calm down! Your brother's got to leg it to Ireland because he's in fear of his life, and why? Because of that bloody article of yours, that's why."

Liam jumped to Quinn's defense. "Get off his ass, Mom. After the truck incident, Quinn offered to kill the article, and I told him not to."

Mrs. O'Brien's mouth fell open. "Are you daft?"

"No. I think it's an important story."

"So important you've got to leave your family whom you might never see again," his mother pointed out tearfully.

Liam pulled a put-upon face. "Don't be melodramatic, Ma. You and Dad go back to Ireland once a year. And I'll be coming back eventually."

"Still."

Quinn tried to change the subject. "I think it's time you told us who the Major is."

Quinn's mother looked to his father, who nodded.

"The Major's father fought with Michael Collins after the Easter Rebellion. It's said he was an assassin. In the Irish Civil War, his father was Collins's chief of counterintelligence, hunting down and killing spies. The stories are that when the Major was a little boy, his father brought him along on his work. When he reached manhood, the son replaced the father. It was in the Second World War that he became a major. They say he hunted down and killed dozens of German and Irish spies for both the Irish Free State and Britain. The stories are all a little confusing. All I know for sure is that he was sent to the States because he was wanted for something by someone. We were asked to give him a place to stay and to help him get settled. And so we did. It's said that to this day men in the know both here and in Ireland grow pale just at the mention of his name. End of story."

"Wait a minute," Quinn said. "Who asked you to help him, and what did you do?"

Quinn's father flashed an enigmatic smile, the likes of which neither of the boys had ever seen before. "That's none of your business, son," he said matter-of-factly. "I said that was the end of the story."

Quinn's mother defused the tension. "When are you thinking of going, Liam?"

Liam looked overwhelmed. "Day after tomorrow. That'll give me tomorrow to pack things and find out about flights."

"I'll call Aunt Bridget and Uncle Paul and let them know you're coming," Mrs. O'Brien said. She looked to her husband. "Do I tell them why he's coming?"

"Just tell them the Major is sending him."

Mrs. O'Brien looked like she'd aged ten years in ten minutes. Their father, too.

Mr. O'Brien rubbed his chin thoughtfully. "We'll tell the regulars Liam's gone on vacation, and then that he decided to stay."

Quinn nodded approvingly.

"I'll tend the bar till we find someone else," said Mr. O'Brien.

"Oh, that'll be grand for your back," Mrs. O'Brien chortled.

Mr. O'Brien lifted an eyebrow. "And who else do we have to do it, *macushla*? You? I'll be fine."

"Famous last words," she grumbled. She looked depressed as she gazed at Liam. "I'll call your siblings and tell them to come over here tomorrow night after closing time. We have to give you a wee send-off."

Liam began choking up. "I hate this."

"If the Major says you have no choice, you have no choice," Mrs. O'Brien replied stoically. "We're not losing you." She stood up slowly, helping Quinn's father off the couch, one of her hands massaging the small of his back. "We're exhausted, boys. We need to get to bed."

Liam hugged his parents, then Quinn hugged them. But as Quinn stepped back from his mother's embrace, he saw accusation in her eyes. *Your fault,* her expression said. *You and your article.*

He turned away, heartsick.

She was right.

* * *

Quinn was surprised when Natalie followed him upstairs to his parents' apartment after closing time. Clearly she knew what was going on, and clearly his parents considered her family. He was sure that if they could, his parents would disown him and adopt her.

His stomach hurt when he came into the kitchen and caught sight of his mother. There were deep circles under her eyes. On the counter was a large chocolate layer cake, Liam's favorite since he was a little boy. Natalie walked over to his mom and hugged her tight from behind. His mother burst into tears and turned in Natalie's arms.

Quinn felt like he was intruding, so he went into the living room. Both his sisters, their eyes swollen from crying, regarded him coldly. Everyone thought Liam's having to leave was his fault. Everyone was right.

"Where's Dad?" Quinn asked.

"He's in the bathroom," his brother-in-law Brendan answered, "taking some aspirin for his back." Quinn noticed that once again, he was hiding behind the *Sent* to stay out of the cross fire.

"Can one of you persuade him to go to the doctor, please?" Quinn pleaded. "I've tried, and he's turned a deaf ear. Maybe one of his 'darlin' daughters' would have more success."

"We've all tried," Maggie answered wearily. "He won't

listen. Face it: he's never gonna change. Neither of them are."

Quinn's father appeared and clapped a hand on his shoulder. "How you doing?"

"Apart from my mother and sisters hating me?" he murmured. "Fine."

"Ah, don't mind them," he murmured back. "It'll blow over. And for what it's worth, I don't blame you for any of this. It's that Tommy Dolan that's at fault. I'm glad you're writing the article, and I'm glad it's going to run. I hope it winds up putting that evil bastard Connors behind bars, which is where he deserves to be."

Thank God someone is on my side, thought Quinn. His father went to talk to Brendan about the Mets game. Quinn looked at Sinead, sitting beside Maggie on the couch, the two of them with their heads together, whispering. He couldn't remember the last time he and Sinead had a long talk. She'd always been the tense one, the one who held it all inside both personally and professionally. In his opinion, she was even more driven than he was.

He realized that in the past few months, the sibling he'd become closest to was Liam. It was something he never could have imagined happening, but now that it had, he was grateful. He just wished the circumstances were different.

He felt a tug to go back into the kitchen and talk to Natalie, but he was in no mood to face dirty looks from his mother. As it turned out, he didn't have to: Natalie came into the living room.

"Is she okay?" he asked.

"*Non,*" Natalie replied bluntly. "How could she be? But she's trying to be strong."

"I suppose like everyone else in this room apart from my father, you think Liam's having to leave is my fault."

"What does it matter what I think?"

Out of the corner of his eye, Quinn could see his sisters

discreetly watching them. Did they know he and Natalie had split up? They had to. Their mother was gossip central.

"It matters to me."

"Yes, I do think it's partially your fault," Natalie said. "And so do you. I see it in your eyes. There's guilt there."

Distressed, Quinn walked away, joining his father and brother-in-law in the sports discussion. He really wished to hell his mother hadn't invited Natalie. Saying good-bye to his brother was going to be hard enough without having to deal with his ex-girlfriend—who hated him—being there, too.

"Hey, everyone."

Liam entered the room, looking and sounding surprisingly cheerful. He kissed Natalie and his sisters before hugging Quinn, Brendan, and his father in turn. "Why the long faces?"

They all stared at him as if he was crazy. "Oh, c'mon," he said, trying to lighten the mood. "I'm going on an extended vacation, people. You should be envious of me."

Mr. O'Brien looked alarmed. "I better not hear from your aunt and uncle that you're lying around on your arse all day."

Liam frowned. "As if that's a possibility. No, I'm sure I'll find a job pumping gas," he said sarcastically. "Or at the pub. Or shearing sheep. Or maybe I'll become the world's oldest altar boy. We all know there's so much to do in Ballycraig."

"World's oldest altar boy. Now that I'd pay to see," said Brendan. Everyone laughed.

*   *   *

His family was trying to put a good face on things as they sat around the dining room table eating cake in the early hours of the morning, but the subcurrent of melancholy was just too strong. As Quinn thought would be the case, it was Liam who decided when it was time to call it a night.

He looked awkward as he stood up. "I really should get to bed. My flight leaves early tomorrow—actually, today," he said in so quiet a voice it was difficult to hear.

There was the sound of chairs scraping back from the table accompanied by a heavy, profound silence. His mother, along with Maggie and Sinead, had started weeping. Liam, their father, and Natalie were all teary-eyed. Quinn yearned to cry, but for some reason, her presence held him back.

He noticed Natalie's discomfort and came up to her as everyone began to take his or her turns hugging Liam. "Are you all right?"

"I shouldn't be here," she whispered. She removed herself slightly from the ring of family.

"You wouldn't be here if my parents didn't think it was appropriate."

"I feel so badly for your parents."

"Yeah, me, too," said Quinn, a lump forming in his throat. "But they'll go see him in the summer."

"And will you? Or do you even take vacations?"

Quinn blinked and said nothing. His mother was wailing in his father's arms, a sound that pierced his heart. *Your fault,* the voice in his head accused. *All your fault.*

Finally, it was his turn to embrace his brother. "I ever tell you how proud I am of you?" Quinn said, jaw clenched tight so he didn't cry. "Probably not enough."

"Yeah, 'cause you're a dick."

They laughed, still holding on to each other.

"I need you to do me a favor," Liam said as they broke apart.

"What's that?"

"I want you to write the best effin' article you can," Liam said fiercely. "You got that?"

"Got it," Quinn choked out. He stepped back so his mother could again hug Liam.

"I gotta get outta here," Quinn said to his father, starting to feel overwhelmed. He hugged him tight. "I'll see you and Mom tomorrow."

His father nodded, and Quinn headed for the door, bounding down the stairs. Only then did he let himself break down.

33

The white lie Mr. O'Brien told the regulars worked: they
had animated discussions about where Liam should go and
what he should do on his vacation in Ireland. Mr. O'Brien
was working the bar and doing quite well, despite his obvious back pain. Every time he bent down to get something
and winced, Natalie winced, too. *There was no way he
could do this long term,* she thought. They'd have to find a
replacement for Liam and fast. She made a mental note to
ask Anthony if he might know someone.

The O'Briens kept up a surprisingly good facade. Liam's
absence seemed to hit Quinn especially hard. A few times
Natalie caught him looking broody as he stared down into
his whiskey. *He feels guilty,* she thought, *and well he
should.* She tried to muster some sympathy for him but
couldn't. Right now, her opinion was that his damn article
had hurt both her and Liam. She hoped it was worth it.

As usual, the dining room was hopping. Were she managing the restaurant, she would definitely employ another
waitress, but it wasn't for her to say. She knew better than
to make suggestions to Mrs. O'Brien about anything.

A table of firefighters, whom she had become fond of because they were very funny and down to earth, asked for their usual, and she hustled to the bar to give Mr. O'Brien their orders. He was patiently listening to Mrs. Colgan rattle on tipsily about how she might get a new parrot and name it Rudy the Second. He seemed glad of a reason to cut the conversation short.

"Mad as a bloody hatter, that one," he said under his breath to Natalie.

"You all encourage her, though!"

"Ah, she's harmless enough. And her late husband was a good sort. Hardworking man, construction. Bit of a bastard when he drank, though, from what I understand."

"You encourage PJ, too. And the Mouth."

Mr. O'Brien shrugged diffidently. "Lonely souls. If they get a bit of comfort and company being here, there's no harm in it, right?"

Natalie agreed. This was one of the reasons she'd become so fond of Quinn's family: they all had such good hearts. So did Anthony's family, come to think of it. She felt a warm glow inside as she realized how lucky she was, knowing so many warm, wonderful, kind people in New York. It was lovely.

As she'd vowed, she'd returned all the items from her spending spree. It was hard, but she felt so much lighter for doing the right thing. She also attended a Shopaholics Anonymous meeting, realizing she should have been going all along. It was good to be reminded that she wasn't the only one who backslid. No one was perfect; it would always be a struggle. But it was one she intended to win.

"Natalie?"

Mason. She made her way down to his end of the bar, expecting he'd want her to get him another Stella Artois. But his bottle was still half full.

Natalie smiled. "Hello, Mason. What can I do for you?"

"I was wondering what you were doing Sunday night."

The question was so unexpected, she was momentarily tongue-tied. "Um . . ."

Mason forged ahead. "There's a new Spanish restaurant opening on the Upper West Side that's gotten amazing reviews. I know you appreciate fine dining. Would you like to go to dinner with me?"

Natalie felt helpless. "Mason . . ." She knit her hands together nervously beneath the bar. "I'm not really interested in dating right now."

"It's not a date," he insisted with that charming smile of his. "Just a friendly meal."

Another delusional man, Natalie thought. He was telling her what she wanted to hear to try to convince her to go out with him, but she knew how he felt about her. There was longing in his eyes every time they spoke. If she agreed to dinner, there would be others until eventually, he would try to turn it into something amorous. She couldn't lead him on that way, even though the wicked part of her that longed to get back at Quinn was tempted to accept his offer, since she knew Mason would tell Quinn about it just to torture him. But it wasn't right to use someone that way.

"I'm sorry, Mason, but I can't," Natalie said gently. "I have too much on my plate right now. But I appreciate you asking me."

"Mmm," he said stiffly. "Perhaps when you're over O'Brien—"

"This has nothing to do with Quinn," Natalie cut in frigidly.

Clement's stony silence spoke volumes.

Natalie picked up the tray of firefighters' beers and walked away.

* * *

"I want your story next week."

Quinn stared at Mason, who'd called him into his office the second Quinn hit the newsroom. Quinn assumed he was in for another pathetic admonishment about how little time he'd been spending at the office tending to his "light" editorial duties.

Quinn sat down this time, casually putting his feet up on Clement's desk as he tilted back in his chair, lacing his fingers behind his head. "Kinda cutting off your nose to spite your face, wanting an article that isn't quite done, isn't it?"

"I want it. I've seen pieces of legislation move faster than this."

"Read my lips: it's not done."

"Could you get your feet off my desk?" Mason asked, pursing his lips distastefully.

"Insubordination, huh?" Quinn swung his legs off the desk. "Better?"

"I've had enough of your bullshit, O'Brien."

"Funny you should say that, because I've had enough of yours. I quit."

Clement laughed curtly. "Pardon?"

"I quit—you know, as in 'You can go fuck yourself, I'm out the door?' Would I like my piece to run in the paper that made me what I am? Hell yeah. But you're turning the *Sent* into a piece of shit. Besides, I know you: you'll hack my article to shreds. Why? (A) Because you can't edit worth a damn, (B) because you don't want to make waves with the mayor's office, and (C) because it's your pathetic way of trying to remind me who's boss around here. I've already talked to the *Standard*: they want me, and they're willing to wait to run the article until it's good and ready. I love it here. Correction: loved it here. But if I can't do my job, there's no point in staying."

Clement sighed, looking at Quinn as if he were an idiot. "I never said you couldn't do your job. I just said you'd be reporting on a much smaller scale because of taking over Rogan's position."

Quinn snorted loudly in disbelief. "I'm not taking over

the job you fired my friend from! Are you serious? Why do you think I haven't given a shit about being around the office? I just told you that so you'd get off my ass about the article." He stood up, stretching. "Guess I'll be hitting the road."

"Not alone." Clement picked up the phone. "I'm calling one of the guards at the front desk to come upstairs and watch you as you box up your things to make sure you don't steal anything that's *Sent* property. And then he's going to escort you out of the building."

"Wow. I wonder what will happen if I try to sneak a stapler past him. Will he shoot me?"

Clement ignored him. "Put your ID tag down on the desk, please."

Quinn pulled out his building ID from the back pocket of his jeans and slapped it down on Clement's desk with a big grin on his face. "Here ya go, my man. Have a good one."

* * *

"What the fuck? You couldn't tell us you were planning this?!"

Kenny Durham looked so distraught as Quinn threw his crap into a box that Quinn was tempted to go over to photo and beg a few Valium for his friend off Darby. He felt bad that he hadn't said a word about his defection to his friends, but the *Sent* was a helluva lot like the Wild Hart when it came to gossip: it traveled faster than a Japanese bullet train.

"Of course I couldn't tell you. Within a day it would have been all over the newsroom. Plus I didn't want to depress you. Or freak you out."

"Oh, and I'm not depressed and freaked out now?" Durham shook his head despondently. "Oh, man, you so can't go. You know what it's going to be like around here without you?"

"No one's making you stay. Find a job at another paper and tell Kangaroo Jack to shove it up his ass."

"There's not a huge need for crossword puzzle writers, Quinn. All the papers already have one."

"You'll be fine," said Quinn as he continued mindlessly chucking his stuff into a box: photos, his dictionary, old press clippings, and his thesaurus. "You've got Rodriguez. You've got Cindy. And we'll still be hanging at the pub."

"Yeah right." Durham looked forlorn. "But I bet you're gonna start hanging at Tico's Grill with the rest of the *Standard* guys."

"Maybe a few nights a week. But the rest of the time I'll be at the Hart—if I'm not working." Actually, hanging with his new coworkers off-hours hadn't crossed his mind. But now that Durham mentioned it, it would probably be a smart thing to do, especially since he already knew and liked a couple of guys over there.

Quinn glanced at the bone-thin, milk-pale guard named Tom, who was busy watching CNN on one of the myriad TVs hanging from the newsroom ceiling. He didn't give a rat's ass what Quinn packed and what he didn't. Quinn held up a stapler. "Should I take this?" he asked Durham, who shrugged.

"Tom, should I take this?"

"Do you need it?"

Quinn turned the stapler over in his hands. "No." He tossed it in the box anyway.

"Cindy is gonna freak when she gets in and hears you quit, pal," said Durham.

"No she won't. She'll be envious."

"Probably," Durham said glumly. "So when do you start at the *Standard*?"

"Tomorrow." Quinn grinned. "And you know what? I can't goddamn wait."

* * *

Talk about—what was the word?—synchronicity. Here Natalie had realized she'd been lax in her search for a job managing a restaurant, and voilà! There was an ad in the paper looking for a restaurant manager for a medium-sized French restaurant. A simple phone call, and she was on her way to an interview.

She'd actually heard of the restaurant before: Le Bristol. She'd called Anthony to see if he knew anything about the chef. He told her the head chef, who was also the owner, was immensely talented, but at one time, he'd been a bit of a bad boy: womanizing, a heroin addict. "The Keith Richards of chefs," was how Anthony described him. "But he's clean now," he assured her.

Natalie entered the empty restaurant, and as she had twice before, she sat down at an empty table. She was surprised to realize that she liked empty restaurants. They were so peaceful, not a hint of the hustle and bustle and buzz of conversation to come. The calm before the storm.

The chef emerged from the kitchen right on time. He was tall and thin with a thick mane of gray hair, wearing cowboy boots, faded jeans, and a plain white T-shirt. A cigarette dangled sensuously from between his lips.

Natalie went to stand, but he waved her down. "Sit. I don't do formal."

He pulled out a chair. "You don't mind if I smoke, do you?"

"Not at all."

"You smoke?"

"I used to."

He held a hand out to her. "Rick Lemieux."

"Natalie Bocuse."

"Nice accent. Customers would love it. You got a résumé?"

Merde. She had never thought of writing up an actual résumé. What an idiot.

"I thought I'd just tell you . . ."

"Go ahead."

While Lemieux puffed away on his cigarette, blowing funnels of smoke up to the ceiling, Natalie recited her short but sweet résumé.

He narrowed his eyes. "You're not a vegetarian, are you?"

Natalie was surprised by the question. "No."

"Good. Because I fuckin' hate vegetarians. You ever eat pig cheek? Entrails?"

Natalie thought for a moment. "No, but I love sweet-breads."

"Are you willing to try new things?"

"Yes, of course."

He tilted back in his chair. "Who's your favorite band?"

Natalie was confused. "Pardon?"

"Favorite band. You dig the Ramones?"

"I don't know them."

"Hmm. Not good." He snuffed out his cigarette. "If you were stranded on a desert island, what's the one CD you'd bring with you?"

What does this have to do with food? she wanted to ask. She thought hard, trying to come up with something fast.

"The Beatles' *White Album*," she offered tentatively.

Lemieux looked at her with begrudging respect. "I'll take that." He lit another cigarette. "You're on death row. What would your final meal be?"

Anthony must have been wrong. Lemieux was obviously still on drugs. Again she felt like she had no time to think. "Mmm. rabbit pâté to start . . . then, for the main course . . . roast quail with a simple asparagus mold as the legume . . . and for dessert, clafouti à la liqueur."

"You're hired."

Natalie blinked. "What?"

"You're the new manager. You're obviously smart, you know French food, and you've got some management experience. You might be in over your head at first, but in my opinion, that's the only way people learn. It can get nuts in here, so I might need you to seat people sometimes, too. When can you start?"

Natalie's head was spinning. "Uh . . . I need to give my current job at least one week's notice so they can find a replacement."

"Sounds good. Call me during the week if you run into any trouble with that. Otherwise, I'll see you next Wednesday. And pick up the Ramones' first CD. It'll change your life."

* * *

"I'm so sorry. Don't hate me."

That night at work when she gave the O'Briens her notice, Natalie unexpectedly found herself weeping. Here she'd finally gotten what she wanted on the employment front, but instead of feeling happy, she felt sad and guilty.

She hung her head, not wanting to look at them as they sat on either side of her at the kitchen table. Mrs. O'Brien gently lifted her chin with an index finger and looked into her eyes.

"Don't be daft. Do you think we thought you'd stay here forever? I'm just worried that it's Quinn driving you out, even though you'll deny it to high heaven."

"I swear it isn't. Managing is what I've wanted to do for a long time, but I got very lazy looking for a job because I love working here."

Mrs. O'Brien brushed her tears away. "We wish you all the luck in the world, darlin'."

"He wants me to start in a week. But if you can't find someone by then, I'm sure I can stay on a bit longer. He told me to call him if that's the case."

"I think we'll be able to. A friend of Maggie's just lost her job and needs something fast. We'll hire her."

"That's good."

Natalie actually felt wounded by the rapidity with which

the O'Briens were sure they could replace her, which was ridiculous. What was she expecting them to tell her? That she was irreplaceable?

"Should I throw you a little going-away party, love?"

"No, please," Natalie said quickly—maybe too quickly. "It's not that I'm ungrateful for all you've done for me. I'm just not comfortable with it." With another party Quinn would no doubt miss.

"That's perfectly fine," Mrs. O'Brien assured her.

Mr. O'Brien shook his head sadly. "Liam gone, and now you leaving . . . it just won't be the same around here."

Natalie was touched.

"You'll come back and visit, won't you?" he continued hopefully.

"Don't pressure her," Mrs. O'Brien chided. "Especially since I'm sure that stupid son of ours is the last thing she wants to see."

"Of course I'll visit," Natalie assured him. She never thought she'd feel this way, but she was actually going to miss the lunatic contingent at the bar. And Quinn's friends. And the firefighters. All felt like family now.

"You look tired," Natalie said. "I'll go now." She kissed them both on the cheek. "Thank you again for all you've done for me."

"And thank you for trying to make our son happy. I'm just sorry he's too stupid to realize what he's lost."

Natalie fought the tears welling up. "Me, too, Mrs. O'Brien. Believe me."

34

"You've driven her out."

That's how Quinn found out Natalie had taken the managing job at Le Bristol. He'd stopped by the Wild Hart in the morning to let his parents know the good news that he'd quit the *Sent* and had jumped over to the *Standard.* Instead, he found himself staring at long faces and putting up with abuse from his mother's razor-sharp tongue. He had the feeling he was going to be on her shit list for life.

His first day at the *Standard* had gone well. He was still riding the high of telling Clement to stick it, and he felt even better knowing his new editor in chief, Carl Koski, considered Quinn's defection quite a feather in his cap and couldn't wait to run his article when it was ready. It didn't hurt that Quinn knew most of the reportorial staff, the newspaper biz in New York being one big round of musical chairs.

After working until about eleven that night, he again headed over to the pub. It was jarring seeing his dad behind the bar; the old man was moving slowly. Quinn slipped behind the bar to pour his own whiskey. "Dad, you have to—"

"I know," his father said, irritated. "I've got Brendan on the case, and the guys from the firehouse. We'll have someone soon."

"You need help right now."

His father drew himself up, insulted. "I'm not a helpless thing, you know. I can manage."

Quinn held up his hands in a gesture of surrender. "Okay, okay. Didn't mean to offend."

He poured the whiskey shot down his throat, noticing that Clement wasn't at his usual seat at the bar. Predictable. Now that he didn't have Quinn to annoy anymore, he'd probably stop coming in.

He quickly scanned the dining room for Natalie and spotted her talking to the table of firemen. It pissed him off sometimes, the way they all looked at her ass when she walked away. Well, he didn't have a right to feel ticked anymore, did he?

"We heard from your brother again this afternoon," his father said. Liam had already called once to let them know when he arrived in Ireland.

"And—?"

"Goin' mad with boredom already, or so he says. He'll wind up in Dublin, mark my words."

Quinn nodded, making a mental note to give Liam a call to see how he was doing and let him know he was now at the *Standard*. He couldn't believe how much he missed his broody little brother. He chuckled; he was sure that whole dark, Heathcliff thing would play well with the ladies in Ireland, same as it had here. Women seemed to love men who gave the impression they were tortured souls. And the fact that Liam was so handsome—hell, if there were any single women left in Ballycraig, he'd have his pick.

Natalie eventually came to the bar to place orders. Quinn

was shocked by the twinge of pain jabbing him when she came near.

"Hey," he said quietly.

"Hello." She began pulling out bottles of Sam Adams.

"I hear you're leaving next week."

"Yes. I have a managing job at Le Bristol."

"Congrats."

"Thank you."

"Look," Quinn said, "I hope you're not leaving on my account."

Natalie laughed incredulously. "Always with the ego! You've known all along that managing is what I've wanted to do."

"I know." Jesus, why was everyone jumping down his throat tonight? "It's just that the timing is suspicious."

"Let's just say I had a number of epiphanies the night I broke up with you."

Ouch. "I have a new job, too."

"Yes, I know. Your friends told me earlier this evening. They left early because they figured you'd be out with your new coworkers tonight. Anyway . . . congratulations."

"Thank you."

He wanted to say something to amuse her, to tease her the way he used to, to try to break the tension, but he knew it would be no use. He deserved any frostiness that came his way.

"Good luck finishing your article," she said, walking away with the firefighters' drink order. His father was checking the ice machine, pretending he wasn't listening. When their eyes did meet, Quinn held up a warning hand.

"Save it."

* * *

Her first day at Le Bristol, Natalie had to actively fight the nausea she'd woken up with. She got in hours before the restaurant opened so Lemieux could explain the "basic deal" to her: how she'd be responsible for scheduling and making sure there were enough waitstaff available to work peak times; how she'd work with him on the food and supply orders; how she'd be the one dealing with food vendors and service providers. Last but not least, she was the one who'd have to deal with customer service. "Basically, babe, you're the smiling face of the restaurant so I can stay in the kitchen and do my thing," Lemieux told her. The thought terrified her.

By 6 p.m., every table at the restaurant, all reserved months in advance, was taken. The clientele was entirely different than the casual customers who ate at Vivi's, or at Dante's, for that matter. It was an affluent crowd of variant ethnicities. At first this pleased Natalie; this was just the kind of upscale restaurant she'd dreamed of managing. But over the course of the evening, she came to realize that casual had its advantages. Worse, Lemieux was insane.

The first problem came with an older couple in their late fifties, one of those couples who seemed to have been married so long they had exhausted the art of conversation years ago. Their waiter came over to Natalie where she stood at the small podium at the front of the restaurant, talking with the hostess.

"Table number five says their food is taking too long."

"I see." Natalie patted the young man's shoulder. He was new, too, and he looked as overwhelmed as she felt.

Natalie made her way to the table, where the couple sat in cranky silence.

"Sir, madam—Adam tells me you are unhappy?"

"The food," the woman said with a sour face. "We've been waiting over half an hour for dinner."

"I see. I'll go and try to find out what the holdup is."

"Thank you," the woman said coldly.

Filling with dread, Natalie entered the kitchen, assaulted by a wave of heat and sound as she pushed through the doors. The cacophony was overwhelming: people yelling orders, people yelling at each other, meat sizzling . . . again, so different from Vivi's. Then again, Vivi's kitchen staff only consisted of two other people beside herself.

She had to admit, though, that the mingling aromas wafting through the kitchen were mouthwatering, even though it was hard to pick out individual smells. Even so, she detected some garlic and some sage. Something was being sautéed in wine. Fine French food.

One of the line cooks saw her enter and hustled over. "What's up?"

"There's a couple out there complaining their main dish is taking too long."

The cook sighed. "Mario!" he barked.

Mario was the sous-chef, in charge of running the kitchen. Natalie had met him earlier in the day. He looked annoyed at being interrupted as he yelled at one of the kitchen staff who was swirling chocolate syrup on a plate, and crying.

Mario came over to Vivi and the line cook. "Yeah?"

"There's some couple out there complaining their food is taking too long," explained the line cook.

Mario looked at Natalie. "How long they been waiting?"

"Half an hour."

"Idiots."

"What do you want me to tell them?" Natalie asked.

"Rick will talk to them."

Natalie thrust her head forward slightly as if she hadn't heard correctly. "Rick?"

"Yeah. It's his place, he likes to talk to the customers himself when there's a complaint."

Natalie nodded as Mario screamed, "Rick!" at the top of his lungs. She was surprised to see him working the line, chopping vegetables. She took this as a sign of solidarity with his staff, as well as humility. She was wrong about the latter.

Natalie explained the situation to him.

"What table are these pains in the ass at?" he asked her.

"Five."

"Follow me."

Heart in throat, she followed him to the table.

"Hi," he said to the couple tersely. "I'm Rick Lemieux, the executive chef. I hear you have a problem?"

The woman drew herself up imperiously. "We've been waiting over half an hour for our food."

"What did you order?"

"Casserole of roasted pork with potato and onions. My husband ordered casserole of roasted duck with turnips."

"Good choices. Now tell me why you're here."

The man blinked. "What?"

"Tell me why you're eating here tonight."

The man replied as if it were self-evident. "Because the restaurant has a wonderful reputation."

"Give the man a cigar." Rick put his hands on the table and leaned forward. "Can I let you folks in on a little secret?" he whispered. The couple froze. "The reason my restaurant has a wonderful reputation is because everything here is cooked to order. Fresh. Made with love and care. Made with pride. That means it takes time. You want fast food, go to McDonald's."

Natalie suppressed a gasp, but the woman at the table didn't.

"There's no call to be rude!"

"You want the best French food in the city or not? If you do, then cool your jets and relax. Have another glass of wine or something, all right?"

Natalie held her breath, waiting for them to leave. They didn't. She followed Rick back toward the kitchen. "Fucking idiots," he muttered. "I hate cooking for fucking idiots. I wish I could give every customer who comes through the door an intelligence test first."

Natalie's heart was about to burst through her chest with anxiety, but she had to speak her piece, because she was confused. "I thought one of the first rules of customer service was 'The customer is always right,'" she said quietly.

"Not here, babe. The rule here is, 'Rick is always right.' If people don't like it, they can go eat elsewhere. We're booked six months in advance, and we have a waiting list of people hoping for cancellations. Those putzes over there who think they're better than everyone else? They don't deserve to eat here."

* * *

By the middle of her second week at Le Bristol, Natalie not only knew Lemieux had indeed tossed her in the deep end of the pool, but also that she was drowning. Setting up hours for the waitstaff was no problem. But she had no idea what she was doing when it came to dealing with the food vendors. Rick and Mario really did the ordering, but she was responsible for following up and complaining, and God knew that Rick had lots of complaints. She asked Mario for guidance, but she could tell he was becoming exasperated because he really didn't have the time to help her out. And then there was the issue of Rick Lemieux himself.

She suspected he was a bit odd when he had asked her those irrelevant questions at her interview about death row meals and desert island discs. But now, seeing him in action, it was confirmed. Every time there was a complaint from a customer (and thankfully, there weren't many), her stomach knotted, knowing he was going to saunter through the kitchen doors and start lobbing insults. On her second night, someone complained that their fruit compote wasn't warm enough, and sent it back. Rick reheated it until it was bubbling and then brought it out to them himself. "Hot enough now?" he asked, once again cowing another diner into silence. On her fourth night, a smarmy, sniffy, solo male diner complained that his glazed carrots weren't glazed enough. Rick came out of the kitchen and handed him his apron. "You know so much about glazed carrots, pal? Come back in the kitchen with me and show me how to prepare them."

The man recoiled, appalled. "How dare you?"

"I own the restaurant. And guess what? You're done. I'm kicking you the hell out of here. You don't even have to pay. Just go."

The man rose, threw his napkin down on the table, and stormed out.

"*Au revoir,* dickhead," Rick said to applause from some of the other diners. Natalie didn't understand how he got away with it. The public had to *know* they risked abuse by coming here. Yet night after night, the place was packed.

She realized she wasn't only shocked by her boss's behavior; she was scared of him. He was a tyrant. No one, staff included, dared disagree with him. Yet those who worked for him took whatever abuse he dished out because they thought it was a great honor to learn to cook under this lunatic, and the customers kept coming because the food truly was magnificent.

Her grace period lasted approximately one week before Lemieux started hurling insults at her as well. How stupid was she? He yelled. How fucking hard was it to yell at the produce guy? Each night she'd come home and cry, too upset to sleep. *This is what you wanted,* she reminded herself. But not this way, being belittled day after day. It wasn't her dream to work with Lemieux. And so she quit. She didn't care if it meant having to completely reevaluate whether managing a restaurant was what she really wanted to do. Life was too short to be miserable on a daily basis. She would go back to the Wild Hart and ask for her old job back.

* * *

"Back already? That was quick."

Quinn saw the spark of irritation in Natalie's eyes as she put his shot of whiskey down in front of him at the bar. Just to amuse himself, he was sitting in Mason Clement's usual spot. Clement hadn't shown up once since Quinn had quit, thus proving his theory that the bastard only hung out there to torture Quinn and ogle Natalie, which had apparently gotten him nowhere.

The past two weeks had been both exhilarating and depressing. Exhilarating because in a week or so, his article was going to run and cause a major sensation, and depressing because every time he'd come into the Hart, Natalie wasn't there. He tried to convince himself it was just Liam that he missed, but it was futile; he missed watching his beautiful girlfriend at work; he missed seeing how his family adored her; most of all, he missed the nights they went home together. Try as he might to focus solely on work, her absence in his life was a distraction. He was tempted to swing by Le Bristol one night to see how she was faring, but he knew Natalie: she'd get pissed off.

It was a fantastic surprise, then, when he walked into the Hart, and there she was. There was no denying the change in atmosphere; everyone seemed cheerier, glad of her return. He felt bad that his sister Maggie's friend was let go after only two weeks, but she wasn't waitress material anyway: by the third night she was complaining about how all the hustling and standing was hell on her legs, and his mother was about to kill her. Natalie's return couldn't have been timelier.

"Hey," said Quinn, realizing that what he'd said about her being back at the pub so quickly might be perceived as somewhat sarcastic. "I didn't mean to sound like I was putting you down."

"Thank you."

Quinn gestured at the bar customers. "Everyone is really glad you're back." He paused. "I'm glad you're back."

Natalie cocked her head inquisitively. "Really? And why is that?"

"It just didn't feel right without you here," he admitted. "My folks must be thrilled."

"They're pleased." Natalie gestured discreetly at Quinn's father. "He shouldn't be bartending. Your mother said he wakes up in the morning and can barely walk. It's not good."

"Try telling him that."

"I asked Anthony if he knew anyone looking for a bartending job. He said he'd ask around."

"I think Brendan is asking around, too. He knows a lot of people." *This is good,* Quinn thought, the fact they were having a cordial conversation. He'd never been able to be friends with one of his exes before, but maybe this would be the exception.

"I see your boyfriend is nowhere to be found," Quinn noted dryly.

Natalie rolled her eyes.

"I think he stopped coming in because I left the paper." Quinn poured himself a whiskey. "He ask you out once he knew we'd split up?" he asked casually.

"That's none of your business."

"That means yes. But you're right, it is none of my business."

Egotistical ass, Quinn thought. What, Clement thought Quinn's relationship with Natalie had been so inconsequential that Natalie would start dating again right away? Even though Clement wasn't there, and even though Quinn was no longer working under him, Quinn still despised him.

He watched his father massage his lower back as he bent to scoop up some ice for a gin and tonic for the Mouth, who was going on to PJ Leary about the likelihood of life on other planets. PJ looked on the verge of sleep. Quinn knew his father would be pissed, but he came around the bar and started helping out with orders.

"No need to do that," his father said with a scowl.

"My ass," Quinn replied. "If you don't find someone by the end of this week, I'm calling Uncle Jimmy and telling him to come in and take over."

His father muttered a few choice curse words under his breath and walked away. Uncle Jimmy was his father's younger brother, the only one of his parents' siblings to also emigrate. Jimmy used to tend bar when his parents first opened the pub, but eventually he left to become a cop. He was retired now, bored and restless. Quinn knew his uncle would jump at the chance to help out. He also knew his father would kill him if he contacted his uncle, since the two had always rubbed each other the wrong way if they spent too much time together. Hopefully, his threat would light a fire under his dad's butt.

He caught Natalie looking at him with admiration for helping his father out, and his heart swelled against his will. Perhaps she didn't completely hate him after all. Perhaps she could see that he wasn't a completely selfish person.

Quinn handed one of the cops who came in a Guinness and turned to her. "So, what happened at Le Bristol, if you don't mind me asking?"

She hesitated. "I was in over my head," she confessed. "The chef was a madman. Verbally abusive to the staff— and to the customers! Every day I'd walk in there, and my stomach would be in knots, and every night I'd come home and cry. I decided if that's what it's like managing a restaurant, then maybe I'm not cut out for it. I don't know." She glanced away.

"It sounds to me like you made the right decision, Nat."

No response.

"And maybe managing isn't what you're meant to do. It's a far cry from what you did in France, working in the foreign ministry."

"I only chose that path because I thought it would impress my politician father," she pointed out sharply. "You know that."

"I know." Quinn immediately regretted bringing it up, since it was a painful subject for her. But he was desperate to figure out a way to help.

"Maybe you're one of those people who take a while to figure out what they're meant to do," Quinn continued carefully. "There's nothing wrong with that."

"That's easy for you to say. You've always known what you wanted to do. So has Vivi. And Anthony. And Michael."

"Maggie took a while to figure out what she wanted to do. And now look at her: she's thriving in massage school."

"True." Natalie looked down at her feet. "I just—I feel like a failure," she said, a slight quaver in her voice. She sounded as though she might cry.

"You're not a failure." God, he wished he could hold her in his arms and comfort her.

Natalie looked back up, shaking her shoulders as if trying to shrug off her glum mood. "That's very nice of you to say," she murmured. She slid a bag of potato chips down the bar to PJ Leary, who was now dominating the conversation with the Mouth with talk of Brian Boru, whose ghost was making an appearance in his never-ending book.

Quinn turned to Natalie. "Just in case you're curious, Brian Boru is the best-known, ancient high king of Ireland."

"Ah." She paused. "Speaking of things Irish, how is your article coming along?" she asked stiffly.

He was surprised she asked, even though he suspected she was only doing so to be polite.

"It should be running next week."

Natalie picked up a tray of beers and mixed drinks for one of the tables in the dining room.

"I'll be sure to read it," she said unemotionally. Then she walked away.

35

"Holy shit, pal. Great story."

Sitting with his friends at their usual booth in the pub, Quinn basked in Kenny Durham's praise. After what felt like years of endless interviews, endless research, and endless investigation, the first of Quinn's five-part exposé on the Irish mob's being behind the gentrification of Hell's Kitchen was today's front cover of the *Standard*, complete with a picture of Whitey Connors being taken away in handcuffs. Whitey and his crew were charged with multiple counts of assault, arson, and larceny for threatening and intimidating tenants into leaving so buildings could be gutted, renovated, and sold for large profits. The Shields Brothers were booked as well for conspiracy. It was all over the media; Quinn's phone had been ringing all day with requests for television and magazine interviews. It wasn't the first cover-page story he'd ever written, but it sure as hell was his most important. Yet the elation he felt was short-lived, and he wasn't sure why.

He thanked his friend for the compliment and then raised his shot glass in a silent toast to his absent brother.

Without Liam's help, he doubted he would have been able to put all the pieces of the puzzle together. He'd called him earlier to let him know the article was finally running, but his uncle Paul told him Liam was out jogging, which completely mystified the older man ("Now tell me this: Why on earth would you go running about if you didn't have to?"). Quinn chatted with his uncle for a while, eventually wrapping up the conversation by telling him he'd try to get hold of Liam tomorrow.

"Anyone up for another round?" Quinn asked.

"Only if it's on you," said Rogan, who was looking for another newspaper job. He'd expanded his search beyond Manhattan to the west and south, and had an interview the day after tomorrow at a newspaper in South Carolina. It depressed Quinn to think of his friend leaving the city, but facts were facts: the guy had to be able to support himself.

"Of course it's on me. Isn't it always?" Quinn needled his friends.

Rodriquez and Durham snorted in response.

Seeing Natalie busy with a dining room full of customers, he went to the bar to fill the order himself. As he'd threatened, he'd brought in his uncle to work with his father. His father paid lip service to resentment, but Quinn noticed that he hadn't put up much of a fight. Meanwhile, the search for a younger bartender was still on.

"How are you and Dad getting on?" Quinn asked his uncle quietly as he began filling the drink order for his table.

"He's a gobaloon, and he's always been a gobaloon," his uncle grumbled. "But he's blood. Can't change that."

Out of the corner of his eye, Quinn saw PJ beckoning him with his index finger.

"What's up, my man?" Quinn asked.

"I read the first installment of your article. Very impressive."

"Thank you."

"I've finished my book," PJ continued happily. "It's only seven hundred pages."

Jesus God, thought Quinn. "You might want to edit it down before sending it out."

"Hmm," PJ said thoughtfully. "Perhaps I'll cut the chapters with the talking eels."

"I, too, thought your article was very impressive," the Mouth chimed in. "Reminds me of the good old days of New York journalism: Breslin, Hamill. The days when—"

"Jaysus, would you ever shut your yap," Quinn's father begged. He looked at Quinn with tortured eyes. "He's been going on about it all night. My ears are about to fall off my head."

Quinn thanked the Mouth anyway.

"Quinn?"

His father's expression was serious as he gently tugged him away from the lip of the bar.

"Yeah?"

"Your article . . ." His father's eyes glistened with pride. "Your mother and I are very proud. I think it might be your best, son."

Quinn coughed uncomfortably, overwhelmed with emotion. He'd been worried that his parents might withhold kudos because of the Liam situation. "Thank you, Dad," he managed. "It really means a lot to me that you said that."

"I rang Liam earlier to let him know the piece was on today's front page."

"I did, too. He was out."

"Well, I caught him in. He said your cousin had a computer, and he would try to read it online. I told him how great it is, and he sounded dead pleased."

"I'm going to try to catch him tomorrow."

They'd talked twice in the past week. Liam had gotten a bartending job at Ballycraig's only pub, the Royal Oak. The pub's owner, Old Jack, was an old friend of their parents, and like their father, he was starting to slow down a bit. He'd jumped at the chance to employ Liam. Liam, in turn, had jumped at the chance to work.

His father patted his shoulder affectionately and moved toward Mrs. Colgan, who was holding her empty glass up in the air, bellowing, "When Rudy was alive I got faster service."

"Daft cow," Quinn heard his father say under his breath. He was right: Mrs. Colgan was nuts. All the regulars were nuts, which was part of the reason he loved them. Colorful was better than boring.

Drink orders filled, Quinn was moving out from behind the bar when the Major lightly touched his arm.

"Good job, boyo."

Quinn squeezed the old man's shoulder. "Thank you."

"I hear your brother is doing well."

"Yeah, thanks to you." Quinn decided to take a risk. "I'd love to talk to you about your history sometime."

The Major stiffened, and that darkness started to return to his eyes. "I'm sure your parents told you all you need to know. We'll leave it at that."

Then with a blink the darkness was gone, and the old man went back to reading his *Irish Times*. The issue was closed . . . forever.

* * *

Natalie couldn't help but notice how buoyant the mood at Quinn's table was as they closed out the bar, celebrating the publication of Quinn's article, the one that had taken precedence over her in his life. When she'd served them their first round, he'd politely asked her if she'd read it yet, but she hadn't. He seemed disappointed.

She was stacking glasses when she noticed a well-thumbed copy of the *Standard* on the bar. Quinn's father had put it there, proudly showing it to everyone who came in. She hesitated a moment, checking to make sure Quinn was still safely ensconced with his now-drunken friends, then picked up the paper and began reading his article, despite the fact it made her feel as though a cold stone had suddenly lodged in the pit of her stomach.

It was apparent right from the beginning of the article that Quinn was an extraordinary reporter. Oddly, she'd never made an effort to read his work before; perhaps deep down, she'd always known on some level that his job would always come first, and she didn't want to deal with her opponent, even if it was just cheap paper and ink.

She closed the paper. She should have known from how long he'd been working on the article that it would be in-depth and couldn't be contained in one edition of the paper, and so it was running over the course of days. She stared at his byline beneath the blaring headline: "by Quinn O'Brien." Quinn O'Brien, the best reporter in New York. She knew it was true, yet the appellation made her resentful. She was still angry with him. Still hurt. Even so, she knew she had to acknowledge the article and congratulate him. Otherwise, it would look as though she were going out of her way to ignore it. She didn't want to appear petty, even though that was exactly how she was feeling.

Quinn's uncle and father had gone down to the basement, leaving her to finish cleaning up, which she didn't mind. She was almost done at the bar when Quinn walked over to her. He looked exhausted, as usual. She had never known a time when he hadn't.

"Busy tonight," he noted.

"Very. Your mother should hire another waitress."

Quinn looked amused. "I dare you to tell her that."

"No, thank you. I've learned my lesson on that front."

"You're family now, right? She might listen to you."

They stood there, awkwardly facing each other. "You and your friends seem to be having a good time celebrating."

"Yeah . . ." He seemed somewhat unenthusiastic, which baffled her. This was his big day of triumph, was it not?

Time to be gracious. "Your article was very good."

"Thank you for reading it." He gazed at her intently. "I put a lot of work into it, as you can see."

"I hope it was worth losing me over and getting your brother sent off to Ireland," Natalie blurted. She apologized immediately. "I'm sorry. That was a cruel thing to say."

"It's how you feel," Quinn murmured. "Don't apologize. I have to confess: I was hoping that if you read it, you'd understand why I couldn't give you the attention you deserved while I was writing it."

"Which means what? Now that you're done with it, you can?" she asked sharply.

"Natalie." Quinn looked remorseful. "You know I never meant to hurt you."

"What are you working on now?" she made herself ask.

Quinn smiled sadly. "Do you really care?"

"No. I'm just trying to be polite." A quiet desperation overtook her as she looked around the bar and realized that she wasn't sure how much longer she could bear working here. Seeing him all the time was torture. Maybe she'd move back to Brooklyn and go back to work at Vivi's. So what if there was nothing for her to do in Bensonhurst? Anything was better than the anger and ache roiling inside her when she saw him. Quinn cocked his head toward his friends. "Guess I'll get back to the guys."

"Congratulations again," Natalie forced herself to say. "I hope everything turned out the way you wanted."

* * *

Quinn headed back to his friends, all of whom were feeling no pain.

"Onward and upward," said Durham, draining the last dregs of his beer. "I vote we hit Ronnie's Lounge next."

Ronnie's was a lounge four blocks away from the Hart,

a popular hangout for journalists working for all the papers in New York.

"I don't know," Quinn said uncertainly.

"What the hell is wrong with you?" asked Rodriguez. "When have you ever not wanted to celebrate?"

"Yeah," Rogan chimed in. "This is your night, pal. To savor. To boast. C'mon, don't be a wet blanket."

"Okay, okay," Quinn acquiesced, feeling pressured not to let his friends down. "We'll go to Ronnie's."

* * *

The bar was packed as always. When Quinn walked in, there was a slight change in mood. His colleagues at the *Standard* applauded, while reporters from the other papers glanced at him with a mix of envy and admiration. Still, even those whom he had scooped managed to make their way over to him and congratulate him, albeit somewhat begrudgingly.

One of his new colleagues, Tim Stewart, came over and draped his arm around his neck. "You bastard," he said affectionately. "You realize you just made life harder for the rest of us, right? You're the standard we're gonna be measured by."

"I thought I was the standard everyone was measured by for years."

"Arrogant SOB. Anyway, all drinks are on us tonight, you got it?"

Quinn smiled weakly. "Got it."

Jesus Christ, what the hell was wrong with him? He should have been exuberantly shitfaced by now. It was his night, but part of him couldn't care less.

He accepted the whiskey from his colleague. Seconds later he found himself pinned against the bar being grilled by some cub reporter from the *Post*. Quinn was only half listening, his eyes drawn to his *Sent* friends. There was

Rogan, divorced for years because his wife couldn't take the erratic nature of his job. There was Durham, who was now sleeping on Quinn's couch because his wife had thrown him out and he had nowhere else to go. Quinn's eyes roved over the rest of the crowd; more than half the people he knew were lone wolves like him: journalists who lived from story to story with nothing else in their lives. Over half of them were guys in their fifties; they were either divorced or incapable of balancing a personal life with the adrenaline rush of their job. Like him, they'd go home alone tonight. They'd lie in their beds with their cell phones on, waiting for a call from an editor or a tip from a source. If nothing were going on, they'd get up the next day and head directly to the newsroom to see if anything juicy might come over the scanners. They'd race to scoop their opponents. And then they'd do it all over again the next day, and the next, and the next.

That's when he realized that Natalie was right: his life was sad, selfish, and stupid. Even though he had tremendous respect for many of his colleagues, he was forced to ask himself: Is this really how he wanted to end up? Drunk in a bar with his fellow reporters, talking shop because they had nothing else in their lives? The answer hit him like a brick smashing down on his head: no. He'd had it all—the job, a woman who loved him—and he'd blown it, because he was so stupid and myopic he chose to put work first. Because he was so selfish he refused to bend while she gave and gave and gave, far past the point he deserved. His all-important article hadn't been worth losing her and Liam. God, what a fucking moron he was.

He had to get her back.

It was all he could think about as he waved away another shot of whiskey. Perhaps he'd give her some more time without him, give her a chance to miss him. Besides, he needed a little time to figure out when and how to tell her he'd been a fool, and she'd been right all along. He had a feeling that if he went rushing back to her now and begged her to give him another chance, she'd tell him to take a hike. He was a man of instinct; he'd know when the time was right to plead his case. He just hoped that when that time came, it wasn't already too late.

36

Natalie hadn't thought she would start crying this early, but the minute she got to Anthony and Vivi's house to dress on the morning of the wedding, she began sniffling. At least she wasn't alone: Vivi's mother and grandmother were there, too, and when Vivi walked down the stairs in her grandmother's wedding gown, out came the tissues. "We're going to ruin our makeup!" chided Vivi, who was also teary. For the most part, they were all weeping tears of joy, but there was also a subcurrent of sadness there, too, since Natalie and Vivi's father wasn't alive to walk Vivi down the aisle.

"He's here in spirit, *cherie*, you know he is," Natalie whispered to Vivi in the limo when it pulled up in front of Saint Finbar's church, where their father's good friend, Bernard Rousseau, stood waiting for them. Bernard was going to give Vivi away. Natalie was thankful he let her remain in his apartment while he was in town for the wedding; she'd been sure he would want his privacy. But he was only in New York for a few days, and then it was back to Paris. He told her that he liked her living in his flat and keeping an eye on it for him and that she was welcome to stay for as long as she liked.

The church was packed. Vivi was right: Anthony had invited all of Bensonhurst. Standing in the vestibule at the back, she spotted Quinn sitting in the eighth pew from the front on the left, right on the aisle. She wasn't sure, but from behind it looked like he was wearing a new suit. When he turned to talk to the woman to the left of him (a good-looking woman in a fabulous form-fitting champagne-colored dress), her gut clenched. Had he brought a date to the wedding? No, Vivi would have told her.

She couldn't stop looking at him. He was clean-shaven, and his hair was combed. He looked undeniably handsome, and she could see the woman he was talking to noticing it, too. She forced herself to look away.

"Hey, how's it going?"

Michael Dante appeared, pulling at the collar of his tuxedo. "I hate these monkey suits."

"I've never met a man who doesn't."

Michael narrowed his eyes as he looked at the doors to the church, where his cousin Gemma's husband, Sean, stood directing guests. Beside him was Aldo, the ancient headwaiter/manager of Dante's.

"Look at that *gavone*," Michael said with a scowl, gesturing at Aldo. The old man was tapping his foot impatiently and checking his watch.

"I'm sure he'll stop once we start down the aisle."

"Pain in my ass. Pain in Anthony's ass. He always has been."

"I think it's sweet that Anthony wanted him up there."

"Oh, please. He would have torched the restaurant kitchen if Ant had done otherwise." Michael looked sentimental as he gazed around the church. "Did you know this is where Ant and I were both baptized? We had our first Holy Communions here, too. And our confirmations. I got married here, too. My kids were baptized here." He paused.

"I was a wreck when I got married. Puked twice before we even left the house and once here."

"But I bet the feeling went away when you saw Theresa, right?"

"Yup," said Michael, as his gaze tenderly drifted to the front pew where Theresa sat with their three children. "Smartest thing I ever did, marrying that mouthy broad."

Natalie smiled, even though her heart felt as though it were made of glass about to shatter at any moment with sadness. The wedding . . . Michael's unabashed love for his wife . . . Natalie felt the absence of love in her own life acutely. She reminded herself that this day was not about her. It was about Vivi and Anthony—their love, their commitment to each other. She would not let the failure of her relationship with Quinn mar the joy of the day for her.

She moved to Vivi, who was talking to Bernard Rousseau.

"Nervous?"

"Not at all." Vivi was radiant.

Michael had momentarily disappeared. When he returned, his eyes were bright and excited. "The padre says we're ready to roll," he told Natalie, Vivi, and Bernard. "We just need to wait for the Bach to begin so Natalie and I can walk up the aisle. Then the wedding march will start, and it's showtime. Anthony's at the altar, waiting."

Natalie took Michael's arm, and they stood side by side in the back of the church, waiting for Bach's "Jesu, Joy of Man's Desiring" to begin on the organ. She felt surprisingly nervous. What if she tripped walking up the aisle? What if she cried like a baby as she listened to Vivi and Anthony exchange vows?

The church organ, which had been playing softly as the church filled up, fell silent for a moment. Natalie took a deep breath, glancing anxiously at Michael as the opening notes of one of J. S. Bach's most beautiful pieces of music began quietly playing. "Ready?" Michael whispered.

"Ready."

Slowly, almost regally, they started up the aisle, heads turning to watch them. All eyes were on them, including Quinn's. Natalie could feel his gaze locking on her and holding. Her eyes cut to him quickly as she walked by, but not so quickly that she failed to notice the longing in his eyes or that he was wearing the shirt she'd given him months back. Shaken, she forced her gaze back to the front of the church, where Anthony stood expectantly, looking extremely handsome in his tux. Aldo and Sean were standing midway down the aisle on either side. The fiery little waiter had stopped fidgeting and now tears were rolling down his cheeks. When she and Michael reached the altar, Michael went to stand beside Anthony, while Natalie moved to the other side to wait for Vivi.

The opening strains of the traditional wedding march began, and everyone in the pews rose and turned toward the back of the church to watch Vivi as she made her way up the aisle—everyone but Quinn, that is, who was still staring at Natalie. She refused to look at him.

Vivi was beaming, her mother and grandmother weeping quietly. Natalie felt overwhelmed with sudden emotion and bit down hard on her lower lip to stop herself from bursting into tears.

A few rows from the altar, Bernard and Vivi stopped. Anthony left the altar and walked down the aisle to where they had stopped. Bernard was smiling broadly, and so was Anthony. Bernard shook Anthony's hand and with his other hand, clutched Anthony's forearm. Natalie could see Anthony's eyes begin to well up with tears. Anthony took Vivi's arm, and the two of them walked together to the altar.

And throughout the ceremony, Natalie could feel Quinn's eyes on her, his gaze intense and unwavering.

* * *

"Help me. I don't know what to do."

Vivi and Anthony's wedding reception was in full swing in the banquet room at Dante's. The two of them had reached a compromise when it came to the food: guests had a choice between an Italian or French dish for each course.

Natalie was seated at a table with Vivi, Anthony, Theresa, Michael, their kids, Gemma, and Sean. Quinn was seated at a table of hockey players, which he seemed to be enjoying immensely when he wasn't busy staring at her. It was starting to unnerve Natalie, especially since it was also stirring up excitement within her. It felt different than when his eyes followed her at the bar; here they were all dressed up, and played out against the background of Vivi and Anthony's wedding, there was an added romantic element to his attention that Natalie couldn't ignore.

Vivi and Anthony had danced their first dance, and the dance floor was now filling with other couples, who were staring dreamily into one another's eyes as the band played one classic love song after another. The minute Vivi left the dance floor, Natalie asked her to come with her to the ladies' room for a minute.

"What's the matter?" Vivi asked as soon as the bathroom door swung closed behind them, her brows furrowed in concern.

Natalie wrung her hands. "It's going to sound trivial, but Quinn keeps staring at me, and it's unnerving me."

"That's because he loves you," said Vivi, fixing the hem of her dress.

"Yes, but—"

"You have two choices," Vivi cut in softly. "You can ignore him, or you can talk to him."

"Talking to him will confuse me," Natalie admitted, catching a brief glimpse of herself in the bathroom mirror. She looked distressed.

"That's because you still love him."

"But I don't want to," Natalie said miserably.

"So stop," Vivi teased. "Tell your heart, 'Stop loving him.' I'm sure you'll be able to turn it off just like that." Vivi snapped her fingers.

"Very funny."

Vivi cupped her cheek. "What do you want, Natalie? I mean, truly, deep down."

"I can't have what I want," said Natalie, putting a hand over Vivi's. "That's the problem."

"You don't know that."

"I do, Vivi." They lowered their hands, twined their fingers together.

"Talk to him. What harm will it do? You talk to him all the time at work anyway, don't you?"

"Not all the time. I've been trying to minimize contact." She rubbed her arms as if a chill had just entered the room. "But today is different. There's all this romance swirling in the air. I feel . . . susceptible. You know how charming he is."

"Yes, I do. But I also know that from the moment you two met, there was an undeniable spark there."

Natalie covered her face with her hands, sighing. "My mind feels so jumbled."

"Then talk to him. Either you'll sort things out, or you won't. At least you'll be out of limbo."

"Yes, you're right." Natalie opened the bathroom door. "I should let you get back to your husband. Thank you for letting me take you away from your party for a few minutes," she said sheepishly.

"You're so silly sometimes." Vivi playfully tugged on one of Natalie's earrings. "Come along, *ma soeur*. Everything will work out the way it's supposed to. It always does."

37

"Would you like to dance?"

Quinn looked almost shy as he approached Natalie, where she sat talking to Theresa about fashion. So far, she'd danced with Anthony, Michael, Sean, Bernard, and even Aldo, who complained the whole time about how Anthony should have made the food for the reception himself rather than hire Spallone Catering. She hated to admit it, but every time she was on the dance floor, she hoped Quinn was watching with envy, because God knows, she herself was filled with an unjustified sense of possessiveness when he danced with Vivi, Theresa, and Gemma. She'd had a feeling he would eventually ask her to dance, and when she did catch him out of the corner of her eye coming toward the table, her heart lurched against her will.

She hesitated a moment as Quinn gazed at her hopefully, his vulnerability making it impossible for her to refuse. She stood, taking the hand he'd extended to her. They found an open spot on the crowded dance floor. Natalie could tell he wanted to draw her closer to him, but she resisted, keeping a small distance between them.

"You having fun?" Quinn asked as they began dancing. For some reason, she thought he'd be one of those men who really couldn't dance and would lead her around in a slow shuffle. But he was light on his feet and seemed to know what he was doing.

"Yes. You?"

Quinn looked thoughtful. "Yes. The food is great. So is the band."

"Vivi picked the band. Apparently Anthony was lobbying for a band called the Tarantulas made up of hockey players." Natalie pursed her lips disapprovingly. "Honestly, I don't know what he was thinking."

Quinn tilted his head in the direction of Anthony and Vivi, who were making the rounds from table to table, talking to their guests. "They look really happy."

"Yes," Natalie agreed.

"Despite quite a few bumps in the road before they finally got together," Quinn pointed out.

Natalie said nothing, trying to ignore the innuendo in his voice as well as her heart picking up pace. He drew her a little closer, and she let him, but she resisted the urge to let their bodies touch completely.

"You look really beautiful," Quinn said, awed.

"Is that why you've been looking at me all day?" she asked quietly.

"Partially. But mainly I've been looking at you because I love you."

Natalie closed her eyes, trying to harden her heart. "Please. Don't."

Quinn ignored her. "I know you still love me, *ma petite blaireau.*"

My little badger. He was trying to charm her, like the old days. She refused to give in.

"Oh?" she replied coolly. "And how do you know that?"

"Because every time we talk, there's still a spark between us. I can feel you fighting with yourself, trying not to look at me. I'm a reporter, remember?"

"How could I forget?" Natalie said dryly.

Quinn looked frustrated. "Let me finish." He drew her closer, their bodies lightly touching now. "As I was saying: as a reporter I have a highly developed sense of intuition and instinct. And mine tells me you still care."

"It doesn't matter."

"Yes, it does. When my article finally ran, I should have been on the top of the world, but I wasn't. You know why? Because it finally dawned on me that without you, I really don't have a life."

"You didn't want one."

"I didn't know how to have one." He pulled her as close to him as she could get, and her heart began pounding. "Listen to me. Remember when you told me I was stupid?"

"Oui."

"Well, you were right. I was a jerk. The night the article ran, after the guys and I left the pub, we went over to another bar where a lot of reporters hang out. Everyone was congratulating me, and yeah, it was nice. But as I looked around, I saw a vision of my future. Half the guys there were divorced or had never been married because they live for their job. I realized I do not want to end up like that." His gaze was intense. "Without you in my life, I have no life at all. I've been a total idiot, Nat. But if you give me another chance, I swear to you that I will never put my work before you again."

Natalie shook her head sadly. "People don't change."

"How can you of all people say that?" Quinn rebutted incredulously.

Natalie was taken aback. "What do you mean?"

"You were a total snob when you came to this country. Now you're not. You had a problem with spending. Now you don't."

"That's different, Quinn. That's an addiction I struggle with every day."

"Yeah, and work has been my addiction. But people learn to manage their addictions so it doesn't ruin their lives." He tenderly brushed his face against her hair. "One more chance, Nat. Please."

Natalie felt her resolve weakening. "Quinn . . ."

"I know you're afraid of getting hurt. But I swear that won't happen again. I swear it."

Natalie swallowed hard as she held his gaze. The love for her that she saw in his eyes was so intense she had to look away. He was right: people could change. And she was indeed proof of that. Didn't he deserve the benefit of the doubt?

"All right," she whispered, her defenses crumbling. "You can have another chance. But if you—"

He didn't allow her to finish, silencing her with a kiss. Natalie succumbed to it, fully allowing yearning to conquer fear. She loved this man, and he loved her. They could have what Vivi and Anthony had. They could.

The kiss ended far too soon. Were it up to Natalie, they would keep kissing as romantic music swirled around them. "I love you, *ma petite jambon*."

She kissed his nose. "I am not 'your little ham.' And God knows why, but I love you, too."

38

SIX MONTHS LATER

"You're offering me a job?"

Natalie couldn't hide her bewilderment as she sat across from Anthony at Dante's. Three weeks ago, Aldo, the restaurant's beloved headwaiter and Anthony's right-hand man, died of a sudden heart attack. It was a shock to everyone but most especially to Anthony and Michael, who had known the old man all their lives. Vivi had told Natalie that Anthony had been walking around in a daze since the old man's death but that in the past few days he'd seemed to pull out of it, more out of necessity than anything else. Natalie was puzzled when Anthony asked her to stop by on her day off, assuming it had to do with Vivi. She was shocked when they sat down and he asked her if she wanted to manage the restaurant.

Anthony nodded.

"But you know how little experience I have," Natalie pointed out, puzzled.

"Yeah, but you're never gonna get experience unless someone gives you a shot. And now that Aldo's gone . . ." Anthony's voice trailed off sadly.

Natalie was confused. "I thought Aldo was the head-waiter."

"He was, but he was also the manager, even though he never officially held that title."

"And you're willing to let me fill his shoes?"

"Someone's got to. Why not you? I know you. I trust you."

Natalie's mind was churning. "But what if I make a mess of things? Make mistakes?"

"Then I'll scream at you," Anthony said matter-of-factly, "but you'll know I don't mean it, and eventually, you'll stop making mistakes."

"You don't expect me to waitress, too, do you?"

"No. Just manage."

Natalie peered at him skeptically. "Did Vivi put you up to this?"

"No." Anthony looked mildly offended. "I am capable of an original thought, you know."

Natalie settled against the back of her chair, quickly calculating the pros and cons of Anthony's offer. Pros: It was a chance to get experience managing a midlevel restaurant where she knew the chef was temperamental but not abusive, crazy, or a lecher. She'd be right across the street from her sister. It would be more money. Cons: She'd have to do a reverse commute, but that wouldn't be a problem, now that she and Quinn had bought Vivi's old Honda Civic.

"I'd need to give Quinn's parents time to find someone to replace me."

"Obviously."

"Can I talk to Quinn and get back to you?" she asked tentatively.

"Of course. But I need an answer really soon. I'm tearing my hair out here trying to manage both the kitchen and the front of the house, and Mikey isn't helping any, always putting his two cents in where it isn't needed. *Madonn'*, he's a pain in my ass."

"I understand." Natalie jumped up and gave her brother-in-law a quick peck on the cheek. "I really appreciate this."

"Hey, you're family. We help each other out, right?"

Natalie nodded. "I'll ring you tomorrow, *oui*?"

"Yep." Anthony stood. "Back to the fifth circle of hell," he joked, jerking a thumb in the direction of the kitchen. "Talk to you tomorrow."

* * *

Natalie was surprised to find Quinn already there when she arrived home after her shift. As had been the pattern when he worked at the *Sent*, he and his cohorts from the *Standard* usually went out to unwind after work, though they hung out at a different bar. He still came into the pub a few nights a week to spend time with his old friends. On those nights, he and she would go home together. But on the nights he was with his coworkers from the *Standard*, he usually arrived home after her.

Once they'd reconciled, they decided to move in together. They didn't feel comfortable living in Bernard's apartment, and Quinn's place was simply too small. Providence came in the form of Jeff Rogan, who'd taken a newspaper job down in South Carolina. Quinn and Natalie took his apartment down in the Financial District, a spacious two bedroom at a surprisingly affordable rent. The area was dead at night, but it didn't matter. She worked most nights, and the nights Quinn wasn't running around chasing a story, he liked to stay at home and surf the Internet for possible ideas or lounge on the couch and watch political pundits scream at each other. The nights they were together, they either stayed in or went out to a movie, though occasionally she was able to convince Quinn to check out an off-Broadway play or a new art gallery. Mr. News Junkie would never be a total culture vulture, but at least he was open to new things—as was she. She'd gone to two hockey games with him and was bored to tears, which Quinn found amusing. "You're still a snob when it comes to some things," he teased affectionately. She replied that she didn't see the allure in games so violent. Grown men crashing into each other? She'd never understand it.

Quinn had kept his promise to her, putting their relationship before work. Natalie could tell it was hard on him at first. Work had been his only love for years, and it was tough to break old habits. But he did it: no longer was his cell phone on all night, because he knew there were reporters and editors who worked the overnight shift who could handle whatever came in. He was still the one sent out on most major stories, and yes, sometimes his hours were erratic and dragged on late into the night. But he no longer seemed compelled to try to cover every single breaking story in the city. She knew he missed spending time in the newsroom with his friends at the *Sent*, but he often professed how glad he was to be out of there, especially since Mason Clement had fulfilled his mission on behalf of Hewitt Corporation, completely transforming the paper into an entertainment-driven tabloid.

Quinn looked up at her from his desk, where his face was practically touching the computer screen. "*Bonjour*, beautiful. How was work?"

"Fine. PJ Leary wants you to call him. He says he needs help editing his book."

Quinn groaned.

"He admires you."

"Clearly."

Natalie hung up her coat and kicked off her shoes. "Has it occurred to you that you might need glasses?"

Quinn blinked. "No."

"Then why were you leaning so close to the screen?"

"I wasn't."

"You were."

She sat down on the couch, patting the space beside

her. Quinn got up but parked himself on the opposite end, gesturing for her to stretch out and put her feet in his lap. Natalie complied, giving a deep sigh of pleasure as he began massaging her feet. It had become a nightly ritual.

Natalie wiggled her toes. "Anthony offered me the manager's job at Dante's today."

Quinn looked delighted. "That's fantastic!"

"You really think so?" she asked uncertainly.

Quinn's expression turned baffled. "Of course I do. It's the perfect situation: you two know each other—"

"But Anthony can be a bit crazy. And he has a bad temper."

"Most chefs are crazy. Haven't you figured that out by now?"

"Vivi isn't crazy."

"Maybe crazy is a bad word. He's temperamental. And so is she."

"I'm afraid he's going to yell at me," Natalie admitted sheepishly.

"Of course he will. But so what? At least you'll be getting yelled at by someone you know and like. And once you get the hang of things, he'll stop."

"That's what he said."

He squeezed her feet. "Take it, Nat. It's what you've wanted."

"All right." She lifted one of her feet from his lap, running her toes up and down his chest. "How was your day?"

"Two cops in Queens shot some guy on a rooftop with their Taser guns, and the guy plummeted to his death," he said excitedly. "There's gonna be a big investigation."

"Sounds like it's right up your alley."

"Hell yeah," Quinn agreed, looking pleased. He lifted her foot to his lips, giving her toes a quick nibble before putting her foot back in his lap. "I wanted to talk to you about something."

He sounded serious, immediately catapulting Natalie into nervous mode. "Okay."

"I think we should get married."

Natalie sat up, stunned. "What?"

"I think we should get married," Quinn repeated firmly. "I've been thinking about it a lot, and my gut tells me it's time."

Natalie was completely flummoxed. She hadn't seen this coming at all.

Quinn's brows knit together. "You seem surprised."

"I am."

"I don't see why. I love you, you love me. What are we waiting for?"

Good question.

"We both said we want what Vivi and Anthony and my folks have," he continued. "And we're not getting any younger."

Natalie's mouth fell open. "I beg your pardon!"

Quinn laughed. "I'm just teasing."

"You'd better be."

"So, what do you say?"

"I say this isn't a very romantic proposal."

Quinn shook his head. "I knew you'd say that. You want me to get down on my knee, don't you?"

"No! But you could at least put your arms around me!"

"True." Quinn wrapped his arms around her. "Miss Natalie Bocuse, will you do me the great honor of becoming my wife?"

Natalie sniffed. "Maybe."

Quinn drew back in alarm. "What?"

Natalie rolled her eyes. "I'm kidding. Of course I'll be your wife."

"I was hoping you'd say that." He fished in the front pocket of his jeans, pulling out a very simple gold engagement ring with a fairly small diamond. He looked sentimental. "This was the first engagement ring my father gave my mother, back in Ireland."

"The first?"

"Yeah. Years later, when they started making decent money, he bought a fancier one for her for their anniversary. But my mother held on to this one in the hopes of passing it on to me or Liam, whichever one of us decided to get married first."

Natalie took the ring, looking at it. "I love it," she whispered. "I love that it has a history. I think it will bring us very good luck." She handed it back to Quinn, extending her left hand. Quinn slipped the ring on her finger. She'd have to have it sized down, but that didn't matter. What mattered was their love and the commitment they were going to make to one another.

Quinn brushed his lips across hers. "This is the best night of my life."

"Mine, too."

"I say we do it soon."

Natalie was puzzled. "Why the rush?"

"I want to make you mine before you change your mind."

She felt a rush of affection for him. "If I haven't changed it yet, I never will."

"I'm thinking we'll keep it small," Quinn continued. "Family, my friends from the *Sent*, anyone you want to come from Paris, the regulars . . ."

Natalie shook her head vehemently. "No. *Non*. I do not want a contingent of crazy people at my wedding."

"But they're like family," Quinn protested.

"No."

"All right, all right," Quinn capitulated with a sigh.

"You seem to have already given this a lot of thought," Natalie noted with amusement. "Any thoughts about where you'd like to have this celebration? And don't say at the pub."

"My sister Sinead owns a gorgeous house up in Sullivan County that she only uses on weekends. It's very modern, open, with lots of glass because the views are spectacular. I think we should have it there."

"I've never even seen it!"

"Yeah, but once you do, I think you'll fall in love with it."

"How come you haven't taken me there yet?"

Quinn looked grim. "She's kind of been hibernating there, pretty much wanting to be left alone since she and her husband split up. But she said she'd stay in the city next weekend so we could check it out."

"So your whole family already knows about this."

"Basically," Quinn mumbled. "I mean, the cat was out of the bag the minute I asked my mother for the ring."

"And when was that?"

"Two days ago."

"No wonder she's been so cheery at work! She's been waiting for this to happen!"

"Yep. So how long do you think we need to pull this thing together? Two months?"

"Are you mad?" Natalie squawked, marveling at how utterly clueless men could be sometimes. "I have to find a dress! We have to find caterers, music, flowers, someone to marry us, plan a honeymoon . . ."

"Four months?"

"Five. Even if it's a small wedding, I don't want to be rushed."

"Agreed." He twined his fingers through hers. "It would really mean a lot to me if we invited PJ, the Mouth, and Mrs. Cogan."

"Quinn."

"C'mon, you know that deep in your heart you love them, too," he ribbed. "Admit it."

Natalie sighed heavily. "If it's that important to you . . ."

"It is."

She tenderly ran an index finger down his cheek. "Why is it that I can't deny you anything?"

"I'm guessing because I'm so adorable." He picked up his cell phone.

"What are you doing?"

"Calling my mother. I told her I was going to pop the question tonight. I'm sure she's waiting breathlessly by the phone."

"Good thing I didn't say no," said Natalie dryly, getting up from the couch. "I'm going to wait until the morning to call Vivi. If I call her now, she'll be so excited she'll never get to sleep." Natalie held out her left hand, admiring her beautiful engagement ring. What a wonderful day she'd had: first Anthony's job offer, and now this. It couldn't get much better.

She looked back at Quinn, moved by how happy he sounded as he told his mother their good news. If anyone had told her two years ago that she'd be marrying the rude journalist who'd made disparaging remarks about Parisians the first time they'd met, she would have snorted loudly, told them they were insane, and walked away. Yet here they were, madly in love, and she was happier than she'd ever been in her life. She hugged herself with glee and then continued on to their bedroom, intent on getting some sleep. From now on, she'd need all the rest she could get. After all, she had a wedding to plan.

FIVE MONTHS LATER

"Darlin', you're one of the most beautiful brides I've ever seen, and I swear that on the heads of my children. Whenever you're ready."

Natalie choked back tears as Quinn's father offered her

his arm in preparation to walk her "up the aisle." Just as Quinn had promised, Sinead's house was gorgeous, perched high atop a hill in Bearsville with spectacular views of rolling hills and small mountains. Since they'd decided on July for the wedding, they were getting married outside beneath a white trellis adorned with pink roses and baby's breath. Rows of white folding chairs had been set up on either side of the trellis, constituting "the aisle." They'd asked one of the guitarists from the band who'd played Vivi and Anthony's reception to play the "Wedding March" on acoustic guitar for them. He'd happily agreed.

The reception was being held on the front lawn beneath a large white tent with a small dance floor in the middle. They had hired the same band that had played Vivi's wedding, as well as the same caterers, Spallone. Anthony's pastry chef made the three-tiered wedding cake. Ken Durham was Quinn's best man; Vivi was Natalie's matron of honor. Hoping to bury the hatchet once and for all, Natalie had invited her mother, but she'd refused to come. Natalie was mildly stung, but she knew it was better this way. Her mother's sour, judgmental disposition would have clouded her happiness.

Since it was a more low-key affair than Vivi and Anthony's wedding, Quinn, his father, and his groomsman were all wearing suits rather than tuxes. At Natalie's behest, Quinn had bought a new suit for the wedding. The only one in a tux was PJ Leary, who was doing very well. After Whitey was jailed, he decided he didn't want to rent his old writing room back, and was now writing in his apartment to save money. The others who'd been Whitey's victims were doing well, too: Franco the tailor decided he indeed wanted to retire after all; he sold his business, made a mint, and moved to Florida. The Sweeneys collected their insurance money and reopened their hardware store in the same locale, while the owners of the video store used their insurance money to open shop in a different neighborhood. Dominick Tallia's business remained firmly in his control.

Natalie felt a wellspring of emotion deep in the pit of her belly as she watched Vivi walk up the aisle with Kenny Durham. For a split second, it all seemed surreal; she couldn't quite believe her wedding day had finally arrived. But when she saw Quinn come outside to stand beneath the trellis and wait for her, the joyous reality of the day washed over her.

Natalie nodded her head at the guitarist, and he began playing. Slowly, she walked toward the trellis on her future father-in-law's arm toward Quinn, who was looking at her with such love it took her breath away. Her father-in-law kissed her when they reached the trellis, turning her over to Quinn before he went to sit down.

Quinn took her hand, twining his fingers through hers in a strong grip. "God, you look beautiful, *ma petite homard*," he whispered.

"And you look incredibly handsome, though I'm having second thoughts about marrying a man who calls me his little lobster."

Quinn grinned, squeezing her hand.

The second the ceremony started, the world faded away. The only two people who existed were she and Quinn, their eyes locked in a loving gaze. Natalie couldn't help herself: she began crying tears of joy. By the time Quinn asked her to be his wife, she was sobbing and had to compose herself before she could answer. It was only when they were pronounced man and wife that she once again became aware that they'd shared the moment with family and friends. Quinn tenderly wiped her tears away, and they started back down the aisle. She'd never, ever, been this happy in her life.

* * *

Natalie felt slightly dazed at the reception as she and Quinn made the rounds of the tables, thanking everyone for coming. For obvious reasons, they'd seated the bar regulars together. Mrs. Colgan told them that when she married her husband, "His family hissed at me as I walked up the aisle because they thought I wasn't good enough for him." The Mouth began pontificating on the sanctity of marriage, until he finally noticed Quinn's eyes were glazing over and he hushed up with a mumbled apology. PJ Leary stared glumly into his whiskey. The Major sat quietly next to PJ, taking it all in.

"Thanks for letting them come," said Quinn gratefully.

"You were right: they're family. Kind of like the crazy relatives you can't avoid but whom you love anyway."

"Precisely."

They made their way to their seats at the family table where all the O'Briens sat, along with Anthony and Vivi. Natalie was surprised when she sat down but Quinn remained standing, signaling for the band to stop playing. The tent fell silent as all eyes turned to Quinn. "I just want to thank all of you for coming to share in what's the happiest day in my life. But there's someone I love who couldn't be here with us today, and whose absence is keenly felt: my brother, Liam." He paused a moment, obviously choked up. Then he held his champagne flute high. "A toast to my brother. To Liam!"

"To Liam!" everyone echoed, as the band resumed playing.

Quinn took a sip of champagne, sitting down as he wiped a small tear from his eye. His parents and sisters were crying openly.

"That was beautiful, *chere*," said Natalie, moved.

Quinn looked distraught. "I wish to hell he was here."

"I know. But he's here in spirit."

His father patted his shoulder. "She's right, son. And what matters is that he's safe for now."

"I pray to God he's home soon," said Quinn's mother, "but your father's right." She clapped her hands together lightly. "No more sad thoughts now, everybody. This is a happy day. Let's enjoy ourselves."

"Agreed," said Quinn. He put his arm around Natalie, pulling her close. "This truly is the happiest day of my life," he murmured.

"Me, too."

Natalie snuggled against him. She'd found a good man, a loving man, the right man. Her dream had finally come true.

Recipes Inspired
by *With a Twist*

Irish Champ

8 medium potatoes
1 cup whole milk
5 tablespoons butter
One bunch scallions or green onions, chopped
Salt and pepper to taste

Peel and cube potatoes. Boil in salted water until tender.
Drain and mash slightly. In a small pan, heat milk and
butter until butter is melted. Add chopped scallions. Fold
into potato mixture until well blended. Potatoes will still
be somewhat lumpy. Season with salt and pepper to taste.

Irish Soda Bread

4 cups sifted all-purpose flour
¼ cup sugar
1 teaspoon salt
1 teaspoon baking powder
½ cup butter
1 to 1½ cup seedless raisins
Caraway seeds to taste
1⅓ cups buttermilk
2 eggs
1 teaspoon baking soda

Preheat oven to 350 degrees. Mix and sift flour, sugar, salt, and baking powder. Cut butter into flour mixture until it resembles coarse cornmeal. Stir in raisins and caraway seeds. In another bowl combine buttermilk, eggs, and baking soda. Beat this second mixture with a fork. Stir second mixture into first until well blended. Form the dough into a round loaf and put it on a baking sheet. Bake forty-five to fifty minutes or until a knife inserted in the center comes out clean. (Note: some people prefer to make the bread in a large, greased loaf pan.)

Go ahead. Try…

Just a Taste

By *New York Times* bestselling author

Deirdre Martin

Since his wife's untimely death, Anthony Dante has thrown himself into his cooking, making his restaurant, Dante's, a Brooklyn institution. So far, his biggest problem has been keeping his brother, the retired hockey star, out of the kitchen. But now, a mademoiselle is invading his turf.

Stunning Vivi Robitaille can't wait to showcase her taste-bud-tingling recipes in her brand new bistro, Vivi's. Her only problem is an arrogant Italian chef across the street who actually thinks he's competition.

The table is set for a culinary war—until things start getting spicy outside of the kitchen…

It's a...

Total Rush

Free spirit Gemma Dante wishes her love life were going as well as her New Age business. So she casts a spell to catch her Mr. Right. But when the cosmic wires get crossed, into her life walks a clean-cut fireman who's anything but her type.

Sean Kennealy doesn't know what to make of his pretty neighbor who burns incense. He only knows that being near her sparks a fire in him that even the guys at Ladder 29, Engine 31 can't put out.

From
New York Times Bestselling Author

Deirdre Martin

M205T0209